The Girl in the Boston Box

A Mystery Times Two

Chuck Latovich

To Joan

I hope you enjoy my book!

Chuck Latovich

Way We Live Publishers

CAMBRIDGE, MASSACHUSETTS

Way We Live Publishers
Cambridge, MA 02138

Publisher's Note: This is a work of fiction. Names, characters, places, and incidents are a product of the author's imagination. Locales and public names are sometimes used for atmospheric purposes. Any resemblance to actual people, living or dead, or to businesses, companies, events, institu-tions, or locales is completely coincidental.

Book Layout © 2017 BookDesignTemplates.com
Cover Design: Alex Peltz for Peltz Creative LLC, Woodbury, VT
Author Photograph: Susan R. Symonds for Beacon LTD Portraits

The Girl in the Boston Box/ Chuck Latovich -- 1st ed.
ISBN 978-1-7352304-0-5
ISBN 978-1-7352304-1-2 (eBook)

For Christine M. Latovich

PART ONE

Caitlyn: March 2016 – December 2016

Mark: April 2017

CHAPTER ONE

CAITLYN

March 2016

Whenever Caitlyn was stuck, she reminded herself that many paths in life were suggested by the universe, and that if she only paid attention to what was around her, some kind of invisible spirit would murmur in her ear and tell her what direction to follow. So to open up to new ideas, she decided to leave her apartment, where she'd been staring for a few days at the blank computer screen that was supposed to display the topic for her qualifying paper in architectural history at Harvard. And it was during this attempt to free her mind that Caitlyn first heard about the Boston Box.

She learned about the Box from a tall man, perhaps in his mid-forties, who, along with Caitlyn, was taking a house tour of a Boston landmark, the Harrison Gray Otis House. The man had a craggy, handsome face and buck teeth, and a wife and two adolescent sons who never wandered more than a few feet away from him as the tour group moved from room to room. Caitlyn was the only other visitor. The Otis House was near Beacon Hill, and Caitlyn had visited it once before, returning to it now like an avid reader returned to a favorite book. The mansion was the work of Charles Bulfinch, an architect whose vision as a city manager in Boston's earliest years had helped to determine the city's character. Many of the rooms in the Otis House had been restored and were colorful and clean. One of them had ornamentation reminiscent of Pompeii, bright yellow walls and blue gilding, a style that was a mania when the house was built.

Near the middle of the tour, the guide, who was a well-dressed, bubbly woman, faced the group and checked if anyone had a question. She looked to be in her late twenties—five or six years older than Caitlyn—and with brown hair several shades lighter than Caitlyn's own. They all stood in a sparsely furnished room that had served as an office for the house's first occupants. The guide had just shown a safe concealed behind the panels of a fireplace. The buck-toothed man raised his voice. "I once read about something called the Boston Box. Is that what the safe is? Can you say anything about that?"

The tour guide looked amused. "What have you heard?"

The buck-toothed man shrugged. "Something about hidden rooms, or hidden compartments...something like that?"

The guide answered, "Well, let's see. You know the phrase 'urban myth'? Right? Or urban legend? Like a rumor? Most of these stories are creepy, or gross, and they aren't true, but they catch on and refuse to die. As far as I can tell, the Boston Box is one of those. A nineteenth-century version of an urban legend."

"What is it, exactly?" Caitlyn asked. "The Boston Box?"

"So, the best I can recall, it goes something like this," the guide said. "Back in the Civil War era, mid-nineteenth century, a Boston architect supposedly made sure that there were secret or hidden rooms somewhere in the buildings that he designed. This is conjecture. Their purpose, that's never been clear. Sometimes it was said they were to hide runaway slaves. Possibly more than one architect was involved. The worst version that I heard was that there was a man who murdered women and he would use a hidden chamber in his home to torture his victims." The guide looked at the buck-toothed man. "I'm sorry," she said, "I don't want to scare your sons."

The man chuckled. "They see worse on video games. But wouldn't this safe be like a Boston Box?"

"I can only say that we've never used the term here," the guide responded. "It's not big. A Boston Box should be much larger, right? At least the size of a closet or small room. In theory. There's nothing of that sort here at the Otis House. Of course, the house itself was moved. It used to be a lot closer to the curb. It was relocated when they widened Cambridge Street. So if there was a Boston Box in the basement..." She laughed. "If there was one, it would be long gone. But we've no indication of anything like that here."

"The safe seems like it could be one," the man insisted. The oldest of his sons was fidgety.

"You can call it whatever you want," the guide said, "but that doesn't really make it one. The story goes that there's...well, who knows how rumors get spread? If a Boston Box really existed, they would have found it by now. There are some hidden rooms around town, but mostly for the Underground Railroad, I think. Not rooms for death. No pattern."

"I'm studying architectural history," Caitlyn said. "Especially Boston. The term is new to me. Surprising."

"Not really," said the guide. "It's not a very reputable idea, right? There's no proof. It's a footnote. Inauthentic."

The tour went on for another half-hour. Afterward, Caitlyn walked about a block to a Whole Foods Supermarket squeezed into a 60s-style shopping plaza. The market wasn't crowded. She bought a coffee and ignored the leer of a young barista. Diet and grad school had helped her to lose more than twenty pounds recently, and she was often uncomfortable with some of the attention that followed, since too much of it came from guys who looked like they mostly spoke in grunts.

A small table was empty in an enclosed dining area near a plate glass window. Caitlyn sat down. She retrieved her iPad from a maroon Harvard backpack and propped it in front of her. A mid-afternoon sun both warmed the area and caused a glare on her tablet screen. She entered "Boston Box" into a search engine. Over 400,000,000 possible responses came up, the first ones about a presentation tool developed by a local consulting company, others about nearby boxing clubs, and many about buying tickets to different theatrical or sporting events. Boston Box Office. Only a few citations on the second page related to what she had heard on the tour.

She went first to a Wikipedia article that didn't offer much more information than the guide had at the Otis House, and its few facts carried the site's standard warning about being an unverified entry. However, the article did suggest that the first mention of a Boston Box came in connection with the work of Gregory Chester Adamston, a second-tier architect who lived in the nineteenth century and who had designed a few buildings in Boston that still existed, most notably a church in the South End and a row of brownstones in the same neighborhood.

One possible "Boston Box" might have been built because of a mistake that Adamston had made in the construction of three connected houses alongside the Public Garden. A miscalculation had resulted in a gap in one of them, an error that Adamston had remedied by fashioning a narrow chamber accessible behind a fake bookcase. The home was one that he himself had lived in for several years. The room wasn't good for much. He used it for storage. The article implied that a few other Boston architects had mimicked the room, calling them "Boston Boxes." But no examples were cited. The Adamston home was torn down over a hundred years ago after a fire so the story could not be confirmed by pictures or an examination of the premises. No other examples had been cited or documented or tied to the term, nor was there any mention of murders.

Caitlyn raked her fingers through her hair and wondered if that was how fables got started. The entry hadn't exactly detailed the "urban legend" that the tour guide had spoken of, and it was certainly vague.

She clicked on an item about Adamston himself. She had read little about his work before this and needed some reminders.

Adamston had had a number of modest successes during his life. Most of his work was more ordinary commissions, the nineteenth century equivalent of common home constructions and office buildings, much of it elsewhere in New England. Some historians suggested that he often took the credit for designs done by others who worked for him, in particular a Black architect named Josiah Hawkins who had trained in Paris. Adamston's career had ended in financial ruin. He had overextended himself in the financing of one of his projects, that row of brownstones in the South End, which hadn't sold. Plagued by debt, Adamston had died a broken man.

Grim history.

Caitlyn's cell phone hummed with a text alert. It was her mother. *How are you, Squirrel?*

Caitlyn typed back. *"Gd. working on my thesis."*

Good! How was your date?

"doing research. shd probably focus. not a date just friends drinks. how r u? how's dad?"

All is well here. I'll let you do your work.

"K. TTYL."

Sometimes Caitlyn regretted showing her mother how to text. She loved her mom, but she had thought that by moving to Boston for a while that the apron strings would be cut. Instead, it was more like they'd been stretched but not severed. Her mom usually sent several texts a day to Caitlyn, who didn't have the heart to ignore them. Did her mother have a life?

Caitlyn gazed out the window. Another customer walked by with prepared food in a small cardboard box with folded flaps. A young UPS delivery man carried a boxed package. A tower of cardboard boxes, full of canned goods and stacked on a hand truck, waited on the sidewalk for a stock handler to come and wheel it into the store. Boxes everywhere. The universe had come through once more. She had found the topic for her paper.

CHAPTER TWO

MARK

April 2017

Even in his dying, my brother was a jerk.

"Are you related to David Chieswicz?" The voice on the phone, male, surprisingly soft, belonged to a Boston Police detective named Jake Taylor. The mention of my brother's name put me on alert. The last time I'd had some news about Dave's whereabouts had been several years earlier. I'd done an internet search on my own name and saw an article about Dave being arrested in Florida. Again. A swindle of some sort. Or was it theft? Housebreaking was big with him. No matter. The rift between Dave and me had already lasted over a decade by that point. Dave's crime had been in a very small town, however, and the story had no follow-up.

"Is that 'Chieswicz' with an 'i-e'?" I asked Taylor. An odd question, I know, but Dave and I were the sole survivors with that spelling of our last name, the end of the line after our parents' deaths. My unusual name also would make it easy for someone from the Boston Police to find me. I was impressed that Taylor pronounced it correctly: CHESS-wich.

He confirmed the spelling. I'd been standing when the phone rang. In anticipation of a long call, I slid onto my secondhand couch. A few broken springs in its seat cushions made me slouch whether I wanted to or not.

"What's wrong?" I asked.

"I am afraid I have some bad news, Mr. Chieswicz," Taylor said. "Your brother, David, he was found dead."

"Oh my God," I murmured. "Where? In Florida?"

Taylor paused. "No. In Dorchester." That neighborhood is one of the biggest in Boston.

For a moment, I wondered if I'd made a mistake in claiming I was related. "Just a second. He was here in town?"

Taylor made an airy sound, puzzled and surprised. "Yes. He lived near Fenway." Absorbing that news, I was silent. Finally, Taylor said, "You didn't know?"

"My brother and I aren't close. We haven't spoken for a long time." To myself, I added, *He was in Boston, where he knew I lived, and didn't bother to get in touch.*

Taylor said, "Are there any other survivors? Someone else I should speak with?"

"As far as I know, no. He isn't married. Wasn't? This is all so confusing. But no kids. Again, that's to my knowledge."

"I'm sorry to tell you this over the phone. Searching for a relative. There was no info. We just found your name in a directory. I would have sent a car. But if there's no one else. We have to speak to next of kin."

"About?"

"We've identified his body through fingerprints, but we need the confirmation of someone who knew him."

"What happened?" I asked.

Taylor's voice took on a gentle tone. "It might be better to go over the circumstances when we meet face-to-face."

"He was killed?"

"I'd prefer to talk in person."

His reluctance spoke for itself: the details of Dave's death were ugly. Since Taylor and I were able to negotiate a meeting in a couple of hours—I was off-shift from my part-time job, and my schedule was open—I didn't ask any more questions. Our appointment would take place at the Office of the State Medical Examiner downtown, not a building I knew, but the address was on a major street and easy enough to find. I refused Taylor's offer to send an escort. We hung up.

In the past, I had sometimes feared a moment such as this, when I'd be told without warning about the death of someone close. I'd learned about my parents dying almost incidentally, a sideways circumstance that, in the end, didn't seem as primal as my imagined "dreaded call in the middle of the night." Right now, I couldn't say if I was caught by surprise and unsettled, or numb, or just didn't care.

Dave's death made me the last living member of my immediate family, and this realization brought on a type of loneliness, almost abstract. At forty-seven, to think of myself as an orphan was peculiar, yet that's the odd phrase that came to my mind: a forty-seven-year-old orphan. I wanted to talk with someone about it. I thought of calling my ex, but our breakup had been rough, and I didn't knock on that door too often. And the friends who'd known us as a couple hadn't aligned with me.

I finished a shower, toweled down. I had several day's scruff, which I might have shaved off in the past, but these days I delude myself that I'm fashionable, and my razor stayed untouched. At least my brown-turning-gray hair was clean. Sometimes I wonder if the darkness under my eyes, a product of the last crummy year, will ever go away. I'm thinner than I used to be, if not exactly slim.

I did a fast internet check on my laptop for a story that might hint about Dave. A possibility, since the police were involved, but I found nothing. I left my apartment in the Boston neighborhood of Brighton and headed toward a street level subway stop on the Green Line. "The T." The calendar said it was April, but here in New England that's no guarantee of spring. I reached an open kiosk pretending to be a shelter but providing absolutely no defense against an invasive wind. In ten minutes, a double car finally hummed and clanked to a halt in front of me.

After some transfers, I eventually got off near Symphony Hall, a grand structure that deserves a better setting than the grubby intersection around it. I had to walk another quarter mile to the medical examiner's office, which was in a modern brick building that also housed a medical school and other organizations. Fancy for a morgue. A noisy elevator took me to the fourth floor where an unsmiling receptionist instructed me to have a seat while she summoned Taylor. I settled into an oaken chair with flat arms that looked like they had been clawed by some animal.

In a few minutes, Taylor came out. It disconcerted me to meet an authority figure younger than me by fifteen or twenty years. Taylor had close-cropped hair that made his face, while handsome, look like that of a thousand other slender guys with perfect noses and high cheekbones, as impossible to tell apart as army grunts from the Corn Belt. He approached me and pulled at the cuffs of his long-sleeved white shirt, neatening himself. His handshake was two pumps and a fast release. After that, his eyes moved toward a hand sanitizer on the reception desk.

"No worries," I said. "No colds or flu."

"Working with hospital staff has made me a germaphobe," said Taylor. He led me to a small office where every piece of paper seemed to be in its correct location. He took a place behind a gray metal desk and I sat in front of it. A big bottle of Purell was on a shelf. Behind him was a sealed, unshaded window looking over a construction site, a hospital expansion, at the moment just naked, rusty girders with no sign of activity. This place didn't seem like a police station. "Can you tell me exactly who you are?" I asked Taylor.

"I'm a detective. Police. Enough happens most days next door at Boston Medical, BMC, shootings, injuries, for us to have some desks here."

"Okay. Where's my brother?"

"There's a morgue in BMC. We'll go over soon. I wanted to speak with you first."

"What happened to him?"

"This isn't a pleasant matter. Are you prepared?"

"Thanks," I said. "We weren't close. I'm ready."

"He was found in a lot near the expressway. His body had been dumped there. He was stabbed several times."

"Stabbed?" I gasped. "Jesus. Dumped?"

"From what we can tell, the lot wasn't where he was killed. We located his car elsewhere. Not far from here, in fact. It had parking tickets. We've not determined where the stabbing actually happened. Not in the car."

"That's awful." I pushed down a surge of nausea. Despite my separation from my brother, we had once shared a childhood, a rickety house in Pennsylvania, rides in the back seat of the Chevy that my dad had owned. All these things—and more. I hadn't cared about Dave for a long time and I didn't want to mourn him, but he had been part of my life, and grief tried to chip away at my indifference. I shoved the sadness aside as best I could. "Who did it?"

"We don't know," he said. "We'd hoped you could shed some light."

I repeated that Dave and I had been estranged.

"Can you tell me why?"

For all I knew, Taylor's motives were straightforward, but I wasn't about to confess anything that could be twisted if the cops got desperate. The first thing they'd investigate were people who were acquainted with Dave. In fact, my break with my family was a piddling event, a story told ten thousand times. I had no connection to Dave's death, but until I understood more, I wasn't going to give the cops a chance to make it seem otherwise. "I could," I said, "but it's personal. It's impossible that it had anything to do with this. My family wasn't in my fan club. That's all there is to it. I'm not big on airing dirty linen with police for no reason."

"Even if your linen is clean, your brother was murdered. Reason enough?"

"I didn't even know he was here in Boston. I haven't spoken to him in twenty years. Or more." I did a mental calculation. To be exact, twenty-six years. Hell. Time moves too fast.

"Let's come back to it," he said. "Do you have any questions for me?"

"You said that Dave lived in Boston? Are there things I need to take care of?"

Taylor explained that the police had obtained a warrant to search Dave's apartment, and it had been thoroughly combed, and they were examining the evidence they'd appropriated. He added that while I might be able to gain access to Dave's place by talking to the building management, I'd probably need a lawyer in order to claim any of Dave's assets. He offered to call the apartment's superintendent on my behalf.

"He had assets?" I asked.

"Oh, yes. Nice apartment." My curiosity was piqued. He continued. "We'll talk more after the identification."

"You've not released his name? There's been nothing in the papers, TV."

"Looking for you. Family." I couldn't think of anything else to ask him and remained quiet. He stood up. "Are you ready for the identification?" He smiled sympathetically. "To view the body. At BMC."

I got up, and we walked off together. An elevator deposited us on the second floor, where a glass-enclosed walkway connected the medical examiner's building to an adjacent one. Our journey continued for another five minutes along a mix of passages, more elevators, and tunnels until we ended up below ground level. We reached a secluded office. There, a burly male attendant in a lab coat sat in a cubicle and greeted Taylor familiarly. Taylor offered my brother's name, the attendant nodded, and we all went through to a nearby empty room. A pair of swinging traffic doors apparently led to the morgue and the attendant left through them to retrieve Dave's body while Taylor and I waited. A fluorescent light fixture hummed above our heads. The room was cold.

"This place is so clean," Taylor said. The conversation started and ended there.

In a few moments, the attendant wheeled a gurney into the room, the contours of a body pushing against a crisp, white sheet. I neared the stretcher, as did Taylor. The attendant looked at me with an expression that asked for my permission to proceed. I responded with a single dip of my chin. The attendant rolled back the sheet, stopping at Dave's naked shoulders and sparing me the sight of any wounds.

Dave had aged, of course, since I'd seen him last. His hair was steely gray. It didn't matter. His face was as familiar to me as my own. The dark mole on his neck was still there.

They say that some people look at peace in death. For Dave, there was nothing, no expression for me to interpret, no sign of the horror of being killed, no indication of resignation, or calm, or fear. Although bitterness simmered in me, I instinctively wanted to find a way to comfort him. I fought an urge to stroke his hair, touch his face, as if he were still alive. Instead, I reached over and placed my hand on his arm, covered by the sheet. His body felt hard under the coarse material.

"Is this your brother?" Taylor asked. "David Chieswicz?"

Again, a small nod.

"Is that a 'yes'?"

"Yes." I said.

"There's a strong family resemblance," he said. "Except for the hair. But I needed to hear you say it aloud. No misinterpretation."

We remained there in silence for less than a minute. I removed my hand from Dave's body. "Can I leave now?" I didn't wait for Taylor's response and went back to the office alcove. A Breuer chair was placed near the attendant's cubicle, and I fell into it and buried my face in my hands because I didn't want to cry and I didn't want to vomit and I didn't want to scream.

I sensed that Taylor had followed me. "I'm so sorry," he said.

"He was a jerk," I said. "They all were."

I had believed that I'd moved beyond all of the pain of Dave's rejection, of my family's rejection, that it didn't matter. I'd buried the feelings of anger and hurt so deeply that on most days I didn't even notice that they were there. Seeing Dave again, however, made them blaze once more. I hated my brother, and my parents, and what they had done.

But once upon a time, I had loved them, too.

CHAPTER THREE

CAITLYN

March 2016

Over the next ten days, before meeting with her advisor, Caitlyn researched the Boston Box. Developing and honing her proposal had complications. Because not much academic exploration had been done on the subject, primary research—a lot of it—would be required. For instance, she would have to match buildings of the period with architectural drawings, if she could find them. That could cause problems since many of the blueprints were probably long gone. In addition to studying Adamston, she'd have to investigate other architects of the era. And given the vagueness of the Boston Box and its purpose, she wasn't entirely certain that she'd succeed. She'd be compiling random bits of information and hoping they would cohere.

Nevertheless, obstacles weren't necessarily bad. With a blank canvas, she might actually make a meaningful contribution if she uncovered fresh material. And research was about explorations, after all. It shouldn't be expected that she would have answers about everything before she did the work. Her preliminary paper would have to have some heft, ten thousand words, but she wouldn't be required to fill hundreds and hundreds of pages, at least yet. Most importantly, she was fascinated by the subject, and where it might lead, and having that strong interest would motivate her.

Two days before her appointment, Caitlyn sent her advisor a brief conceptual paper so that he'd have the opportunity to review her proposal and help with refining the subject. She had some trepidations. The professor, Dr. Allen Bacht, had never warmed to her; indeed, Bacht never seemed to warm to anybody, but that understanding about his personality wasn't much comfort when she had to speak with him.

She shouldn't have bothered showing up early for their meeting in Sandler Hall, a modern office building behind Harvard Yard that housed faculty offices for the Art & Architectural History Department. Bacht was late. He walked past her and into his office while talking to a colleague, acknowledging her presence with a brief glance but no greeting and then closing the door. Five minutes later, the door to the office swung open, the colleague exited, and Bacht signaled for her to enter with a jerk of his head. Knowing him, she didn't expect that he'd apologize for his lateness.

He was a good-looking man, lean and elegant and with neat, silver hair that contradicted his age, which she guessed was less than forty. Bacht sat at his desk and she took a chair by it, an almost intimate arrangement that would allow them to consult on what she had written. She could smell his cologne.

"Nice scent," she said. He raised an eyebrow. *Oh, Jesus,* Caitlyn thought. *Does he think I'm flirting?*

"Tom Ford," Bacht said as he glanced back at his notes, frowning.

Uneasy, she waited for him to say more. While he flipped through some pages, she stared at a bookcase behind him that held copies of books that he had written—she'd read a couple of them, and they were brilliant—and leather-bound histories of Harvard.

"Let me see if I understand you, Ms. Gautry," he finally said. "You want to write your thesis on a third-rater like Adamston and some fantasy facet of design that has no credibility beyond internet scaremongers? Did I get that right? Buried bodies in closets?"

Caitlyn stammered, "What? No. That's not exactly right."

"Explain it to me then. Explain to me precisely what I got wrong."

"There's a broader context here," she answered. "I'm not saying that there was, or is, such a thing as the Boston Box. At least explicitly called that. Not yet. But maybe. And the concept is out there, secret rooms. It's an aspect of Boston architectural lore, whether or not they exist. I admit it's unusual, but their genesis, the Boxes, and the resulting conversation about them, could be illuminating. I think so. Might even be humorous. And while Adamston is a first focus, he's not the only one who has been connected to the Boston Box. I would talk about him, of course, but other architects associated with the time, the legend. I'd write about them, too. There's a lot of imprecision that could be sharpened."

"You'd be looking at others?" Bacht asked.

"Yes."

"You're a social scientist now, Ms. Gautry?" He read from her document. "'Explore contemporary events and mores that required concealment.' Digging up scandals? I had the impression you were trying to be an architectural historian, not a gossip columnist. Would you care to clarify?"

"That is so totally not fair," Caitlyn said. She felt her face redden. "There's an overlap."

"I'm so totally sorry. Am I not being fair? Would you like a tissue?"

"This was a preliminary exploration of a topic. I think it has validity. Very preliminary. Before I go forward, I came to you to discuss it."

"I think my opinions on your subject and approach are clear. Of course, you are free to do whatever you choose. My advice is to find something worth the time, but it is *your* attempt to get an advanced degree. Anything else?"

Caitlyn wanted to spit out *What would be the point?* but simply said, "No." She gathered up her papers and rose to leave.

"You'll thank me someday, Caitlyn."

For what? Being a dick? I doubt that. "Back to the drawing board." She tried to force a smile.

Caitlyn remained quiet until she descended some stairs and went to the office she used as a graduate teaching fellow, located directly below Bacht's. Closing the door, she grabbed the three pages of her discussion document and tore them into shreds. The move was cathartic but reversible since she had copies of the paper on electronic file. The man and his arrogance were infuriating! *Would you like a tissue!*

More frustrating was his complete dismissal of her proposal. The Boston Box would have been a subject that she could have buried herself in. Yet she could only ignore Bacht with the risk that he'd trash her research when it was presented.

She'd have to look for another topic. Could she salvage something from the last two weeks? If she were unable to start her work soon, she wouldn't meet the academic timetable for her program. And could she find an advisor other than Bacht? Because this much was certain: he wasn't a supportive mentor. She needed someone with a functioning heart.

CHAPTER FOUR

MARK

April 2017

By the time Taylor and I returned to his office, my outward composure had returned, but my guts were still knotted. We resumed our seats. A small pile of manila folders was stacked on Taylor's desk and he shoved it toward me. "We made copies of the financial material that we found at your brother's apartment. You can have the originals back."

Casually, I opened the first file. Atop an inch of paper sheets was a recent bank statement. Dave's account balance was printed prominently. $633,215.28.

My eyes must have widened.

"Legitimate," Taylor said.

"How the hell?"

"We did some digging. Fast check. Your brother gambled. Mostly horse racing. Over the last three years he had a string of wins. Big payouts. All of them duly reported to the IRS. Taxes paid. We found some racing crib sheets in the apartment— you'll see copies in the file—but we've seen no indication he'd gambled and won here up north. Hasn't been here that long, and not many outlets for that. No recent deposits. Most of this comes from Florida."

The thought of all that cash made me dizzy. With the realization that my reaction—a mix of wonder and delight at my possible inheritance—was apparent, I found myself embarrassed, almost blushing. "After taxes?"

"Yes."

After calculating what Dave would have had to throw to the government, plus what he had spent on an apartment and other things, his winnings must have been over a million dollars, maybe as much as two. "That's impossible," I said. "Nobody's that lucky."

"Well, your brother was. At least on the surface."

"Explain that."

"You're right," said Taylor. "Extraordinary good fortune, isn't it? It does seem suspicious, and we haven't had the chance to go back and examine every angle. But from the few deposits we've looked at so far, it's all legit. We're checking his arrest record. He'd lost a lot in the past. Maybe this latest run just evened out his streaks. Or maybe he just finally figured out a winning formula for playing the horses."

"Shit," I said, in disbelief.

"You should take some time to examine those statements. Let us know if you find anything."

"I will," I mumbled.

"We have some other matters to talk about," Taylor said.

I was still absorbing the revelation about all that money. I wasn't able to focus. Outside the office window, the construction site had come alive. A building crane slowly lifted a girder for placement. I couldn't hear anything, though, and to see this monstrous machine move, so close by, without any corresponding sound, was disorienting. "The windows here must be thick," I said.

Taylor's All-American face scrunched up, and a question mark practically appeared on his forehead.

"Sorry," I said. "The construction. I'm a little blown away by this. I'll try to concentrate."

"Can you tell me where you were over the weekend? Let's say Thursday."

As fate would have it, a friend from out of town had been in Boston, and we'd had dinner and drinks. I had a work shift on Friday. I gave Taylor my alibis and then added, "Am I a suspect? No offense, but if you want to investigate me, it's a waste of your time."

He shrugged. "Just doing my job."

"Is that it? Are we done?"

"No. We got back an initial autopsy report. I knew about a possibility, but we needed some test results before I said anything." He paused. "Basically, the story is…well, your brother was dying."

"You mean he wasn't killed?" I asked. "I don't understand."

"No, he was murdered, all right. But he had cancer. Probably terminal. He was about to do treatment here in Boston. Aggressive. We found meds at the apartment. And we talked briefly to a doctor. The cancer also showed up during the autopsy. His prognosis was bad, and according to the doctor, he knew it."

"What does that mean?" I said. "I don't get it."

"On one hand, I'm not telling you anything other than your brother was sick. Very sick. As you learn more yourself, you'd probably find that out. But it's just…if I were you, you should be aware. I don't know. I thought you should know. Your brother had a death sentence hanging over him. I wouldn't be surprised to find out he was erratic. That's all. Behaving oddly."

"You've seen something?" I asked. "That he was causing trouble?" I flashed on an image of Robert DeNiro in *Mean Streets*, throwing explosives into mailboxes just for the hell of it. "No. I'm just saying in the past I've witnessed men, people, in this condition act abnormally. Doing weird things. Sudden changes. I've had to bring seriously ill people to trial when a disease screwed them up. But I suppose it's just as possible that he came to Boston to get treatment or tie up some loose ends. Like reconnecting."

If he was prompting me to go into the details of our estrangement, I didn't bite. "I'll keep it in mind," I said.

"Do." Taylor stood and we shook hands, and then I grabbed the stack of folders. As I did so, the edge of one of the files hit a pen holder on Taylor's desk and nudged it about an inch. Taylor reached over and put the holder back in its original position, an adjustment that no one but him would ever notice.

Back in Brighton, dusk approaching, my perceptions were jumbled. Normally, the small space of my apartment, the lack of sunlight, the furniture that didn't match, the inadequate kitchen counter that always looked dirty no matter how many times I wiped it, all those things, I didn't let them get to me. Now, as I looked quickly through the folders with Dave's financial information, a thought fractured my mental block about my circumstances.

$633,215.28.

I'd had to deplete my savings after my breakup and was living close to the edge, money-wise. I had a job now but hadn't yet gotten back on my feet. I'd become isolated. The idea that I could be lifted out of my financial hole, that I could be given another chance—by my brother, my lousy no-good brother...I couldn't make sense of it. I felt as if I'd won the lottery without buying a ticket.

$633,215.28.

I popped open a beer, swigged it, and tried to stop the fantasies that swirled through my head like golden-winged butterflies. The money wasn't in hand yet. But then I surrendered to the dreams. At least for a few days, or a few weeks or months, I could imagine a better life, thanks to Dave's legacy. I could live in nicer digs. Get new clothes. Replenish my savings.

My mood changed, and then changed again. In less than a day there had been the news about Dave's murder, and a reopening of old wounds, and this unexpected windfall. I felt some shame because I was celebrating good luck that came to me because my brother was in a morgue. Moreover, grief, of a sort, mixed with the revived anger that came when I remembered my family.

I was anxious as well. I wanted the money, but it was all too simple, too loaded. In the back of my brain, a voice—that of my superego, or my guilt, or perhaps that of my self-righteous mother—chanted a platitude over and over. It sang: *The Lord giveth, and the Lord taketh away.*

CHAPTER FIVE

CAITLYN

October 2016

After the debacle of her meeting with Bacht, Caitlyn shifted, a little late, to a different theme for her qualifying paper, under the guidance of another advisor obtained over the summer after careful and exhausting negotiations with the department chair. Her new topic, French Academic influences in the construction of the Back Bay, would allow her to slip in some research on the Boston Box. And who knew? Maybe with time and friendlier coaching, the Box could again become the center of her studies.

Bacht had agreed to the advisory reassignment with a few biting comments. For a while, Caitlyn had worried whether she had made an enemy, but with his announcement of an unanticipated sabbatical, she relaxed. He'd still be on campus, but less often, and not as one of her instructors.

In fact, Bacht had agreed to deliver a lecture before his leave had been approved, and he kept that commitment. In an attempt to demonstrate goodwill, Caitlyn attended the event, titled *The Sense of Humor of Architects*. About fifty others, including some of her fellow doctoral candidates, squeezed into a seminar room with tiered rows of seats arranged in semi-circles facing a podium and screen.

Bacht was a practiced speaker. Amusingly, he began by describing a visit to Disney World as a teenager to which he had agreed at his parents' insistence, a celebration of a younger sister's birthday. He had participated in a mood of teenage grumpiness until he came across the Swan and Dolphin Hotels, when he was suddenly mindful of the concept of architectural whimsy. Now, as an adult, he no longer cared for the work of Michael Graves, the postmodernist architect who had designed the hotels, but at the time of the vacation he had been entranced, and the buildings were a factor in his identification of a life's work. But these opening words were only the setup for a larger consideration of humor in construction, more specifically, little architectural jokes.

At that point, he launched a tirade about the ridiculousness of the Boston Box!

Caitlyn listened, unbelieving. He twisted her words about the exploration being humorous. Bacht talked about the Boston Box as an example of failed wit, a facile inside joke without any basis. He didn't cite many scholarly sources; as she knew from her own early research, there weren't many of those. Much of what he offered was critical riff, more opinion than fact. A couple of Caitlyn's fellow doctoral candidates were aware of her interest, and as Bacht spoke, one of them, a red-haired design student named Henry, looked uneasily at her.

Bacht repeated that his overall point in mentioning the Boston Box was to reinforce the notion that his speech was about actual, constructed architectural whimsy. What would be the point in discussing fictional edifices?

Caitlyn placed her elbow on the arm of her chair, raised her hand to her face to hide any blush of anger. Of course, he hadn't mentioned her by name. He wouldn't dare go that far. Was he upset that she had asked for a different advisor? Had he heard somehow of her continued interest in the Boston Box and been displeased at her rejection of his opinion? She almost got up and left but thought the better of it, fearing to bring too much attention to herself and confirming to her friends that Bacht's comments were aimed at her.

She wondered whether to confront him in some fashion. As the talk continued, she was often off-balance, because outside of his comments about the Boston Box, his lecture was frequently insightful and funny. He had a good time speaking about the Harvard Lampoon Building, which was built as a joke and looked like a zany sphinx. At the end of the speech, Bacht was rewarded with generous applause. When the clapping subsided, Caitlyn was about to raise her hand to ask a question, but before she could flag Bacht's attention, he left the podium with a protest of time and disappeared through a side door.

"That was weird," said Henry, next to her. She acknowledged his sympathy with a shrug. He invited her to join him and some others at Cambridge Common, a crowded, unpretentious bar where they could have beers and a cheap meal. Agitated and in need of a diversion, she agreed.

Six people crammed into a big booth. Caitlyn tried to enjoy this chance to hang loose, as if on a small vacation from her concerns, her work. It was a bit of a busman's holiday because when a bunch of architectural and design students got together, much of what they talked about was buildings. They argued for the thousandth time about Harvard's new law school: it's beautiful, it's monstrous, at least it's green, it doesn't fit in, it looks Fascist.

The genial sparring took her mind off Bacht. Four males were in the group, and an extra charge spiked the air, a playful teasing that she enjoyed. Sometimes Henry held her glance a beat longer than normal. Especially in moments like these, her spirit lightened. She felt that if she settled on Henry or some other guy in the bar, she just might be able to make a connection.

Her fun was interrupted, however, when Bacht showed up. This had happened before at Cambridge Common—rarely, but there were instances. He was single, and he usually had a beautiful woman in tow. His presence led those in the booth almost unconsciously to lower their voices.

"The iceman cometh," said Henry. He had put on a Red Sox cap.

"Please, dear Lord," Caitlyn whispered in response, "make him go away." She poured another glass of beer from a pitcher on the table.

"Christ," said Henry, "Sophie made eye contact. Sophie Wong! Stop that! Get under the table."

Caitlyn chuckled. "Of all the nights to forget my cloak of invisibility."

It was as if their wish to avoid him caused a perverse pull to the table. Bacht approached. "Ah, the candidates," he said. "So delightful in their rituals."

Sophie laughed, but no one else did.

"And Caitlyn," Bacht said. "I trust you are thriving under Madame Venda." Helene Venda was Caitlyn's new advisor. "Did you enjoy my talk?"

"Your comments about the Boston Box were intriguing," Caitlyn said, trying to sound neutral.

"Boston Box. Intrigued? Just the opposite of my intent. I hope Madame Venda will continue to educate you. Well, if you don't mind, my friend has just arrived. Maybe I can convince her to go somewhere else. Not that this isn't a charming establishment. But very crowded. Enjoy your hamburgers. Next time I'll have to insist on joining you." He said the words in a manner that suggested hanging out together was never going to happen. He walked off and descended upon his acquaintance.

When he was out of earshot, Caitlyn said, "That man is a dick."

"He's funny," Sophie said. "He isn't that awful. And he's good." This remark made more than one of the gang at the table pretend to be shocked. "You're all idiots. I meant he knows architecture. He's a genius."

"What's with all the snarky remarks about the Boston Box?" Henry asked.

Caitlyn knew that complaining was useless, but the beer had loosened her inhibitions. "Damned if I know," she said. "He has some kind of hair across his ass about it. And me, apparently."

Another of the group, a nerdish guy named Tony, spoke up. "He didn't seem too encouraging, to say the least. Rather insulting."

"Excuse me," said Sophie, who hadn't been at the lecture. "What's the Boston Box?"

"The stuff of legend," Henry said. "A special torture chamber in Boston homes to hide dead bodies."

"It's not that," Caitlyn protested. "Let's talk about something else."

"You think Charles Bulfinch was a serial killer?" Tony asked.

"I didn't say anything about Bulfinch," Caitlyn replied. "Maybe Bacht, but not Bulfinch."

The group laughed. "In any case, take comfort," Henry said. "He hates male students as much as he hates female ones. None of us are safe."

"Can we change the subject?" Caitlyn said.

"How about sex?" Henry said. "Is anyone getting laid?"

"Tony is," another guy at the table said. "But he's gay so he doesn't count."

Tony shrugged. "I'm told I'm adorable."

Thankfully, sex seemed to carry the group away from the topic of the Boston Box. The conversation with Bacht lingered, however, and spoiled Caitlyn's mood. Forget about making or accepting an overture tonight. In her current state of mind, it'd be asking for disaster.

CHAPTER SIX

MARK

April 2017

When I woke the next morning, the events of the previous day haunted me, but I didn't have time to brood because I had to go to work. Under the circumstances, I probably could have called in, stayed home, but I needed the distraction. And I needed the wages, too. My inheritance wasn't yet in hand. I didn't want to piss off my boss.

Thanks to a former co-worker, last autumn I had landed a gig driving an amphibious tour vehicle, colloquially called a "Duck," around the streets of Boston. The good news was that the tips were exceptional, and I could make a few hundred bucks in a day. Sometimes more. The bad news was that as a low man on the roster I didn't get many shifts, and winter was slow, with a few months' hiatus. The owners assured me that things would pick up in the spring and summer. In the meantime, I had to grab whatever sparse April hours came my way.

I enjoyed the job and had gotten comfortable navigating what was essentially a military vehicle around Boston's narrow streets and, ultimately, afloat on the Charles River. That was the amphibious part—the "Duck" part—the tour's major selling point. My biggest challenge was the city's ruthless drivers,

who never wanted to yield to something as big and as slow as a
Duck. At times their belligerence made it difficult to maintain
the good-humored tour guide attitude that earned big gratuities.

I had contrived a jovial professional personality—all the
drivers did. I liked researching my city, and I was becoming
a fount of Boston lore. I nonchalantly dispensed historical
facts and jokes, pointing out attractions like the State House,
the Harrison Gray Otis House, Mass General Hospital, and the
Longfellow Bridge. I recommended places for a good bowl of
chowder and quacked like a real duck for the company's signature routine. For a laugh, I would pretend to be insulted if somebody called Boston "Beantown." Really, baked beans aren't that
big of a deal here anymore.

I did three tour runs, two of which were full thanks to a
convention of microbiologists in town. Okay tips. Afterward, I
went out for a drink with one of the other guides, but I didn't
know him very well, and our chat was mostly bullshit, no talk
about Dave from me, although my colleague gave me the name
of a lawyer when I asked if he could recommend a good one. I
hedged the reason.

The following morning, after my breakfast of cereal and coffee, I resigned myself to taking care of the consequences of my
brother's death. Might as well. I had no more shifts booked until
the weekend.

Taylor had spoken to me at the OME about the release of
Dave's body. The autopsy was complete, and I could have the
"remains" whenever I wished. A funeral home in my neighborhood was as good as any other, I supposed. I called and then
met with the undertaker, an overweight man dressed in a black
suit and a gray tie flecked with ivory, all very subdued, like his
sympathetic manner. He was at ease with the everyday routines

of death. He probably thought I was heartless as I explained the circumstances, maintained a non-emotional front, and endeavored to hold down the costs. Which, in the end, would still amount to a few thousand dollars. With reluctance, I handed over a credit card and said a silent prayer that Dave's estate would be settled quickly and cover the balance.

Money anxiety led me next to call the lawyer I'd learned about. His name was Larry Dietz, in private practice, and on reaching him by phone I told him about my brother's death and estate. Dietz had a specialty in probate. He said that, even presuming no will existed, it could still take several months for the final disposition of Dave's property. He urged me to visit the apartment and uncover what I could about Dave's finances. I'd been so caught up in the inconvenience of the situation—and in my sullenness about my estranged brother—that I'd practically forgotten about the apartment.

"When can you go there?" Dietz asked.

"Today, I suppose."

"It'd be helpful to get some more information. If you're up for it."

I wasn't exactly "up for it" but had no good excuse to avoid it either.

I reached Detective Taylor and asked if he could notify Dave's landlord that I would visit. Efficient bastard had already done that. I asked if the police had taken anything else besides the bank statements. He told me there had been no computer or laptop. A cell phone hadn't been found, nor was there any sign that Dave had owned one, although a landline was installed at the apartment. Taylor speculated Dave had had a prepaid untraceable cell phone that had been lost or destroyed or kept by his killer. "Why?" was anyone's guess.

When I'd first heard that Dave lived in the Fenway area, I'd imagined an apartment in one of the nondescript row houses that had characterized the neighborhood until recently. Once I saw the address was on Boylston Street, a major thoroughfare, I adjusted my expectations. New residential high-rises had spurted up there, aimed at the personnel who worked at a network of hospitals and clinics a couple of blocks away. Expensive residences. So I wasn't entirely surprised when I arrived at a doorman building, glass-fronted and shiny, a tower. The Fenway Grand. But I was slightly awestruck.

A front desk attendant, who looked like a retired man killing time, summoned the building supervisor, a hefty dirty blond called Joe with an Italian surname that I didn't hear clearly. Joe expressed condolences about Dave. He said my brother was a good guy, no trouble at all, and it struck me that Joe knew my brother better than I did. Or at least my brother in his most recent, and final, incarnation. I thought Joe would accompany me to the unit, but he simply handed me a set of keys and a pass card that would get me through a security door on the first floor. He apparently had little concern about the legalities of my visit. The police's okay was good enough for him.

An elevator took me to the tenth floor, better than midway up. I fumbled with the lock until I found the right number of half-turns that released the tumblers. I took a deep breath, pushed open the door, and prepared myself to sort through the leftovers of my dead brother's life.

CHAPTER SEVEN

CAITLYN

October 2016

Bacht's comments continued to annoy Caitlyn. She wrote an angry email to him that challenged the contentions in his lecture, objected to his insults, accused him of unfairness. Her hand hovered above the "Send" button, but instead she pushed the "Draft" tag, saved her text, and then shut down her laptop. It was too much. She needed to talk to someone before she acted.

The logical confidante was her new advisor. Caitlyn dismissed the idea of texting Helene Venda because the professor had made it clear that she communicated by that method only in emergencies. Instead, Caitlyn sent a short email message, purposefully vague, and asked to speak as soon as possible. Within the hour, Venda responded and offered a meeting for the next day.

At the appointed time, Caitlyn went to Venda's office, which was also at Sandler. Venda was French-born and had an accent. Although bundled under a thick knit sweater, she took up no space. Her hair, in a pageboy cut, was brown, and the color complemented her eyes. In the past, Caitlyn had found her to be kind and shrewd. Venda let Caitlyn speak without interruption, was silent for a few moments, and then asked a question. "What is it exactly that you are saying? In as few words as possible."

"He attacked me," Caitlyn said.

"Okay. Attack is a strong word. Evidently, there is some problem with the subject itself. This box. Is it that he used any research that you did? Or vice-versa? For example, if I were to compare what you wrote to the speech, is it that I would find similar wording, or sources? Please understand. I am just trying to do this evaluation."

"I guess my point is that he totally dismissed my concept as negligible, basically telling everyone that it was stupid, implying that I was a moron for considering it, in front of people who know about my interest."

"He didn't mention you at all."

Caitlyn shook her head back and forth, no, frustrated.

"I am not unsympathetic," Venda said. "Confidentially, the man is maddening. It doesn't shock me that he is petty." These statements surprised Caitlyn. There'd been departmental gossip that the two professors were very close friends. Or more. As if reading her mind, Venda continued. "Such a handsome man, and so intelligent, but sometimes his manner! Nevertheless, unless it is that you say he has a grudge and you have proof, or that he invents facts, you will have many things lined up against you. Those of us in academia argue about matters every day. I could raise the issue with the department chair, but…"

This wasn't what Caitlyn hoped to hear. "I am really angry." She almost whispered the sentence.

Venda offered a complicit smile. "My dear girl, you must not be so shy. I think that is a good thing. We must all find motivation where we can. I am pleased to hear you express your anger. Your spirit. We women do not always. Perhaps we can find a way for you to achieve some justice. We can continue to work together. You and I. It is likely he would be one of your readers, and an obstacle, but you could make this point."

"But how?"

"Dear girl, it is so simple. Show he was wrong."

Caitlyn sat back in her chair and considered this proposition. *Show Bacht was wrong.* He had dismissed all of her ideas, but his speech hadn't offered any solid research for his theories. She had even recognized some errors in his thinking.

She suddenly felt satisfied, lit up with the prospect of combat, of winning. If Bacht wanted to humiliate her, she wouldn't give in. She would prove the existence of the Boston Box.

CHAPTER EIGHT

MARK

April 2017

My first impression was that Dave's apartment was modern and soulless and bare. Although the police had searched the place, it looked neat. Probably a tribute to Taylor's OCD. The main room was a combined kitchen, dining, and living area, an open floor plan; a medium-sized bedroom was off to the side; a classy bathroom had a fancy rain shower and extra spray heads. Dave had made only a perfunctory effort at decorating, just the necessary furniture like a couch and a coffee table and lamps, and nothing but a flat screen TV on the walls. Neither of us seemed to have a gift for nest building.

But closer inspection revealed one trait that separated us: the outlay of money. I began to appreciate the understatement of Taylor's observation that it was a nice apartment. Everything was new. A rich looking rug was, if not Persian, then something like it. The couch was leather. The flat screen TV was a high-end brand and gigantic. The appliances—admittedly installed in the apartment rather than purchased, but still—were stainless steel, and the kitchen counter and a breakfast bar were topped with marble, complemented by a couple of stylish stools. Not much imagination here, but a lot of cash.

The view was spectacular. Floor to ceiling windows. The unit wasn't high up enough to see into Fenway Park, a block or two away, but I almost felt like I could reach out and touch the stadium. Before I set off on my more purposeful search through Dave's belongings, I paused. The sun was low, and Boston's cityscape was spread before me. Breathtaking. A view like this makes a man feel important.

But being in someone else's home is like walking on a tilted floor. With practice, you can maintain your balance, but it takes getting used to. In this case, the unfamiliarity was heightened because I had no one to tell me where things were or how they worked. I spent the next twenty minutes finding the thermostats, making sense of the remotes, locating the trash baskets. At the end of these efforts, ventilation flowed and warmed the air, and some smooth jazz from a cable music channel came through the excellent speakers of the television.

As I headed to the kitchen area, I wasn't entirely clear what I was looking for. I figured the police would have already grabbed those items that offered any clues about my brother's finances or his murder. I rummaged through the cabinets and cutlery drawers, and what struck me once again was how new everything was. Dave had managed to gather the basics, like dishes and flatware and a set of pots and pans. Calphalon Non-Stick. The shelves had salt and pepper grinders and Cheerios. A bottle of vodka. A can of Folgers Coffee. It was apparent that when he had moved here, he hadn't brought much with him except an old photograph of my parents at their wedding, 5 x 7, framed, which I noted then ignored. The only other item that revealed any character was a Red Sox ticket stuck on the refrigerator door with a magnet. I guessed Dave had continued to like baseball, as he had as a kid. I wasn't a big fan myself, but I made another mental note to use the ticket—which had cost almost $200—when the early May game rolled around in a few weeks.

A portable phone handset rested on the kitchen counter. No messages were on the answering machine except from the door-man, saying food deliveries were at the desk for pick-up. Dave used a pre-recorded message, so I couldn't hear his voice.

I went to the bedroom. A heavy oak chest had two small drawers, one of them full of socks, and four large ones containing briefs, tee shirts, and some pajamas. Maybe I'd use the socks. I'd throw out the underwear.

A coffee table book about Boston was on a nightstand, along with a pair of reading glasses. Dave had never been too studious, so I presumed he was just trying to get to know the city better, although I wondered why he hadn't used a more traditional guidebook. A folded page corner showed that he'd made it about halfway through. Up to that point were several of these markers. I hated when people damaged books in that way.

Under the bed were a pair of bedroom slippers, and some dust, and some porn. Nothing too kinky in my brother's taste in erotic reading. A plastic bottle of hand lotion was also on the nightstand. Like all guys, Dave must have still enjoyed jerking off. Mercifully, no other signs of that activity were in evidence. I flashed back to our adolescence when he had shown me a contemporary version of this kind of material. An issue of *Penthouse*. I remembered my confusion. It seemed like it was a big deal for my brother and his pals. I knew it was supposed to be sinful, but I didn't find it especially interesting or understand their leers.

So far, not much success in finding clues or helpful information. Everything was what it appeared to be. I entered a small walk-in closet and shuffled the items that were on hangers. A dozen or so shirts hung there, professionally laundered, as well as a brown leather jacket, a few sport coats, several pairs of shoes, and a stack of sweaters piled on a shelf, almost all of them shades of blue. No hidden compartments, or boxes of mementos, or anything other than clothes and shoes. At least if my claims on Dave's property were successful, my wardrobe would be improved significantly. Some pretty nice labels.

I put on one of Dave's blue sweaters, a cardigan, and looked at myself in a floor length mirror on the wall of the closet. It fit perfectly. Someone watching me might think I was ghoulish, but this stuff was too good to donate to charity just yet. Because I'd never seen Dave in any of the clothes, it was as if I were in a department store.

As I removed the sweater, paper crinkled. I searched in a pocket and found a piece of a newspaper with two words, or word fragments, written on it in pencil. The script was smeared and almost illegible. It looked like "Boston Bok" or, more likely, "Boston Box." Probably meaningless, and I almost threw the note away, but after a moment's reflection I kept it for Taylor. I checked the pockets of other pieces of clothing and found nothing but lint and loose change.

I muttered to myself. This was going nowhere. I still had a coat closet to inspect and the bathroom. Getting another beer, I went into the living room, sat on the couch, and put my feet on a coffee table. With a remote I changed the channel on the TV to HBO. A costumed superhero, sixty on-screen inches of him, battled an alien creature in a big city, the two of them careening through the air like out of control jets. I was mesmerized by the scale of the image, the rumbling stereo sound.

Outside the enormous windows, it was after sunset. Boston's lights started to twinkle. I sipped my beer. To match that skyline, this luxury, I should be drinking champagne, or fine wine.

I noticed that the coffee table had a narrow drawer, so I sat up and pulled it open. Inside was an electronic car key, probably the spare. The BMW insignia was easy to identify.

I've always wanted a BMW.

I found nothing more of interest. On my way out of the building, I stopped by the superintendent's office to give back the keys, but he told me to keep them.

"I'll need to talk to you about vacating," I said. "The end of the month is soon. I have to talk to a lawyer about it."

"No worries," Joe said. "The rent's paid through the end of the year."

"My brother paid in advance?"

"That's the way he wanted to do it. With his application, he included a full year's rent. Solved a small issue with his credit. Only been here since January. The police said you're his family. As far as I can see, that means you have access. They're done here. They told me they were all set. You might as well use it. The rent's paid. You let me know if you need anything else."

I shook my head and left. It struck me that the super's generosity could have a more dubious motive: there was probably legal justification for me to break the lease and get the rent back, perhaps as much as $50,000. With all the construction that was going on in Boston, maybe luxury spaces weren't so easy to rent. I'd have to see what was possible, what made sense.

I went outside and stared up at the shimmering Fenway Grand. If I wanted, this could be my home until the lease was settled, for several weeks or maybe even months.

It didn't take long to decide. I headed to my apartment and packed a bag.

CHAPTER NINE

CAITLYN

October 2016

At her apartment, a cluttered one bedroom not far from Harvard's campus, Caitlyn decided to reenergize her research into the Boston Box by arranging a visit to the most public of Gregory Adamston's surviving works, a Presbyterian church called the Old Pilgrim in Boston's South End. After an internet search, she sent off an email to the church's administrator, and received a prompt reply that welcomed her the following day.

At the church but before introducing herself, Caitlyn walked around the building. The Gothic Revival edifice, in pink wine puddingstone, had a great spire and what seemed like a dozen eaves and peaks, and worn slate on its roof. The structure was probably Adamston's best. In all likelihood, its location had had almost a country aspect in the nineteenth century, but now it was in the middle of urban sprawl. A housing development occupied the adjacent block, and towers in Back Bay like the Pru and the Hancock jutted against the sky not far away. Caitlyn wasn't afraid of hard, detailed work, and poking around the big church would be more like fun, but she realized that the time she'd allotted for the visit, a few hours, would have to be used wisely.

Her phone vibrated. A text from her mother: *How are you?*

"*OMW to a meeting can't chat. Ltr?*"

Sure. Miss you! Can't wait for Thanksgiving. Study hard, Squirrel!

Caitlyn slipped the phone back into a jacket pocket, entered the church through a side door, and made her way down a narrow staircase to the parish offices in the basement. Linoleum floors and painted sheetrock corridors hinted at another, probable complication for her research: some of the interior space had been renovated, perhaps several times.

The office had scuffed walls and mismatched furniture. A casually dressed male receptionist pushed a series of buttons on an ancient intercom phone set, chatted briefly, and then hung up. "Dr. Roman will come and get you. You can have a seat."

"Who is Dr. Roman?" Caitlyn asked.

"The pastor," said the receptionist.

Caitlyn had expected to meet with a custodian.

Dr. Roman arrived shortly. He was a tall man, Black, substantial heft, and his friendliness was almost tangible. He put forth his hand to shake. His ring finger had been amputated above the second knuckle. "The Harvard scholar?"

Caitlyn introduced herself and then said, "Scholar in training, I suppose."

"I studied at the divinity school for a spell," Dr. Roman said. "With Peter Gomes. What a remarkable man!"

"I'm afraid I didn't know him."

"What can I do for you?" Before getting her answer, Dr. Roman faced the receptionist. "Scotty, would you call Pat and have him join us?"

Then Dr. Roman led Caitlyn back upstairs. They entered the nave, a great space, all of the walls a flat white, with wainscoting, railings, and pews in carved cherrywood. Some plaster was peeling, particularly close to a water stain in the right corner near the roof. The altar was almost like a stage thrust forward into the congregation, with a lectern in the center of it, and a pulpit to the left. At the rear was a spectacular pipe organ. Almost no religious imagery adorned the church.

Dr. Roman continued to a front pew, where they sat. "So, what can I help with?" His voice echoed in the emptiness.

"I'm researching Adamston's style for a project," Caitlyn said. "The church's architect."

"A thesis?"

"No, another project. Some writing. Especially his interior design."

"I see. You certainly can look around here. Feel free. As much as you want. Easy to arrange. It's a wonderful building. But there've been so many renovations to the interior. The exterior, in contrast, is fundamentally the same as when it was built. Exquisite, I think. Except for the roof. Not enough funds when time came for replacement. It's patched. The church has changed denominations over 150 years. It was a community center in the twenties and thirties. Even now, it's multi-purpose. We let some of the local immigrant religious groups, wonderful people, use it on Sundays, in the evenings."

"Can I ask a strange question?"

"Oh, dear," Dr. Roman said, laughing. "By all means."

"Are you aware of any hidden chambers or rooms? Or was there a time, maybe, when you heard of something like that?"

Dr. Roman shook his head. "That's interesting. No. Sorry to disappoint you. The church is from the 1860's. Too late for the Underground Railroad and runaway slaves. Mostly closets. Not even a crypt. I'm not sure if there's much in the loft. I've never had occasion to crawl up to it myself. I don't think anyone does."

Caitlyn cast a glance around the ceiling. Above a side altar on the left was what looked like a small door, painted to match the wall and blend in. It wasn't a Boston Box—one could hardly claim that it was hidden. She pointed at it. "Is that the loft?"

Dr. Roman was about to answer the question when they were joined by a wiry man in jeans and a heavyweight forest green shirt with stitching above a pocket that identified him as "Pat." He had the air of an intense man with much to do. Dr. Roman introduced him to Caitlyn.

"I wondered about the loft," Caitlyn said. "Like what's in it."

"Never go there," answered Pat. "Nothing much. Some decorations, old papers, and stuff. I checked it once. A bother for storage. Too difficult to reach."

"Papers?" Caitlyn asked.

"Invoices, bills, things like that, building repairs. It's all out of date. Should probably be junked. Might be a fire hazard, now that I think of it."

Caitlyn said, "If there was anything about the church's construction, it might be useful to me. I'm looking at the history."

Obviously not keen on the idea, Pat replied, "It's filthy. You need a ladder. I have the current prints in my office."

"I could do it," Caitlyn said. "If I could get up there. You wouldn't have to hang around. I'm sorry. I'm being so much trouble. But I could take pictures. For your reference. It's simply that older files might be more helpful to me than new."

Dr. Roman spoke. "Oh, what do you say, Pat? Do you have time to help her out?"

Pat eyed Dr. Roman and hesitated, as if weighing whether to argue with his boss before finally determining there was no point. He nodded and went off to get a ladder. Caitlyn and Dr. Roman waited in the nave and chatted, sometimes drifting away from talk about the Old Pilgrim. Dr. Roman alluded to time in the military, and maybe that accounted for his severed finger, but he offered no explanation, and Caitlyn didn't ask about it.

Pat came back with an aluminum extension ladder and leaned it against the wall where the loft was located. The climb, over twenty feet, would be dizzying yet considerably less dangerous than others Caitlyn had done in the past, like during an internship in Italy. Pat offered to join her, but she insisted it wasn't necessary; she was wary of his impatience. Before she climbed the ladder, Dr. Roman excused himself but asked that she speak with him when she was finished.

With the ladder solidly moored by Pat, Caitlyn mounted its rungs. Three-quarters of the way, she turned around. The height made her lightheaded. "I won't be long," she called out. At the top, she pushed the painted panel of the loft door, lightly at first, but it was stuck, and a harder shove was needed to open it. She crawled from the ladder into the space and then shouted to Pat below. "You can come back in twenty if you like, but I think I can manage."

"I'll wait," Pat yelled back. "Have to fix a window back there. I'll work on that."

Caitlyn sighed. His vigil would be like a ticking clock and force her to hurry, but nothing she could do about it. She turned her attention to the loft. Its wooden ceiling was low and angled, smooth unpainted boards interrupted by a few heavy beams. No light shone other than what came through a round, stained glass window that threw rays of yellow, red, and blue unevenly around the room. She heard a scratching sound. A bird on the roof? A mouse? She saw nothing move.

Caitlyn used her phone as a flashlight. Starting at the door, she rotated slowly and aimed the phone's beam into the loft's nooks. Near one corner was a pigeon's dried carcass, a clump of feathers. The bird had probably been trapped a long time ago. Disgusting, but so old that at least it didn't smell. Continuing to turn, a figure loomed out of the shadows and startled her. A plaster Christ, almost the height of a real man, extended his arms toward her. For Jesus, he didn't look particularly friendly, which surely accounted for his banishment into an attic. How he got into this space might be a miracle worth investigating.

Although the loft was forbidding, not much of its contents was out of the ordinary. At about the third quarter of the way in her turn, she spotted several boxes stacked close to a wall.

A voice came from behind her in the church. "Are you okay up there?"

As Caitlyn moved back to the door, she scraped her head on a rafter and felt a touch of pain that caused her to swear. She looked down through the door. Pat was at foot of the ladder. "I'm fine," she yelled. "Fifteen minutes. Thanks so much!"

Crouching to avoid another knock on her head, she stepped back to the stack of boxes and lifted the lid of the uppermost one. It held a number of file folders that she quickly leafed through. They contained old invoices related to the maintenance of the church. Some were from the 1930's. She wondered if they had any importance or value. Not for her study, necessarily, but these days, people paid all kinds of insane money on eBay for weird, arcane objects.

She moved the box to the side and then checked the next carton in the stack. More files, but one of them was very thick and labeled "Building." With amazement, Caitlyn grasped that the file contained folded architectural drawings. A number of them were faded and water stained, but one notation suggested that it came from the time of construction.

She was elated. If they were originals, and if the church once had a Boston Box, these might show it. But reviewing the drawings in detail required better lighting than the loft offered, and—due to the damage—better tools than she had at hand. After finding nothing more of interest in the other boxes, and taking some pictures, she returned to the door.

Pat had remained in the nave, and he anchored the ladder again as she climbed down. The bulky file was awkward to hold while grasping the rungs, so her descent was clumsy and slow but safe.

Back at the parish offices, she caught up with Dr. Roman. When she told him what she'd found, he said, "Why that's marvelous!" She asked to borrow the files. A scanning device back at Harvard could make electronic copies for her to analyze. "By all means, you can use them," he said.

They separated. Caitlyn spent a little more time at the Old Pilgrim, but she concluded that it made more sense to examine the blueprints before exploring further, and she soon left. Outdoors, the autumn day was moderate. She recalled that a row of Adamston's residential buildings was located a few blocks away in Chadwick Square. She consulted her phone for directions to that neighborhood.

In less than ten minutes, she was at Chadwick Square. The Adamston row was six adjacent brownstone residences with shared window designs and mansard roofs. They were all very symmetrical, with some distinctive semi-circular arches over the entry doors, each capped with an engraved keystone.

Nevertheless, the buildings seemed of a piece with the most charming aspects of the square, where several other sequences of brownstones surrounded a well-maintained, although small, strip of parkland in the center of the street. Caitlyn knew that for most of its history Boston's South End hadn't been a fashionable area to live, despite ornamental features like the park. That is, until recent years, when gentrification and proximity to stylish Back Bay had finally certified the neighborhood's desirability. Of the Adamston row, five of the six homes looked to have been restored and probably carved up into condominiums.

The single exception was at the far end, Nine Chadwick Square. It was more tattered than the others, yet evidently still occupied. A discolored Christmas ornament hung in a window on the highest floor, and she could imagine that the decoration wasn't an early celebration of the upcoming season, but a leftover from last year, or even several years past. Caitlyn felt like the place had an aura only she could sense. Was something signaling to her? No. But how odd to have that feeling! She decided that, out of all of the row, it was the strongest prospect to have a Boston Box, given its state of disrepair and lack of modernization, and that accounted for its mysterious pull on her.

Near the front entrance of one of the remodeled buildings in the row was a "Condo for Sale" sign. On impulse, Caitlyn dialed the number of the realtor, a woman named Susan Slaughter. Caitlyn's call went into voicemail. She left a message inquiring about the unit, pretending to be a buyer. She wasn't sure if there'd be much benefit to a tour, at least in looking for a Boston Box, because the interior had likely been redone, but since the opportunity to snoop had arisen, she'd take advantage of it. Maybe she could learn about the shabby building, too.

MARK

April 2017

When I returned to the Fenway Grand the next day, duffle bag in hand, I stopped by the superintendent's office to let him know I'd be in and out over the coming weeks. Joe reminded me that Dave had a mailbox in the lobby and that it hadn't been emptied for several days. A key had been included with the others he had given me. I went to the box and retrieved about a dozen items, mostly bulk mail plus a few bills.

A different desk attendant was on duty as I was about to go through the security door with the card that Joe had given me. The attendant was swarthy, olive-skinned, and his shirt didn't fit. Too tight. He eyed me with suspicion. "Excuse me," he said. "Can I help you?"

"I have a pass card," I said. "My name is Mark Chieswicz. The brother of Dave Chieswicz. 1004."

"Do you mind if I see it?"

I displayed the card. "I spoke with Joe," I said.

The attendant looked at the card and then seemed to evaluate me. Finally, he waved. "Go on through, sir. Sorry. I didn't recognize you. Usually, guests have to sign in. I see the resemblance now."

"I'll be here a lot probably until things get settled," I told him. "What's your name?"

"Hesh."

"Cool. Nice to meet you." Hesh observed me as I went to the elevators.

In the apartment, after shedding my jacket, I sat on one of the stools at the breakfast bar in the kitchen. I turned on my laptop, logged onto a Wi-Fi connection provided as one of the benefits of living at the Fenway Grand, and then spread the mail in front of me. Most of it—catalogs, circulars, a solicitation from an auto club—went directly into the trash. I opened a credit card bill. The balance was several hundred dollars, all of it from expenses accrued over the last cycle. Dave apparently paid down his account to zero every month. Despite what I knew about Dave and how he earned his money, I felt a perverse form of sibling rivalry, one that showed me at a disadvantage. Dave's lack of debt became a judgment on my own inability to make ends meet.

The list of charges on the first page of the bill included over four hundred dollars to the Red Sox. Because the ticket that hung on the refrigerator only accounted for half of that amount, Dave must have gone recently to another game, one of the first of the season, just before he died. Other than that, lots of restaurant deliveries—Dave must have liked Thai food and pizza—and laundry charges.

On the second page, however, was an item that caused my stomach to clench.

Dave had bought a ticket to a Duck tour from the company where I worked. I checked the date of the purchase and brought up my personal calendar on my laptop. The date matched a day when I was on duty.

I told myself it was impossible that Dave would have been on one of my tours without my knowing. Even though I'd not seen him in decades, I'd recognized him immediately at the morgue. I would have noticed him on a tour. I'd bet my life on it. Possibly the ticket was a coincidence. Maybe the posting date of the purchase didn't match the actual day of his tour because of delayed office paperwork or an advance buy. Or maybe he rode with a different driver.

Then the doubts crept in. I wouldn't have expected him, and that might have hindered me from identifying him. I knew that in other circumstances somebody could look at an object a hundred times and not notice a detail. Or Dave could have disguised himself. In that case, however, wouldn't I have found some evidence here in the apartment? A toupee, or a false mustache? The reading glasses on his bed table wouldn't have provided much camouflage. Was his tour random? Did he even know I worked there? But just as I was sure I didn't see him, I was equally sure of something else. Call it brotherly intuition, or my absorption of adages like "Where there's smoke, there's fire," but in the end I convinced myself that *Dave had spied on me.*

Perhaps curiosity had motivated him—like whatever became of his long-lost brother, as casual an interest in me as my internet search about him had been over ten years ago. Perhaps his illness brought about remorse, or he needed me once he was in treatment. Or perhaps it was Taylor's supposition, that Dave wasn't totally rational. In any case, snooping fit Dave's character. He was a thief, and definitely someone who snuck around.

I wasn't sure what to do with my speculation. Confused, letting it ferment, I moved on to figuring out how to claim Dave's car. Taylor was a good start for that task. I reached him by phone. He said the BMW had been towed from the South End for parking violations. After my brother's body had been discovered, the police did a crosscheck and made the connection. The car had been examined for evidence and I could claim it from the lot where it was being held. "There are probably some charges," he said. "Fines."

"Really?" I asked. "A city surcharge? For being murdered and not moving your car?"

I could almost hear his frown over the phone. "Got it. I'll make a call. The lot's info is on the web."

"There's something else." I told him about the paper that I'd found with "Boston Box" written on it. He grilled me about whether the phrase had any meaning for me and then asked that I take a picture of the note with my phone and text it to him. I was to hold onto the paper until he could dispatch someone to pick it up.

"Do you think it's related?" I asked.

"That's what we'll check," Taylor said.

The call ended. As instructed, I texted a shot of the scrap of paper to Taylor. Then I went onto the Boston Police website to get information on retrieving a towed car. Luckily, the license plate number of Dave's BMW had been written on a tag with the spare electronic key, which enabled me to confirm online that the car was being held, and where. The lot, on a frontage road in South Boston, was open till 7PM. It was only mid-afternoon.

By using a combination of subway and taxi rides, I reached the lot an hour and a half later. I gave Taylor credit; he was again efficient. I didn't have to pay any fines or other charges. Once the necessary paperwork was finished—just signing a few receipts—I had to walk through the lot on my own to find the car, a challenge since I only knew the make and the license number. I continued down a row of maybe thirty vehicles.

And then I saw it. Dave's car. A thing of beauty. A BMW M235i, metallic gray, a bullet in the shape of a coupe. Somehow it sparkled even in the cloudy weather that darkened the skies, so sleek that it was almost scary. I opened the door with the electronic key and slipped into the cockpit. The car had less than 10,000 miles and smelled new. Because Dave and I were similar in size, I hardly needed to adjust the seat before I hit the ignition and touched the gas pedal. Power. This monster was going to fly. As the lot attendant waved me through the gate, I waited for an appreciative glance, but he probably saw beauties like this all the time since he barely registered my departure.

Although I was ready for takeoff, Boston didn't cooperate. When I reached the Southeast Expressway, rush hour had begun, and traffic crawled. I might as well have been driving an old Chevette. Let me reconsider that. If I had to stare at Boston's biggest piece of artwork, a gas tank that an artist had decorated with enormous swatches of color, the best way to do it was while listening to a Bose sound system, warmed by climate controlled air, on leather seats, with the comforting vibration of a turbocharged V6 almost giving me an erection.

Delete that "almost."

I wanted to show the car off. After a moment's consideration, I succumbed to a foolish impulse by contacting my ex. It's illegal to text and drive in Massachusetts but traffic wasn't moving, and no state police cars were in view. Not that the law would have stopped me.

"You free for a drink? I have something to talk to you about."

I waited for a couple of minutes. No reply. Oh, well. I pondered whether the Beemer offered a way to do "hands-free" texting. I'd have to check the manual, which promised to be the most enjoyable book I'd read in ages.

And then a response. *What?*

"A surprise. It's important."

I'm at work until six.

"I'll swing by. Meet you at the entrance."

Several moments passed before the response: *OK.*

"Great."

My ex worked in Cambridge in Kendall Square, an area that has prospered during the high tech and biomedical booms. Notwithstanding traffic jams, I could make it there in time, but the pace would be slow. Somehow, I figured out how to give instructions to the car's in-dash GPS and was directed to a nearby off-ramp that took me down Mass Ave. Soon the rotunda of the Massachusetts Institute of Technology—MIT—came into view across the river in Cambridge. The university's army of science and engineering expertise was responsible, in large part, for the recent, rapid development in the neighborhood.

Miraculously, I found a parking place on a side street about a half-block away from where my ex worked. Still had about fifteen minutes to kill. Travelling and traffic and the excitement of the BMW had occupied my mind until that moment, but faced with this imminent reunion, the first that my ex and I would have in about two months, I contemplated what to say, what to do when I saw him.

Paul and I had been together for almost a decade. He was a couple of years younger than me, more ambitious, and certainly more outgoing. Sex was phenomenal, at least in the beginning, and we were compatible in other ways, like he cooked, but I was handy with repairs. He used to say my laid-back attitude gave him the dash of relief he needed from his stressful job. We enjoyed the same kinds of movies. I loved him deeply. These were the happiest years of my life.

Even so, I never quite understood what he saw in me. Although I liked money, career building has never been one of my priorities. I have a liberal arts degree from a state college and, before I met Paul, I had managed to survive mostly by doing administrative work. During our relationship, he picked up more checks than I did, and he didn't seem to care as long as I kicked in now and then.

When I lost my job following a merger, Paul started to look at me differently. Comments about my lack of ambition occurred more and more frequently. Whatever the cause of my ongoing failure at finding re-employment—and I'd claim I was a victim of the economy at the time—his lack of faith didn't help. I got depressed. Eventually, he viewed me as damaged goods and gave up on me. I could almost see the love drip out of his eyes. The breakup devastated me. I felt like I'd lost my family all over again, this second time reminding me of my first rejection. I moved out, collapsed, went to a doctor, got some pills.

Since our split ten or eleven months ago, I'd tried to stay in contact. Getting together was usually because I made the effort, not him. My overtures produced unreliable results. Today was one of the times that I got lucky.

I left the car and walked over to the entrance of the building where he worked, yet another gleaming tower, remarkable in my eyes because one day it wasn't there, and the next day it was, like a dozen other Boomtown structures in Kendall Square. I texted Paul that I was outside, and he appeared in five minutes. I noted smugly he had gained some weight since I'd seen him last. His heritage was Italian, and he had the kind of plain face that good grooming advances to attractiveness. His black hair had a few strands of silver and was combed back off his face. He wore casual business clothing, light cords and an expensive Canada Goose jacket, ash-gray, the uniform of a mid-level exec in information technology.

I moved forward to kiss him on the cheek, but he blocked that attempt by extending his hand for me to shake. Ouch.

"So where should we go?" he said.

"I have something to show you first," I said. "Come with me."

"What's this about?"

"You'll see." We crossed a broad avenue and then rounded a corner to the street where the Beemer was parked. As we approached it, I reached into my pocket and pushed the remote key, causing the lights of the car to flash a few times. "What do you think?" I said.

Paul's expression was surprised and then skeptical. "This is yours?"

I nodded yes.

"Where did you get this?"

"Long story. Care to go for a spin?"

He hesitated. "I was thinking we could have a drink nearby."

To a point, I understood his suggestion. Several new restaurants had opened in the area and dropping into one of them meant we wouldn't have to travel. On the other hand, I wanted to show off the car. "You're sure you wouldn't like to drive it?"

"Let's have a drink. Not till you tell me about it first."

We settled on a place that was minutes away on foot, one that catered to the IT crowd employed in the vicinity, mostly Gen Yers and Millennials. The restaurant had an industrial look that was supposed to be modern but that I found cold. Uncrowded, probably because nearby were six other places just like it. The host looked disappointed when we said we only wanted drinks and not food, but she guided us to a high-top table near the bar. A handsome server took our order, a vodka martini for Paul, top shelf, and a pull of Sam Adams for me.

"Okay, what's the car about?" Paul asked.

"I inherited it," I told him. "From my brother."

"Wait. The brother who you never talk to? The one who wouldn't have anything to do with you? The homophobic asshole?"

"No one but," I said. "It's complicated." I used the next fifteen minutes to narrate the tale of the last few days, about Dave's death, the apartment, the car. I painted the picture with broad strokes, eliminating some details because I wanted to present the situation in the most favorable light. Granted, because of the manner Dave had died, this was not easy. But money was a language that Paul knew, and I was trying to speak it.

He looked unconvinced. "You still have to take care of the legalities?"

"Not all of them," I said. "I have a lawyer."

"What does he say?"

"We've only talked a couple of times." Once actually, and on the phone, but Paul wouldn't know that. "He thought I could come out okay."

"Dave was murdered? That's very scary."

"That part's unreal. But he practically didn't exist to me anymore. You know that. You can't lose the same limb twice."

Paul sipped his martini. "Mark. Do me a favor, okay? Just be careful. Cautious. For lots of reasons. You don't have a deal until you have a deal. Things fall apart all the time. In my work, I mean. You think you have something, and then you don't."

I'd heard this kind of admonition from him before. *Grow up, Mark. There's no magic bullet, Mark.* Amazing how easy it was for the Ghost of Conversations Past to take a seat at our table. And then it struck me that one of the reasons I'd reached out to Paul this afternoon was that I needed to hear those cautions. Okay. I wouldn't be able to resist some extravagance. I knew myself too well. I wanted to drive that car. But he reminded me that some restraint was in order.

"Thanks for warning me about the precipice," I said.

Mollified, Paul said, "Sure." He paused. "If it's true, if you get it, what will you do?"

"I'm not sure yet. I haven't really had much time to think about it. I'll do the tours for now. I like that."

"I'm glad you found something you like."

"How's Barbara?" I asked. Barbara was his sister. I'd gotten to know his family during our relationship, but that closeness ended when Paul and I did. I felt the loss.

"Good." Paul launched into a too long story about one of Barbara's children, a high schooler on the brink of college.

When he finished, I said, "Tell them all I said hello." Then a pause. "And what's up with you? You seeing anybody?"

The curtain descended. "You really want to talk about that?"

No, I didn't. An answer from him in the affirmative would tear me to shreds. "Yes," I said. "I wouldn't have asked."

"Nothing serious," he said. Enough of an equivocation to cause a pang. He downed the martini. No query from him about my dating life. Not that I had anything to report.

"So," I said, "ready for a ride?"

"I think I'll pass. I'm wiped from work. I'll catch the subway."

I might have a BMW, but it didn't make any difference to him. "You still think I'm a loser," I blurted.

"I don't think you're a loser," he said, irritated. "Look. I have to go. Just be safe. It's very scary. Send me an email." He reached into his pocket for his wallet.

"I'll get it," I said. He appeared dubious. "I had a shift yesterday. Flush with tips."

Paul shrugged. "Okay. If you're sure." He pushed away from the table. "Bye." Before he stepped away, he said, "You're not a loser, okay?" No hug or goodbye peck on the cheek.

Once he was gone, I ordered another beer and some calamari. Seeing Paul always made me want to get drunk. I could have moved from the table to the bar and perhaps engaged in conversation, but as was typical in Boston these days, most of the crowd was ten years younger than me, or more, and I've never been any good at bar talk anyway. I stopped after the second beer. The BMW waited, and two drinks were plenty before I got behind the wheel of the beast. I settled the check. Ah, Boston! Two beers, one drink, and an appetizer, with tip and tax, over fifty bucks.

The sun was down, and the streetlamps threw an unpleasant cast upon everything. I turned the corner to the side street where the BMW was parked. After business hours, the area was deserted. As I approached the car, it sat close to the ground. I presumed the racing tires with their low profile accounted for this impression, even though I hadn't noticed anything so unusual before. But nearer to the car, I saw the tires were indeed extremely low. In fact, they were flat. Because someone had slashed them.

CHAPTER ELEVEN

CAITLYN

October 2016

At her apartment the next evening, Caitlyn used her laptop to examine the electronic scans she'd ordered of the architectural drawings of the Old Pilgrim Church. She displayed them on an enormous monitor, a present from her parents and a real boost when working with blueprints.

Caitlyn moved nearer to the screen and peered at it. The visual texture of the old drawings was very different from modern, computer-aided documents. A separate page was devoted to each of the church's four elevations. In addition to line drawings with dimensions, an artist had drawn representations of the exterior and of random highlighted features, such as the pattern for laying the stone. The illustrator was talented, and the drawings almost suitable for framing.

Floor plans for the nave were included on the sheet that portrayed the front face of the church. This particular drawing also indicated the proposed locations for some interior walls. Other inset illustrations on the sheet suggested designs for ornamental features like the light fixtures, the main altar, and a lovely pattern for an outer wall decoration, almost like a chain. The plan for the basement showed the locations for columns but otherwise indicated only open floor space. Walls on this subfloor must have been demarcated while the church was being built.

It wasn't uncommon at the time for architects only to supply what were, in essence, grand schemes for the buildings they designed. Specific details were determined at the site, with someone like a modern-day foreman providing exact measurements. The architect, or a trusted lieutenant, was often present as well to offer expertise and make decisions. What that meant, however, was that the usable information on these old plans for Caitlyn's research was patchy. If a Boston Box existed, or had once existed, at the Old Pilgrim, the room was probably improvised and built during construction, and not from following a diagram on the drawings.

In the lower right corner of each page, Caitlyn noticed two sets of initials. In uppercase was "GCA," obviously, Gregory Chester Adamston. The other, in lowercase, was "jrh," which must be Josiah Hawkins, the Black architect who had helped Adamston, and the man whom some historians felt was denied credit for his contributions to the senior architect's work. Caitlyn tried to imagine what it would be like to be in that situation. For a Black man of the time to have such a professional position must have been a source of pride for Hawkins, to accomplish so much despite the obstacles. On the other hand, resentment must have simmered in his soul because another man was honored for his work. She vowed to learn more about Hawkins as part of this project.

In a while, Caitlyn turned away from the blueprints. No outlines for a concealed room were on them. If time allowed, she would visit the church again and match measurements against the actual structure. But with regard to a Boston Box, the drawings by themselves were a dead end.

CHAPTER TWELVE

MARK

April 2017

I circled the car. Each of the tires had about a three-inch slice in its sidewall. Clean cuts. The vandal, whoever he or she was, had known what to do, and could have finished the slashing in a couple of minutes with a good sharp blade. Obviously, I had no way to know why this happened. The most plausible explanation was that it had been random, senseless, that the shiny BMW caught some delinquent's eye. Yet the crime's expert execution, and the fact that nothing else nearby had been damaged, made me think that my car had been targeted intentionally, and that my brother was at the root of it. I had no proof to back up my suspicion and I couldn't come up with any logical reason that someone would want to frighten or punish Dave. I mean, he was already dead.

In any case, it didn't matter. I was pissed. The beers mixed with the leftover feelings from my meeting with Paul, and now this. I wanted to strike something, but no suitable target for my temper was at hand. I swore aloud.

I swallowed my bile and called 9-1-1. A human operator with a mechanical voice asked for some details and then my location. She told me to stay on the line while a patrol car was dispatched. During the wait, I slipped into the BMW, popped open the glove compartment, and retrieved a plastic folio that I hoped contained the car's registration and other information. It did. I fretted about whether my brother's death would affect insurance coverage, but my worry was interrupted by a siren. Its shrill shriek heralded the flashing blue and white lights that soon appeared about a block away. I positioned myself outside the BMW and waved. The cruiser swung over by me and came to a halt, blocking a lane and creating an obstacle but without much consequence since the street wasn't busy. I told the 9-1-1 operator that the police had arrived, and we ended the call.

Two uniformed cops got out of the vehicle. One of them was a short-haired blonde woman who moved slowly and had a sympathetic, if resigned, expression on her round face. Her partner was a younger man, hefty and solid, taller than the other officer by about eight inches. Although he looked formidable, she was in charge.

She neared me and spoke. "Mr. Chieswicz?" She pronounced it "Cheesewich," like I was a snack. "I'm Janet Gill. What have we got?" Her partner inspected the car while we talked.

"I met a friend at Quarter Four," I explained. "I parked here about two hours ago. When I came back, this is what I found."

"Car looks brand new," she said.

"It is. It was my brother's. He died recently."

"I'm sorry to hear that, sir."

I measured what more to say. I didn't want to speak to Officer Gill about Dave's murder, which might draw out the report of the incident. My aim was to have the slashing on a police log for insurance purposes and then to arrange for the car's towing and repair so I could return home. Fortunately, Gill and her partner treated the crime as a random act, in part because when they asked if I knew anyone who would do something like this, I said—truthfully—"no." I might think a connection existed between Dave and the incident, but I had no proof, only my haphazard grasping for a reason. I was aware that if the Cambridge cops plugged my information later into a computer, stories about Dave might appear, by virtue of our last name, and that might bring about further scrutiny. To cover myself, I'd call Detective Taylor in the morning. Tonight, however, I just wanted to sidestep that complication.

Completing the report took about a half-hour. When I asked the cops for advice about next steps, they noted that some BMWs come with a roadside assistance program. Another call for help sounded on their radio. They didn't need to hang around while I made plans for the car's repair. I thanked them and they sped away.

Following a look at the owner's manual, I restarted the car and pressed a shiny SOS button on the dash. Before long I was connected to an extremely sympathetic service representative whose voice came through the car's speakers. She assured me that life would return to normal very soon. After our brief conversation concluded, I played on my phone until a noisy truck pulled up a short time later. Its very hairy driver proceeded to chain the car and load it onto a flatbed—no towing allowed for a new BMW. I refused a ride in the cab of the truck to the apartment. My heart broke a little as the beautiful Beemer went on its way to a dealership and receded from view.

In the damp night, I started by foot to the Fenway Grand, which wasn't far, maybe a mile or two. With every step, I mourned the joyride in the BMW that had been denied me. My anxiety about insurance lingered, about whether I'd have to pay for a new set of tires. As I crossed the Mass Avenue Bridge over a silent Charles River, Boston's skyline was all lit up, the Prudential building's windows aglow in green and white to celebrate something I didn't know about. A Celtics basketball game, probably. To my right, the CITGO sign, Boston's oddest landmark, displayed its rhythmic patterns of pseudo-neon. The city's beauty provided solace, yet I yearned for even more comfort, yearned to call Paul again, yearned for some love, I guess, but I already understood that he'd not answer, not for the second time in a day, so I just kept walking along.

CHAPTER THIRTEEN

CAITLYN

November 2016

Caitlyn called her mom to say that she would remain in Cambridge for Thanksgiving, a little more than three weeks away. Caitlyn offered her reasons: the trip was expensive; she was busy and needed the time for study; she'd be heading home for the winter holiday less than a month later. Her mom didn't take the news well and became very emotional, crying. Unusual behavior for her. Caitlyn hadn't lived at home for more than six years, and she had canceled trips in the past. While those decisions had often met with mild expressions of disappointment, they'd never caused this kind of reaction before.

Hanging up, Caitlyn was upset. Could it be her mother's menopause? The disturbing conversation gnawed at Caitlyn as she went to bed, and not even the sweet smell and fresh feel of newly laundered sheets kept her from a restless night.

The next morning, Caitlyn sent her mom a text. *"sorry about Thxgvng. everything OK?"*

Just disappointed. Wanted to talk to my squirrel.

"talk about?"

Things. Nothing important. We can talk at Christmas.

"*ur ok? dad's ok?*"

Everything's fine. We'll catch up when you're home.

"*catch up?*" After all, they texted every day and spoke at least once a week.

Don't worry. There's nothing.

"*maybe I shd come home.*"

I'm fine. We'll talk in December. Have to run.

Caitlyn wasn't reassured. What was there to talk over? She wondered again if menopause was causing her mom to act weird. That would be a relief, in a way. Menopause wasn't negligible, but at least it was in a category of expected events. Or maybe it was just the martyrdom streak that showed up in her mom now and then, especially under stress, annoying but not extraordinary. Or was she simply imagining that her mother was being odd? On the other hand, what if this behavior continued? Should she reverse her decision about going home? What if something was wrong?

CHAPTER FOURTEEN

MARK

April 2017

I'm not big on "to do" lists, but because of Dave, the morning after the slashing, I needed one. I had to take care of insurance companies, automobile dealers, lawyers, police, funeral directors, and probably something else that I'd forgotten. Everything seemed urgent except for Dave's funeral, which had to be done soon to contain costs but didn't demand my immediate attention. I was indifferent about my responsibilities to my brother and I felt guilty about that, yet the chip firmly affixed to my shoulder was hard to knock off.

I started with the car. After a couple of phone calls, I determined that Dave's insurance was paid through year end and still in effect, and that it would cover any costs that resulted from the vandalism, minus a $500 deductible. Mostly good news, but the $500 was going to hurt, another swipe of one of my credit cards. I was also told that, with the notification of his death, the countdown on the policy was now ticking. I'd have to make alternate arrangements soon because the insurance company would cancel coverage in sixty days. The service rep discussed some options. Buried in her talk was a sales pitch. I eventually understood that even if a refund was issued for the remainder of the policy's term, I'd need to make another outlay of my personal funds.

I next contacted the dealership where the car had been towed. The BMW used nice, expensive racing wheels, and replacements for the four tires were going to ring up at over $2,200. Since the costs after the deductible were neutral to me, bargaining was pointless. I was almost tempted to ask whether a higher-grade tire was available.

As my Dave-related expenses mounted, I was learning that living high required big money, even if some base costs like rent were covered. The swelling balance on my credit card led me next to Dietz. We set up a time to meet the next day, and I was told to bring Dave's files along with me. Dietz thought getting the court's permission to access Dave's balances for expenses would be easy.

With money matters addressed, I called Taylor's office to talk about the tire slashing, and I was put through to him at once. For a detective, he spent a good deal of his time at a desk. He listened to my story without much comment until I finished and then said, "Do you think it was deliberate, Mr. Chieswicz?"

The "mister" made me feel ancient. "I don't know," I said. "The thing is, I don't have any enemies, and even if I did, none of them would know about the car. I only had it for a few hours. And if it was an enemy of Dave's, he's dead. Not sure what they thought they'd accomplish. His killer would put himself at risk by doing something like this, don't you think so?"

"You said none of the other cars were damaged?"

I told him no.

"Did you notice anyone following you?"

Up until that moment, I hadn't considered the idea that someone had trailed me. Yet if the bastard who had slashed the tires had targeted the BMW, he or she would have had to track me from the towing lot, or more probably, from the Fenway Grand. Hell, someone could be spying on me now. "No," I said. "That's a disturbing thought. What good would that do? Why would they?"

"I'm not trying to scare you," Taylor said. "Unless there's a family vendetta that you haven't told me about."

"Nothing like that. As I said, I hadn't spoken to my brother for a long time. And there was no family feud. And nobody is out to get me."

"And you have no idea if your brother was up to something?"

"No. I just know what you told me. I've taken a look at the folders. I haven't done a deep dive. You probably know more about him than I do." I paused. "There was a parking place for the car here at the apartment. So he must have been stabbed in the South End, right? If his car was there. And then moved?"

"It's clear he didn't die where we found him. Told you that already. His body was dumped. But saying that the murder took place in the South End...it's a big neighborhood. We've knocked on doors near the car, around the block, but no surprise here, no one noticed anything. Parking a car isn't very interesting and doesn't attract attention. And depending on the time of day, if it was late, even less likely."

"You've talked to the people here at the apartment building?"

"Yes, Mr. Chieswicz. We've been doing our job."

"But there's no family vendetta. Whether there was some other kind of vendetta, I don't know. Against Dave, I mean. Like I said, you'd think killing him would settle it, wouldn't it? Between me and my family, it was an estrangement. We didn't talk. I never did anything to hurt them physically, or vice-versa." The real knives stayed in the kitchen drawers. Emotional stab wounds were another matter. I continued. "About Dave and his acquaintances, or people who didn't like him, he didn't do anything extra, more security, at the apartment. He kept his name. If he was hiding, wouldn't he have changed it?"

"Maybe," said Taylor. "With the money, maybe not. Might have made the transfers more difficult. It takes time to change your name. Legally. Maybe he just didn't care. Being sick. He took a few steps to hide his tracks, like his cell phone, presuming he had one. Which we've not found. The landline at the apartment, as far as we can see, he didn't use it for anything but stuff like utilities. A number he could put on applications. He told the folks at the Fenway he needed to get a new phone, and then gave them that number."

"Did he have a computer?"

"We didn't take one."

I'd no more questions and said so.

"Before we go," Taylor said, "please keep your eyes and ears open, but be careful. From what you just told me, and under the circumstances of your brother's death, it may be that something shady is happening. If anything suspicious occurs, please contact me at once."

"Got it."

"The tires could be a coincidence, but we don't know. I'll talk to the Cambridge Police. See if there's been a rash of vandalism. Keep alert. Don't take any risks. Call me if you see anything."

I told him I appreciated his concern and hung up.

I checked my email. A message from the dealership relayed that the BMW was ready. It doesn't take long to mount four tires and balance them. But before I went to retrieve the car and attempt another joyride, I needed to make my final call of the morning: the funeral director.

I looked at the picture of my mom and dad that Dave had placed on an end table. They looked happy. My mother, especially, was beautiful, in a bridal gown, holding a bouquet of beribboned white roses. I wish I could say I felt a warm surge of affection, but all that came forth was anger and resentment.

The story of me and my family wasn't complicated. I told them I was gay when I was twenty years old. They told me they never wanted to see me again. Shut me out. End of story. There were some details, I suppose. Like that my mother and father were "religious," which, in their case, meant being self-righteous and nasty about selected sins while overlooking teachings like "Love Your Neighbor." Like how Dave was out of work and under their thumbs at the time, but a fag hater, nonetheless. Like how I made several efforts to stay in touch until I just gave up because I couldn't stand it anymore. Like how I heard about my parents' deaths one day while scanning obituaries on the internet site of my hometown newspaper. Obituaries that failed to mention me. Like how I was depressed for several years, going through the motions of life, work, bars, until some magic pills lifted me out of it. Pills that I eventually stopped using except for the short relapse after my breakup. Sometimes I think that my rebound from the split with Paul has been longer and harder than normal because my ego isn't as strong as it should be after my family's rejection.

Going to your final resting place, Dave? Go there alone.

My final "fuck you."

And yet.

Unintentionally, with his money, Dave was about to rescue me, give me a second chance. Was there a karmic debt? Moreover, I needed to ask myself what kind of man I wanted to be: one who was unforgiving, who despised people he once

loved for what they had done to him, who would carry unre-
solved anger in his gut forever? Or was this an opportunity to
become a better me, one who didn't forget but forgave, who
was grateful that his brother had bequeathed to him a small
fortune and a new start?

I was devoted to the idea of family, of unconditional love. I
had been denied the opportunity to practice it most of my adult
life, except briefly, with Paul and his sister and her kids. And
that loss added to the pain of my split with him.

The war between these two visions of me was easy to resolve
intellectually. The better me would win, of course. But emotionally, acting in a finer way towards Dave was much more difficult
to choose. To compare it to an absurd example, I might recognize a need to lose a few pounds, and rationally I know then not
to eat a donut, but I want that donut nevertheless, its disreputable, unhealthy sweetness. I wanted the disreputable, unhealthy
sweetness of spite.

For a second, I had a glimpse of myself, sometime in the
future, going to my death alone. Were I to die today, that's how
it would happen. I'd be in my bed or in my kitchen or on the
street, all by myself, jumping into the great void. A gloomy destiny, one that I wouldn't wish on anyone. Even my worst enemy.

Then again, maybe I *would* wish it on my worst enemy.

If I thought of Dave not as he was, but just as another human being, as an abstraction of family, perhaps I could put aside
my narrow, tainted image of him and follow the finer path, to
win the war over my bitterness. Not make my way to forgiveness, but to decency.

To be a better me.

I spoke to the funeral director. He told me that everything
was taken care of, and that he was awaiting my instructions on

the final step, the cremation. Undoubtedly, he had sensed my ambivalence about my brother in our other conversation, and he said, if I wished, Dave's body could be cremated without my presence or participation. And I wanted to agree to that plan, to let the funeral director take care of everything. I could pick up Dave's ashes at some time in the future, another chore, like getting the BMW. In that arrangement, I had the satisfying prospect of payback for Dave's past rejection of me.

Instead, I said, "I think I should be there."

"When would be a good time?" I perceived warmth in his voice.

"Two days?"

"That would be no problem," he said. He told me the address of the crematorium, discussed a few other details, and rung off.

In the end, I wasn't sure if I was going to Dave's cremation for him or for myself. Dave was dead, insensate, and I didn't believe he would watch the conversion of his body to ash from a cloud while playing a harp. With all the therapy I've done, I knew that people fundamentally acted out of self-interest, that even the holiest among us did things for love, for recognition, for a place in heaven. I was no different. I wasn't feeling noble. I would backslide into anger. But to give myself some credit, I allowed the idea that my presence at Dave's cremation might be the right thing to do for both of us. A small step for me, and a small victory for Dave to claim if he had to defend himself to a higher authority in front of the Pearly Gates. "See?" he could say. "I helped my queer fag brother to be a nice guy."

Before I headed off to retrieve the BMW, I cruised the internet for a few minutes, at one point checking the words "Boston

Box" in a search engine. I wondered if there might be something in the term that would jog a long-forgotten memory and help with finding Dave's killer. In response to my query, I was offered 400,000,000 responses. A healthy lifetime's work.

The upfront answers were about a business tool, somewhat esoteric, and I was pretty certain that Dave didn't have any reason to do PowerPoint presentations. Some story about secret rooms was entertaining but not very substantial and largely fiction. Another link mentioned a boxing class held somewhere in Back Bay that combined boxing, hip-hop, and martial arts. How do people come up with these things? Since Dave was sick, I couldn't imagine he'd want to break, lock, and pop while learning Asian methods of self-defense, but I made a second notation on my phone, the vendor's name, so I could keep it in mind while I looked over Dave's bank and credit card statements.

After that, most of the items on the list were for box offices. Dave had bought those Red Sox tickets. Could that be it? Shorthand? Boston Sox? Boston Red Sox Box Office?

I'm just not a detective. I have no patience, no persistence. I hoped there was someone, maybe in Taylor's office, who would stick with this investigation and have the time to search through 400,000,000 clues for a Boston Box.

CHAPTER FIFTEEN

CAITLYN

November 2016

Susan Slaughter, the realtor for the condo on sale in Chadwick Square, contacted Caitlyn about her query. Slaughter congratulated Caitlyn on her good fortune because an accepted bid on the property had collapsed and it was back on the market. The realtor urged an immediate viewing. Of course, Caitlyn had no intention of buying the place and felt slightly guilty about wasting the realtor's time, but she told herself the small deception was justified by her search for info about Adamston and the Boston Box.

They met in Chadwick Square in late afternoon. Slaughter was in her mid-forties, and she wore enough make-up for it to be evident but not tawdry. Her manner was professionally friendly and assertive. They climbed the front steps and entered a vestibule where two doors led to condos on the first floor, and another door, marked "Exit" by a lit red sign, led to the basement. The walls were smooth, an ivory shade. "The staircase and banisters are all original," Slaughter said. "In the eighties, just about everything else was replaced. Do you own now?"

"I rent," Caitlyn said. "I'm at school in Harvard."

"Ah, well. That's a distance. Why are you looking here?"

"Thinking ahead," she improvised. "I like the neighborhood. Investment."

"It *is* a charming area. Lots of restaurants. And convenient. Millennials like you love it. This unit is very special."

Caitlyn bristled at being called a "Millennial" but held her tongue. They walked up two flights of stairs to the top story where the unit on sale was located. The condo's interior had some charm, with an exposed brick wall, but the layout had to be completely different from the original construction in the 1860's. An open area—a combination kitchen, dining, and living room—was about 350 square feet, and a bedroom with a narrow walk-in closet was around 200 square feet. A small bathroom with shower but no tub was laid out smartly with attractive patterned tile. The current occupant's furnishings were still in place and, although clean, they weren't much more impressive than Caitlyn's own ramshackle student belongings.

"They did a good job on the redesign, don't you think so?" Slaughter said. Caitlyn agreed. Slaughter continued. "The owner here did an upgrade in the kitchen but had to relocate. It's being rented at the moment. Lease is month-to-month, so you can move in as soon as you close."

A packet on a countertop in the kitchen indicated the cost was $650,000. "That's with parking," Slaughter said. "What were you thinking about financing?"

Caitlyn wasn't prepared for the question. "My father...he'd be co-signing," she stammered. "Twenty percent down?"

Slaughter sensed the hesitation. "Have you pre-qualified?"

"Not yet, but there should be no problem." Caitlyn looked at the packet, a diversion. "I passed by the unit the other day and got interested. It says the condo association has twelve members. I only counted six units."

"Six here and six next door. Three of the other adjoining buildings are associated in a separate condo organization, but it's pretty friendly between the two."

This offered the opportunity to probe about the home at the end of the Adamston row that hadn't been renovated. "What about the sixth?"

"Nine Chadwick? Privately owned, single home. Very rare. The guy who lives in it is sitting on a fortune. The parking places alone are worth a bundle. But he's been there for decades. A little odd but harmless. Don't get why he hasn't cashed out yet."

"You think it's not been remodeled?" Caitlyn asked.

"Never seen the inside." The realtor gave her an odd look, as if confused by Caitlyn's interest. "Anyway, what do you think about this place? Have you seen much else?"

"It's very nice," Caitlyn said. "No. Just started looking. Is there any negotiation on the price?"

"In this market, I'll have three offers before the weekend. It will go for asking, at a minimum. Might even get an all-cash offer. If you like this, you have to grab it."

"It's a lot of money."

"I'm trying to be helpful. Honest. Don't think long. Talk to your father tonight. Even if you roll it over after Harvard, this is a good investment."

Caitlyn pictured a conversation with her parents about buying a $650,000 condo, roughly $1,000 per square foot. She didn't get far beyond imagining their hysterical laughter. "Okay. Let me talk it over with them." She quickly added, "Tonight. I'll call tonight. Any storage?"

"There's a small space in the basement, like a big closet."

"Can I see it?"

"Sure. There's not much. Do you have any questions here?"

Caitlyn said no. She'd love to live in a place like this while she was single, but it was too far from Harvard, and a fantasy until she finished her doctorate. She reminded herself this viewing was about the Boston Box, not purchasing real estate. Being nosy was fun as long as Slaughter didn't catch on.

"Let's head to the basement," said Slaughter.

The storage area smelled musty. Eight doors ran off a narrow hall made of ordinary drywall covered with a base coat, an unfinished appearance. Slaughter tried to open the compartment that went with the condo on sale, but the lock refused to give. "Sorry," she said. "I'll make sure I have access when you do an inspection."

"What's over there?" Caitlyn pointed at two unnumbered doors.

"One leads out back to parking. The other is furnaces and water heaters."

"Can I see the utility room?" Caitlyn asked. It was her last hope to find a hidden chamber.

"Really?"

"I study architecture. It interests me."

"Architecture, huh?" Slaughter looked as if she were measuring Caitlyn's seriousness about making a purchase. She sighed. "There's not much, but sure. That door's not locked."

Caitlyn stepped into the utility room, looked around, and then pulled a string cord that turned on a naked overhead bulb. Slaughter hovered behind her. The room had a small, high-efficiency furnace, seven boxed meters, and a cluster of water heaters, all crammed around two perimeter walls of exposed stone and cement. No evidence of a Boston Box. Caitlyn turned off the light with another tug of the string and they left the room in silence.

Outside on the sidewalk, Slaughter handed Caitlyn a business card and said, "If this place doesn't work for you, get in touch. Happy to help you find something else. Call me tomorrow after you talk to your father." She headed to her nearby parked car, but Caitlyn lingered at the doorstep and pretended to check email on her phone until she saw Slaughter drive away.

Caitlyn then turned her attention to the house at the end of the row, Nine Chadwick. She doubted whether the owner would invite a stranger to come in on a moment's notice, but she hoped that if she explained her project, he would perhaps agree to another time.

Dusk had arrived and the light near Nine Chadwick was murky. The home needed paint on its doors and window frames. A small garden patch adjacent to the stoop was untended, mostly weeds and dirt, and those windows not obscured by drawn shades were dark.

The name over the doorbell was "Rumberg." Caitlyn pressed a yellowed, unilluminated button. Caitlyn thought a shuffling noise came from inside the house, and she waited. A minute passed. No one answered. She debated whether to ring again and decided against it. She didn't want to bother the occupant if he wasn't in a condition to speak with a visitor. Walking down the steps and away from the entrance, she retrieved her phone from a pocket and said, "Make a note. Rumberg." She spelled the name, added the street address, and then clicked off the application. The information would help her to look up the property deeds and contact the listed owner.

Caitlyn saw a shade in a first-floor window move just an inch or two, and someone caught her eye for a split second and then stepped away. The watcher's age or sex was indeterminable. Caitlyn remained motionless and waited again to see if the door opened. Nothing happened. So odd! She shivered and started down the brick sidewalk with a quickened gait, suddenly eager to get back to Cambridge.

CHAPTER SIXTEEN

MARK

April 2017

When I left the Fenway Grand to pick up the repaired BMW, it was drizzling. April showers. Forewarned by the view from the apartment, I had brought along a collapsible umbrella, one of Dave's, found in his coat closet. The subway would be the easiest, cheapest way for me to get to the dealership where the car waited. The subway that I needed to catch, on the Green Line, would take about ten minutes to walk to, over by Boston University, on Commonwealth Avenue.

As I jaywalked not far from the Fenway Grand, I squeezed between a parked, black Mercedes Benz and another vehicle on my way to the sidewalk. A Mercedes is a common sight in Boston, and although this one was new and sleek enough to notice, it wasn't so special that I'd stop and gawk. No one was in the car. A block or so farther along, the same black Mercedes passed me. Again, nothing unusual. The windows were tinted but I could tell the driver was male. His features were a blur, however, and the car traveled on, never slowing. I blamed a moment of uneasiness to paranoia brought on by the combination of Taylor's warning, Dave's possible spying on me, and—not least of all—his unsolved murder.

I reached the subway stop. The light rain made the day feel raw, and while I had been smart enough to bring the umbrella, I had left behind my nerdy wraparound ear-warmers. The cold was like little pinpricks on my face. The green and white subway car arrived in a minute. I stuffed myself into it with about two dozen other waiting passengers, mostly BU students. Normally, this would be a quiet ride, each of the riders lost in their own little worlds with a book or a cellphone or staring into space. But on this trip the students laughed and chatted and covered the electronic drone of the subway with a layer of lively, irritating noise.

Progress was slow. At the third stop, near a traffic light, I thought I saw the Mercedes on the street. I convinced myself that this was not the same car as the one I'd seen before, that it was an older model. My fears eased as the car disappeared from view, overtaken in my attention by a student whose backpack kept slamming into me.

The subway finally reached the street near the dealership, my stop. Pretty BMWs of all shapes and sizes were displayed in the showroom, but none of them were more beautiful than the one I was about to claim. Finishing the paperwork took time because of documents I needed for the insurance company. Eventually, a clerk in the repair shop drove my car to a door outside of the waiting area. I slid onto the heated seat. My return trip promised to be much more enjoyable than the subway ride.

The BMW was a contented, purring cat. Or maybe it was me who purred. The tank was full. I eased from the garage's ramp onto crowded Comm Ave, not a road for joyriding. Too many stoplights, too many pedestrians, too many bikes, too much slickness from the rain. I needed to get to open highway, someplace I could tap on the gas pedal.

On the brink of fulfilling my fantasy of speed, I couldn't think of any place to go. While I decided on a destination, I guided the car to Storrow Drive, a riverside parkway which would lead to an interstate. An ad came on the radio for a burger joint on the South Shore, run by the relatives of Mark Wahlberg, the movie star. I said the name of the restaurant aloud, feeding it into the car's GPS, and it gave directions.

Then, moving onto the expressway, as I merged into moderately fast traffic, a black Mercedes, a new sedan like the other, appeared in the rearview mirror.

I didn't know what to do. Try to evade it? Call the police? Pull over and confront the driver? With a full tank, maybe I could simply drive and drive and drive. By the time I would reach Rhode Island or another distant location, my suspicions that I was being followed would be confirmed or denied. Once again, I wondered if my nervousness had caused me to imagine the whole situation. The world was full of black Mercedes. I hadn't made a mental note of any license number so I couldn't be positive the car was the same as before. But it sure was similar.

I went into a tunnel. Traffic was moderate. In a reckless moment, I accelerated and swerved into a center lane, cutting too close to another vehicle, and then I repeated the maneuver and entered the passing lane. The BMW handled smoothly, responding to my commands without a jiggle or lurch. The driver of the car that I'd cut off sped up and passed me on the right, offering me a deserved finger as he did so.

The turn signals on the Mercedes flashed. Whoever trailed me must have gone to Drivers Ed. A very considerate stalker. He, too, got into the passing lane, about three cars behind me. His LED safety headlights shone steadily, two white eyes, unblinking, watching me.

The car directly in front of me moved out of my way, and the road ahead was clear for about a quarter mile. I pushed down on the accelerator and zoomed off. The Mercedes was trapped by surrounding cars and a tractor-trailer and was unable to maneuver. No drag race would take place between us, no test of the relative merits of different brands of German engineering.

Having gained some distance, I switched lanes again, to the right this time, and then again, and I found myself nearing an exit. I swung over one more lane and left the expressway. I didn't know where I'd end up. The tractor trailer must have blocked the Mercedes's view of me because as I turned off the highway my presumed pursuer continued onward. Maybe I was wrong, after all, about being tailed. The female voice on the GPS announced she was recalculating, and she sounded annoyed about that. I was directed to follow a route of side streets to the hamburger joint, ten miles away.

Traffic on this route was thicker and slower than the four-lane highway. I moved along these streets—some residential, some business—for about a mile and watched for the Mercedes. All appeared to be clear. I entered an almost empty lot in front of a Kentucky Fried Chicken franchise, parked, and stopped to take a breath, convinced of my safety.

My pulse pounded. For the twentieth time, I wondered if I was being paranoid. Why would anyone want to follow me anyway? I wasn't the most diligent contributor to society, but I hadn't hurt anyone, didn't owe money except to banks for credit cards. And if the reason for being hounded bounced back to Dave, what more harm could they possibly do to him? I convinced myself I was mistaken.

I wasn't hungry for a celebrity hamburger any longer. The windows of the KFC were splashed with signs announcing cheap buckets of chicken and biscuits. I like crispy, fatty foods as much as the next guy, so I left the car, went into the gaudy restaurant, and queued up. Soon I toted several thousand calories of guilt-inducing deliciousness back to the BMW, somehow a bad match with fried chicken.

Before shutting the door, I twisted and put the bucket of chicken on the floor in front of the passenger seat. Bent over, I sensed a presence.

"Mr. Chieswicz," a male voice said. "Good afternoon."

I turned to face the man who spoke to me. Behind him, parked on the street, near the curb, was something I hadn't noticed on leaving the KFC.

A black Mercedes.

CHAPTER SEVENTEEN

CAITLYN

November 2016

When Caitlyn returned home from the South End, she was hungry because she hadn't eaten much all day. She made a toasted cheese sandwich and read her email while she munched. None of the messages were important. The sandwich finished, she switched to the website of the Suffolk County Registry of Deeds, where ownership of Boston properties was recorded, and typed the name "Rumberg" into a search box. A list appeared that stretched over twelve screen pages. She scrolled through the list and came to the line for Nine Chadwick Square. The first name of the present owner was George, middle initial "T." His possession of the brownstone began in 1992, after it was deeded to him by a "Mary" with the same last name. His mother, Caitlyn guessed. The online records for the building only went back as far as 1975, so there was no way to tell how long the house had been owned by Mary Rumberg or any other members of her family. Since the place had not fundamentally changed hands for over forty years, and probably longer, it augured well for some preservation of its original features, like a Boston Box, if the stars aligned.

A search on "George T Rumberg" yielded his address—unimportant, since she already knew it—but no links to Facebook, or LinkedIn, or Twitter, or any other social media sites. She tried "George Rumberg" and "G. T. Rumberg." An interesting listing in a comment stream from a few years earlier was attributed to a "G Rumberg" from Boston who ranted in several entries about Democrats and liberals. But no other similar comments turned up, so either this tirade was an aberration, or George Rumberg was ordinarily very good at covering his tracks with pseudonyms or anonymity. Or the vitriol had been spewed by someone else.

Caitlyn fantasized about how Rumberg would react to an overture from her. Conservatives and Harvard academics were a volatile mix. After a few minutes of worry, she told herself to settle down. He could be a very nice guy. People were often kinder in person. Because she couldn't find Rumberg's email address, if he had one, she'd have to send her request by regular post. Just to be safe, she would use blank white paper instead of Harvard letterhead and downplay that connection.

About to start the letter, a text from Henry interrupted her. *At CC. Come join us.*

"working on something. ltr?"

Will be here

In a quarter-hour, she had composed a brief letter to George Rumberg that introduced herself, talked about her research in a couple of vague sentences, asked if he would agree to a visit, and offered several different ways for him to reach her. She printed the correspondence and an envelope, stamped and sealed it, and then left it on a conspicuous spot on a tabletop, a prompt to pick up the letter and mail it when she next left the apartment.

Returning to her laptop, on an impulse she typed "Josiah Hawkins" into the search engine. The only significant citation to appear was in the Wikipedia entry about Adamston, the one that she had read several months earlier when she'd first heard about the Boston Box. Looking at it again, however, she fixated on the phrase that indicated Hawkins had studied in Paris. Adamston wasn't credited with any comparable training. From what Caitlyn had seen of Adamston's brownstones, traces could be found of a style popular in the mid-19th century called French Academic, with mansard roofs, symmetry, attention to ornamentation. The term "French Academic" was self-explanatory: it referred to the principles of good design taught in Paris during that era. She'd been studying it for her thesis. Adamston had possibly learned about it by observing the work of his peers, since many Boston practitioners had adapted the style in their buildings. But the question now worth considering was whether it was Josiah Hawkins who had infused the French Academic elements into the constructions credited to Adamston. And if Hawkins was responsible for those characteristics, he might be a key to other elements. Like the Boston Box.

The initials on the Old Pilgrim Church drawings had an "r" in the middle, so Caitlyn tried typing "Josiah R Hawkins," and then "J. R. Hawkins." Neither of those guesses resulted in any additional items related to an architect or architecture. However, genealogical citations indicated the death of someone named Josiah Richard Hawkins in 1891 in Boston. Interesting to Caitlyn was one genealogical table that tracked Hawkins's descendants to the present day. An "Andrew J. Hawkins" had been born about thirty years ago. Josiah Hawkins's great great-grandson.

She entered "Andrew J. Hawkins" into the search bar. Not only was Andrew Hawkins alive, but he was also an architect with a downtown Boston firm. Caitlyn was intrigued by how an occupation might continue over several generations of a family. Certainly, it wouldn't be the first time in the history of mankind when some descendants followed a career path that was a family tradition. Quite common, actually. In fact, she had read studies that said a tendency to a profession could be inherited. Andrew Hawkins—and Josiah, for that matter—could be genetically wired to practice architecture or to work in the building trades.

Was that also true of her, Caitlyn wondered. But the notion didn't work. Her mother wasn't at all interested in architecture, except for house decoration of the simplest kind.

A picture of Andrew Hawkins on the architectural firm's website showed him to be a lean, muscular man, russet-skinned, his head shaved so just a trace of his hairline remained. Very handsome. He wore a striking tie, brown with thick irregular veins of blue coursing through it, wider than current fashion. His biography noted degrees from the Rhode Island School of Design and Cornell, good schools, and his specialty as an architect was work with acoustics in halls, theaters, and the like. His professional contact information was included in his profile. Caitlyn added the web address for this information to an online folder she had created for her Boston Box investigations.

The likelihood that Andrew Hawkins would be familiar with any of his ancestor's occupational history was debatable. Not many of Caitlyn's friends cared much about their family histories. Caitlyn herself knew next to nothing about her own family's background. She thought they were all poor peasants from somewhere in Europe. But since she had just written the letter to Rumberg, the text for a request to meet was fresh and easy to adapt for a note to Andrew Hawkins. She cut and pasted the contents of the Rumberg letter into an email and revised it with references to Josiah Hawkins. She added more background about her Harvard affiliation because—in this case—the connection was probably an advantage. Using the contact info from Andrew Hawkins's profile, she sent the message electronically.

She felt pleased with herself, having completed two tasks. Yet all of her direct academic duties persisted. Should she crack a book or go for a drink?

She definitely should go out and decompress. But before texting Henry, she moved to another webpage that recorded the buildings attributed to Adamston's firm and tried to identify which ones to explore next. Dates of construction were included in the list. Activity seemed to stop in the early 1870's. The "Great Fire" in Boston in 1872 had destroyed almost 800 buildings but Adamston's firm apparently hadn't benefitted from the subsequent rush to rebuild.

She looked at her email box. Andrew Hawkins had sent a response. Fast turnaround.

Hi. I'm very interested in your research. I might be able to add a little and would like to talk. By any chance, are you free tomorrow afternoon? I'm going out of town later in the week. Let me know. Andrew.

A review of her calendar showed no formal commitments for the afternoon, but that was not the same as having nothing to do. She'd mentally booked the time for study related directly to her dissertation and other catch-up. But the opportunity to meet with Andrew Hawkins was too good to refuse. She accepted his invitation, leaving the details to him. His response came fast once again, and he gave a time and an address on Fort Point channel, a trendy business area on the fringe of Boston's financial district.

She looked at a clock. It was already 10:30 PM. Where had the time gone? It'd be after 11 by the time she made it to the bar. She sent a message to Henry: *"Got caught up in studies, sry... hope you had a good night."*

Still here

"tired see you tomw."

☹ ☹ ☹

Henry was disappointed? Well, Caitlyn *was* tired, so she held off from trying to interpret his reaction. The two of them had flirted lately, but that was all. Meaningless.

She spent ten minutes washing a few dishes and picking up junk and papers scattered around her apartment, and another ten on preparing for sleep. In bed, she propped her iPad on her lap and turned to a lightweight novel that she'd begun reading weeks ago. She was drowsy. It had been a full day, and the next several days looked to be the same. Her decision to stay in Boston and work over the Thanksgiving break became firmer. Caitlyn hoped her mother would be okay, would understand. After all, Christmas would be here in a flash.

CHAPTER EIGHTEEN

MARK

April 2017

For a second, I wondered if I had time to step on the gas and speed off. But I decided there was no point. In the parking lot and on crowded streets, I wouldn't be able to make much of a getaway. I would only delay an inevitable confrontation.

Plus the door was open, and my follower was an obstacle. He was big, over six feet tall, and with huge muscles of the sort that developed after regular doses of steroids. His head was shaved but had a shadow of ginger-tinted stubble, about the same length and color as his close-cropped scruff. His jaw was slack. A mouth breather. He wore a pair of jeans and running shoes, Nikes, black with outrageously bright orange stripes that clashed with the rest of his clothing. His leather car coat, also black, was open and revealed a snug rugby shirt tucked in at the belt. I couldn't tell if a pistol or some other weapon was concealed in his inner pockets.

It would have been foolish to be optimistic, and I wasn't, but the encounter might be inconsequential. Best scenario. And frankly, curiosity had taken a hold on me and matched my fear. What was this all about?

Drizzle still fell and a spray of water blew onto me. The man from the Mercedes leaned on the door and put his face near mine. "How are you?" His voice was husky, and from its tone I didn't think his question reflected sincere interest about my state of mind, but I answered it anyway.

"I'm confused right now," I said. "Do I know you? Why are you following me?"

He loomed above me. His eyes were bloodshot. "Mr. Chieswicz," he said. "We haven't had the pleasure. We know someone in common."

The number of my friends is small, and he looked like rough trade, not the sort my few acquaintances would hang out with. "I'm not sure who you mean."

"We have a mutual friend in Florida," he said. "He asked me to say hello."

"There must be some mistake. I've never been to Florida. You must mean my brother."

"Of course, there's a mistake. Nice car you're driving."

"But..."

"Do you like living at the Fenway, by the way?" he asked.

"Seriously, dude, I think there's a mistake. You're thinking of my brother Dave. My name is Mark. My brother is dead."

"Mr. Chieswicz, oh, Mr. Chieswicz, how stupid do you think I am?"

My initial impression was that he looked really stupid, but this was not the time to offer that opinion. "I'm not lying. My brother, Dave, is dead. He was killed. You can read the papers. I'm Mark."

My guess was that my questioner made a good living as a collector and that he had heard many excuses, but mine was not the usual weaseling. He squinted as if working to understand my words. The effort failed. The easiest way to deal for him with my claim was to pretend it didn't exist. He exhaled hard. He had coffee breath. "Our friend wants his money," he said.

"I'm not sure what money you're talking about. Or what friend. I don't have any money."

He didn't seem to appreciate my statement. "Nice car."

"It is. But it's my brother's. Was my brother's. I'm just driving until his estate is taken care of. I'm his only relative, you see. I'm still finding things out."

The collector's gaze hardened. "His estate? How grand. Cut the crap, Mr. Chieswicz. It's not going to work."

What else could I say? Enough of a familial resemblance existed between me and my brother to make such a mistake understandable, particularly if the collector was acting on secondhand identification, like an old picture, or information like an address. "I can prove who I am," I said. I reached for my wallet in my jacket pocket so I could show him my driver's license.

This was the wrong thing to do.

The collector grabbed my hair and jerked his arm back, banging my forehead above the right eye against the upper part of the door. "Shit," I yelled. The pain was sharp. I felt dizzy. I tried to shut the door, but he continued to grip me, and then he yanked me again for a second blow against the door frame.

"Listen, you son of a bitch," he growled. "I'm getting tired of you."

"I was just getting my wallet," I whined.

From somewhere in the lot, near the KFC, a voice called out. "Hey! What's going on?" Through blurred vision, I saw a customer at the door of the restaurant. He stood motionless, a red and white bag gripped in his left hand. "I'm going to call the police!" he yelled.

The collector tried to knock my head one last time, but I resisted, pulling my weight back. He released me with a hard shove. "That was just a taste. You'll hear from me again." He turned and walked calmly toward his Mercedes.

"I'll call the police!" said the customer. My eyes began to focus. The customer had silver hair that gleamed like a knight's armor.

The collector turned to him. "Shut the fuck up," he said. He lurched in the customer's direction, a feint, and his move made the customer instinctively jerk back. The collector entered his car, started it, and drove off.

As he did so, the customer jogged over to me. "Man, you okay? You're bleeding." His silver hair was misleading, just prematurely gray, feathered with black. He was perhaps in his mid-thirties, about five eight, medium build. He wore black hornrims.

I lowered the driver's side sun visor and uncovered the vanity mirror. On my forehead, above my right eye, a sizeable lump grew, with a half-inch cut in the center of it. "Shit," I murmured. The blood flowed like crazy, bright red, and was about to drip into my eyes and obstruct my sight. A box of tissues rested on the back seat and I grabbed it. Some drops of blood fell upon the car's upholstery. Did leather stain? I bunched some tissues together, wiped the blood on my face, and then, with a second glob of tissues, applied light pressure to my wound.

"Do you want me to call the police?" the customer said.

"No!" The customer looked surprised. "No, thanks," I said, more calmly. "I'm okay. Family stuff," I lied. "He's a hothead."

"You sure? I think I should."

"No. Thanks. Thanks for speaking up."

"Can you drive?"

"Yeah. I just need a minute or two. I'm fine. Seriously. But I really appreciate your help."

He looked dubious. "I didn't get his registration number."

"I know him," I said, repeating my lie, a stall.

"Oh, right." The customer pulled out a business card holder and gave me one of his. His name was Clark Hodder, and he was an assistant vice president at a local bank. "Take this. If you decide to file charges or something. Maybe the store has security cameras. You should ask."

"I'm okay. Clark. Thanks. I'm Mark. Clark and Mark. Ha. You were a great help. I mean it." I forced a smile while holding the bloody compress of wadded tissues against my forehead. Another customer who left the franchise stared at us before proceeding to her car.

"All right," he said. "If you're okay, I'll go."

I nodded.

"I have band-aids in my trunk," he said. "A first aid kit. You might need stitches."

"I'm fine. Thank you so much."

Clark gave me a reassuring smile, walked away, and got into a small car, a Hyundai, on the other side of the lot. He glanced in my direction before entering traffic. A rainbow decal was affixed to his rear bumper.

I dropped the wad of tissues and made another, cleaner compress and held it against my head. The bleeding slowed, but the wound was ugly, crusty, smeared with red. I had nothing wet to use and wash away the blood, so I spit onto a tissue and tried to wipe off the worst of it.

I couldn't think straight. I was in shock, and scared. I wanted to roll up into a ball until I recovered, but I couldn't do that at the KFC. Following a brief wait, sure that my wound no longer oozed, I gripped the steering wheel, pulled out of the parking lot, and headed toward the Fenway Grand. My head still swam from the blows. The smells from the bucket of fried chicken made my stomach turn.

Back on the road, the rain fell harder.

So far, the BMW wasn't much of a good luck charm.

In case you're wondering, why didn't I call the cops?

The collector hadn't known that Dave was dead. He had mistaken me for my brother. And if neither the collector, nor apparently his Florida friend, was aware that my brother was murdered, then they must not have had any direct involvement in that crime. Their lack of knowledge absolved them of Dave's murder. On the other hand, I could have sought an arrest for the assault on me, but I had a very good reason to avoid that.

The money.

Speaking with Taylor meant that I would have to reveal a tarnish on the funds in Dave's bank accounts because somebody in Florida, somebody who played rough, put a claim on them. That information could result in greater scrutiny of my inheritance. At present, the cops thought the money wasn't obtained through criminal behavior. If an illegality were uncovered, the money could disappear.

I wasn't going to give it up that easily.

This decision, however, came with some clear drawbacks. First, Mr. Florida and his friends wanted the money, or some part of it. I didn't know why. And I doubted very much that today's encounter with the collector was going to be the last. Convincing them of Dave's death would be an easy enough matter. A couple newspaper clippings, the death certificate, my driver's license, were all proof of my story and identity. I wasn't sure what to say about the $633,215.28 in the bank account, though, or how to prevent them from going after me to recover their money, whatever that amount would be. I'd have to work on constructing a cover.

Another matter frightened me. Dave's killer. Until now, the idea that someone might have been in pursuit of him for restitution wasn't part of my calculations. Oh, knowing Dave, I hadn't dismissed the possibility that he was murdered by a person with a motive. Dave was a guy who hung out with criminals, and I had no doubt that over his lifetime he'd pissed off people whose qualities didn't include restraint. But because the murder happened in Boston, where he wasn't known, I had believed his death could be more random, that he'd put himself in the wrong place at the wrong time. What I hadn't considered was that his killer might be looking for money. Or revenge. And if that was true—and I wasn't sure of it, but *if*—then the killer's quest for some kind of payback might continue.

That meant Mr. Florida wasn't my only worry.

Of course, this was all speculation. Dave's murder might have had nothing to with the money. I didn't know. That was the problem. My brain was overloading. Too much was mysterious. Except for one certainty: muscular guys on steroids aren't known for their gentle behavior, or for letting a matter rest.

CHAPTER NINETEEN

CAITLYN

November 2016

Close to Boston's harbor, Fort Point Channel seemed busier each time Caitlyn visited it. A recently built convention center not far away was attracting hotels, upscale restaurants and bars, and chic retailers to the area. Other new construction was everywhere.

Andrew Hawkins's firm was located in a former cotton warehouse that had been converted to offices. The building's glass entrance doors had been shaped to fit under a patterned yellow stone arch. A directory guided her to the fifth floor, where a friendly young woman at a front desk led Caitlyn to a closet to hang her coat. Caitlyn wished she could check herself in a mirror. She had tried on four different outfits before deciding on a blue and white plaid skirt and a navy-blue V-neck sweater over a white blouse. She had exchanged her daily stud earrings for a pair of small gold hoops and added a scarf purchased in Italy. Despite the dressier touches, she worried that she looked like a schoolgirl.

Andrew appeared in a few moments. He was not as tall as she had imagined from his picture, perhaps an inch or two less than six feet, but other than that, he matched the impression from his online profile. An easy smile revealed perfect teeth and deep dimples. He had an earring: a ruby stud. An attractive man.

"Cool scarf. Hermes?" he said.

"Thanks. Italian. It's old. I've had it forever."

Andrew raised an eyebrow. "Doesn't look old. Quality lasts. Take the compliment. Let's go this way." He led her past a maze of gray cloth cubicles to an office on the perimeter of the floor and then invited her to sit at a strapped leather chair near a coffee table. He offered her a beverage, which she refused, before sitting opposite her. "I have some things to show you. But tell me about your project first."

"I'm not sure where it will go," she said. "Several months ago, I became fascinated by something called the Boston Box. Have you heard of it?" Andrew shook his head no. "I'm not even sure it's real," she continued. Caitlyn then told him about her research, her reasons for focusing on Adamston at first, how that brought her to his ancestor, and the little that she'd uncovered so far.

Andrew spoke. "The Boston Box, huh? And you're at Harvard?"

"This is more of an unofficial project for me. It keys into some of the research I'm doing for my thesis, but not the main focus. At the school, there are some people who think it's a waste, but other professors are supportive."

"I'm sure you'll learn along the way. The journey, not the destination."

"I suppose," Caitlyn answered.

"Just trying to be upbeat."

"No, I understand. That's actually very astute. There are times when I can't let go of the destination. That's all. Anyway, about your ancestor?"

"Old Josiah was quite the dog," he said. "I've not heard about any Boston Box. But it wouldn't surprise me. You know, he was in Boston before the Civil War. He studied in France, came home. This is family lore, that he helped with the Underground Railroad."

"For hiding runaway slaves."

"Not all of them were slaves, exactly. Sometimes, these men and their families were free, but traders or owners ignored their claims. Evil. I'm not saying runaway slaves didn't have a good reason to try and escape, of course. Just there were many kinds of people of color on the railroad, people who wanted to be out of danger. Do you know all this? No? Boston was a major stop on the way to Canada. A hidden room might be used for something like that. I don't have proof Josiah made any of them. Or designed them. But it would make sense. He was an unofficial part of something called the Committee of Vigilance. I have a picture of him."

"Really?"

Andrew got out of his chair and walked to a corner of the office to a small bookcase. He retrieved a framed photograph and handed it to Caitlyn. "Here's the old boy. My hero." He continued to stand by her side, awaiting her reaction.

In some ways, the photograph looked like a classic vintage shot. Josiah wore a frock coat and vest, not finely tailored, and his shirt had a high, stiff collar. But the picture had been put through a restoration process and had none of the aging or fading that sometimes distances a viewer. The photo's clarity and some colorization made Josiah appear startlingly modern, as did his hair, which was close-cropped and almost contemporary in style to the present. She guessed he was approximately fifty years old. His expression was confident, surprisingly sexy.

"He was a good-looking man," Caitlyn said.

Andrew nodded. "I think so."

"You resemble him." After the sentence was out of her mouth, she realized that it might be misconstrued. Or construed, if that was a word. She lowered her eyes, away from Andrew's glance, and prayed that her cheeks weren't as scarlet as they felt.

Andrew took the picture from her hands and placed it on a small table. Caitlyn caught a glimmer of amusement in his eyes. Before he sat again, he said, "Are you sure you wouldn't like something to drink? The ventilation here is a problem."

She grabbed at the lifeline he threw her. "Maybe water would be good after all." While he left the office to get the beverage, she took a few breaths and attempted to recover her composure. Josiah Hawkins's vivid expression in the framed picture looked more self-satisfied than before. "Don't you look at me that way," she said.

Andrew reappeared at the open door. "Excuse me?" He handed her a plastic bottle of water and a cup.

"Josiah and me," she mumbled. "We were talking. Oh, thanks so much. I mean, can you tell me more about him?" She poured the water and gulped a swallow.

"Josiah was a free Black," Andrew said. "Never a slave. We don't know much about the generations before him, although the story is that his parents traveled here with a Spanish sailing vessel in the early 1800's. Josiah himself was bright. A local family, the Carters, the father did construction, took Josiah under his wing. Kind man. Theodore Carter. Progressive for the time. Actually sent Josiah to France as a practical matter. Carter needed help with the business, only had a very young son and daughters, and thought it would be good for Josiah to learn about methods, style. I think Theodore Carter himself mostly built things in Boston's West End, not sure, but they all got torn down during the urban renewal projects in the fifties, sixties. You know about that?"

"A little."

"Wholesale razing of the neighborhood to make way for City Hall and other construction. Would never get away with it now, although I gather a lot of the places were tenements. Anyhow, Josiah goes to France, and the Carter business languishes. So Josiah is more or less stranded for a while in Paris, but he makes the best of it."

"How do you know all this?"

"That's a very good question. Josiah told this to my granddad when he was a boy who told my dad about it."

"Oral tradition."

"In a way. There's some other material about Josiah that's less verifiable. I'll get to that. Josiah made a go of it in France. He was already midway through his education when the Carters had their rough patch. Family legend is that Josiah found a patron, a woman in France, whether she was an aristocrat or a courtesan, it's not totally clear. This is the unverifiable part. It makes sense in one way because that was the other thing about Josiah."

"What's that?" Caitlyn asked.

"He was a ladies' man. He had three wives over time."

"I see."

"A few families claim him as an ancestor. Mine is the first lineage, first marriage, but every once in a while, I trip over someone who says she or he's my cousin. Distant cousin or something. Through another of his wives." Andrew's eyes glistened. "Anyway, Josiah finished his training in Europe and headed back home. Things were pretty volatile at the time in

Boston, with abolitionists. And his opportunity with the Carters didn't exist anymore due to slow business. Eventually, however, he found someone who needed him. Gregory Adamston."

"I know that they had a working relationship."

"According to my great-great-grandfather, Adamston was a drunk. Not a bad man, but just could not handle liquor. Always wasted. On the other hand, despite those Bostonians who fought the moral war against slavery, it wasn't easy for Josiah to get commissions. People didn't really believe Black men had any brains. So Adamston drummed up the business, he had connections, and Josiah did most of the work for a share of the money. Not a fair share, but a better salary than many Black men earned at the time, even many white men, and more interesting work than if he tried to set up shop on his own. And that's how it worked until Adamston died. Josiah kept working after that, but it was trivial stuff, compared to what he was used to."

"A waste of talent."

"Yeah, well, that's true of centuries of Black people in America," Andrew said. "At least Josiah had saved his money. Jobs came after Adamston's death, just not big ones."

"I'd heard that there was a scandal when Adamston died. Just through Wikipedia. Do you know anything about that?"

"Yeah. The drinking got worse. He lost money on a building. Killed him. Harsh."

"But you never heard anything about a Boston Box?" Caitlyn said.

"No."

"Do you know anything about your great-grandfather's buildings? Or Adamston's?"

"I've gone to the church. You know it? Ah, good. I think there are some very nice touches there. My dad lived in what was supposed to be the family house on Fort Hill when he was younger. It was sold. I'm not sure if it was a work of Josiah's. There are some warehouse type buildings in towns around Massachusetts. The thing is, it's been a hundred years. Over a hundred and fifty in some cases. Unless you're lucky, it'll be difficult to find a place that hasn't been renovated. From afar, it would appear your best bet would be to concentrate on the smaller buildings. Like the brownstones. More manageable."

"I didn't think it would be simple. I enjoy the research. But that's worth considering. Thanks."

"Just a thought."

"Were there other architects in your family? Your father, or cousins?"

"I'm the first since Josiah. There may have been others in other branches of the clan, but I don't know. My dad was a teacher. So was my granddad. I have two sisters. One's a lawyer and the baby is going to Columbia."

"Non-achievers," Caitlyn joked.

Andrew laughed. "My dad, for obvious reasons, stressed education. We grew up in Cambridge."

"Okay," Caitlyn said. "To make sure I understand. You think that Josiah was the talent in Adamston's business. I don't doubt it. From what I've read, it rings true. You don't know anything about the Boston Box, but you could imagine a connection with your great-great-grandfather's work with the Underground Railroad. Creating secret places for Black people to hide on their way to Canada. At least in the beginning."

"That could be a premise."

"But you have no evidence."

"None on the railroad," Andrew said with a hunch of his shoulders.

"Anything else?"

"Well, if you visit some of Josiah's buildings, I'd be interested in joining you. Even if I'd seen them before, I'd like to revisit, pay some homage to my bloodlines. I might be able to help."

"Yes," Caitlyn said. "Of course. I'd enjoy the company."

Andrew paused. "You free now, by any chance? Time to close up here for the day. There's a great bar across the street. Do you have time for a drink? A real one."

Caitlyn knew she should turn down the invitation. She had too much work to do. But Andrew was so damned good-looking. "Sure. A drink would be fun."

"Very cool," Andrew said. "Let me wrap up and we can head over. This is a great place. You tell them what kind of drinks you like, and they make one up for you."

"I'm not too sophisticated when it comes to cocktails. Mostly I drink beer or wine."

Andrew said, "Tell them that. They'll figure it out. Time to broaden your horizons."

He really did have a beautiful smile.

CHAPTER TWENTY

MARK

April 2017

By the time I reached the Fenway Grand, the right side of my face looked like the paint chips for shades of purple at a Benjamin Moore store. I had a tour shift coming in three days. I could only hope that I was presentable by that time. I'd go to a drugstore later and get some gauze compresses. I didn't want to visit an emergency room for stitches. I was too exhausted.

I holed up in the apartment for the rest of the day, not wanting to explain to anyone why I was black and blue and cut-up. My purchase of the fried chicken now seemed fortuitous, as it freed me from any need to cook or go out for a meal. I slept off and on, sometimes from fatigue, sometimes as an escape, and sometimes in shock, often curled in a fetal position under bedcovers. The collector showed up in a dream. I feared that a reunion with him was just a matter of time.

I woke before dawn, headachy, and then snuck over to an all-night CVS across the street to buy some bandages big enough to hide my wounds. While I was outside, looking over my shoulder became so habitual that I probably appeared like I had a nervous tick. It was too early for bruisers in Benzes to stake me out and I returned to the apartment without incident.

I ate a fried chicken breast for breakfast while I viewed the sunrise through the floor-to-ceiling windows. I'd brought along my sedatives when I moved to the apartment, just in case, but I resisted a temptation to take one.

When I left a few hours later for my appointment with Dietz, my forehead injury was hidden behind a patch of white gauze, and I had a very noticeable black eye. I brought along the stack of files that Taylor had given me. Dietz's office was on Newbury Street, where people went shopping when money was no object. I drove and found a parking place on the street, highly visible and highly trafficked, so any attempt to damage the BMW again would be noticed. As far as I could tell, no one followed me.

It was sunny, and a few hardy individuals sat outdoors and sipped coffee at one of the street's many cafes. After a long winter, fifty-five degrees in April can feel like a heat wave in Boston. I walked past a row of expensive boutiques and came to Dietz's address. On the first floor of the brownstone that housed his office was a gallery which sold antique advertising prints. In the main window hung a French poster for Peugeot featuring a grinning pink, yellow, and gray clown. What clowns had to do with cars, I didn't know.

I went up a set of red concrete steps, pressed a button on a directory, and was buzzed into the building. Dietz's suite was on the third floor. In private practice, he shared space with another lawyer, a couple of associates, and a fortyish pinch-faced receptionist, the only person visible when I entered.

Dietz, who came from a small office to greet me, was tall and lanky, in his mid-forties, with a long face dominated by round eyeglasses and one of the fullest beards I'd seen outside of Amish country. Eying my bandages, he asked what happened. I said that I'd fallen yesterday on a rain-slick street.

"Did you go to a hospital?" he asked.

I shook my head no.

His expression was wry. "It looks like it was a pretty aggressive sidewalk," he said. "Hope you fought back."

For a moment I was bothered by his guess that I wasn't telling the truth. But then I accepted the justice of his suspicion. After all, I *was* lying, so who could blame him for doubting me? At a minimum, I had to give him credit for detecting bullshit. My evasiveness was part of my stopgap strategy to hide any illegality of Dave's accounts. Since I didn't really know Dietz or the guidelines for our discussions, I was unsure if any of my disclosures would be protected by client confidentiality.

In a minute, Dietz and I sat across from one another in a small conference room. He asked me to tell about the overall situation as I saw it, so I did: my lack of communication with Dave for more than two decades; the news earlier in the week about his death; the accounts; my living at the Fenway Grand; my status as sole survivor. After that, Dietz took his turn to speak and outlined his next steps. He said he'd get a power of attorney for Dave's estate and a court order that gave me limited access to the money to cover costs. He recommended that I set up a separate account somewhere and use it only for expenses related to the estate. I was to keep receipts for every cent I spent. Dietz said that unless there were challenges to my claim, the matter should be straightforward, but the process could take time, even several months, and perhaps as long as a year or more. He would answer any procedural questions as they arose, and I shouldn't hesitate to contact him if I ran into difficulties.

"What about things like the apartment, the car?" I asked.

"I'll address those with the judge," he said. "What you have going for you, from what you said, is that there's nobody to contest your claim. No will. The apartment and clothing, nothing lost for anyone there. As for the car, we have to see what the title says. Do you know if it's been paid off? Leased?"

"No."

"Then I wouldn't take any cross-country trips," he said. I must have looked deflated because he added, "Don't get blue just yet. Let me check all this and do what I can. The power of attorney should help."

"What about the files?"

"My assistant will make a copy and review them. This is the only set, right? You can have them back in a couple of days."

"The cops have a set."

Dietz spent the next half-hour explaining the process, the forms, the timing, what I needed to do. I told him about the expenses that I'd already incurred, like the funeral, and the costs for the deductible.

"Deductible?" he asked.

I had omitted, so far, any reference to the tire slashing. It hadn't exactly fit into the narrative that he'd requested at the beginning of our meeting.

"Just so I understand this," he said, his face deadpan. "There's been a murder. The car's been vandalized. You fell on the sidewalk and got a black eye. In a week's time."

"Yes. A little less."

"Your brother was a crook?"

"At one point," I answered. "The police say the money is legit. But his history was sketchy."

"And where did you fall? Your head wound?"

"I was buying fried chicken in Quincy."

"Quincy? Did the store take any information? If you incur medical expenses, they could be liable."

"I don't want that," I answered. Why does one lie always beget another?

"Do you often go to Quincy?"

"Never. The new car. I was on a joyride."

"Quincy?" he asked. I guessed he found it hard to believe much joy was to be had there. "Anything else you want to say to me?"

"No, right now, nothing."

Dietz pushed back against his chair. "Ouch," he said. Seeing my confusion, he added, "I have a weak muscle in my back. Here's the thing, Mark. If you want to talk things over, or tell me anything else, you should. I work for you."

"What's confidential?"

"All of it. If you were intending to commit a crime, things get squishy, but you seem like an honest guy."

Given our conversation, I wasn't sure if he meant that ironically, but I told him thanks and that I would keep his offer in mind.

Dietz ended by explaining his fees. He charged $325 an hour. His assistant was $220. He expected the process to take about 30 hours, about $9,000. He would forego his $5,000 retainer until we went before the probate court so that funds from Dave's account could be used to cover his expenses, but he would expect payment immediately afterward.

"How much of this is public record?" I asked.

"All of it," he answered. "Is that a problem?"

It could be for me, I thought. I'd have to see what Mr. Florida, whoever he was, believed he was owed. If he wanted a big share of Dave's money, he might not appreciate any attempt that I made to disguise what I knew about the account, and how much money it held. For the moment, I could claim ignorance and say that Dave's papers weren't in order, but once the court documentation was filed, there'd be no way for me to hide my deception.

I smiled. "No. No problem at all."

CHAPTER TWENTY-ONE

CAITLYN

November 2016

The drink with Andrew—a martini with Cherry Heering and vodka and Jägermeister made just for Caitlyn—had progressed into dinner and wine, more good conversation, and a pass. Andrew had asked if Caitlyn would like to see his condo, not far away from Fort Point in Boston's Leather District. Her refusal had the alcohol as its rationale: "I don't usually drink so much." He asked once more very lightly—*You're sure?*—but when it was clear that her "no" meant "no," he gave up.

Back at her apartment, as she prepared for bed, Caitlyn second-guessed her decision about not sleeping with him. He was hot. She hadn't been with anyone in so many months that it was embarrassing. At that very moment, instead of brushing her teeth in front of her bathroom mirror, she could have been enjoying herself.

She sighed. Too late now. Maybe there'd be a "next time," a hope that she'd expressed before they parted. They kissed on the cheeks, friendly-like. He would return from his out-of-town trip, a business jaunt overseas, early next week. His interest in his ancestor's work would provide a reason for her to be in touch with him. If a reunion occurred, she would stay sober.

Or sober-ish. And maybe she would be the seducer. Or maybe it could be more than that. She briefly wondered if mixing her "scholarly" investigation of the Boston Box, a professional undertaking, with a relationship was a good idea. She dismissed the concern as just another lame excuse not to follow her instincts, overthinking a romantic prospect, delaying, coming up with the negatives till the opportunity no longer existed. She always did that. Time to stop.

She liked Andrew. He was charming and smart and gorgeous. But she had just met the guy and shouldn't order a wedding gown yet. About to fall asleep, she fantasized that he would be really good in bed.

In the morning, walking to Harvard, Caitlyn replayed a part of her dinner conversation. Andrew had questioned her approach to the Boston Box. He noted that finding one instance of its existence was hardly enough to prove her contention that many Boston architects had created secret rooms almost as a regular practice. She would need to locate several examples, and by more than one firm or builder. She groaned. Investigating Adamston and, by extension, Josiah Hawkins, was already time-consuming. Fun, certainly, but demanding. How in the world could she expand her research? Maybe this was the time to tie the Boston Box more closely to her thesis subject. Contemplating this possibility, she mentally complained about Bacht once more for his rejection of her first proposal.

While she had every intention of continuing her on-site examinations of buildings, and of using field trips as primary data in her study, she also wondered what secondary resources were available for her to analyze or review. She knew of several academic surveys of Boston architecture. Not to mention articles, so many that she became a bit overwhelmed in contemplating their number. But, putting that feeling aside, might it be possible for her to take already compiled information and reinterpret it? To discover something that the original researchers missed because they just weren't aware of the Boston Box? Could she look at those other studies through Boston Box-colored glasses? Hm.

Entering Sandler, Caitlyn saw Professor Venda in the foyer, sunglasses propped on her head, not conceding to the approach of winter. She asked about Caitlyn's "special project."

"Chugging along," Caitlyn said. "There's so much to do."

"Dear girl, this is not an excuse you should use."

"I mean, I love it. But trying to balance everything..."

"You are capable."

You don't understand, Caitlyn thought. The residue of the previous night's drinks made her cranky.

"I can see your conflict," Venda said. "I am a woman, too. There are many things we must try to do at once. These are the facts of our lives."

Caitlyn sighed. Venda might be melodramatic, but she was also encouraging, and meant well. "Okay. Let me ask you something," Caitlyn said, and then she recapped the conversation she had had with Andrew, or, more accurately, her interest in some secondary sources. In response, Venda recommended a book from the seventies by a former Harvard professor, Bailey Munce. It was out-of-print, but the university had several copies. Venda also promised to give the question further thought.

"Keep strong," Venda said, and walked off.

Although running immediately to get the Munce book went against a commitment, made to herself, to concentrate on her other schoolwork, Caitlyn found herself dashing to Widener

Library, which was, after all, only five minutes away, a minor detour. She easily located the book, *Back Bay Houses*, soft-covered, and checked it out.

On the return walk, she thumbed the book's slightly soiled pages and glanced at its illustrations, pleased because getting the volume had taken less than a half-hour. She was almost back at Sandler when she spotted Bacht about to enter the building. She shouldn't have been surprised. Professors on sabbatical visited their offices for one reason or another from time to time. Caitlyn hadn't encountered Bacht since the night at the bar, and she absolutely did not want to speak with him now. She decided to go to a nearby Starbucks in order to avoid him. She purchased some coffee. By the time of her second—or was it third?—attempt to enter the building, he wasn't in sight.

Caitlyn reached her office and left the door ajar. At her desk, a stack of envelopes awaited her. A paper was due before the Thanksgiving break in a class she assisted, and several students who hoped to leave early had dropped off their assignments. She brought up a time management calendar on her laptop to be sure this task was on the list. Indeed, it was, along with roughly forty other items with upcoming due dates. She spent about fifteen minutes re-ordering her tasks, trying to figure out what was urgent, what was mandatory, what could wait.

Despite the pressing duties of her thesis and her teaching fellowship, *Back Bay Houses*, lying near her hand, beckoned. The book wasn't a direct hit for her thesis topic, but she couldn't keep herself from picking it up.

A doctoral thesis converted into a professionally published manuscript, Munce's book documented every home built in the Back Bay over a seventy-five-year period, 1845-1920. There were variations in how thoroughly Munce described the homes, with "notable" specimens given more detail than others. Interwoven with the text of the book were sample floor plans for a selection of the brownstones. According to Munce, interior layouts were often standardized. City planners had limited the plots for the homes to widths between nineteen and twenty-five feet, narrow, and in the days before electricity, given these restrictions, not many designs allowed a front-to-back stream of sunlight.

Generally, the study was a gold mine, particularly an appendix at the back of the book that listed each house according to address, along with its architect if known, its style, and year of construction. Using the appendix, Caitlyn calculated some further guidelines for her study. It made sense to focus on the years between 1845 and 1880, roughly the time of Adamston's and Josiah Hawkins's professional lives. The early period, before and during the Civil War, would match the period of the Underground Railroad. The later years keyed in with an impression Caitlyn had that the Boston Box persisted in the post-Civil War era, perhaps out of a panic in the aftermath of all of the death and destruction. People might build hiding places in the event of danger, one of many possible uses for secret rooms.

Homes in Back Bay during the pre-Civil War period, candidates for a Boston Box, were easy to deal with. There weren't many. The landfill project that had created Commonwealth Avenue—that had created much of Back Bay for that matter—hadn't begun until the late 1850's. If Adamston or Hawkins or anyone else designed a Boston Box in this period, it would be elsewhere, maybe Beacon Hill, or the area around the Public Garden, or closer to the harbor.

In the second period of her study, however, a boom happened mostly in the lower end of Back Bay, as the landfill progressed and the new neighborhood eclipsed Beacon Hill as the "hot" area to live. According to the appendix, Adamston wasn't responsible for any of these properties, which she had suspected already, but she wished for a different outcome, one that would make her life a little easier.

She said aloud, "Oh, damn," and sighed.

"Are you having a bad day, Ms. Gautry?"

The familiar voice came from behind her, at the doorway. Without turning around, Caitlyn knew who it was. She tried to conceal her dismay and faced him. "Is there something I can help you with, Dr. Bacht?"

"A little chat?" he said.

She wanted to protest, *I'm very busy.* There was no point, however, in denying his request. He'd ignore the refusal. Nevertheless, she didn't invite him to sit down. Trying to sound neutral, she said, "What would you like to talk about?"

"I understand you continue your work on secret rooms."

She paused. *Admit nothing. He'll sabotage you.* "Um, I'm not following."

"You don't mind if I join you for a moment, do you?" Bacht didn't wait for her permission and took a seat across from her. "Have you discovered anything?"

His skin was bronzed. He'd be sexy if he weren't such an asshole. "Oh, have you been on vacation?" she asked. Bacht looked confused by her response. "Your tan," she added.

"Costa Rica," he said. "A conference." He scanned the material on her desk and spotted the Munce book. "Munce was very good. Very thorough. What are you finding?"

"He's a source for my thesis. Professor Venda recommended him. I just began reading him."

"Of course, Helene would know him. I don't recall any hidden rooms in his survey."

"Really, I just picked him up," she responded, perhaps too quickly.

"My questions aren't offending you, are they, Ms. Gautry?"

"Dr. Bacht, please."

"I'm trying to save you from wasting your time."

Why was he digging like this? In truth, she hadn't yet discovered much about the Boston Box, but she worried that the simple fact of her ongoing investigations might irritate him. "I appreciate your concern," she said, a clipped note in her voice.

Bacht's eyes locked on hers, and maintaining her composure took effort. Her thoughts became muddy. Should she own up to her continued research? Or would that blow up in her face, expose her to more of his ridicule or interference? Or would it blow up anyway? Those eyes! She was almost blushing. Disoriented, she was on the verge of answering him honestly, of telling him, that yes, she was still investigating the Boston Box.

"Missteps could derail your advancement," he said. "I'm trying to prevent that."

Was he threatening her?

A quick knock on the door interrupted them.

Professor Venda stood there, smiling. "Allen. You cannot stay away?"

Bacht looked at her. "Helene. Marvelous to see you. No. Not back yet. I'm attending to some matters for a few hours on campus and had an item to discuss with Ms. Gautry."

"I see," Venda said. "Good luck for me. I was just passing. I wonder if I might have a moment with you. A departmental matter."

"Certainly, Helene. I'll be finished here shortly."

"Unfortunately," Venda said, "my time is very small. Might I pull you away?" There was almost a sensuousness in the way she spoke and posed in the doorway. Caitlyn admired how certain French women didn't hesitate to employ that weapon, even if, at the same time, she questioned whether it was exactly ethical, or perhaps not how a good feminist should act.

Bacht started to protest. "Surely…"

Venda said, "Thank you so much. I am certain that Caitlyn can spare you."

"Of course," Bacht said, a hint of irritation on his face. He addressed Caitlyn. "To be continued in a bit, I hope?" It was more of a statement than a question. He stood and walked toward the door. As the two of them stepped away, Venda glanced at Caitlyn, raised her eyebrows archly, an expression that mixed exasperation with *what the fuck?*

"I have an appointment," Caitlyn said, probably too late for him to hear. She took a deep breath and savored her reprieve, but just for a second. She had almost thrown her ball to the opposing team. She packed up her laptop and headed out the door. For the rest of the day, she holed up in a remote corner of Lamont Library, hidden from Dr. Bacht.

CHAPTER TWENTY-TWO

MARK

April 2017

Having made a couple of excursions outdoors without incident, my nerves inched toward recovery. Not my banged-up face, however, so after my meeting with Dietz, I sequestered myself once more at the Fenway Grand, a very comfortable place to heal and convalesce. My cocooning was aided by the HD cable connection and the last of the chicken. I had no commitments till the next day, Saturday, for Dave's cremation.

By morning, my injuries, notably the discoloration, had improved. Because of the solemnity attached to a funeral service, I felt like I needed to be groomed, so I went for a haircut to my usual barber, who was in a bad mood and didn't ask much about my wounds. Then I traveled to my apartment in Brighton to put on my suit, a four-year-old blue pinstripe, the only one I owned. This didn't seem a time to raid Dave's closet.

The crematorium was a short drive away. It was noon when I arrived. The viewing room was windowless but brightly lit, with a few padded folding chairs. Dave's closed plain white coffin sat upon a rolling bier at the front of the room. The funeral director, at my request, had arranged for a priest to come by. I wasn't religious any longer, and I doubted that Dave had been, but I covered the Catholic base out of superstition, and just in case Dave might have wanted it. Counting a funeral assistant, who hovered in the background, we were four living beings, and one dead.

The funeral director offered me a last look, and I agreed. Maybe I wanted to see Dave once more, or maybe I didn't but felt I should. The funeral director lifted the lid of the coffin and stood aside. I was unprepared for the surge of feeling—not anger, or love even, just a wave of something like grief, yet not really for Dave, or just for Dave, but for my loss of family, the final possibility for a relationship that was innate, in the blood, in a history together since birth. What ran through my mind over and over again was *I wish it had been different.* I may have muttered that aloud. But I didn't cry. No kneeler had been set up where I could say a prayer or do something other than look, so after several minutes, or what seemed like several to me, I just stepped back.

The priest, in his late sixties, read some prayers from a missal and then sprinkled Dave with holy water from a small glass bottle that had fit in his pocket like a flask. He had no reason to make any remarks since I was the only mourner and the priest knew nothing about Dave or me, but he offered a few personal words of condolence and stayed by my side while the funeral director shut the casket.

The funeral director gave an envelope with a cash token of my gratitude to the priest, who left after saying some final words to me. I asked the director when Dave's ashes could be claimed, and he said it wouldn't be long. I could come by later that day if I wished. We arranged a time in a few hours. In the end, after all my deliberations, the event itself was matter-of-fact and fleeting, although I wouldn't say it was painless.

I left the crematorium and walked down the block, where I found a bar attached to a bright, upscale, almost empty restaurant. I sat at a stool, drank a couple of beers, ate something, toasted Dave in my mind. I tried to buy a round for the other patrons at the bar, both of them. One young man refused because he had just come by for a lunch burger and wasn't having any alcohol, saying he had to go back to work. But after I told him why I was there he agreed to an O'Doul's, a pretend beer. The other patron took me up on the offer with a Tanqueray martini.

I was a little drunk when I walked back to get the stainless-steel urn with Dave's ashes. The director placed it in a white plastic bag with a drawstring. I hadn't given much consideration to what I would do with him, it, them. I could just throw the bag into the ocean. I was confident the urn would sink. In any case, not today. I put the urn on the passenger seat of the BMW. Its weight made the seat belt alarm beep as I drove us back to the Fenway Grand.

CHAPTER TWENTY-THREE

CAITLYN

December 2016

Being in New England at holiday time, after a few light snow-falls, should have been magical, but Caitlyn had tests to prepare, papers to review, grades to calculate, and her own studies to complete. And a deadline loomed on a preliminary document for her dissertation. Furthermore, mixed with the professional and scholastic obligations were seasonal activities: departmental parties, a few gatherings at faculty homes, and a large number of Christmas-themed concerts and performances. It was good academic politics to attend some of them, and she did, and she had fun, but ultimately these year-end events just added to her stress.

Her letter to Rumberg about a tour of Nine Chadwick Square was never answered. In the best of all worlds, she would have already written a follow-up—try, try, again—but her schedule was so crazy that attempting a contact seemed foolish since she was already overwhelmed. She resolved instead to send a second letter immediately in the new year. Likewise, a return to the Old Pilgrim, with its Christmas celebrations, was out of the question. The church and its staff were too busy. Besides, as Andrew had said, a focus on smaller properties made more sense.

As for Andrew, yet another fail. They'd exchanged a couple of messages, but his work and holiday plans clashed with hers. One more time, moving forward was put off until after the holidays. The lack of progress with Andrew was doubly disappointing: both for her research and for her love life. Or, more accurately, for her dismal, non-existent, sexless love life. With Andrew out of the picture, she'd probably be without a date on New Year's Eve. At least Henry was throwing a party, so she'd have a place to go. She briefly considered inviting Andrew to join her, but when she remembered the casual junkiness of Henry's past gatherings—grad student affairs—she decided against it.

Caitlyn didn't neglect the Boston Box entirely. One afternoon in her office, she used the Munce book and winnowed the number of architects in the index to ten firms active during the period she researched. The resulting list couldn't be called exhaustive. Architects other than those in Munce's book might be uncovered, and attributions for some homes were missing. Nonetheless, she believed most of the men important to her study were now identified.

With a manageable number of names, she did an online search on each, a mechanical task that required only a small amount of brain power, which was a relief, since a small amount of brain power was what she had available. The investigations of the first five men came up empty, with barely a note on their buildings and nothing on their private lives.

Of the remaining names, the most intriguing was a man named Thaddeus Simpson, who had been responsible for designing a small number of brownstones in Back Bay during a short career in Massachusetts. Most of them were solid work. He was best remembered, however, for an incident that had nothing to do with architecture: accused of murder, he had been at the center of a scandal.

A woman, Sally Morris, had been found dead on the banks of the Charles River. Morris, fifteen years of age and poor, had moved from Connecticut to northeast Massachusetts to look for factory work after she had lost an earlier job due to accusations of "lewd behavior." Following a cursory examination, her death was initially ruled as the result of a hemorrhage after a fall. But then a brief letter from Simpson was found among some of Morris's belongings, and the text indicated that the note had accompanied a small amount of money. It would be revealed that Simpson had met Morris while assisting in the construction of a dress mill in Lowell, near Boston. A friend of Morris's told the police that the dead woman was expecting Simpson's child. Morris's body was exhumed and re-examined, and it was determined that she had indeed been five months pregnant, and that a crude attempt at an abortion had led to her death.

Simpson's defenders—and apparently there were many—portrayed him as a loving father, a widower who took great care of his children, and someone of great moral fiber. He apparently was part of the Boston anti-slavery movement, a possible connection to Josiah Hawkins. Simpson's detractors claimed he was a practiced womanizer and seducer of young girls. But except for that note, no strong evidence of a relationship between Simpson and Morris was uncovered. Simpson said he'd sent money after she approached him at the mill site. Kindness to a stranger. He was ultimately acquitted, but public opinion was against him, and following unsuccessful attempts to repair his reputation in Boston, Simpson had moved to another state.

What Caitlyn learned about the Morris case was taken from a not very detailed write-up on a website. She put a reminder in her calendar to search for a fuller version after the holidays. Simpson had lived on Commonwealth Avenue at the time of the trial in a home that he had designed himself. If the house still stood, she must investigate it. She wanted to know whether a man like Simpson—potentially a sexual predator—would build a Boston Box for his own use.

CHAPTER TWENTY-FOUR

MARK

April 2017

At work, the day after Dave's funeral, my colleagues at the tour company ribbed me about my patched-up face. My supervisor Gerry, a gruff, husky man, shook his head and said, "For Christ's sake. Don't scare any of the tourists." He advised me to come up with some clever bit to put my passengers at ease.

I told my first group that I'd had a Duck full of Yankee fans the day before and as usual, I had to take some extreme measures to maintain a proper level of respect. Folks were in good humor, and they laughed. One guy yelled out, "I'm a Yankee fan."

"Remind me of that when we're out on the river, okay?" I said.

He chuckled. Yankee and Red Sox fans enjoy hating one another.

A Sunday, the weather was decent, which boded well for full, happy runs. The line in front of *Cheers* was long; the Swan Boats were running; the golden dome of the State House gleamed. Because trees were not yet in full spring bloom, the vistas of Boston Common and the Public Garden were open and clear. You could even make out the statues that celebrated *Make Way for Ducklings* and the toddlers who played on them, which was unusual. Later in the season, they'd be obscured from the tour by blossomed, leafy trees.

During a short break between my second and third runs, I was leaning on a wall near the ticket booth when one of the other drivers, a cubbish man named Neal, approached me. "Someone was here asking for you," he said.

I nodded. "Who?"

"Didn't leave a name."

"What did he look like?"

"A guy," Neal said. "Well dressed. Older than me."

"I'm older than you, Neal. Lots of people are. How old?"

"Older than you, too, I think. Like in his fifties."

At least that ruled out the collector. "Thanks," I said. "Maybe it was a friend." But whoever it was, he didn't know me well enough to text, email, or call in advance.

I stepped back onto my Duck and welcomed the newest round of tourists, my last of the day, as they boarded. I gave my opening comments and was about to pull away when Neal banged on the side of the Duck and said, "The guy with the purple shirt."

"What's that?" I said.

"Purple shirt. That's him."

Actually, I'd noticed the man in question when he boarded. He was good-looking, Nordic features, blond hair on its way to gray, the straight point collar of his purple—lavender, really—shirt peeking out from the neck of his beige ski jacket. Looked healthy. I glanced into the rearview mirror. He had taken a seat near the back of the Duck. A week ago, I might have been titillated that he asked about me. Now, after all that had happened, it was disconcerting. He saw me glimpse at him, and our eyes met, deliberately on his part, with no hint of underlying feeling, no anger, no sex, no nothing.

I was off my game as I narrated the tour. Purple Shirt and I played eye tag, somewhat involuntarily for me. I couldn't help looking. My train of thought was off the rails. At one point, I struggled to remember the name of the Zakim Bridge.

If the tips that I earned from these tour riders were an indication, my jumpiness must have been well disguised, because they were generous. Purple Shirt hung back, partly a function of his seat near the rear. The Duck was almost empty when he rose and aimed toward the front, the last person to leave. He retrieved his wallet and pulled out some cash. "Good tour," he said. He handed me a $100 bill.

I was stunned. "God," I said. "Thanks. Wow. That's a record."

"Sure. Now that I have your attention. Maybe we could meet for a drink."

My wariness increased. This was not a pick-up. I'm not bad looking, but there was no way I was dating material with a bandage and a black eye. "I'm not sure I understand," I said.

Purple Shirt smiled. "I knew David." My expression must have shown the apprehension that I immediately felt. "We'll go somewhere public. You're in no danger. Consider the money as a sign of my good will." I still didn't think this was a great idea. Sensing my hesitancy, he added, "This invitation is friendly." I wasn't sure if his words contained a threat was that the next request might not be so cordial. "Trust me," he continued. "We can work this out really simply. I just need some information. You can pick the place."

I held his gaze. "You live in Florida?"

"Miami."

After I had been assaulted at the KFC, I knew that another encounter would happen. This was it. At any rate, the conditions suggested by Purple Shirt were probably as favorable as I could hope. His manner was much less brutal than the collector's.

"As you can see," I said, "I'm not exactly in shape for much socializing." A test. Would he, even subtly, acknowledge any connection to my injuries?

"I am truly sorry about that," he said, his tone an attempt at sincerity. "I'm sure nothing will happen."

Not quite an admission of guilt, but the fact that he didn't ask about how my bruises had happened suggested that he already knew the circumstances. A veneer of honesty.

"What's your name?" I said.

"Russ." He extended his hand, and we shook.

"Russ, I have to take care of some business here. There's a bar at the Legal over in Copley Place. I can meet you there in forty-five minutes."

"Okay. That can work."

"Forty-five minutes or so. Wrapping up is not a precise science." I gave myself a good cushion when I suggested the time, not eager to have my head smashed again if Russ was the type who watched the clock.

He walked off.

I would be stupid not to believe I took a risk in meeting with Russ, but I didn't see I had much choice. I couldn't call the police and say, *Some guy is forcing me to have a drink at Legal Sea Foods. That's right, officer. He said this is a friendly invitation.* And without knowing his story, I couldn't accuse him of any wrongdoing.

Of course, the last time I gave into the notion that a meeting was inevitable, with the collector, my face got smashed. I told myself now I was protected because we would be in a public place. I doubted that any physical violence would erupt. Russ didn't seem that kind of reckless. If I feared for my life at some point, I'd stay put and call Taylor to ask for help. Or I'd go to the restaurant manager. Or I'd call Dietz. I'd do *something*.

While I waited to validate a timesheet with Gerry, I contemplated my tactics for the meeting. At this point, I had a good story to tell Russ. I'd no knowledge of Dave's activities and I couldn't be held accountable for whatever he'd done. As for the money, I was going to play dumb, to say that Dave's accounts hadn't yet been found. My biggest problem was that I'm not a great liar. Oh, okay. Up until now, I may not have given the whole truth all the time to Taylor or Dietz, but the situations were not as charged as this one. Here I'd be telling a flat-out lie to a man who played rough. A slip-up could have dire consequences.

On the other hand, if I could be convincing, maybe I'd be home free. It can't be that hard to act dumb. Maybe I'd find out that Russ's claim against Dave was minuscule, or that Russ was reasonable, or that he'd buy my story that the money was missing, and he'd go away and forget about it. Maybe he had so much money that recovering $633,215.28 was a matter of pride, not of desperation. I could dream.

I finished my duties with the Duck crew and spent a few minutes organizing my tips. Thanks to Russ and the $100 bill, I had my best haul ever. I decided to buy the first round, kill him with kindness, soften him up. So what if my generosity was basically with his money? I just prayed, perhaps illogically, that he didn't think I owed him more than a drink.

CHAPTER TWENTY-FIVE

CAITLYN

December 2016

By the twenty-first of December, Caitlyn had met all of her immediate school deadlines. Some longer-term work still pended, but the university was going to shut down, so she put academia aside. While at home she wanted to rest and renew, to turn off her brain for a week.

Over the past month, an occasional text or comment suggested that something continued to bother her mother. Yet when Caitlyn addressed these hints, her mother would backtrack and insist everything was okay. Caitlyn brought up the issue with her dad, who also downplayed the matter, but a note in his voice implied the whole truth had yet to be told. After their denials, however, Caitlyn concluded that if a problem existed, she would not learn about it until she was home for break.

She flew into Philadelphia early on the 22nd and was met by her parents. Her mom, Sylvia, in her early fifties, looked good. Her brown hair had been cut, full but only a little longer than ear length, and with her glasses she looked almost stereotypically intellectual. The style gave the wrong impression. Her mother had finished a year of college but had never completed her studies. Ed, her dad, was a few years older than Sylvia but looked younger, a handsome man, baby-soft skin, dark hair with only a trace of gray. He colored it. Their immediate family was just the three of them.

At home in West Chester, a college town outside of Philly, Caitlyn relaxed, slept, ate, slept, chatted, slept. The television was on constantly, a continuous loop of local news, Hallmark Christmas movies, and game shows. It was amazing how she figuratively returned to the womb, with her mom doting on her and catering to every need. A total regression.

After adjusting to this rhythm, and prepared for whatever might be wrong, Caitlyn asked Sylvia directly about her cryptic comments. The question was dismissed once more with an "everything's fine," followed by a declaration that she simply missed her squirrel, her baby, and that she was so glad that Caitlyn was home. But she avoided looking at Caitlyn as she spoke and made a point of asking Caitlyn to be available on the day after Christmas for a special holiday lunch, a troubling request because of the mysterious signals. Of course, Caitlyn agreed.

On the 23rd, Caitlyn braved the nearby malls for some last-minute shopping. Amid the crowds, waiting forever for clerks who could check out her purchases, she felt far away from Harvard. That evening, she met with a few of her high school friends at a local pub. The get-together was fun, and worth the guilt caused by her mother's sad look after she realized Caitlyn would not spend the time at home.

For the next two days, traditions took over. Christmas Eve started at an early church service, and the rest of the evening was spent with her dad's side of the family in a nearby town. Gifts were given. A few pieces of clothing that Caitlyn received were obviously meant for her past, heftier self and would have to be exchanged. Her parents also gave her money, for which she was grateful. It wasn't the $650,000 she needed for a condo in the South End, LOL, but it would help with other expenses.

Christmas Day was dedicated to her mom's relatives. This was a much bigger group, with several cousins close to Caitlyn in age, and lots of laughter, and too much food. If she wasn't careful, those wrongly sized gifts would come in handy.

While helping in the kitchen with clean-up, her mom reminded her of the lunch date.

"Mom," Caitlyn said. "How could I forget?"

"I just want to be sure," Sylvia said. "Looking forward to a girls' day out."

Her need for reassurance was mystifying, and Caitlyn was about to address it, but then her mom hugged her and said, "I love you."

As Caitlyn was drying a dinner plate, hugging her mother in return was awkward, but she did the best she could. "I love you, too, Mom. Merry Christmas." And she did love her mother, but this perpetual undertone of anxiety was wearing her out.

The next morning, Caitlyn felt like a blimp. A hungover blimp, at that. She went to the kitchen in pajamas and a robe in search of a cup of strong coffee. Her father wasn't around. Her mom was much too chipper in her greeting, and her cheerfulness was difficult for Caitlyn to tolerate before she herself was fully awake.

"I've made reservations at that bistro for lunch," Sylvia said. "Marcel's."

"Oh, joy, more food," Caitlyn said. Her comment was meant as humorous. She sipped coffee.

"I want some time with you," her mom said sharply. "I need some time with you."

Surprised at the outburst, Caitlyn said, "Mom. I'm here now. We've been together for four days. What's the big deal?" Her mother's shoulders suddenly slumped. The pretense of normalcy had finally cracked. "What's wrong?" Caitlyn said.

"We'll talk at lunch."

"Mom," Caitlyn said, pleading. "No. We'll talk now. Please. You've been doing this to me for months now." She reached over and touched her mother's sweater-covered arm and led her to a breakfast table in the corner of the kitchen. They sat close to one another. "What is it?" Caitlyn said. "Are you ill?"

"No. It's about your father."

"Dad? Dad is sick?"

"No, not him. Not Dad. Your father."

It took a moment for Caitlyn to understand. Not Ed. Not her adoptive dad. But her father. Her biological father.

CHAPTER TWENTY-SIX

MARK

April 2017

The restaurant where I was to meet Russ, Legal Sea Foods, is a tourist trap, but one of the best kind, locally-based, with several outlets and more than decent food. This location was usually very busy, which is why I chose it. Russ couldn't try anything extreme unless he didn't care about dozens of witnesses.

Small groups, waiting for tables, gathered by the entrance. I pushed my way past them to the bar and scanned it. Russ wasn't there. A hand tapped my shoulder, and I turned. "I got a table for us," Russ said. "I'm hungry. Follow me. My treat." That immediate offer—or was it a command?—did away with any idea I had about picking up a tab. Ah, well. So much for my strategy. In any case, he looked like he could afford the check better than me. Russ crossed the crowded floor to a corner with a secluded booth offering a good view of the restaurant, the kind of table you get when you slip a twenty to the maître d'.

Our server, a tall and thin young man named Sandy, came to us as soon as we sat down. Sandy asked me about beverages. I enjoyed some banter about what was on tap, an easy subject for immediate small talk, a bridge to more charged subjects. In the end, I ordered a craft beer. Russ must have waited for a while because he already had a drink made with some clear brown spirit like bourbon, now half-gone. Maybe an Old-Fashioned. Sandy left.

"Let's get this out of the way," Russ said. "Apologies are necessary." He spoke matter-of-factly, and for the first time I noticed the tinge of a Southern drawl.

"Go on," I said.

"My colleague made a mistake. He was supposed to find your brother. I told him not to get rough about it. About the damage. It's regrettable."

Damage made it sound like I was a car and not a human being, but I had to admit his apology was an effective opening gambit. "The wounds hurt," I said. "I'm not exactly in a place yet where I'm feeling gracious about being beat up. Even if it wasn't precisely your idea."

"In my world, an apology is usually accepted," he said.

"I don't know what your world is."

Sandy delivered my beer and asked if we had any questions about the menu. The answer from me was "no" because I hadn't looked at it. He said he'd return in a few minutes.

"I'm a businessman," Russ said. The look on my face must have betrayed my dissatisfaction, or at least my wish for further explanations. "I manage a racetrack, some other properties."

"A racetrack. Interesting."

"It's work."

"That's how you know Dave?"

"Yes. But his death. A shock. What happened?"

"He was stabbed. I don't know why. Or who did it. Not me or the police know. They're investigating." I provided a few more details about Dave's death.

"A mystery," he said.

"Yes. Now you and Dave. The racetrack. Gambling? Is that the money you're looking for?"

"How do you know about any money?"

"Your friend," I lied. "The one who beat me up. He mentioned it. What's his name?"

"Clarence."

I snickered. "Not the kind of name I associate with thugs."

"I'll do you a favor," he said. "I won't tell Clarence you laughed. His mother liked *It's a Wonderful Life*. The angel. He has a nickname that might change your attitude, but I don't usually use it in public."

Sandy showed up at the table again, and we broke for two minutes, examined our menus, and ordered. I recommended lobster but Russ said he didn't feel like dealing with the mess and chose broiled swordfish. I got crab cakes. We each ordered a bowl of clam chowder, a staple.

"The money," I said.

"David and I had a deal," Russ said. "He didn't keep up his side of the bargain."

"Gambling losses?"

"Not exactly. More like wins."

"Did he borrow money from you?"

He snorted. "It may end up that way. It better not."

In the interest of keeping things cool, I chose not to confront the threat. "For what it's worth," I said, "I have no idea about Dave or what he was up to. We hadn't talked for years. Decades. Did he steal? You know more about him than I do. You've seen him more recently."

"How did you end up with that car?"

"The police contacted me," I said. "I'm his sole surviving relative." That comment seemed to surprise him. "I'm staying at the apartment because the rent is paid and it's nicer than the one I'm living in. A hell of a lot nicer. I'm still trying to make sense of his estate. No will."

"Well, if you find any money, let me know."

I sipped the beer. "Why should I?"

"Because it's mine."

"You were saying. Why should I believe you?"

"Because I'm telling you. Because it's true."

I shrugged. "Then how did Dave get it? Did he steal from you? How much?"

"Just under a million and a half."

I kept my face immobile. The money in Dave's account wouldn't satisfy that much debt. In an odd way, there was comfort in knowing that Russ could make as many demands as he liked, but he wasn't going to get a million and a half, and he could hardly hold me responsible for his losses. But he might try for the leftovers.

"How did that happen?" I said. He hesitated. "Look," I continued, "I already know that all of your activities aren't exactly on the up-and-up. I have the bruises to prove it. If I was going to turn you in, we wouldn't be sitting here now."

Russ remained silent.

I held his gaze. "I may not have seen my brother for a while, but Dave was never very clever. Maybe tricky, but he almost flunked out of grade school. I know he was a crook. I don't know anything about a million dollars, or a million and a half, but there's the car. The apartment. I'm curious about the explanation. And since your, ah, assistant Clarence didn't realize that Dave was dead, and you hired him to shake Dave down, forgive the jargon, I'm guessing you were surprised to learn he was murdered. So I won't go to the police with what you tell me."

"I wouldn't advise it," Russ said. "Your brother's death was news to me."

"Got it," I said. My mouth became sour, a taste of anxiety.

"Why didn't you and David get along?"

"I'm gay. Dave didn't like faggots. His words. He was a jerk." Russ shrugged. "As you say."

"Up until this week, he was pretty much dead to me." Russ snorted. "I mean, for all intents and purposes, he was dead. He's dead to me different now. And you and Dave?"

"David was around," Russ said. "Small time. Never quite had the brains to pull off the schemes he came up with. He served jail time now and then, but his grifts were so measly, he'd be in for a few months and then out on parole."

"What kind of schemes?"

"He broke into homes a lot. And bounced checks were big with him. Or forged ones. Some neighborhood thugs, more small timers, would use him as a runner once in a while. Small timers using an even smaller timer. I think he tried a two-bit Ponzi scheme once that landed him a year or so. Hadn't served time for a while though."

"Are you a big timer?" I asked.

"Stupid question, and I'll ignore it. David thought he could get on your good side by giving you something. Show you what a nice guy he was. And then in two minutes he'd do an ask. A big ask. No finesse. Insisted on being called 'David,' by the way. Thought it was classy."

"Yeah? He was 'Dave' to me. Not that it matters anymore."

Sandy showed up with our chowders, and Russ tasted his. "It's still good."

"You been here before," I said.

"I went to school here for a semester. In Boston."

"Harvard?"

"Bentley. Summer program. I was a kid." Over in a corner of the restaurant was a round table of eight, and they were rowdy. Among them was a minor celebrity, the host of a game show. Russ twisted and looked. "Noisy son of a bitch," he said, and then returned to his chowder.

"Where did you and Dave cross paths?"

"As I said, I'm a businessman. The racetrack. David was familiar to some of my colleagues there. For a long time, I knew him by hearsay. Only met him face-to-face a few years ago. Obviously, I insist on your discretion."

I nodded. The sourness in my mouth intensified. How much guilt would fall on me if I knew the details of a crime? "Dave liked to gamble?"

"He always looked for the easy way. With a lot of people, a day at the tracks is an outing. Others, it's a sickness. David seriously thought it was a way to make a living. But he wasn't any good at it. Didn't have the brains. Bad at the sheets. Mostly played whatever a crony told him was a good bet. It wasn't a long-term winning strategy. After we met, he'd send me bottles of gin, to get on my good side. Like if I knew the winners."

"Did you?"

He didn't answer, pondering a response.

"He owed you money, then," I said. "He lost. Did you lend it to him?"

His eyes searched the restaurant. "If you see our waiter, I need another drink. The thing is that David and I reached an agreement. I helped him with some of his bets, let's say. Helped him to win. And for his cooperation, he was supposed to get a percentage. A little one. The rest was to stay in a bank for safekeeping."

"Why would you do something like that?"

"Had a little extra cash on hand. He was convenient."

I was silent. If I was figuring this out correctly, Dave—because of debts to Russ—was placing bets on some fixed races. Dave was to hold the winnings, pay taxes and clear them, before eventually returning them to Russ. I was about to label it aloud as money laundering when I stopped myself. "I haven't seen anything about his accounts yet," I lied. "The cops have all of Dave's papers."

"Shit."

"I can assure you nothing was buried in his mattress. Haven't found a million dollars in the apartment. No secret keys to safe deposit boxes or anything under the rugs."

"You didn't talk to your brother?"

"Truth. The last time I saw Dave was over twenty-five years ago. Except for identifying his body."

"Shit."

Sandy cleared away the soup bowls, and our entrees were brought to the table. Russ placed his order for the second drink. My crab cakes, another specialty, were crisp and delicious.

"We're in discovery," I said. "That phase of settling his estate. Because we, my brother and me, didn't communicate, I've no idea what money he had. That he spent."

"David disappeared about six months ago," he said.

And took the money with him, I thought. "Did you know he was sick?" I asked.

Russ looked surprised. "No kidding?"

"Cancer. Autopsy found it. He was seeing doctors."

"Cancer. Tough." He bit his swordfish. "So you never met his kid?"

"Excuse me," I said. "What?"

"His kid. He said he had a kid. You never met his kid?"

I spoke slowly. "What are you talking about? He didn't have a kid."

"Not what he told me. In a bar, he said he had a kid."

I was dazed. "Son? Girl?"

"Don't know," Russ replied. "He didn't say. Just that he'd once had a girlfriend who had his kid. He was a little morose, maybe he knew he was ill, this wasn't long ago, but there was this kid out there. Said how he should've done better with the kid."

"How old?"

"He didn't say. Or, if he did, I don't remember. Years ago? I don't recall."

I sipped my beer and tried to absorb what Russ told me. *Dave had a kid?* But there was no information about sex, age... even last name. "Was Dave married?"

"No. He said it was an old girlfriend. Youthful fucking around. My interpretation, not his words. So maybe he wasn't so young. Don't know. Certainly didn't have any wife around him in Florida. Hung with some women but no kids."

"Hell. This is crazy."

"I was surprised when you said you were his only relative." He watched me. "Do you want dessert? Another beer?"

I shook my head no. A pause. "He never told me. He never told me anything. Especially this."

Russ nodded. "It's terrible, Mark. Really. Nothing else then? Eat? Drink?" Another nod. "Well, here's the thing. You seem like an honest guy, right? If you're saying you know nothing about the money, I believe you. And nothing to do about that."

Still disturbed by Russ's news about the child, I waited for the punchline.

"Of course, you'll probably find some things out. And I'd appreciate it if you contact me when that happens."

"How would I do that? Clarence?" I said, sarcastically.

Russ retrieved a business card from his wallet and handed it to me. His last name was Celano. His company was identified as iPlecks Enterprises. "Celano? Italian?" I asked.

He nodded. "Northern."

"If I learn anything, I'll be sure to call."

"You'll forgive me if I'm pushy about this," he said.

"What does that mean?"

"I may occasionally check in with you. In the event of a discovery, I'm sure we could reach some accommodation."

"You calling off Clarence?"

He smiled. "I'm heading back to Florida in the morning." It was obvious that he didn't say "yes."

After Russ and I parted, I rushed back to the Fenway Grand. My brain raced. I lost no time in pulling out my laptop and plugging my last name into a search engine. As usual, there were a few references to me, mostly some links to social media sites. A small number of stories about Dave's murder also popped up. But no listings appeared for anyone else named "Chieswicz." I reversed the "i" and the "e," but that didn't bring up any different results. I leaned back in my seat. The failure of the internet to locate anyone didn't change the shattering detail that Russ had revealed.

Dave had a kid.

CHAPTER TWENTY-SEVEN

CAITLYN

December 2016

Caitlyn had known for most of her life that Ed was not her birth father. As a child, about eight years old, she had seen a copy of her birth certificate that was blank in the space where a man's name was supposed to be. When she asked her mother about it, about why Ed wasn't listed, Sylvia responded in a deliberate manner that suggested her answer had been rehearsed. She explained that children could sometimes be made when their parents weren't married, and that was the story when Caitlyn was born. The man who had fathered Caitlyn wasn't ready to be a dad, so Sylvia decided to go on alone until she was lucky enough to meet Ed when Caitlyn was a baby and they became a family. She said that Ed had adopted her, and he was her father in every way that mattered. That Ed was a wonderful dad, who loved her very much. The story had a very happy ending.

For a long time, the answer was enough, but as she grew older, Caitlyn became more curious about her biological father. Her questions weren't always welcomed. During her high school years, her relationship with her mom was stormy, and the matter of her conception became a battle that was part of a much bigger, ongoing war. Whether out of wisdom, or fear, Sylvia refused to say more about the unknown man. She told Caitlyn that until she was eighteen, the subject was closed. Caitlyn must show that she had enough sense to deal with what she would learn.

Funny enough, by the time she became eighteen, Caitlyn wasn't interested. At least for a while. There was college at Penn State and a new life and a chance to develop her mind and boys and sex. Caitlyn's relationship with her mom changed: more peaceful, congenial, less fraught.

In Caitlyn's second year away from home, however, once college was routine, the subject of her father came up again. She had talked it over with her boyfriend at the time—her first real lover—and the situation had fascinated him. He convinced her that she needed to learn more about her biological father if she was ever to know herself. He was into psychology. It was drama.

At first, Caitlyn was dubious. She saw a therapist through the counseling services at the university. She didn't want to endanger the balance in her life. She adored her dad—a loving, kind man. And she wondered whether meeting her biological father would cause emotional upheavals and doubts and conflicts. It took her a few months to decide to make the effort, and then after only after heart-to-heart talks with her parents. Her dad said he understood. Her mother was worried but cooperated.

Sylvia revealed the name of her biological father: David Chieswicz. Sylvia said she had met him one summer, that they had an affair, that he was a little wild and at the time, for some reason, she'd found that attractive. When she became pregnant, he split. She tried to find him but wasn't successful. After telling this story, Sylvia said she was concerned that David Chieswicz might not want to meet Caitlyn. Because of that, she had waited till Caitlyn was more mature and able to handle the situation.

Caitlyn searched for her father on the internet. She found a couple of stories that suggested he'd been arrested, which made her waver, but just for a moment. He was also mentioned in an obituary, that of his mother. He apparently had no other siblings or immediate family members. A "Mark Chieswicz" in Boston must not be related.

It was easy to obtain a phone number for David Chieswicz through a website that specialized in this service. Ten bucks. The number had a Florida area code, although these days that didn't mean much. He could be anywhere.

Days went by before she decided to call. Caitlyn had plotted the timing carefully. Her boyfriend would be available. Her roommate and some other friends were nearby and on alert. She also had a regular session scheduled with her counselor the next day so she could deal with whatever emotions that the call unleashed. All of the cushioning for a soft landing was plumped and waiting for her if she needed it.

On a Tuesday evening, alone in her dorm room, Caitlyn took a few deep breaths, braced herself, and finally tapped David Chieswicz's number into her phone.

Several rings occurred before an answer. "Hello?"

"Hello," Caitlyn said. "I'm trying to reach David Chieswicz."

"Who is this?"

"My name is Caitlyn Gautry." She almost made the statement sound like a question. "You don't know me. This is David, right? But I think you knew my mother. Sylvia. Her maiden name was Sylvia Keynes."

"Yes? Oh, Christ. Sylvia. That was long ago. How is Sylvia?" His voice was deep, and he had some kind of accent. He sounded tough.

"She's fine."

"So? What's this about?"

"The reason I'm calling is I think you may be my father. That's all. I mean, I have a father, but I think you may be my biological father. That's all."

A silence of several seconds happened. "Oh," David finally said. "Holy shit."

"Hello," Caitlyn said, shyly.

"Are you sure?"

"My mom says."

"I don't have anything I can give you," he said.

"I wasn't looking for anything," Caitlyn said. "I just wanted to make contact with you. To say hello."

"Where are you?"

"In college. Penn State." A pause. "Where are you?"

"I'm south. College, huh? Good for you."

"It would be nice to meet sometime."

"Yes. That would be great. But listen, sweetheart, this is a surprise. I'm in the middle of something. This is not a good time to talk. Seriously. I'm with a man. Business. Can I call you back? Lots to talk about. Now is not good though."

"Of course. I'm sorry for interrupting. Do you want my number?"

"It's here on the phone, I think. Yeah." He read the number. "I'll get back to you."

"Good. Great. So we'll talk again?"

"Yes, sweetheart. I'll call you in a few days. What's your name again?"

"Caitlyn."

"Caitlyn. That's pretty."

"Thanks." He didn't say anything. She continued. "So, like, okay. Bye. We'll talk soon, I hope."

"Sure. Goodbye. Hey. Holy Jesus Christ. Thanks for calling."

The call ended with a push of a button. After months of preparation, the conversation felt anticlimactic, unfinished, almost as if it didn't happen. Caitlyn went down the hallway to the room where her friends waited, but on entering, she shrugged. She didn't have much to say.

For the next few days, Caitlyn felt nauseous, anxious for the phone to ring. A week went by with no return call. In the event that David Chieswicz had somehow misplaced the number or deleted it, she tried to reach him once more. The call rolled over to voicemail, a pre-recorded, default greeting. She left a message with her name and phone number. He didn't call back. While she didn't want to make excuses for him, she decided that some mix-up was still a possibility. Maybe he didn't know how to retrieve items from voicemail. A month later, she made another attempt, her final. This time, no nervousness troubled her. She didn't really think he would speak to her. A message relayed that the number was no longer in service.

In the therapy sessions that followed, her deep disappointment surfaced, and her anger. She struggled to understand her rage over a rejection from someone she didn't know, didn't respect, didn't love. Someone who didn't participate in her day-to-day life in any fundamental way, who could disappear off the face of the earth and not cause her to lose a minute's sleep or a penny from her pocket. Analyzing her emotions took several months. Something elemental was embedded in the situation, reactions buried in the structure of her DNA rather than in logic. She entered a period of easy sex, and then, after berating herself for that behavior, she gained weight. It was as if David Chieswicz's rejection had cracked her psyche and all of the important matters of her life dripped through the fissure and splattered on the ground. She dissected her relationships with her mother and father, her sexual habits, her self-esteem, her approach to life. After all of it, Caitlyn felt she had done important work in figuring out who she was and how she wanted to live. She felt cleansed. And she made one important decision.

Fuck David Chieswicz! She never wanted to speak with that selfish bastard again. He was nothing to her. Her life was better without him. But it took a couple years for her to drop the weight she'd gained.

CHAPTER TWENTY-EIGHT

MARK

April 2017

I was in turmoil. The information that Russ Celano had given me was so paltry that unless David's kid used our last name, finding him or her would be next to impossible. I wasn't even sure if the kid lived in the United States. Dave's girlfriend could have been Mexican, or Canadian. Or perhaps the kid didn't even know about Dave, or might even be dead by now. Perhaps the kid didn't need the money or would be better off ignorant about Dave for some reason. And from what Celano had told me, Dave himself wasn't in touch with the kid. Good old Dave. True to his pattern with family to the very end.

My greedy side was satisfied that the threat to my claim on Dave's estate was small. With so little to go on, I could hardly be blamed for failing to find another heir. And I wasn't sure what legal claims an illegitimate child would have, if any. And yes, I immediately felt guilty about having those impulses. After yesterday, and the funeral, my sense of family—moral obligations—held onto me. Family was important. But what could I do? Hire a detective? I'd nothing to go on.

I wondered what a child who had been fathered by Dave would be like. Another slug like him? A petty larcenist? A juvenile delinquent? Or, by some miracle, a sweetheart? The baby might even be gay. Homosexual chromosomes obviously resided somewhere in the Chieswicz gene pool. I could have gay family. I'd been so isolated. I wondered whether he or she would want me as a relative or be a bigot like the others.

My thoughts turned to the rest of the conversation with Russ Celano. His slick veneer didn't hide the implied threats to me. Dave's death might have put up a barrier to Russ's recovery of the money, but that complication wasn't going to stop him. He might give me a temporary pass, based on my claim that I'd not found any fortune. Once the probate papers were filed, however, with their details about the accounts, Russ would be after me.

I did an internet search on his name, using the information on his business card. iPlecks Enterprises, and its connection to the racetrack, were all direct. iPlecks appeared to own a few bars in Florida as well. Oddly, Russ was not listed among the senior officers of the company. That left open a few possibilities. The names on the company masthead could be figureheads. Or maybe Russ was a pseudonym. I couldn't tell since no pictures of him or the other managers were available.

I was dancing on the edge of criminal behavior, thanks to my knowledge of Dave's scheme with Russ. At least I wasn't hiding any evidence that might lead to a solution to the murder. Small comfort. Somewhere out there Dave's killer still ran free. I wasn't so concerned about justice. I simply wanted safety. And the money.

I had put the plastic bag with Dave's urn in a corner of the kitchen. I wanted to toss the goddam thing out of a window, to be rid of it. I took the urn from the bag and stood by the sink. I turned the water on, full force, and hit the switch for the garbage disposal. Its motor growled, an eager beast waiting to be fed. I opened the urn and tipped it toward the drain. Dave's ashes edged to the lip of the container and I was disgusted by the idea that they might touch my skin.

Before I poured him down the drain, I imagined Dave's body and spirit mixing with Boston waste and flowing out to the bay. The burial he deserved. What was the difference between getting rid of him this way and scattering his ashes on the ocean?

I stopped. What if I met the kid? What if the kid asked about Dave? What would I respond? That I'd ground up his daddy in a garbage disposal?

CHAPTER TWENTY-NINE

CAITLYN

December 2016

In the kitchen, Caitlyn sat across from Sylvia, not exactly breathless because of what her mother had stated, but in a state of confusion. "I don't understand," Caitlyn said.

"I thought we could go for a nice lunch," Sylvia said. "Have a glass of wine perhaps. We could talk about this in a relaxed atmosphere. I didn't want this to be a shock. I'm sorry."

"Mom," Caitlyn said. "Please just tell me already. You're wearing me out."

Her mother nodded. "I understand. I'm sorry. Are you okay? Do you want more coffee?"

"Mom."

"All right. David called me. Out of the blue one day. It was in the fall. He asked if he could come to see me. I told him there wasn't any point in that. After the way he didn't get back to you before I just didn't see why. But then he told me he was sick, and he just wanted to talk. I said I'd ask your father about it."

"Where is Dad now?"

"He ran to the office for something. He'll be back soon. I talked to your dad. He left it up to me. They'd never met, you know. Eddie and I, we spoke about it for a long time, and Eddie said he wasn't interested, but that it was up to me. David offered to come to Philadelphia."

"Did he say why? Did you meet with him?"

"I went into town. He was staying at the Four Seasons. I was surprised. You know those places are dear. We met for lunch. I hadn't seen him for over twenty years. He didn't look sick. But he did look older. I kept thinking how much he must think I've changed, too. It was so long ago, the two of us. He has a mole on his neck. Like you. I'd forgotten that. I saw him and I guess I realized how much you resemble him in some ways. Physically. It was a bit of a shock."

This wasn't necessarily welcomed news to Caitlyn. She nodded. "What did you talk about?"

Sylvia continued. "He asked about you. He said he was sorry that he didn't get in touch when you called but it was a shock and it was all for the best. I told him some, about how you're in Harvard and how proud I was, that you worked hard. He said you must get that, your brains, from my side of the family, that his parents hadn't had much education. Mostly he didn't talk about himself. He said he'd been living in Florida and that he'd had some luck and some money. The thing is, he was sick, and he was going to beat it but it was changing his perspective on life and how he looked at things. He had a tumor and it was malignant, but he was going for treatment and his chance was good to get better, but it made him start to think about you. To be honest, we were there for an hour and a half and I was the one who said the most. Maybe he wasn't feeling well that day. It was difficult. I could have been nervous and chattering."

"I don't get it," Caitlyn said. "Did he want something? Just to have lunch?"

"There was more."

"Go on."

"He said he wanted to meet you. He tried your number and it didn't work."

"I have a different phone now," Caitlyn said. "Since I called him."

"Well, that's it. He wanted to meet you. I said I'd have to talk to you about it because I know you were pretty upset when he didn't contact you in college. That it was your decision, you're a grown woman, but that I'd talk to you. I'm sorry I didn't say anything on the phone, but I just thought this was a matter that we should discuss when we were together like now. In person. And then I thought I didn't want to ruin your Christmas. That's why I waited. I thought if we had a nice lunch." Sylvia started to cry.

Caitlyn touched her mom's hand and waited for her to stop. "So that's it? Now he wants to meet me?" Caitlyn tried to weigh the benefits of seeing David Chieswicz. She had been curious once. She wasn't any longer. She'd buried that idea after the months of therapy. And the residue of her past disappointment clung to her. Going through those emotions once was enough. Fuck David Chieswicz. "I don't think I want to do that."

"He could be dying, Caitlyn," her mother said. "This could be your last chance if you have any desire at all. I can't tell you what to do. But I told him I would ask you. It wasn't a choice for me to make." Her head shifted, as if listening. "I think Eddie is home."

Ed's car had pulled into the garage, and soon a door in the kitchen opened. He hung his coat on a hook and then faced them. "How are my girls this morning?" Then he seemed to sense the feelings contained in the delay of an answer. "Okay. What's up?"

"We were talking about David," Sylvia said.

"Oh," he replied. Ed hesitated, then looked at Caitlyn. "How are you?"

Caitlyn paused, unable to answer.

"Caitlyn?" Ed said.

She rose and hugged him, and she suddenly found herself sobbing in his arms. "You're the only father I want." She soaked Ed's shoulder with her tears.

All the while, Ed held her, kissing the top of her head. "Okay, baby. Okay." He said the words over and over again. "It's okay, Squirrel, it's okay."

"I don't want to see him," Caitlyn said. She cried for several minutes more, holding onto her father—her real father, her only father—until her eyes were dry.

CHAPTER THIRTY

MARK

April 2017

It's said that things are often clearer in the morning. For me, partly true. On waking, I brewed as strong a cup of coffee as I could from the old, opened can of Folgers that was in Dave's kitchen cabinet. Then I tried to figure out some of yesterday's dilemmas.

I started with a premise: I wanted the money. And after that: I needed to do whatever I could to keep it. And then: I wanted to be able to look at myself in a mirror. And then: there was a line I wouldn't cross.

That line was the kid.

Keeping the cash out of the hands of Russ was the first, and in some ways the easiest, ethical dodge. Russ and Clarence were criminals, and if I stretched the truth with them and took evasive action, too bad. My inheritance from Dave could compensate me for the beating; I'd save everyone the bother of filing a civil lawsuit. Whether this was bluster on my part, time would tell. No doubt my resolve would be tested when I faced these gangsters during our inevitable confrontation. But I didn't give a shit about Russ's claim on the money. He screwed up by trusting Dave. Not my problem.

Regarding the legal authorities, another simple sidestep. They believed Dave's money was above board. I wasn't to blame for the cops' mistake. I hadn't led them to that conclusion. They did it all on their own. My conduct would be lawful. I would pay whatever taxes were required and give a buck or two to charity. But I wasn't concerned about any other interest that the Feds or the cops might have in the whole story. Their ignorance became my ignorance. Dave's money wouldn't go far in fixing the national economy, but it would take care of Mark Chieswicz. The money would help me become a more productive member of society again. I'd serve the greater good. Somehow.

Those matters were easy. The situation with the kid was more problematic. I didn't want to be a bastard like the other members of my family, to cheat someone from their due. I didn't know whether the kid's illegitimacy diminished his or her legal standing. I had done a quick look on the web about the laws and the situation wasn't clear-cut, varying from state to state, sometimes depending on when a claim was made.

The kid could be a positive force in my life. I wanted family! But I didn't even know what to call the kid. He? She? It? The kid was some blob in my mind, a concept, someone without a name, a face, a gender, an age. I'd make a serious effort to learn about…oh, hell, I'd call him "Junior." In a few weeks I'd weigh whether to hire a detective, but right now I didn't have the money. And I needed time to think.

I decided to dig a bit on my own. There were lots of missing pieces, incomplete parts. But where to start: Dave? His murder? Junior? Russ? Clarence? Maybe the Boston Box? Or did that even matter? Perhaps every single element was part of the same story and in some way related. In college, whenever an odd connection between events or people happened, one of my dormmates would say *"The world is a circle."* Everything is connected. I wasn't sure if I accepted the idea completely but—sipping my third cup of coffee, awful stuff after sitting on a hot plate—that phrase spun in my brain. At least a few of the events of my past week must be linked.

At the last second, I had stopped from pouring Dave's ashes into the garbage disposal, and now, as I tried to make sense of it all, I wanted to shake the urn, make it talk to me, make disembodied Dave give me some answers.

How was he murdered? Did someone else want his money? Was his death connected to Junior? Or was it random? No acquaintances had emerged over the past week except for Russ. Did Dave live in a vacuum during his stay in Boston?

And there was the Boston Box, whatever that was.

And then there was the weather, and some loose ionized particles in the air, and that new movie at the Fenway Cinemas. In other words, despite the wistful philosophy behind my dormmate's slogan, maybe the world wasn't a circle, maybe everything wasn't connected by a thread, but it was all the flotsam and jetsam of life, united only by the fact that these things had happened around me. I was what connected them, not any logic or story.

Dave? His murder? Junior? Russ? Clarence? The Boston Box? The world is a circle, indeed.

Unless, somehow, I was the circle.

PART TWO

Caitlyn: December 2016 – March 2017

Mark: April 2017

CHAPTER THIRTY-ONE

CAITLYN

December 2016

After the discussion with Sylvia, Caitlyn spent another two days in Pennsylvania. Her mother was less tense but still concerned, watching whether the revelations about David Chieswicz—not her father really, Caitlyn decided, just a sperm donor—would cause an emotional crash. But she had already done that in college. The news about the meeting may have opened an old wound, but the new scratch wasn't deep, and it closed up fast. No severe bleeding. Eventually, the atmosphere at home again became as warm as the glowing log in the family room fireplace, comfortable, and even jokey. Her mom's secret about David Chieswicz, once known, lost its power. He was not mentioned again.

Returning to Cambridge, Caitlyn was relaxed, and energized. Winter break continued for most students, and the city was quieter than usual, so she was able to concentrate on her own studies. Her research on the Box had fermented in her mind over the holidays, and in order to reorient herself, she reviewed the material that she'd already gathered about a number of subjects: Gregory Adamston, whose supposedly accidental prototype of a Boston Box had been torn down after a fire;

the chance that a secret room remained in existence at a South End brownstone that she was attempting to visit; the probable role of Josiah Hawkins, a Black architect, in sustaining the concept; the possibility that a peer of Adamston and Hawkins named Thaddeus Simpson had used a Boston Box for a crime. Connections among these men, and actual proof of the Boston Box, had yet to be established, so Caitlyn had a good deal of work ahead of her.

She let her mind wander. She couldn't help but think about sex. Hawkins had three wives. Simpson was accused of adultery and manslaughter. Was this a track for Caitlyn to follow? The sex lives of nineteenth-century Boston architects, hiding their activities in secret rooms?

Or was she just horny?

Caitlyn definitely had sex on her mind. She was not overworked or overcommitted, and her body was begging her to bonk. But sex had to be channeled where it belonged. She thought she could see a pattern—one of lust—in her discoveries about the Boston Box. The question was whether this pattern was true and provable, or just a detour that she had imposed on her findings because her hormonal gyroscope was spinning so wildly. The answer could only be revealed with more research. Or masturbation to release some energy and clear her head. Or a hook-up, although easy sex hadn't been her style since her undergrad days.

So, for now, research.

It was past time to try again for a meeting with George Rumberg, and she composed a second letter to him and asked once more for permission to visit his Chadwick Square brownstone. She heightened the importance of his home to Boston history without, she hoped, nagging.

If Rumberg granted her request, she wondered exactly what she would look for. Rumberg himself might know of a hidden chamber, but conceivably he could be totally unaware of any such secret room. As years had gone by and the house had passed from hand to hand, knowledge of a Boston Box may have been forgotten or disregarded. Maybe it had become a closet.

She searched "secret rooms" on the internet. In the places outside of Boston where hidden chambers had been built, a few tricks had been used over and over to conceal them, such as fake or movable bookcases or small doors under staircases. False walls, although possible, were devised less often. Not uncommon were trapdoors covered by rugs.

She discovered that Harvard had an example of this last type, in Williams House, a huge clapboard house that was once a stop on the Underground Railroad. A trapdoor under a rug on the second floor opened to a short passage that led to a ladder to the basement, where a small room was concealed. Since the home's original owner was an abolitionist who donated the house to the university after his death in 1838, it was assumed that the chamber was used to hide runaway slaves. In the 1850's, the passage was sealed up "for safety reasons." Caitlyn deduced that students had discovered the room and used it for illicit activities. Sex again? Drinking parties? In any event, she could find no cross reference between the room and the term "Boston Box," nor could she identify the architect of the house.

Williams House was now used for departmental offices. The room's being sealed would make it impossible to see, and the timing of its construction wasn't quite right. Too bad. It would be a powerful argument, especially against Bacht, if she could make a connection between Harvard and the Boston Box.

CHAPTER THIRTY-TWO

MARK

April 2017

In trying to find Junior, with almost nothing to go on, the Boston Box became a straw for me to grasp at. Even if it ended up being meaningless, a question about it to Taylor was a pretext for a conversation that might yield information which inspired me. Unlikely, I knew, but it was a start. And, in any case, I reckoned that as Dave's next of kin, I had permission to call from time to time for an update.

After an exchange of rote greetings, I asked Taylor about any progress, and whether he'd figured out what the Boston Box was.

"We're continuing to investigate," he said.

In other words, "no" on both counts. "I saw some things on the web," I said. "A Boston boxing club of some kind. I think it was near the South End. Did you check on that?"

"Mr. Chieswicz."

"Just asking."

"Your brother wasn't known to them."

"Process of elimination, at least," I said. "Have you learned anything else?"

"Nothing yet."

"Nobody has shown up here at the apartment. No friends or anything." Technically, since Russ wasn't a friend, and Clarence hadn't come into the apartment, I told the truth. "Did the hospital list anyone? Don't you have to put emergency contacts?"

"Your name, it appears."

"Really?" *Confirmed: Dave knew I was in Boston.*

"The hospital actually hadn't done much with him yet," Taylor said. "The more intensive treatments hadn't begun."

"Do you know what else he said? About me?"

"No," Taylor answered. "You might want to talk with them directly. You sticking to your story that he wasn't in contact?"

That pissed me off. "It wasn't a story. It's the truth."

"Lucky for you, we gather from the hospital that was the case. Just checking."

In my mind, I called Taylor an asshole. "Is the Boston Box something about houses? Some kind of room or building?"

"There's no need for you to investigate any clues, Mr. Chieswicz. If you come across something is all. Tell us. While you're going through your brother's property."

"Okay, sure. But you'll call me if you learn anything?"

"Of course," Taylor said. "If we find something definite."

"One last thing. Where was the car? When you towed it? The exact address. Speaking of the South End."

"On Washington. I don't remember the number. It should be on the receipt, the one you got from the towing lot. Why?"

"Just wondering," I said. "I mean, that must be where Dave was. That's all. Maybe I'm getting sentimental. Tracing his last steps. Chasing a ghost."

"There are a few security cameras at spots near where the car was. We viewed the tapes."

"Nothing?"

"Nothing useful."

"Okay, then," I said. "Thanks. I'll call again."

On hanging up, I tried to digest the news that Dave had listed me on his hospital document. I wondered if I could call his doctor for more details, but with all the regulations about the release of medical information, that course of action was probably a dead end for now. Maybe Dietz could help. He was due to call me about probate court. I'd ask him then.

As for the receipt for the car, I checked the only place where I had put any kind of paperwork, a pile on the counter, and it wasn't there. In my initial excitement about the BMW, I hadn't been too attentive to documents and had no clear memory of what I'd done with them. I had probably just tucked the receipt into a door pocket or the glove compartment.

I was about to go to the car when I remembered that Dietz had told me to open a checking account in anticipation of managing Dave's funds. I thought of Clark Hodder, the guy who helped me at the KFC and who worked at a bank. I decided to give him the business as a way of thanking him. I retrieved his card from my wallet. His office was in Dorchester Lower Mills, a neighborhood not too far from where I'd been beaten up. I called and was told he couldn't come to the phone, that he was with a customer, but that he'd be in his office all day.

I went to the BMW, which was parked in the Fenway Grand's garage. It took only a moment to locate the towing receipt in the pocket of the driver's door. The address in the South End where the car had been found was nearby. Thinking to go there, I exited the garage and realized the weather was all too typical for an April day in Boston, that is, drizzly and chilly and not ideal for amateur private-eying on foot, so I defaulted to my other purpose, and aimed in the direction of Clark Hodder.

CHAPTER THIRTY-THREE

CAITLYN

December 2016

On New Year's Eve, Caitlyn climbed the steps to Henry's apartment while carrying a baking pan of macaroni and cheese, sure-fire, her contribution to a potluck buffet. Henry, wearing his Red Sox baseball cap, greeted her at the door with a kiss on the cheek. The apartment was a floor-through on the second story of a multi-family house. The place was clean, the furniture second-hand but presentable. No pictures hung on the walls. Before mingling, Caitlyn placed her casserole on a table with six or seven other dishes. She threw her coat onto a pile on the queen-sized bed in Henry's room and then returned to the party.

Henry handed her a plastic cup of champagne "to get her started." "Happy New Year," he said, knocking his cup to hers.

"The same," she responded, and took a sip. The wine was dry and extra fizzy. "This is good."

"Glad you like it," he said. "It's Spanish. A cava."

"Oh my God. Spanish?" She held the cup at a distance. "Not French? How could you?"

"Well, yeah, I could get it for eight bucks a bottle. So what's new? How was your trip home?"

"Mostly good. You know. Family."

"Yeah," he said. "They're never all good, are they? I'm happy you're here." In the doorway stood another new guest, whom Henry ignored. "I'll let Michael take care of him. It's only Pettick." Michael was his roommate, and Pettick one of the usual crowd, a grad student in music.

"How about you?" Caitlyn asked. "How was break?"

"I just slipped over to western Mass with the family. The folks were fine, my brother good. I got a new sound bar for the television. Hear that magnificent sound? Geek stuff. Some skiing up at North Conway." A sigh. "Another year gone."

"Yes. Sucks. I'm getting old."

"I noticed the crow's feet," Henry said. "You don't stand as straight as you used to. You're falling apart." Caitlyn laughed. "You have resolutions?" he asked.

"Let's see. Go to the gym and fight gravity. Write my thesis. Fall in love. Same as last year."

"How did you do last year?"

"I went to the gym for a few months. And then no. And then again." She was rueful. "Partial success. Progress on the thesis. Love was a total fail."

"We should work on that."

Caitlyn laughed. "What do you suggest? A support group?"

Henry looked exasperated. "Not what I was thinking."

"Oh, what were you thinking? What are your resolutions? Resolutions are totally useless."

"You're such a dunce," he said, wide-eyed. "My resolutions? Go to the gym. Finish my thesis. Fall in love."

"We should collaborate. No points for originality, though."

Another guest—a very thin Swede named Svenda but who everyone called Slenda behind her back—lingered aside them, so they widened their sphere to include her. She had the appearance of a country maiden. "Why do you make resolutions?" she said. Another guest, Slenda's German boyfriend, joined the conversation.

The crowd thickened, mostly a Harvard group, a greater concentration of international students than usual since many of the foreigners didn't travel home during break. A few guests spoke French in a corner, two Asian men dawdled near the table of food, a Spanish lesbian couple giggled as they touched one another.

"Why don't they get a room?" Henry whispered to Caitlyn.

"Don't go there," Caitlyn whispered back.

More talk, and Caitlyn tried, with some success, to control her drinking, a glass per hour, switching between Pellegrino and wine. As midnight neared, Henry played host and made sure that everyone had some kind of liquid in hand, preferably alcoholic, but he complained aloud that too many people were puritanical these days. When the countdown to midnight began, broadcast on the television, Henry stood near her. The ball in Times Square dropped, and he led the toast of "Happy New Year!" No one sang "Auld Lang Syne" except some revelers on the screen. Then, as the round of good wishes began among the partygoers, Henry kissed her softly on the lips. He rested his arms on her shoulders. "That was good. I wanted to start the New Year off on a positive note. Help you with your resolutions."

The implication of some of Henry's earlier comments broke through to her. "Oh."

"Do you mind if I do that again?" he asked.

She didn't mind at all, because the first kiss had been delicate and sweet, and it was New Year's Eve, and she had a mild buzz, and she was aroused. She moved closer to him. The second kiss was more forceful, his arms around her, and her hand moved to his face and hit the brim of his baseball cap, which fell to the floor. He pulled his face away from hers, and while still holding her, he said, "I'm going to wish a few more people a good year. Hosting duties. I'll be back, okay?" He swooped down to get his cap before leaving her side.

Caitlyn watched as Henry gave hugs and pecks on the cheek to other guests. He didn't kiss anyone else in the same manner as he had her. She appraised him. He was slender and had a small butt. His red hair was intriguing. He'd cleaned up for the holidays, and he was cute. She'd always thought that was evident, his cuteness. Could she think of Henry as a lover? Maybe. Or they could be friends with benefits. Better idea?

Eventually, he returned to her. "Can I get you anything?" he asked.

"More cava?"

"Easy." He went to a nearby table and filled a wine glass to the brim.

Caitlyn looked at it skeptically. "Are you trying to get me drunk?"

"Maybe. Are you drunk now?"

"No," she said.

"In full sobriety, then, do I have permission to proceed?"

"Not fully sober," she said. He looked anxious. "But mostly. Permission granted."

Henry grinned. "Great." He leaned in for another kiss.

CHAPTER THIRTY-FOUR

MARK

April 2017

Lower Mills is a historic district that bridges the border between Boston's Dorchester neighborhood and Milton, a town of some wealth. A number of factories—most notably, one that produced chocolate—had been converted to business offices, condos, and storefronts. The narrow Neponset River runs through the center of Lower Mills, and the sounds of its waters give the neighborhood a tranquil atmosphere.

I parked on a side street and headed to the Dorchester Community Bank, which was located in one of the factory offices and wasn't very big. A young woman greeted me when I entered, and I gave her Clark's name. I was asked to take a seat in a small waiting area while she checked on his availability. In a few minutes, Clark emerged from an office in the rear of the branch and approached me.

In the chaos that had followed Clarence's assault on me, I hadn't evaluated Clark's appearance beyond the basics: clipped beard, glasses, some nerdishness, a solicitous demeanor, prematurely gray hair. Without a bloody wound distracting me, I could now appreciate that he was very good looking: big brown eyes, long lashes, and very straight nose. Full lips. He wore a long-sleeved white shirt and a tie, and some dark arm hair peeked from beyond the cuffs. Small waist and trim. I had presumed he was gay from his car's rainbow bumper sticker, a diversity symbol that usually signaled LGBTQ-friendliness at a minimum, and often more. I wondered if he had yet reached the same conclusion about me.

"Still some black and blue?" he said, shaking my hand.

"Getting better," I said. "I want to thank you again."

"Your family was pretty rough."

Until that moment, I'd forgotten that I'd lied about Clarence's relation to me. Damn. "To be honest, he's not exactly family. Just the acquaintance of my late brother's. It's complicated." Not quite the whole truth, but closer, anyway.

He shrugged. "Huh. I guess I figured something was off. Let's go to my office."

Clark led me to a seat across from his desk and then closed the door behind us. The inner wall of the office was all glass and looked out on the teller stations. A picture of Quincy Market, painted with broad strokes, hung on a wall behind his chair. A photograph of Clark hugging a boy in a basketball jersey was propped on his desktop.

Clark took a seat. "So how can I help you?"

"To start, I need a checking account," I said. I told him, perhaps in more detail than was necessary, about Dave's estate, and Dietz's recommendation that I keep a separate account until court matters were settled. "There could be more business down the line after probate is done."

"Easy enough." The account opening didn't take too long. He outlined a few options and I picked the simplest one. All very businesslike. When Clark finished, he said, "I'm sorry to hear about your brother."

"We weren't close," I said. I pointed at the picture. "Is that your nephew?"

"Oliver? No, he's my son."

I didn't see a wedding ring. "Oh, excuse me." I felt a dash of disappointment. "How long have you been married?"

"I'm not anymore. I'm divorced. Miserable split, but there's Oliver. He's my light."

"Oh, that's good. Not that you're divorced, I mean, but your son. Do you share custody with your wife? I'm sorry. I'm being nosy."

He was amused. "Not at all. Actually, I had a husband. We moved too fast. We share some custody, but I'm primary caregiver. This is probably too much information." He watched for my reaction.

"Oh, no problem. That's interesting. You're single?"

He nodded. "Being a dad takes most of my free time. Scares guys off, too."

I paused. "Do you have time for a cup of coffee? I owe you a favor for rescuing me."

"Rescue? Bit of an exaggeration. But now? No. Sorry. I can't leave right now. And the new account is plenty of thanks. I'd like to have coffee some other time, though." He grabbed a business card from a small holder on his desk and wrote on the back of it. "There's my personal email. Send me some dates. Or a text. We can figure it out."

"Great. Will do. My email address is on the account sheet." I rose.

"I'll walk you to your car," he said.

I was pleasantly surprised by his offer and almost suggested there was no need before I came to my senses. We went outdoors toward the BMW and chatted nonchalantly about the weather, which was still cold, but the rain had stopped. When we reached my parking place, I put out my hand to shake his. "I have your card," I said. "I'll send a message. We'll fix something up." I got into the car.

"Real soon, I hope." Did I see a wink? He stood by the curbside, watched me pull away, and then raised his hand in a gentle wave.

CHAPTER THIRTY-FIVE

CAITLYN

January 2017

Asleep and snoring just a little, Henry was spooning Caitlyn. His breath tickled her neck. His forearm was over her breasts, and his body was warm and moist under a tumble of blankets. In his sleep, he was hard again.

They'd left his place at about one and gone to Caitlyn's apartment, necessary if they wanted to be together because Henry's bed was buried under all those coats and two dozen people still partied. A host abandoning his guests was bad form, but Henry's roommate agreed to handle the situation, and, in any case, no one seemed to be monitoring etiquette.

Henry had carted along another bottle of cava, and drinking it helped with the self-consciousness that came with this change in their relationship. The lovemaking had some first-time clumsiness but, for the most part, it was comfortable, giggly, and pleasurable. Afterward, Caitlyn had slept deeply, as had he. Now, snuggling against him, she wondered if he'd want to play again. She wondered if *she* wanted to play again. If so, she should freshen up. She wriggled carefully from his embrace, hoping not to wake him, and maneuvered her way through a mess of strewn clothing to the bathroom.

Caitlyn wasn't pleased with what she saw in the mirror. Her face was sleep sodden, her hair disheveled. She had a moment of doubt. Was this wise? She liked Henry, but did this open a door to something more? The situation could be awkward. But the sex had been good. And needed. Could they be friends with benefits? No strings attached? She decided to stop fretting. She didn't want to regret the last several hours.

She washed her face, ran a comb through the worst tangles in her hair, peed, rinsed her mouth with a capful of minty Listerine. Opening the bathroom door, she saw Henry stretch under the blankets. He greeted her with a yawn and a smile. "Happy New Year," he said. His heavy-lidded eyes told her another go was available if she wanted it.

She decided that she did. "Happy New Year," she said, and she returned to the bed.

Caitlyn didn't have the right food at her apartment for a decent breakfast, so after cuddling, they bundled up and walked to a nearby café. The day was overcast but dry. The streets were holiday empty.

The restaurant had high ceilings, tables with plain white linens, and the same brunch menu as every other café in the city. Henry ordered Eggs Benedict, and she got a salad. He asked about her plans for the day.

"Well, I'm not up for watching football games," she said. "I'll probably study this afternoon. I need to do some reading."

"About?"

"Back Bay. Beacon Hill, maybe."

"Why?"

"Couple of architects there who later did the French style that I'm studying. What about you? What are you doing?"

"I'm sure there's some cleaning. Michael probably has it done, the apartment. He'll get irritated though unless I pretend to kick in. I was thinking of a movie later. *Star Wars* or something light."

"Sounds good," she said.

"So you'll come?"

"Ah? No. Didn't realize that was an invite. I don't much care for spaceships."

"Then pick something else."

"I need to figure it out later," she said. "Can we check in this afternoon?"

"C'mon. It's a holiday."

She felt uneasy and tried to tease. "What? You can't live without me now?"

"I just thought we could spend the day. It's a holiday. You have a better offer?"

She didn't. "I need to study. That's all. Check in with me later. How about that? Maybe a movie."

He brightened. "Great."

"No spaceships."

"Plenty to see. There are several about oppression. Or do you want something girly? You know, love conquers all." He batted his eyes.

She laughed. "Screw you."

"Hey, you want to fall in love, right?"

"Oh, let's not go there."

He moved closer and whispered to her. "The sex was prime, right?"

She whispered back, matching his inflection, but adding mischievousness. "The sex was very good." Then she made a face. "Not sure how I feel about gingers."

He frowned. "You are a killer. You know that?" He stabbed a large home fry and put it in his mouth, chomping, gulping.

"Oh, please. Yes. Behind me is a trail of broken hearts that must be several inches long."

He was silent for a moment, moving home fries on his plate with a fork as if lining up soldiers for a war game. "Okay. No prob. It's all cool, right? It was fun. Let's see a movie. Maybe we can play again sometime."

"Maybe. One step at a time. I'm sure I'll run into you. Classes and all." Her tone was gently mocking.

He didn't laugh. "But a movie. Tonight. No spaceships. Something that'll make us suffer."

She rolled her eyes. "I'm a killer, you said? There might be some middle ground between spaceships and suffering. It's Christmas. Isn't there a musical?"

He named the film, a good possibility, a compromise, and Caitlyn was intrigued, but she wondered whether he would want to sleep together again, and if that was a good idea. Moving too fast.

They ended up seeing the musical, which was fine, and the movie was followed by another night in bed, which was fun again. But the morning brought a stronger swell of second thoughts. *Caitlyn. Slow down. This situation could be tricky.* She avoided a round of wake-up lovemaking, and although she maintained a friendly demeanor while Henry hung around for a cup of coffee, she gently insisted that she needed to study, to be on her own. Henry said he'd text her later, and she agreed. To herself, she determined that a text would not mean spending a third night in a row together. She didn't want to fall into a relationship, even a casual one, without more thought. She would not let her sex drive rule her head. Enough play. She had to concentrate on her doctorate for the foreseeable future. First things first. She would read and write for the next several days.

Almost as soon as she made that resolution, Andrew Hawkins sent her an email that declared he had found something exciting to show her. The prospect appealed to her for a number of reasons, not all of them academic. To justify the break from her studies, Caitlyn convinced herself that meeting Andrew was research. They arranged to get together in forty-eight hours.

CHAPTER THIRTY-SIX

MARK

April 2017

I smiled as I drove back to the Fenway. Since my breakup with Paul, I'd not had so much as a drop of romance in my life. A little sex, when I couldn't stand it anymore, from online connections, but no love. Admittedly, Clark's attention was just that: a drop of romance. For all I knew, maybe he just wanted a hookup. Nevertheless, I could fantasize. Clark was a pleasant change from the more troublesome parts of my life.

An incoming call from Dietz was broadcast via a Bluetooth device through the speakers of the car. I wasn't used to this particular gadget, chatting without a handset. The call was brief, and I tried to focus on it while navigating the Jamaicaway, a narrow, twisty-turny road evidently engineered by someone who liked car crashes. The gist of Dietz's call was that a hearing with the probate court was scheduled the next day—there had been a cancellation, he'd pulled a string—and that I needed to be present. My calendar was clear, big surprise. Dietz told me to look for an email with details about the time, location, and process. He said I should dress up.

The probable outcome of the court date was that I'd have access to enough of Dave's money to pay off some expenses, like the funeral. Combined with Clark's overture, it was a day of favorable signs. I lowered my speed, taking extra care on the dangerous Jamaicaway, not wanting to break my streak. I arrived safely at the garage of the Fenway Grand and felt a greater contentment than I had in a long time.

At the apartment, I hung my coat on the back of a chair and then grabbed the coffee table book about Boston that Dave had been reading. I carried the book into the living area, stretched on the couch, put the book on my stomach, and started to thumb through it.

The last pages that Dave had marked by bending the corners had colorful photos of the town squares of the South End. Maybe Dave's visit to that neighborhood was more purposeful than I'd initially imagined. But, so what? Could the book in my hands have a clue to the location of Dave's murder? He may have been sightseeing and then gotten mugged, robbed, killed, a small crime gone awry. Dave as a tourist did not fit the image that I had of him but after all, he was *my* brother, and *I* liked local history, so one of his genes might contain a predisposition to explore the city. He didn't have much else to do. Why not make the best of being in Boston?

Dave? History maven? Nah. It didn't fit. Not without some motive.

I continued to turn the pages. Then I held it upside down and shook it. Nothing as easy as a scrap of paper with an address fell out. Life was never that simple.

Nevertheless, I wanted to feel like I was onto something. But what? I checked the book's author: a woman, middle-aged, not counting the addition of more years suggested by a dated copyright. I could eliminate the far-fetched possibility that Junior had written the book.

I went online and redid my search for the Boston Box. No current South End addresses or other examples were named. Instead, the text confirmed that the Boston Box didn't exist. Boston Box. A room. The book. The South End. Dave. His death. Junior. Yet again, I couldn't connect them.

CHAPTER THIRTY-SEVEN

CAITLYN

January 2017

Andrew asked to meet at Quincy Market. No nearby buildings were built by Josiah or Adamston, but Andrew insisted on the location and said that visits to his ancestor's designs could be deferred to another day. But when Caitlyn pressed him for a reason, he wouldn't offer any, other than to say she wouldn't be sorry.

Located right behind Faneuil Hall—a historic meeting house from pre-Revolutionary times—Quincy Market was just shy of 200 years old, made of granite, Greek Revival in style, and almost 500 feet long. Two complimentary buildings, also granite, lined either side of the central market. The entire complex had been converted into an urban shopping center in the 1970s and was now one of the biggest tourist sites in the city, replete with shops and food stands.

The day was cold. Caitlyn was to meet Andrew at a stone-paved plaza between Faneuil Hall and the market entrance. She stood outside near a column, a visible spot, but not seeing Andrew, she moved into the market for warmth and then stationed herself by a food stand that sold elaborate snacks built with bagels: sandwiches, pizzas, something called a bagel dog.

She was nervous. The encounters with Henry hadn't lessened her interest in Andrew. In fact, she almost felt as if being with Henry had intensified her attraction to Andrew, as if some energy had been unleashed but not yet completely exhausted.

Andrew came into view. He was dressed more casually than before, a leather jacket, a pair of crisp jeans, a stocking cap. A leather messenger bag was strapped over one of his shoulders. He looked great—athletic and lithe. His head twisted and he scanned the plaza for her. His ruby earring caught the sun. While she knew she should step forward immediately to greet him, she enjoyed watching him unaware for a moment. After some seconds of appreciating his handsomeness, she pushed past the heavy market doors and called to him.

He smiled and pecked her on the cheek. "Happy New Year."

Caitlyn returned the wish and said, "So good to see you! Mr. Mystery! What do you have planned?"

"I'm going to take you to meet someone."

She was dismayed. "You should have mentioned…"

Andrew interrupted her. "Don't worry. Painless."

"Why am I not reassured?"

"Trust me."

'Well, okay," she said, dubious. "Lead the way."

They walked in tandem across a busy avenue, and then Andrew guided them through a much narrower street in an adjacent neighborhood, a place of cramped pre-Revolutionary houses, most of them now converted to businesses. Few other pedestrians were near them. Passing the Union Oyster House, a restaurant once frequented by Benjamin Franklin, Andrew interrupted banter about the holidays to ask, "Have you ever seen the Boston Stone?"

"No," Caitlyn answered.

Some steps after the Oyster House, Andrew pointed at a brick row home with a round reddish stone embedded in its foundation. The stone was perched upon a base made of the same reddish stone and also set into the building, and in the middle of it was a small hole. Engraved on the base were words, "BOSTON STONE 1737."

"Huh," Caitlyn said. "What is this? I never heard of it before."

"Some guy in the late 1600's used it to grind paint pigments," Andrew explained. "I don't know why or how it ended up here. One of the legends about it is that it was a measuring point, that all distances from Boston were calculated from this spot."

"This is new to me."

"There's something like it in London. Cool, right?" He paused. "There are other legends. Like you should put your finger in the hole and make a wish, but the wish can only be for one thing."

"To come back to Boston?" Caitlyn thought that most of the superstitions of this sort were all about returning to the spot, like the Trevi Fountain in Rome.

"No," Andrew said. "But I'll only tell you if you promise to do it."

"Oh, please."

"Okay. Let's move on."

"So, really, you're not going to tell me?"

"Will you do it?"

With a look heavenward and a sigh, she capitulated.

He smiled. "You're supposed to wish for true love."

Caitlyn rolled her eyes again. "Oh, that's so lame."

"You think so?" Andrew said. "I'm surprised. Anyway, you have to keep your word. A deal is a deal. C'mon. Look. I'll do it first." He approached the stone, made a big show of mumbling and closing his eyes, and then leaned over and poked his right index finger into the hole. Returning to a full stand, he looked at her.

"This is ridiculous," she said, but she decided to be a good sport. As she bowed down to the stone, she heard a "click." Andrew had taken out his cell phone and had snapped a picture. "Look for this on Instagram," he said.

"Oh, you are horrible," she said, with a laugh. Two young men in suits and topcoats walked by them and appeared amused by the scene.

Caitlyn returned to Andrew's side. "I'm surprised I'd never heard about this. It would seem like the kind of thing that would be promoted. Tourists like that stuff, about making wishes."

"Well," Andrew started, with a grin, "truth is, I made it up."

She wondered if she should be angry, and indeed she was irritated slightly about being tricked, but her strongest response was pleasure. She was having a good time. "Was that why you brought me here?"

"No. That was just an on the spot inspiration."

"Inspiration? You're using the word loosely."

"There are one or two other things I want to show you." Despite more prodding as they moved along, he refused to elaborate.

They walked on, maneuvering through the vendor stalls of Haymarket where fruits and vegetables were being sold, and then they crossed a park, the Rose Kennedy Greenway, open space reclaimed after an elevated highway had been replaced by tunneled roads during the Big Dig. Andrew offered commentary but no hints about where they were going, or why. They ambled along Hanover Street through the North End and dozens of Italian restaurants, ultimately traversing the shadowy Paul Revere Mall and bypassing the Old North Church and its famous bell tower, where the signal of *One if by land and two if by sea* had been given. Then they went up a gentle slope, Hull Street.

Near its crest, Caitlyn said, "Look. The Skinny House." She pointed at what was reputed to be the narrowest home in Boston, barely ten feet wide, supposedly built to spite an abutter by blocking out sunlight.

"That's very bizarre, isn't it?" he said. "I wonder how anyone could live there."

"So where are we going?"

"Follow me."

Directly across the street from the Skinny House was a small set of stone steps that went into the Copp's Hill Burying Ground, an old cemetery. Andrew mounted them and Caitlyn trailed behind, a little uncomfortable: graves were not her favorite things. The burying ground was about a block in size and bordered by a fence of black iron spiked posts. The January light was diffuse, dirty. The graveyard was covered by grass yellowed by winter's cold. Several big bare trees spotted the land.

Nearest to the gate and throughout the cemetery, crooked gravestones of battered gray slate jutted from the plots, the names and dates and quotations on them often worn and nearly illegible. There were also several above-ground tombs. A few of these were ornate, but many of them were no more than white, weather-washed boxes of marble or cement.

Caitlyn tugged at Andrew's jacket. "Okay. Explain."

"It's interesting. Even though it's a cemetery, it's not too creepy. Anyway, we're heading over there." He pointed to an area in the far northeast corner. They followed a paved walkway, crisscrossing the paths of a few tourists who were bundled in winter coats but braving the chill. Eventually Caitlyn and Andrew stopped before one of the above-ground tombs, plain except for a row of interlocking "C"'s decorating a jutting base. The name "Carter" was engraved at the top.

Andrew stood in front of the tomb and stared at it. "Thought you might like to meet Josiah," he said.

Caitlyn gazed at the names carved on the tomb, and sure enough, there was *Josiah R. Hawkins*, along with the years of his birth and death.

"The old man, Theodore Carter, was very fond of Josiah and provided for him to be buried with the family in their grave."

"Wow," Caitlyn said. "They didn't mind…" She hesitated.

"What? That he was Black? No. They didn't mind. I don't know what went on with the rest of the family, but Theodore's wishes were clear, and they were kept. There are other Black people buried here in Copp's Hill. Like an activist named Prince Hall. This place holds rich and poor alike. Black and white."

"I'm sorry. I don't know if I phrased that right."

Andrew glanced at her. "I'm okay. I know what you meant. It's a legitimate question."

"Historically. I just thought people might have been more bigoted." At that point, she decided to keep her mouth shut. Nothing was coming out the way she intended.

He smiled slyly. "So, did you ever think this might be a Boston Box?" He gestured toward the tomb. True, it did look like a box. But nothing she had read ever implied that the Boston Box was anything other than a secret room.

"Noooooo," she said. "I've never thought that. Why would you suggest it?"

"Here's the thing. Over the holiday, one of my cousins got married, from the third family, and we all were together, and we got talking about Josiah. I thought I might find out something that could help you. And a sister of the bride, she said she had heard that Josiah was buried with his journal. Just think. We could be standing a few feet away from the answers to your questions."

Caitlyn turned to the tomb. A cold breeze blew across her cheeks, stinging them. "A fat lot of good that is. We can't exactly rob the grave."

"Can't we?"

She looked at him, nonplussed. "You aren't serious, are you?" After a moment, he broke into a wicked expression. "Oh, you are a devil," Caitlyn said. "Is there even a journal?"

Andrew laughed again.

She moved closer and beat upon him with her fists, no force at all behind her blows, just pretending to strike. He lifted his arms, protecting his head, more laughs.

"Wait, wait," he said. "Behave. This is a cemetery. I'll make it up to you."

Caitlyn pulled away. "Oh, yeah? How? How are you going to make it up to me?"

Andrew put his hands up, a "hold on" gesture. His expression became serious. "I *did* go to a family wedding, and I *did* talk about Josiah with some of my distant relatives, and one of them had something. Not with her, of course, but I picked them up a few days ago." He unfastened the flap of his messenger bag, reached in, and pulled out a small batch of what looked like old letters. They were bound together with a knotted faded blue ribbon, dirty with age.

"What's that?" Caitlyn asked.

"Letters from Josiah," he said. "Things he wrote to my cousin's great-grandmother."

"Oh my God! Really?"

"Really."

"Have you read them?"

Andrew nodded. "Yes."

"And?"

He smiled. "I think you'll find them helpful."

CHAPTER THIRTY-EIGHT

MARK

April 2017

I left the Fenway Grand early the next morning for my probate case. Hesh was on duty at the front desk and I chatted with him briefly before departing. I felt like I was beginning to belong there.

The courthouse looked to have been built as a public works project during the Thirties. The lobby had a pair of curved stairways that led to the second floor and an open foyer, where I found Dietz. He sat upon a high-backed mahogany bench near the door of our courtroom. A pile of documents and a briefcase rested next to him. His eyes were trained upon a crystal chandelier that hung in the center of the foyer, and it took a moment for him to notice and recognize me.

"Hi," he said, languorously, almost as if I had awakened him.

"Hi." I waited. "Are you okay?"

"What? Oh. Yes. My back. I'm trying this technique where I focus on something other than the pain." I must have looked concerned, and I *was*, not so much about his discomfort, but about his ability to represent me. In any case, reading my expression, Dietz said, "Don't worry. I do this instead of pills to keep my head clear. This will be all cut and dried."

"If you say so."

"I say so," he answered. "Let's go in." He spent a minute gathering his files before standing, which he eventually did with a groan. At the door, he added, "There's a case ahead of us. The clerk will call us when it's time. No talking once we're in the courtroom, a sign of respect to the judge. Like the tie I told you to wear." That was a reprimand. I had forgotten dress up as he had instructed. "You'll be called. Let me do all the talking."

I nodded. "Got it."

The room itself was small, at least when compared to the courtrooms of my imagination. The judge's bench and those of the court officers took up about a third of the space; their backs were to a bank of large windows, acrylic shades half-drawn. A low wooden rail separated them from the area where we were to sit, which had about four rows of chairs. The sound of shuffling papers was constant.

Dietz and I took seats in the second row and watched the case before mine unfold. It took about twenty minutes to be resolved. Once those plaintiffs were dismissed, Dietz stood and spoke with an officer, whom Dietz must have known, because their chat was friendly.

A moment later, my name was announced, and Dietz signaled for me to approach the rail. Once I acknowledged that I was, indeed, Mark Chieswicz, Dietz took over. He explained the situation to the judge, a middle-aged woman: robed, of course, and with a compassionate expression. As she asked some questions and spoke with Dietz, I heard someone else enter the courtroom, but didn't dare to look back, out of fear that my inattention would be viewed as rude. In a matter of moments, I was granted immediate access to a percentage of Dave's assets, announced as approximately $600,000, in order to service the needs of the estate. I was to document my expenditures with the stipulation that they would be reckoned in the final settlement, were there any disputes. I was also given the title to the BMW and a power of attorney. I tried my best to conceal my joy. We were then dismissed. The whole process was over in minutes.

I whispered a "thanks" to Dietz and turned. I had expected that the next plaintiffs would be preparing to approach the bench, and they were, but an additional, unwelcomed observer stood like a colossus in the back of the room.

Clarence.

He stared at me.

I turned to Dietz and whispered, "I need to introduce you to someone."

"Who? What?"

"That man in the back of the room," I said, indicating Clarence with a gesture of my thumb.

"Well, we can't talk here," Dietz muttered, and then he hugged his briefcase to his chest. We walked to the exit. "Damn," I heard him whisper, in pain. Clarence watched us as we passed, and I watched Clarence. Instinctively, my hand tightened into a fist.

Outside the room, back in the foyer, Dietz and I halted. "That was simple," I said, waiting for Clarence to appear, which didn't take long. He wore almost the exact same clothing as before. Mostly black. Loud running shoes. And his face exhibited the same angry scowl.

I spoke loudly, addressing Dietz. "Here's the man I want you to meet." My stalker looked perturbed, wary. "Clarence, come here. Meet my lawyer. I'm afraid I don't know your last name."

Clarence was silent.

"What's that?" I said. "I didn't catch it."

Clarence said nothing.

"Okay," I said. "We'll just call you Clarence. This is my lawyer, Larry Dietz. I met Clarence in Quincy last week. In a parking lot."

Since I'd hedged the story of my injuries with Dietz, it took him a moment to piece together the situation. "Your joyride for chicken," he said. "When you fell."

"Right," I said. "Exactly. Thought you should meet. In case I fall again."

Clarence glared. "We'll be in touch, smart guy." He moved by me, making sure that his shoulder hit mine. Who said that brick walls were inanimate objects? He descended the open foyer staircase, at one point twisting his head in my direction, managing to look both threatening and stupid.

As he left the building, Dietz said, "Okay. What was that about?"

"My brother's friend."

"Your brother had some scary friends."

"He owed him some money."

"And you didn't tell me this before," Dietz said.

"Just found out some stuff this weekend, after you and I met."

"Do you want to get the police involved?"

"No. But if you find me at the bottom of a lake, at least you'll know who put me there."

"Mark."

"I was joking. I'll handle it."

Except I wasn't joking. Because now that Clarence and Russ knew about Dave's accounts, I had no freaking idea how to keep them at bay.

CHAPTER THIRTY-NINE

CAITLYN

January 2017

Andrew would not let Caitlyn look at the letters until they found a warm place to sit and talk. Salem Street, nearby, was lined with restaurants and shops, and they came upon a funky café, neither a Starbucks nor particularly Italian, distinctions that made it unusual in the North End. Some walls of the café were brick, others were planked, and the furniture was mismatched. Most of the other customers hacked away at laptop keyboards. Caitlyn and Andrew ordered coffees, black for her, an elaborate foamed milk concoction with a list of specifications—dry, skim, cinnamon, double shot—for him, before they settled into a corner table.

Andrew carefully put the stack of letters onto the tabletop. The stationery was plain, and the handwriting on the uppermost envelope was composed of the uneven blue ink trails of a fountain pen. A small brown blot, rusty water perhaps, stained the lower left corner. The stamps had been removed. The aged ribbon that bound the letters was tied in a simple knot, no bow, little more than a substitute for a piece of string.

"You've read them all?" Caitlyn said.

Andrew pursed his lips and nodded yes.

"And…"

"For the most part, they're not relevant. They're love notes, of a sort. Josiah was involved with the maid of a South End family. Alicia. They're from three or four months, the letters, when she was in Nantasket for the summer, with her employer's wife and children."

Caitlyn glimpsed at the top letter's address. In the present day, Nantasket was about an hour's ride from Boston on the South Shore of Massachusetts. Of course, the trip would have taken longer in the 1800's. "You said I'd find them interesting."

"I'll get to that," Andrew said. "In any case, as love notes, they're acceptable. Mostly. The affair was secret. Josiah was in his fifties. God knows how they escaped the notice of Alicia's employers. They might have been bent out of shape if they knew what was really going on. Not much family folklore about the exact circumstances. Just the letters."

"So…what can I learn from them?"

"Some of the content might be helpful." He paused and sipped his coffee for dramatic effect. Reaching to the stack of letters, he tugged at the ribbon, untied the bundle, and then fanned it across the tabletop. "Let me show you the highlights. But one detail is especially important. Look at what happens when the family comes back to town. Check the address."

Caitlyn examined the stack, and seconds later, saw that the last few letters had a Boston address. She gasped. *It was Nine Chadwick Square! George Rumberg's home in the Adamston row!*

"Oh my God," Caitlyn said. And then, "OH MY GOD!"

Andrew beamed with satisfaction. "Oh my God, for sure."

"I don't believe it," she said.

"While I can't say precisely what happened," Andrew continued, "it went something like this. Alicia's employers were the original owners of the Chadwick Square house. One that Adamston—and, by extension, Josiah—had designed. I'd guess that while the plans were made for the construction of the house Josiah met Alicia and started their affair. Over the summer, the one covered by the letters, the family's Boston furniture was moved from their old residence to their new one. There wasn't anything about a Boston Box explicitly. That is, Josiah doesn't use that term. But there are some lines in there." Andrew became quiet while he shuffled through the letters and pulled one from the middle of the stack. Almost as an aside he said, "You can read them all." Then he gave her the single item he had retrieved.

Caitlyn turned the letter over and lifted the back flap with a slide of her thumb. She pinched the folded sheets of the letter inside and took them from the envelope, three pages, maybe five inches by seven or eight, of onion skin weight. Josiah's handwriting was tight, forward slanting, and precise, but not easy to read because the thin paper had allowed the ink to bleed through and made shadow images behind the script. The penmanship style was that of another time. She squinted, needing to concentrate in order to decipher the strokes of the old-fashioned alphabet.

My sweetest A,

How I do miss you! The summer days of Beacon Hill have been warm and unpleasant, and I fear my temper has been more ill than usual. It is not the heat alone that increases my displeasure. It is the absence of you and your delicious kisses that makes me unhappy. I count the days until your return, when I can once again enjoy you, the flavor that these days is the most delicious of all.

Caitlyn looked up at Andrew. "This is kind of hot."

"That was Josiah," he said. "Read on."

Chadwick Square steals my days and many of my nights. Two homes of the six are now occupied, one is being furnished, and your new haven will be ready for your too distant return. How will I survive the next weeks! The last two remain unsold, much to the despair of Mr. A and his investors. All must be bought for them to profit. He drinks heavily.

I have tried, with some stealth, to make the room that you are to occupy have some small additional ornaments. Douglas seems unaware of my efforts, which is just as well, of course.

"Who's Douglas?" Caitlyn asked. "Do you know?"

"I think Alicia's boss. The homeowner. Mr. Douglas."

I do so much long for a tryst with you, my sweet Alicia! My body and soul ache for unity once more with you. Have I ever had such moments before? I do not believe so.

"About how old was Alicia?" Caitlyn asked. "Do you have any idea?"

"We think she was seventeen or eighteen."

"A dirty old man, sneaking around."

Andrew looked dubious. "Oh, you're an ageist? How interesting. I prefer to think of him as a life force. After all, it's only sex. And there was love."

"Yes, but…at the time?"

"Anyway, it's impossible to judge."

"Perhaps."

"Think of it this way," Andrew said. "Without Josiah's love affairs, a number of happy people would not be alive today. My cousins. Ask them if they believe he should have behaved. And he eventually married her."

"That's a perspective," Caitlyn said. The noise in the café suddenly seemed louder. One table, occupied by a laptop diver when they had arrived, was now crowded with a quartet of college-aged boys, faces shining from the cold, chattering and happy. Elsewhere, a couple of middle-aged women spoke almost conspiratorially with one another. They didn't look like North Enders. A solo man, also middle-aged, turtle-necked sweater, was seated in a nearby lounge chair, and he saw Caitlyn scanning the room. Their eyes met briefly before he turned away and picked up his coffee, an action that prompted her to sip from her own cup. The coffee was strong and giving her a buzz.

"Read on," Andrew encouraged.

The house on Chadwick Square will have a love nest for us. Please do not let your heart give in to moments of doubt or despair. There will be arrangements that will allow us to be together, to steal precious hours of joy and delight.

"Love nest?" Caitlyn said.

"Exactly."

"Do the other letters explain what the love nest was?"

"No. Not in detail."

"You think it was a Boston Box?"

Andrew grabbed the last envelope from the batch and removed the letter from within it. Holding the sheets in two hands as if they were the folds of a newspaper, he moved his eyes across the text until he smiled and said, "Here. This note was written after they'd returned from Nantasket. It's the final one. You can verify but I think I've found everything that was important. Maybe not. But listen to this." He was about to read aloud but then stopped and looked up. "I should explain that Josiah just told Alicia that he would be outdoors after a meeting around nine-thirty in the evening. Most of the last few notes are about logistics for assignations. And then he writes this. *'Put a ribbon in the window if you can meet. Leave the rear door unlocked. I will join you at the trysting place again.'*" Andrew grinned. "Did you catch that? 'Trysting place.' How cool is that?"

"You think the trysting place was a Boston Box?"

Andrew nodded. "I think it's a distinct possibility. He was sneaking into the house. He doesn't say that he'll go to her room or to come outdoors. He says 'trysting place.' So they could be meeting somewhere in the house." He waited for her to speak, and then appeared disappointed. "You don't look convinced. I thought you'd be excited. This could be big."

"So Josiah took this opportunity to design a secret room where he could meet his lover?"

"You're the one who's into secret rooms," Andrew said. "But this is plausible. Maybe Josiah has been used to creating these chambers for the Underground Railroad or something, and after the war, he had the skills, or the smarts, to keep doing it. You're looking for it, right?"

To Caitlyn, verifying the existence of a Boston Box like this seemed too good to be true. And why wasn't she more excited? Did it seem unlikely? Her mind went to Pennsylvania and the conversation with her mother. Even though she'd never seen David Chieswicz, she felt as if his ghost was in the café, trying to haunt her, scare her, take away her achievement. She didn't know why she felt his presence so strongly at that moment, from almost out of nowhere. *Buck up*, she thought.

Caitlyn smiled at Andrew. Handsome Andrew. "I'm sorry," she said. "I think I'm in shock. You know what it's like, when you've wanted something for a while, and you finally have it, and it's almost unreal, you can't quite believe it? When I've imagined this moment, finding a Boston Box, I pictured being somewhere in one of the dark corners of Harvard, or poking around an old building and I'd push a door open, and there it would be. In my mind, dramatic music would be playing." She pretended to strike imaginary piano keys forcefully and seriously.

"I understand. I think. Well, this isn't the final word. You still have work to do. We found something here. But it's a wisp."

"I have to get into Chadwick Square. I wish that man would answer my letters." Caitlyn sipped her coffee. "Oh, Andrew, I am such an ingrate! I should be thanking you. This is awesome. You have done this wonderful thing and I'm acting here like Debbie Downer. What's wrong with me? I am so appreciative." She grabbed his hand.

Andrew smiled and squeezed her hand in response.

A twinkling tone came from Caitlyn's phone, so she released Andrew and retrieved the phone from her pocket. A text from Henry was displayed on the screen: *Sup?*

She looked at Andrew. "Do you mind if I answer this?" With a gesture, he agreed. Caitlyn quickly typed *"with a friend. Ltr"* and then returned her attention to Andrew, but not before a response came from Henry: *Got it. Later please.*

"Just a friend," she offered.

"Aw, c'mon," Andrew said. "It was a booty call."

"It was not!" she answered, but blood rushed to her face.

He laughed. "I was teasing, but look at you, all red. I think it was."

"I'm not in a relationship with anyone. Dates is all."

"Good."

Good? "I guess my next step is to get into Chadwick Square," she said. "I'll just have to nag that guy until he gives in. I really think the interior might be close to the original."

"That would be fortunate. 1860s or 70s though. There would have to be conversions for electricity. Some of the structure must have been updated at one time or another."

"True," she answered. "I can hope." She touched the stack of letters. "I can borrow these?"

"My relatives will kill me if anything happens to them."

"I'll be very, very careful."

"You know, I'm thinking maybe the best thing is that I have a scanner back at my condo. We could copy them for you. It's just a ten-minute walk from here. Wouldn't take long."

"That makes sense," she said.

"We can have dinner after," he suggested.

Caitlyn was about to ask, *After what?*, but she stopped. If she had any say in the matter, she was already certain of the answer to that question.

CHAPTER FORTY

MARK

April 2017

Does money make you popular? After the session at the probate court, once I was back at the apartment, I almost believed it did, for suddenly my phone started to ring. Okay, two calls in the space of three hours. Not much, but for me, practically off the hook. Thinking it over, however, I came up with another proposition. Money just stirs up trouble.

The first call came from Dietz, a surprise, since we had just parted a couple of hours earlier. "I did some digging about your friend," he said.

"Who's that?"

"Clarence," he responded. "He looked familiar."

"Oh."

"Just made a few inquiries. I know some people."

"And…"

"Listen, Mark. This is not a man you want to play around with. His last name is Hudson. A couple of prison terms for assault. Rumors about other stuff. He is one very, very bad character. Those bruises of yours, the ones you got from your 'fall,' as you called it, for Hudson that's nothing. He has a nickname, you know."

"I've heard," I said. "I mean, I don't know what it is, but I heard he had one. What is it?"

"Death Squad," Dietz responded. "That's what they call him. Death Squad Hudson. Independent. For hire. You don't want to get on his bad side."

Unfortunately, I was already there, even though I hadn't done anything to deserve it except to be Dave's brother. And not confess about the amount of the inheritance to Russ, but damn, as I've said, it was Russ's own stupid fault he'd trusted Dave.

"You there?" Dietz asked.

"Yeah, I'm here."

"You want to tell me what this is all about?"

"The best I can understand it, Dave screwed over one of Clarence's friends. They got me confused with him. That's been straightened out. And because of the money, the inheritance, they're looking for some compensation."

"That's it?"

"That's all I know." Nothing was going to force me to admit the illegality of Dave's legacy.

"We should let the police in on this," he said. "Clarence could be wrapped up in your brother's murder."

"No. He's not. He thought I was Dave. He didn't know anything about Dave's dying."

Dietz was silent for a moment. "Mark, your life could be in danger."

"I'll be okay. I'll handle it."

"You have a gun?"

"What?"

"It's not something I normally advise, but for God's sake, make sure you have some kind of protection. This is not a reasonable man, Mark. This is a psycho, a sociopath, nasty piece of work, you pick your label."

"Got it."

Although Dietz didn't have more to say, he seemed reluctant to hang up. I held onto my silent phone before breaking the quiet. "Thanks for your concern, for checking this out, for telling me. I'll be careful. I promise."

"I have a bad feeling about this. Hudson may not be smart, but he's ruthless. You're sure you don't want me to intervene?"

"What could you do? Get an injunction? How? And that won't stop him if he's out for me. He already knows I put you onto him if anything happens. I appreciate the warnings. I'll think things over." After goodbyes, we disconnected.

I shivered and wondered how you buy a gun. I should have asked. Maybe I could charge it to the estate, I thought, sardonically. Protection services.

At my laptop, I did a search on "Clarence Hudson." Too many answers came up after that query, so I tried various combos of "Clarence," "Death Squad," and "Hudson." Some mug shots appeared. The face I'd learned to love. For the most part, Clarence had kept his expression neutral while the photos were taken, but his eyes signaled contempt.

The few articles that I found weren't comforting. The "Death Squad" nickname wasn't based on his recent occupation. Rather, Clarence had been a boxer during a stint in the Army in the 90s. I couldn't locate many details about his length of service or whether he had spent any time overseas or in combat. My recollection is that the era was a time of relative peace, so frontline activity was unlikely. I'd guess the army was a brief interlude in his late teen years, after high school, presuming he graduated, which was by no means certain. And as much as

I was sarcastic about his lack of brains, I was uncomfortably aware that he drove a Mercedes while I was scraping by and dragging on Dave's coattails.

Brief news stories detailed two of Clarence's arrests, one of them for beating up a girlfriend, the other an altercation a decade earlier outside of a downtown nightclub. Clarence's victim in that one didn't die but he was badly messed up, hospitalized, the result of a pounding that was characterized in an article as "brutal." Allusions were made to Clarence's uncontrolled rage, a side effect of steroids and God knows what other kinds of chemicals. Clarence was given five years for assault. The story hinted at a plea bargain, with some other pending cases against Clarence dismissed in the process. Whether he served his entire sentence or—more likely—got paroled early, wasn't clear.

The military. Boxing. Prison. Excellent training to be a "death squad." Add some steroids to the mix and maybe his nickname should be "Time Bomb."

In the middle of my research, a second call came through. The number was from Florida, and I should have ignored it. Curiosity got the better of me.

"Mark," Russ said.

"Oh, hello." I tried to sound jaunty.

"How's the weather up there?" Russ asked. His drawl was strong.

Really? He called to discuss the weather? I guessed the rules of Southern civility govern even during shakedown calls. "Not bad for February," I said. "Too bad it's April."

"Good one."

"How's the weather wherever you are? Florida, is it?" Two could play this game. Maybe we could next chat about the books we were reading.

"Just fine. In the eighties. You should come visit."

"I'll keep that in mind."

"So, Mark, I heard you were in court this morning."

"Yes."

"Anything you want to tell me?"

"I have a feeling it would all be old news."

"You're pretty sharp." I wasn't sure if Russ meant my mind-reading abilities or my razor-like wit, but I didn't ask for a clarification. He continued. "Sounds like you came across some money."

"Yes, there was some. Still figuring it out."

"Care to inform me?"

"As I said, I think you know it all. I found out some things this week. Truth is that the money isn't doing much good. Tied up in probate. It's going to take a year till it's all sorted through. At least. With taxes, and taking care of Dave's estate, God knows if there'll be much left. It's certainly not the million plus that you're looking for."

"I thought we were pals, Mark. I thought you would keep me in the loop. A deal."

"And I thought your friend was going to disappear. I figure there was no need to make any phone calls. Waste of your time. I'm being tracked. What's the point? You already know what I'm doing." I was sounding cockier than I felt. Yet I have to admit my logic was impeccable. "If you ever decide to call off your goon, perhaps we can set up a regular time to speak."

Russ was silent.

"Like I said," I continued, "whatever money Dave had is tied up in the courts. I was given access to part of it because I've been paying for things out of pocket, the funeral, damage to the car...you know about that, right? And I just don't have the cash to cover my brother's expenses. Don't own a racetrack or any-thing. You want a deal? Clarence goes away. And if he doesn't, then no need to be in touch. He can keep you informed."

Silence.

"Hello," I said. No response. "Anybody there?" My phone screen displayed a message: *Call ended.*

I stared out of the apartment window. Traffic was heavy. Game day at Fenway, despite the cool weather. "Fuck," I whis-pered. And then louder: *"Fuckeddy fuck, fuck, fuck!"*

CHAPTER FORTY-ONE

CAITLYN

January 2017

It was after ten when Caitlyn left Andrew's apartment. Drizzle dampened her face as she walked to the T. The mist turned the glow of the streetlamps along the way into a foggy haze.

She was tired. Sexual chemistry with Andrew had been immediate and powerful. He had considerable skill and endurance, and she thought she'd matched him in enthusiasm. At least, that's how she'd felt afterward with him, over take-out pizza and a bottle of good Italian red wine. Now, in the wet night air, almost giddy, she murmured some words of gratitude to the universe. *What a day! The Boston Box, and discoveries, and this!*

By the time she reached the turnstile of the subway, however, she had second thoughts. For one thing, Andrew hadn't offered to walk with her to the subway station. She wouldn't have expected him to go all the way with her to Cambridge— that was ridiculous—but company would have been nice, and a warmer conclusion to the evening. He might even have a car that he could have driven. Or he could have insisted that she order a cab or an Uber. Why was this bothering her? Perhaps, post-sex, being by herself on a lonely street felt like she was doing the Walk of Shame, even if it wasn't seven in the morn-

216 • CHUCK LATOVICH

ing, even if her hair and make-up weren't disheveled and her clothing wasn't messy. Oh, well. She could have gotten her own Uber. And the station really wasn't that far from his condo.

Ten minutes later, in a subway car, looking at the other passengers, she wondered which of them, if any, had had sex in the last few hours. A young couple, snuggling, was the most likely possibility. Could anyone see sex on her? She lifted her coat lapels and slunk behind them.

Another qualification about the evening: Andrew hadn't suggested that she spend the night. Again, she was being foolish. This was not, by any means, a hard-and-fast requirement in the hook-up rulebook. Truth be told, her past experiences didn't always include sleeping together after sex. But Andrew's behavior was an interesting contrast with Henry's.

Henry. She hadn't followed up on his texts, for obvious reasons.

She switched from the subway to a bus that would take her closer to her apartment. Caitlyn couldn't remember the last time she'd slept with two different men over the course of a few days. Undergrad days, perhaps. Nothing wrong with it, logically, ethically, or intellectually—she was entitled to a healthy sex life, and the universe had provided these opportunities, so why not? She thought of those Victorian women who were supposedly driven to hysteria from lack of orgasms. Life wasn't like that anymore. On the pill, Caitlyn had little chance of getting pregnant. Both of her partners had used protection, so a disease, while not technically impossible—it never was—was improbable. This was the new millennium. Women were allowed to enjoy their bodies. Right?

But why now for her? In the past year, she hadn't played much. Deep down, she recognized a pattern from her past, but she hated the thought that the whole David Chieswicz thing had blasted open her libido, had made her needy. She rejected the idea. The circumstances were different now.

She got off the bus. Her stop was near the café where she and Henry had had brunch on New Year's Day. Henry. Andrew. How interesting to compare them! In bed, Henry had been a teddy bear, easy, an old shoe, familiar, even though, until New Years, not that kind of familiar. Warm. When they stood together, his arm draped over her, she fit perfectly. He felt good. On the other hand, Andrew was more polished, confident. He knew what he was doing. Maybe neither of them was right in the long run. Too soon to tell. For now, it was good to have choices.

Caitlyn turned at the coffee shop on the corner of her street and walked to her home. She unlatched her door, shed her coat, and put her shoulder bag on the kitchen table, where an unfinished cup of tea from the morning still rested, an ugly dose of reality. Men! Sex! They were distractions. The important thing was her studies, the work on the Boston Box. Andrew had scanned Josiah's letters and had sent the files to her in an email. She'd glanced briefly at them earlier and felt sure that Andrew had already highlighted the most important details. She was exhausted, if in a good way, so a closer look could wait till morning. She wanted to rest.

CHAPTER FORTY-TWO

MARK

April 2017

How hard was it to buy a gun? Of course, a legal purchase in Massachusetts would take some time. To cover my ass, I'd have to do all that was required: take a class, apply for a license, and so forth. The problem with a legal course was that it took weeks, and I'd no confidence that the intervening period would be without a confrontation. I needed a stopgap.

Initially, I went onto Craig's List. Why not? But it turned out that the only guns for sale—in Massachusetts, anyway—were things like paintball cannons. Next, I did a web search on "Handguns for sale in NH." I thought I'd go out of state in an effort to stay under the radar. My query led me to a site called NHGUNLIST.com where some privately-owned weapons were posted for sale. I examined the variables in several ads: what kind of gun was being offered, what was the cost, how far a drive. I settled on a handgun that a review in an NRA magazine characterized as good for self-defense and perfect for a beginner, which was me, since I'd never held any kind of firearm. The price, used, was $500. Cash sale.

Over the next couple of hours, the seller and I exchanged some emails, and I arranged to travel north and be at his home in Concord, New Hampshire, in early evening. I ran into some rush hour traffic just outside of Boston, but mostly I had an easy ride and open roads, which gave me the opportunity to enjoy the BMW. A purposeful trip with that fringe benefit. No black Mercedes trailed me. Maybe Russ had shared my request for freedom with Clarence. I doubted it. Death Squad Guy was probably out on another job terrorizing a different innocent man.

The gun seller lived in a split-level house on the edges of Concord. Wooded land bordered the yard behind the house. The seller was in-shape, jean-clad, and with a cute, crooked smile; his wife was a friendly gal, and a few young children peeked at me from upstairs while we three adults introduced ourselves. I felt like I'd entered the real Amurrica. The transaction took place in a furnished workroom in the basement. At least the owner kept the gun away from the children under lock and key, and a security device on the revolver added protection. He removed it so that I could grip the gun before I bought it, and I pretended to know what I was doing, but I don't think I fooled him for a second. He didn't seem concerned. For another $50, he threw in a shoulder holster and a box of ammo, a bargain, in his words. He said he'd use the proceeds to buy an upgrade for himself. He had his eye on some model, the name of which he mentioned, and I nodded as if I understood and was impressed. My purchases were put into a paper bag with handles. We shook hands, and I carried the gun and accessories out of the house like a sack of groceries.

And so it was that within a space of about ten hours I went from my first thought about buying a gun to possessing one. God bless the USA.

CHAPTER FORTY-THREE

CAITLYN

January 2017

Caitlyn read through Josiah's correspondence while eating breakfast. They were love letters, with no references to any architectural details of Nine Chadwick Square, other than the citations that she and Andrew had already discussed. Although those few lines implied the existence of a secret room, they were ambiguous. Nonetheless, the discovery was intriguing, and if the references didn't prove the existence of the Boston Box once and for all, especially without an on-site verification, they did provide an important clue.

A response from George Rumberg became even more urgent. He must have had her second letter for several days by now. But he hadn't called, or sent a text, or written an email. She supposed that a timely reply by posted mail was possible. If that was the case, a reasonable waiting period hadn't passed. But why on earth would anyone write a letter nowadays when there were so many easier options? And what if he didn't respond soon? What if he never did? What other avenues did she'd have to explore? Should she just go and knock on his door again?

Patience, she told herself. Research was a process, not a horse race. Her deadlines about the Boston Box were self-imposed. In the meanwhile, other matters and avenues remained to be checked out. One hidden room wouldn't confirm her hypothesis. She needed a few, at least. (Although one could be the origin of a rumor, of an urban legend. Hm.)

Disregarding Chadwick Square for a moment, Caitlyn thought a good question to ask about the Boston Box was "Why?" Why would anyone construct a hidden room? Up to now, a few possible answers had emerged. The first was the origin story: hidden rooms were built as places to hide runaway slaves. But after that, once slavery was abolished, why continue to build them?

There was the proposition of the abominable Bacht: they were examples of architects making jokes, boys being boys. Dubious. What kinds of amusement would this give them? It's not like they could break into houses and use them without the occupants' knowledge.

Yet that's what Josiah Hawkins apparently did.

Here was the value of her research into Hawkins. Another possible purpose: the rooms were built for sex. Caitlyn had this notion that sex in the nineteenth century was staid: Did women even enjoy it? Before birth control? Didn't most men of the time just stick it in and get off and roll over and go to sleep? Maybe the Boston Box was a perfect metaphor for another kind of sex, hidden away from the main functions of a house, illicit, and maybe a rousing good time? After further consideration, she concluded it was condescending and stupid to believe that past generations didn't enjoy sex as much as those of the present. In any case, sex was another answer to "Why?" But could there be other reasons?

Caitlyn pulled out a small pad of paper to brainstorm. Across the top, she wrote "The Possible Uses of a Boston Box." She started with her current hypotheses, and then let her mind run free.

Hiding fugitives
In-jokes for architects
Furtive sex
Gay sex
A man cave
A panic room
Hide something other than a slave: money from thieves, illegal or stolen money, etc.
Punish children
Secret experiments
A sewing room

She paused. There would be no need to hide in order to sew, but this was brainstorming, where you didn't censor your thoughts. An unlikely guess might yet lead you somewhere. If a man could have a "man cave," nineteenth-century version, why couldn't a woman have a sewing room? A woman cave? Did wealthy women ever commission a house? Of course, they did! She knew of the Isabella Stewart Gardner Museum, for instance, and from Caitlyn's thesis studies about the Back Bay, she was aware of others. Would a woman use a secret room? Could a Boston Box be an architectural metaphor for a vagina? A vulgarism?

Yuck. No.

She continued.

Torture chamber (S&M? Actual torture?)
Murder?
Kidnapping?
Storage?
Which came first? The room or the usage?

She imagined a new owner would hesitate to say, "Hey, look, I need a torture chamber. Can you build one behind the bookcase?" Even so, how strange that her mind went in that direction, beyond sex, to violence, kidnapping, torture. Of course, that could be the impact of modern life upon her sensibility, of too many police procedurals on television, the shows that her mother loved to keep in constant rotation on the set at home in West Chester. *CSI: Back Bay. Law and Order: Special Victorian Unit.*

Were there serial killers in Boston in the nineteenth century? She typed "Boston notorious murders" into a search engine. A list popped up on a tourist website whose owners were seemingly unaware of the irony of "celebrating Boston" by displaying the locations of approximately thirty famous murders and crimes. Several of them had taken place in the twentieth century, like the Boston Strangler's reign of terror. She'd certainly heard of him, but others, like the hitchhike killer of the 1970's, were new to her. And there was Chuck Stuart, who murdered his wife and faked an alibi about a racially motivated attack before jumping off the Tobin Bridge, his guilt about to be revealed. There were stories of murdered lovers or vanished children, of a man who had disemboweled his wife after they'd fought about a ziti casserole.

Caitlyn could have easily tumbled into this swirl of lurid modern crime stories. But they weren't of the appropriate era, and she turned to the nineteenth century.

The most notorious case involved the murder of a notable socialite, George Parkman, by a well-known doctor who was indebted to him. The doctor had killed and dismembered Parkman after an argument and then tried to conceal the body parts and bones. Not in a hidden room, however. The doctor used a tea chest. Interestingly, one of Parkman's houses was now an official residence of the mayor of Boston. Anyway, that murder took place prior to the Civil War. Not a direct hit. And the famous case of Lizzie Borden, whacking away with an ax at her mother and father, was too late in the century to be applicable to Caitlyn's studies, not that any of the particulars supported an association with a Boston Box.

However, another story intrigued Caitlyn, that of a man of good family, Pearson Jeffries, who lived on Marlborough Street in the Back Bay, and who was implicated in the deaths of several young women. According to the testimony of a woman who had escaped from him, Jeffries lured prostitutes to his place. Once there, he overcame them and took them to a room where he abused and killed them. The woman who told the story said Jeffries had pulled out several of her teeth. She had escaped when the torture was interrupted by a visitor to the house; the woman, having loosened a gag that Jeffries had hastily put on her, screamed for help. After a struggle with Jeffries, it had taken several minutes for the visitor to locate her. The bones of a number of victims were found in the basement. Jeffries ultimately confessed to four killings. He was convicted and hanged.

More than a hundred years later, these dreadful crimes still had the ability to horrify. Caitlyn was almost reluctant to read more but having made the decision to investigate the Boston Box, she didn't have a choice.

The Jeffries crimes occurred in the early 1870's. The story was illustrated with a picture of Jeffries's home, and the street number, on lower Marlborough, was visible. Caitlyn looked up the house in her copy of *Back Bay Houses*. It was one of the first built on the block, which would have given Jeffries the protection of isolation, although a couple of homes were on lots not far away. For a period, no one would be close enough to hear screams. But then, Caitlyn got a shock. The architect, as listed, was Thaddeus Simpson, the man accused of murdering the young factory worker.

"Oh, wow," Caitlyn said. Was this a connection, an indication that Boston Boxes were more than jokes, more than love nests, but places where some men conspired to have illicit, extreme, deadly sexual encounters? The ties among these men begged to be investigated. Josiah Hawkins didn't quite fit this theory, since he used the Box for simple sex—albeit outside of marriage—and not torture. Could he be connected in another way? Was there a secret society?

Her phone buzzed. A text message from Henry: *Heyy*

"hey back"

Sup? You avoiding me. LOL

"visiting a friend got caught up in research."

Tonight?

"don't think that'll work. tmrw??"

Sounds good.

As soon as that exchange was finished, she hesitated before eventually determining to send a text to Andrew: *"Thanks for the help (& everything else). Was fun. Again sometime soon?"*

She waited a few moments. No immediate response came through. Disappointing, but that was part of the texting game.

Back to research, she checked on the present status of the Jeffries house. It still stood but unfortunately had been cut up into multiple units in the late sixties. Yet checking the place out might still be useful. She found some information about the owners, a condo association with only a P.O. Box for an address. She'd try them.

The upsetting story about abductions gave Caitlyn goosebumps. She breathed deeply. She needed to get a grip on herself. Just because one Boston Box, or some of them, might have been used for grisly purposes, that type of threat no longer existed. She was in no danger. It wasn't as if she would end up in a Boston Box somewhere, struggling for her life, like those poor Victorian women whom Jeffries had tortured.

CHAPTER FORTY-FOUR

MARK

April 2017

When I returned from New Hampshire, I took my new toy to the apartment to play with. The seller didn't have the manual for the gun any longer, but I was able to get one online from the manufacturer's website. The gun was a .357 double-action revolver. "Double-action," I learned, meant that pulling the trigger both cocked the hammer and released it, for faster shooting, I supposed. The body was gleaming stainless steel with a rubber handle, and the gun weighed about a pound and a half. It felt good as I gripped it, comfortable yet with some heft.

I spent time reading, comparing the text with the thing in my hand. I tried to learn the names for its parts. A few of them were common—cylinder, barrel, hammer, trigger. Others were less recognizable—muzzle, frame, crane latch.

Another online site suggested specific exercises for familiarizing oneself with a firearm, so I attempted them. I opened and closed the cylinder until I was used to that routine. Then I stood in front of a mirror and practiced my stance, planting my legs wide apart as if I were a James Bond with a pair of big balls, and then trying to aim by lining up the gun's rear and front sights. It was hard to believe that in a dangerous situation I'd have enough time to do all this stuff, but maybe frequent practice would make it automatic. Staring at myself in the mirror, pointing the revolver at my image, I felt ridiculous, and I laughed at the absurdity of Mark the Gunslinger.

I pulled the trigger a few times, and my mood changed. The barrel was empty, of course. Although the gun wasn't loaded, I felt frightened by its potential power, life or death, and I became nauseous. I'd have to desensitize myself if I ever expected to get over my qualms and shoot the damn thing. I reminded myself that a psychopath may want to harm me. I was in "stand my ground" mode so I had to learn, become adept.

My final drill was to put bullets into the gun. I decided not to load all six chambers. Instead, I just used two bullets, repeatedly inserting them into a couple of the chambers and snapping the barrel shut, then emptying the gun, and then doing the routine all over again. Whenever the revolver had bullets in it, I tried to be mature and careful and calm, yet part of me squirmed. My hand trembled. The gun, when loaded, terrified me, and it took some force of will for me to continue practicing.

After about an hour of this improvised training, my nervousness built instead of lessened, so I unloaded the chambers for a final time, used the safety lock, and placed the gun in a kitchen cupboard. I stored the bullets in a bedroom drawer, several feet away from the revolver, as if by placing the two components in separate rooms, I somehow prevented them from mating in secret during the night and exploding.

To relax before I went to sleep, I got a beer, picked up Dave's coffee table book about Boston, and opened it while I stretched out on the couch. I'd assumed that Dave had turned the page corners to mark his place, but as I examined the folds more closely, I wondered if they had been more purposeful. Coffee table books aren't difficult to read, and some of these markings were only a few pages apart. Perhaps Dave had highlighted them for the information they contained rather than showing his progress.

I looked at the pictures. One double page spread that he'd marked was a vista of Chadwick Square in Boston's South End. The other pages were more complicated montages of the neighborhood that highlighted details, such as a flower box or ornamentation like a carved chain, or a park bench, or a small cemetery, which surprised me, because I hadn't remembered seeing any gravestones when I'd walked in the neighborhood in the past. Not every one of these pictures had a caption, but several did, and these texts occasionally indicated a locale.

I wasn't able to discern any precise pattern to the pages that Dave had marked, but, obviously, Chadwick Square stood out. I got up from the sofa, brought back my laptop, and mapped the addresses that I could identify. Unfortunately, most of them had street names but not numbers, and Boston avenues like Harrison spanned blocks and could go across the entire South End.

Looking again at the online map, I realized the territory to explore was enormous. Yet once more I grabbed onto the thought that somewhere in this vicinity was a clue about Dave's death, and maybe a link to the kid. The chance that I'd learn something was weak, a real longshot. I considered whether I was deluding myself, just telling myself that I was trying to find Junior but really making futile gestures that I hoped would fail. In the end, I gave myself the benefit of the doubt. Longshot or not, Dave *had* marked those pages. He must have had a reason.

CHAPTER FORTY-FIVE

CAITLYN

January 2017

For the next couple of days, Caitlyn returned to her apartment from work or study at the university, eager to check the mailbox, hoping for some reply from Rumberg, only to be repeatedly disappointed. But she made other progress. She'd been able to contact the management company for the Jeffries/Simpson/Marlborough Street building, and its director, Lisa Allsbrook, was much more sympathetic and responsive than the owner of Nine Chadwick Square. Allsbrook mentioned that her husband went to Harvard and she would be glad to help for that reason. But she wasn't encouraging when told of Caitlyn's purpose for a visit. The house had been renovated in the sixties, with little left of the original floor plans.

On the day of the appointment, a freezing rain fell. The building had a brownstone foundation, with red brick used on the upper floors, a traditional Back Bay look. Allsbrook was not on time, and Caitlyn huddled in a narrow alcove at the top of the front steps to avoid the worst of the rain.

Allsbrook showed up in about fifteen minutes, out of breath, clutching some files stuffed with folded architectural drawings. "Sorry, sorry, sorry," she said, with an apologetic laugh. "Last minute emergency. Parking around here." She was older than Caitlyn had pictured in her mind, somewhere in her fifties, jowly, no umbrella, the hood of a winter parka protecting her head against the elements. "Let me get you out of the weather." Allsbrook retrieved a key fob from a pocket and used it to let them into a tiny outer vestibule, and then she punched a code into her smartphone that popped open an inner door to a small, well-lit, and warm foyer.

Allsbrook shook like a dog drying its fur, and drops of water splashed onto Caitlyn. "Oops," Allsbrook said, laughing. "Sorry about that. I hate winter, don't you?"

"It's so kind of you to go to all this trouble."

"Not at all. Except there's not much I can show you." She chortled. "I don't really have permission to go into people's condos for something like this. We have to stay in the common areas, and that's not much. You said you're studying something."

Caitlyn gave a brief description of her research, capping it off with her understanding of the Jeffries murders and the room where they took place. Allsbrook became wide-eyed. "Oh, dear, honey! Don't tell the residents! They'll think the place is haunted and expect me to fix it. Ha! So let me show you what I can." But as she had suggested, there wasn't much to investigate. Obviously, the three individual units—one each on the two lower floors, and a gigantic two-floor unit at the top—took up most of the space, and without being able to enter them, all Caitlyn could see was doorways and carpeted staircases. None of it was left over from the original construction. Even the basement had been reconfigured into storage. Allsbrook frequently inserted a giggle without any provocation. The tour was finished in ten minutes, and they ended up once more in the first-floor entrance hall.

"Caitlyn, so you're interested in Victorian interiors, and that's all gone here. Even these days, almost nobody has one of these places as a single family. Most of them are divided. They got cut up in the fifties and sixties. Everybody wanted to live in the suburbs. But I have something for you." She retrieved the architectural drawings she had carried. "I looked through the files and found these. They're demolition documents."

"Really?" Caitlyn said, thrilled. Demolition documents would show the floor plans of the home as it existed before it had been remodeled, detailing what walls were to be taken down, a guide to the crew that was renovating the property. If a hidden room had been on the property, as the Jeffries story indicated, these might show it. "That's amazing! I can borrow them?"

"I don't think anyone has looked at them in forty, fifty years," Allsbrook said. "I'll lend them. I'd like them back, of course," she laughed, "but for your research, just use them and give them back when you're finished."

"I'll make copies. This is great." She tucked the folded drawings into her knapsack.

"One other thing. Have you seen the Hibbert House? You want Victorian? Correct?"

The Hibbert House sounded familiar but Caitlyn couldn't immediately recall it. "Please remind me."

"House over on Beacon. Mostly preserved. It's a museum now. They give tours. It's not far from this place. I walk by it every day. If you're into Victorian, that's the place to see. Not this."

With Allsbrook's prompt, Caitlyn remembered reading about the museum, and she wasn't sure how she'd let it escape her attention until now. She would take care of the oversight at once. Hibbert House wouldn't have the gruesome history of their current location, and a link to her research was improbable. Still, nothing was lost by checking it out. "Thanks for the idea."

"I'm not sure if it's open now. Could be. Limited schedule."

They parted on the doorstep. Allsbrook rushed off in one direction, stopped, reconsidered, turned around, and then dashed the opposite way. Her head was hidden by the cowl of her coat, but Caitlyn could hear her laughing as she passed.

Caitlyn hung behind, took out her phone, and said, "Tell me about Hibbert House on Beacon Street in Boston." Five seconds later, the phone found a website for the museum, which was open, just a few blocks away, with the next tour to begin on the hour, a time she could easily meet. She opened her umbrella and traipsed in the rain over to the museum.

The exterior of the Hibbert House resembled that of many other Beacon Street residences and was constructed, like the Marlborough building, of brownstone and red brick. Its style was primarily French Academic—very symmetrical—with an elaborate design of interlocking circles above the windows. The house next to it shared the façade, duplicating its design and giving the impression it was one building with two entrances. A wooden sign in the museum's small front garden, presently winter bare, gave its name and the hours for admission. Caitlyn climbed the steps to the entrance. A laminated sheet tucked into the front door said a tour was in progress, and that visitors should wait until the top of the hour to request entry. Once again, Caitlyn found herself on a Back Bay doorstep in the icy rain.

But not for long. The front door was opened in a few minutes by a man in his thirties who seemed surprised to see her. "Oh, come in, come in, get out of the rain." As he ushered Caitlyn into a foyer with a wave of his hand, he held the door for an older couple, who had evidently just completed the tour. "Bye, now," the guide said to them. "Stay dry." They exited.

He and Caitlyn stepped further into the house. He was thin, almost skeletal. His thick knit sweater and corduroy pants were three sizes too big and hung on him loosely. When he moved, it was almost as if his clothing arrived a couple of seconds after him. He was unshaven in a cultivated way, with wire-rimmed glasses. "What a day to be out! Welcome. Where are you from?"

"Cambridge," she answered.

"Oh, good. I love it when a local descends upon us. You a student? Yes? Then you get our magnificent two-dollar discount on the cost of your nine-dollar admission. We'll start in about five minutes. Someone else may show up, although this is not much of a day for touring, is it?"

While the guide settled accounts, Caitlyn took in the hallway, which had a large staircase on the left and extraordinarily rich brown and gold patterned wallpaper. She examined it closely. "Is this leather?" she asked.

The guide said, "Chinese leather, which means it was produced to look like leather, but it isn't. Only the supremely rich could afford actual leather wall coverings. You'd see that in places on Comm Ave. Of course, because this was indeed imported from China," he indicated the wallpaper with a flourish of his hands, "it's a rarity now. Once upon a time, the gold color was really golden. It's darkened with age. The old central heating system didn't help."

"It's gorgeous."

"'Tis true, 'tis true. That's why I love visitors. Keeps me alert to the beauty that surrounds me." He opened his stance and spread his arms as if about to announce, *And here it is!* The loose cuffs of his bulky sweater moved of their own weight practically down to his elbows. "And from whence comes your interest in this abode? Where are you a student?"

Caitlyn nodded. "Yes. Interdisciplinary. Design, architectural history." She mumbled, "Harvard."

"Marvelous. Anything in particular that intrigues you?"

"How places from this period were built. I'm interested in secret rooms."

"ARE YOU? That's marvelous. I've got one for you!"

Caitlyn was stunned. "Really?"

"REALLY. Between you and me, it's not something that we show as part of the regular tour. Liabilities and such. We don't even publicize it. All that modern legal mumbo-jumbo. And as you will see, there is a certain amount of difficulty involved. But for you, and your particular fascination, which I must say is very unusual for a young woman, and…where was I? But for you, a student, doing research, we will explore the inner sanctum of the Hibbert House. Would you like to see that first? Or shall we latch it on at the end? It doesn't appear that we will have any further companions for this tour so we can do as you wish."

"I'd love to see it now," Caitlyn said, avidly.

"Good. Let me start by taking your coat, which we will place in a closet, which you will see is linked to your unique request."

Caitlyn removed her jacket as she followed the guide to a closet located under the staircase. After he hung her coat on a hook and tucked her knapsack into a corner, he turned and pointed at a door on the other end of the closet. Because its location was under the steps, the ceiling was triangulated, and the inner door, made of about a half dozen interlocking beaded boards, was only about four feet high. Behind it, she speculated, would be about sixty cubic feet of storage space. Hardly a room. She was crestfallen. "That's it?"

Disappointment must have colored her tone. "Oh, ye of little faith," the guide said. "What we tell most visitors, if they ask, and they never do, is that it's storage." He twisted the ends of an imaginary mustache. "A little white lie to avoid difficulties. But the truth is, as they say, infinitely more interesting." He bent over to avoid hitting his head and then unlatched the door. He reached inside and switched on a light, a single uncovered bulb that illuminated a narrow staircase, leading downward.

"As you can see, very, very, very, precarious," he continued, "The august members of the Boston Victorian Ladies Society, fearful as they are, have nightmarish visions of children tripping and falling and hitting their heads and breaking their arms and little bodies and worse. Personally, I think they are a mite over-cautious, but I am merely a lowly volunteer at their service. Shall we proceed? And, of course, I must ask you to be extremely careful. There is no handrail."

He maneuvered around the door, which couldn't be fully opened due to the angled ceiling, and then went first down the staircase. Ducking her head, Caitlyn followed. The stairs groaned and creaked. In the dim light, on the uneven treads, maintaining balance was tricky.

At the foot of the steps was a windowless room, about six feet wide, maybe twelve feet long, seven feet high. The walls were covered with a dirty white and pink striped paper that looked cheap when compared to the entrance hall. A wood floor was painted dark gray. A twin-sized bed took up a lot of space, as did a very plain chest of drawers on which stood a ceramic jug and mismatched washbasin. A chamber pot rested in a corner. The room was airless, stuffy, and ugly.

Yet Caitlyn was elated. This is what a Boston Box was like! After searching for three months, to be in one so unexpectedly was exhilarating and unreal. "Wow! Do you know how this was used?" she asked.

"Absolutely no idea. The last owner, who died in 1950, left a shelf of journals and nothing was mentioned. Once we speculated the room served as accommodations for a workman because a male could not, of course, be housed with the female servants on the fifth floor. Oh, heavens, *quelle scandale,* were that to happen! But that guess is problematic. The furnace of the house is on the other side of that wall." He pointed to the inner wall at the foot of the bed. "That's why it's so warm in here. It makes no sense that he would have to climb up and down to get to it. Why not just build a door off the basement hall, were that the purpose?" He rapped on the longest of the inner walls to show where the hallway was.

"Why indeed?" Caitlyn murmured. "When was the house built?"

"1861. Same time as the place next door. Relatives of the Hibberts. Exterior is shared, but the interiors are very different. That's been renovated, unfortunately."

"1861," she repeated. "This could have been used for runaway slaves." Although the Civil War might have begun, the Emancipation Proclamation would not have been signed.

"That's a noble interpretation. Unfortunately, there's no evidence that the Hibberts, although a wonderful family, had any abolitionist sympathies. Mrs. Hibbert, the matriarch who built this place, was a widow of some means who was quite occupied with managing the household and the lives of her two sons."

"Do you mind if I take some pictures?" she said, showing the guide her phone.

"Oh, please, by all means. Shoot away. I'll get out of your way and meet you upstairs."

Caitlyn tried to contain her excitement. Here it was! An example of what she'd been looking for! A genuine Boston Box! Her work was paying off!

The small space was awkward for snapping photos, and dark, so her flash fired repeatedly. She was just about to finish when she thought she heard the door latch at the top of the stairs. A bolt of panic coursed through her gut. What the hell had she done? She'd just let a strange man lock her in a basement. What a fool! Trapped in a Boston Box! She ran up the steps and tried the handle. It was jammed.

She could feel the guide pulling on the other side. "Please, miss, let it go." She released her grip and the door swung open, the guide bowing down and peering at her. "Sorry. It's quite difficult to maneuver here when the door is ajar. It doesn't swing back fully, see? Hits the ceiling and blocks the space." He demonstrated. "And this latch is not the finest example of nineteenth-century craftsmanship. I should have warned you."

Caitlyn was flustered. "I'm a little claustrophobic," she said, which wasn't true, but she wanted to cover up her idiocy. The stories she'd been reading about tortured women and murdered lovers were distorting her outlook. She glanced back into the room with regret. "I'd like to see more."

The guide looked thoughtful. "Let's do the rest of the tour and then discuss what's possible. How does that strike you? A good idea?"

Caitlyn agreed. They left the closet space together. "Who was the architect?" she asked.

"We don't have a name. We know of a firm, Burns Brothers, which was very much a high society choice for jobs like this, I am told. But a lot of architects worked there, and no one was given credit for this specific design. I think that's the story."

"Just curious. Have you ever heard of the term 'Boston Box'?

The guide shook his head. "Nope," he responded. "Not familiar at all."

His denial didn't concern her. At this point, it wasn't important if the architects who built Boston Boxes called them "Boston Boxes," although that would be a fantastic discovery. Nomenclature could be another facet of her study.

As for the Hibbert House, in and of itself, the museum would not prove her theses, but if she found a few more examples, perhaps from the floor plans of Marlborough Street, perhaps in Chadwick Square, she could establish a pattern, especially if she could prove some relationships among the architects.

She put aside her preoccupation with research to enjoy the rest of the tour. The home was remarkably well preserved. The Hibberts had retained ownership from the time of its construction until the death of its most recent permanent resident, John Hibbert. Inspired by visits to other historic homes, John Hibbert became determined to maintain as much of the house's original furnishings and design as he could, with an eye to making Hibbert House an artifact of its time. On his death in 1950, the home was donated to the BVLS, along with a substantial endowment for its maintenance.

The guide was effusive as he pointed out objects of interest like stereopticons and bedchamber intercoms that the lady of the house could use to summon her husband to her side from his separate bedroom. The tour included the basement floor, where the guide pointed out the wall behind which the secret room was hidden. Anyone without some prior knowledge of its existence would never be aware of it.

At the end of the tour, Caitlyn explained to the guide that the secret room that he had shown her could be an important link in her research, and she hoped he would not get into any trouble if she contacted the BVLS for another visit. He assured her there wouldn't be any consequences for him and invited her to do whatever she needed. He handed her a brochure with contact information. Before she left, unsure of protocol, she tipped the guide five dollars, for which he thanked her profusely. "I know what this means to a poor student, and I will spend it wisely," he said.

"I wish I could give more. You really helped me."

"Give me credit when you publish," he said, jokingly. He led her to the door and opened it.

"I don't know your name."

"Hibbert," he said. "Randy Hibbert." He shrugged.

"Wait a second."

"John is my great uncle," he responded. "Long gone by the time I was born. Never met him." As soon as he spoke, a small group of tourists came into the gates of the museum garden, and he greeted them with a smile. "Welcome, welcome," he said. "Come in. Where are you from?" And with that, he closed the door.

CHAPTER FORTY-SIX

MARK

April 2017

I enjoy my work, but weekdays are never the best times, income-wise, especially if school is in session, the weather is variable, and no conventions are in town. Before leaving in the morning I had to give myself the same internal pep talk that anyone who has a job must sometimes deliver. *Get over it. Go to work. You need the money.*

I didn't think my employers would be too happy if I brought along the gun, and I debated whether I should just leave it at the apartment. But I was never more vulnerable than when giving a tour, out in the open, visible, easy to follow. I listened to my nervousness and decided I had purchased the gun for a reason, and I wasn't going to overcome my anxiety if I didn't keep it with me. I rolled the revolver, locked, in a dishtowel and put it in my knapsack. Then I placed a few bullets in an outside pocket of the sack. Lord knows, if Clarence attacked me suddenly, I'd be unable to respond fast. But with any time to react, like what happened at the KFC, I would have a way to defend myself.

I walked from the apartment to the ticketing kiosk at the Prudential Center where my Duck for the day was parked. Knowing that I carried the gun filled my stomach with acid.

I almost expected the pistol to glow and reveal itself through the nylon of my knapsack. Despite evidence in the news to the contrary every day, I couldn't fathom how anyone got used to carrying these things.

The two tours that I ran were uneventful. Even though my pessimism about the number of riders was borne out, those people who did show up were fun. The city was edging into spring and looked good. Sights like the Christian Science Center and its glimmering pool never failed to lift my spirits. And Clarence didn't buy a ticket, as my runaway imagination had conjured up as a possibility.

I finished by mid-afternoon. A couple of hours of daylight remained, and my curiosity was still fueled by my last night's reading of the coffee table book, so I decided to head over to the South End and see the actual locations that Dave had marked. My quixotic first step.

I ambled to Washington Street. The area wasn't far from the hospital where the medical examiner was located and I'd identified Dave's body. In this part of the neighborhood, brownstones mixed with storefronts. I passed the address near where Dave's car had been found, close to a Thai restaurant. A pair of diners sat there in a window under the place's stenciled name, The Thaiphoon, the letters throwing shadows on their faces. From the evidence of the take-out menus at the apartment, I knew Dave liked Thai food. Maybe a charge on his credit card offered a clue to the timing of his arrival in the South End on the night of his murder. I'd have to check.

I'd once had to learn about this part of the city for a special excursion that a corporation had requested from the Duck company. The route had been complicated because the side streets around here are not congenial to big vehicles, but at least

Washington Street could accommodate a Duck. Washington Street itself has a confusing distinction: many perpendicular streets change their names when they cross it, a sign of honor to George, the street's namesake. Here, at Washington, is where East Newton Street became West Newton Street, or in downtown Boston, where Winter Street becomes Summer Street. But to assure a quotient of Boston quirkiness, the rule isn't applied absolutely, and exceptions abounded.

Perhaps Dave ended up in the South End from confusion. He was relatively new in town. Any geographical hints that names with directions—like the "South" End—had once offered to Bostonians have long been useless. There's a South End and a South Boston, and they're not the same. The latter is nicknamed "Southie." There is a North End, but no North Boston. East Boston is actually further north than the North End. There's never been a West Boston, as far as I can tell, but there was a West End. However, it largely exists in memory, obliterated by urban renewal in the Fifties and Sixties and, in any case, it wasn't very far west. In fact, it's to the east of East Cambridge, just across the river. And don't look for the Old South Meeting House in either South Boston or the South End.

Maybe all this NWSE stuff was helpful before landfill created much of the modern Boston, but I've found it better to think of names like the South End just as labels. Bewildering labels, and no help in getting oriented. I pity out-of-towners. Making sense of it all, I'd be fucked.

I wondered if Dave was fucked. With his criminal history, hanging out in South Boston might have been more logical for him, because Southie was historically one of the bases for organized crime in the city. Maybe that's still true, although older Southie residents have cashed in on gentrification, sold their homes for a bundle and moved to the burbs, mostly neutralizing an inhospitable townie population. Maybe Dave, a stranger in the city, got mixed up on his way to Southie, where he hoped to find some cronies.

I strolled around a one-block square called Blackstone Park. In the corner of the park, a small memorial had been constructed from bouquets of flowers, now dying, and burnt out candles, and teddy bears, most of which looked sun bleached and soggy. The picture of a girl, preteen, was covered by plastic wrap and propped in the middle of the display. I learned her name was Emily from a lavender ribbon adorned with gold letters. I couldn't recall any story in the news. Had she been hit by a car? Killed in a drive-by shooting, a wild bullet? When I returned to the apartment, I'd have a look.

I headed to nearby Franklin Square, on the other side of Washington Street, almost the same size as Blackstone. Some older guys were chatting, and one of them, bundled in a canvas coat, caught my eye. He seemed wary of me. Might he have known Dave? Didn't seem likely. I turned my gaze forward and walked to a corner where a crossing guard, maybe sixty years old, was on duty. She smiled and wished me "good day" as I neared her. I was tempted to ask her if she had seen my brother wandering around, but I didn't have a picture to show her, and even if I did, the odds were nil that he was in that precise spot, or that she would have noticed him, or that she would remember him.

I wandered farther without finding some box in the gutter with "BOSTON" embossed on it, a hint at a product, something that would explain the mysterious note in Dave's possession, and miraculously answering every question I had. At last, I came upon Chadwick Square, much smaller than the other two, really just a street with a narrow strip of parkland in its center, lined with rows of brownstones on either side. A couple of the homes were for sale; some were in the midst of renovation; many were in pristine condition; one of them looked dilapidated. If the secret of Dave's death was in any of those homes, it would be impossible to uncover without more clues. There were just too many possibilities, and I wasn't a cop with permission to knock on doors.

I sat in the park for a moment. These types of places, full of charm, dotted the South End. Chadwick Square probably looked better now than it ever had, if you could ignore the cars. A young woman came out of one of the brownstones and set up a stroller. She reminded me of a common complaint that I'd hear from acquaintances when Paul and I were together: that the formerly very gay South End was being taken over by baby carriages. Shudders usually accompanied these comments.

I wished I'd brought along the coffee table book to compare the photographs against reality. In lieu of that, nothing seemed out of the ordinary. The lanes that framed the park didn't have a lot of traffic. A FedEx truck delivered Amazon boxes to a couple of places. All of the parking places were full, and nobody pulled in or out of one. Without a parking sticker for the neighborhood, Dave would have been forced to leave his car blocks away, possibly as far as the Thai restaurant, if this had been his destination.

The shabbiest home had holiday decorations in an attic window, unlit. As I stared at this house, which was about a hundred feet away, the front door opened, and a pudgy middle-aged man came out. Even from afar, I could tell that he wasn't attractive, that he looked like a potato. Most of his scalp was hidden under a knitted ski cap that had a New England Patriots logo on the front. He wore a canvas car coat, dark olive with an opened corduroy collar, and brown khakis, and black running shoes. Not the stereotype of a sophisticated, well-off South-Ender. He spent some time locking the door, needing at least two or three keys to secure the property. Then he proceeded down the front steps and turned right at the sidewalk, his direction away from me. He didn't see me.

The woman with the stroller returned. She stopped and said hello to the pudgy man, and they chatted a minute or two before moving in opposite directions.

My attempts at observation weren't very rewarding, and it was getting dark, so I stood and walked away. Coincidentally, I was about half a block behind the pudgy guy. He stepped into a corner convenience store. His stop triggered my own cravings; I was thirsty. I just hoped that there weren't any metal detectors that would be set off by the heat I was packing. I snorted. *Packing heat?* What a joke! Unless I removed myself from Dave's world soon, I'd surely be talking about "broads" and "mugs" and "rats."

By the time I entered the store, the pudgy guy had finished his transaction, buying a lottery ticket. He had a full round face given shape by a short-cropped goatee. A clerk said, "Bye, George. See you tomorrow." As he turned, we awkwardly blocked each other's paths, danced back and forth, made eye contact. Face to face, he looked startled to see me. He smelled of perspiration.

I nodded and said, "Excuse me."

George didn't respond before heading out of the store. Typical unfriendly Bostonian.

Had the encounter ended then I probably wouldn't have remembered it. But from inside the store, after I had scanned the layout and located the beverage cases, I saw George look at me again as he walked by the store's window. He was almost checking me out. Maybe he was a repressed gay man. Terribly sad. With his lack of hygiene, I wouldn't predict a great romantic future for him unless he started a beauty regimen. I turned away from his stare.

CHAPTER FORTY-SEVEN

CAITLYN

January 2017

You awake?

Caitlyn texted back. *"hey yes. Hi. How r u, Andrew?"*

Been busy.

"Gd to hear from u. What's going on?"

How's the research?

"fantastic. A great day. Lots of new info, gd leads."

You should tell me about it.

"Sure."

How about now?

Caitlyn paused. *"Ah. late."*

Only 10. C'mon. Come over.

"don't do booty calls."

Not a booty call.

"yes it is."

No it's not. I'm interested in your research. Have a glass of wine. We could relax.

"10 o'clock. it's a booty call. can't travel..."

Take Uber. I'll pay. It'd be great to see you.

"can't. by the time I cleaned up, got there, be late."

I'm a night owl. It'd be fun. C'mon.

"it'd be 11. maybe ltr"

Fine. GREAT.

"didn't mean yes"

I want to hear about your research.

"sure you do"

It'd be fun.

Oh, why not? Caitlyn thought. It would be fun. But the good angel on her right shoulder whispered: *He won't respect you.* The bad angel, on her left shoulder, countered: *This isn't about respect.*

She wrote: *"i'll send a text when I leave"*

GREAT! See you soon.

CHAPTER FORTY-EIGHT

MARK

April 2017

Back at my apartment, after putting the gun and the bullets in their respective hatches, I did a web search for information about recent crimes in the South End. The list was long. A housing project was the scene of several drug busts, including one in which caches of heroin, cocaine, and oxycodone had been recovered, not to mention a few guns. In another, more amusing incident, a young man had been arrested for a series of break-ins after he'd left traceable footprints in snow following one of his crimes. A Dunkin' Donuts had been robbed at gunpoint; so had a bank branch. Three young men had been mowed down by a machine gun in a gang-related incident. Another man was stabbed, same cause. Some people were mugged or robbed. Several vehicles were stolen or broken into.

Three women had been sexually assaulted during the past two months, one of them not too far from Chadwick Square. That victim had been beaten as well. The assailant, who wore a ski mask and whose face was not seen, was described as heavy, a description I could have applied to George, the pudgy guy, as well as hundreds of other men who live in Boston. Yes, George wore a ski cap, but no mention was made of a Patriots logo like the one that decorated his.

Just about every major violent crime was represented on the list, and glancing away from the screen, I shivered. When I'd been there, the neighborhood had looked so peaceful and safe. I took some comfort in knowing that most of the crimes happened at night and that I'd compressed two or three months of illegal activity into a ten-minute reading. It came out to less than one major crime per day, and many of them, like the car thefts, while not fun, didn't endanger anyone's physical safety.

The gang deaths were the only murders besides Dave's. I wasn't blasé about these other killings and regretted them, but I might have been more shaken if they hadn't involved groups—street gangs—to which I didn't belong. I was trying to convince myself I was safe if I walked around in the area. On the other hand, my brother had been murdered, my car vandalized, and I had been beaten up, so my mental attempts at distancing myself from violence deserved a reconsideration.

I remembered the memorial I'd spotted so I did a second search, this time on "Emily" and "South End Boston." Several stories immediately popped up, including an entry in Wikipedia.

Emily Packard was an eleven-year-old who had vanished eight months earlier after saying goodbye to a school friend whom she had visited a block away from her home, not far from the memorial. Her parents were a well-to-do professional couple. Of course, a massive effort had been undertaken to find Emily at the time, but neither the girl, nor evidence of a murder, were located. Rumors had circulated about a suspicious van with out of state plates in the neighborhood, but they were never confirmed. The memorial in the park had been created after a service that marked an anniversary of her disappearance.

My memory jogged, I now recollected the uproar in the city, but I hadn't paid much attention to it. My own life had been at a low point at the time. And in terms of Dave, the event was a detour.

The clock was inching toward eleven o'clock, and I had had a busy day. I checked Dave's credit card bills and saw no charge to the Thaiphoon Restaurant. A dead end there. After that, my tired brain just couldn't come up with any other way to investigate Junior's identity. Additional searching would have to wait until tomorrow.

Before shutting down my laptop, I checked my email and found a message from Clark Hodder. His son would be with his ex-husband over the weekend, and Clark wondered whether I was free on Saturday. He suggested a cup of coffee and a walk in the Arnold Arboretum, a park in the Boston neighborhood of Jamaica Plain. I checked my calendar. I'd no social engagements—when do I ever?—but I didn't remember whether I had a work shift. Lucky for me, I was on-duty on Sunday, but not Saturday. I sent off my response: a "yes," of course.

I might be in my late forties, but I still can get excited about a real date with a real, live man, especially an attractive one. For the first time in a while, I fell asleep hugging my pillow, and with a smile on my face.

CHAPTER FORTY-NINE

CAITLYN

February 2017

Caitlyn began to negotiate a return visit to Hibbert House with the Boston Victorian Ladies Society, which had actually been renamed the New England Victorian Society and was now being led by Jack Conroy, a congenial, older Irish-American guy of some crust and blather. Conroy—not even close to being a Victorian lady—was as cautious as Randy Hibbert had suggested. He worried about the accidents that could occur if visitors climbed down the rickety steps of the room. But he supported research, and Caitlyn convinced him that her academic study would not bring a flood of thrill seekers into the museum. Or, if by chance, as she secretly hoped, publicity about her work should occur someday, an influx of money might be the happy result, since more visitors equaled more income for the NEVS. And they would have plenty of time to prepare for curiosity seekers. Whatever Conroy's concerns, Randy Hibbert's backing of her request literally opened the doors. The wishes of a member of the Hibbert family could not be ignored.

She returned to the room in early February on a day that the museum was closed, which meant she didn't need to rush. Her credentials as a scholar convinced the NEVS that she could look at, pick up, touch the furnishings of the room and not damage them or diminish their worth or walk off with a valuable. Her deepest hope was for a clue about how the room had been used. It had to be more than a workroom—had to be—for there would have been no need to hide such a room.

In the glaring, shadowy light of the single hanging bulb, she probed the room inch-by-inch, carefully lifting the mattress to look under the bed, testing the floor for loose boards, examining the wall for telltale dents or marks, taking too many pictures with her phone of every single object. The item that held the biggest promise of a bonanza was the chest of drawers. It was made of stained pine wood, four drawers over a four-footed base, almost no ornamentation save for glass knobs and a beveled lip on its top. She opened each of the drawers carefully while praying that an object of interest remained inside. Predictably, the drawers were empty.

Having examined everything, Caitlyn rested on the floor, her back against a wall, afraid to sit upon the bed in case that would damage it. Had she missed anything? The bedposts were solid wood, no hollow chambers available for concealment. Small scratches marked the top of the posts, and she got up and twisted and turned the newels in an effort to unscrew them, but they didn't give. The walls were papered, with no mismatched seams to indicate a cut-out or compartment. She sighed. The room was very much just what it looked like, all of its story front and center. Perhaps it had been too optimistic to think that a home under the auspices of a museum committee would not have had every mote of dust completely examined and documented.

In a final effort, she lay on her back and reached under the chest of drawers. Its short wooden feet held the main frame of the chest about three inches from the floor. She was barely able to squeeze her hand in the tight space between the floor and the bottom drawer.

As she reached upward on the base, feeling for God knows what, she noticed that the bottom drawer didn't move. The lowest panel of the chest was separate from the drawer. Caitlyn sat up and pulled the bottom drawer out of the chest frame; it slid easily, without a catch. Impressive. Even cheap furniture of the time had craftsmanship superior to the mass manufacturing of the present. With the lower frame of the chest exposed, she realized that about two inches of space, hidden in the base beneath the lowest drawer, was not accounted for. She moved her fingers around the baseboard of the chest and felt something move. She pressed down and could sense a movement. She pushed again and heard a sound like the unlatching of a hook. A board popped up, as if on a spring, revealing a compartment.

Inside was a pamphlet entitled *Available Pleasures*. The silhouette of a woman's head, cameo-style, decorated the cover. "Mrs. Marian's Castle" was printed on the bottom of the page in ornate type. The booklet was very old, the paper brown with age. Nevertheless, it appeared sturdy enough to withstand an inspection. She'd brought along a pair of disposable latex gloves, so before proceeding, she put them on, and then lifted the item from the drawer.

On the frontispiece was a short index, and each item on the list was matched with a page number: *Displaying, Fucking, Parties, Special Tastes, Our Ladies*, and several more. The second page noted that Mrs. Marian's hostesses could be enjoyed at her place of residence in the North End on Unity Street or at a customer's home.

Under *Displaying*, the "pleasures" included a special private dance, living tableaux with two or more "sensual ladies," or, if a customer wished, the opportunity to dress in frilly garments. *Fucking* offered basic missionary position intercourse. Surcharges would be applied for other, less common positions, like doggie style or hostess on top.

Caitlyn read along, rapt. Sections outlined activities such as bondage and discipline, threesomes, massages, sponge baths, and more. Boys were available. The final pages gave little biographies of the women who worked for Mrs. Marian. The range of body types, races, and skills was impressive in its breadth. Pencil marks indicated that someone had checked off many of the names on the list, like a scorecard.

The pamphlet was a Victorian sex take-out menu.

Caitlyn examined the little book for an hour and then, on hearing some movement above, photographed its pages before she put it back where she had found it. After an exhale, she snickered, titillated, imagining Victorian sexual escapades. Those scratches on the bedposts now brought to mind *50 Shades of Gray*.

A volunteer attendant, auburn-haired and docile, was on duty at the Hibbert House's offices. Caitlyn joined her upstairs and asked about how the artifacts of the museum had been documented. The woman told her that the final occupant, John Hibbert, was extremely careful in his later years to keep things as they were. Many of the purchase records for the furniture survived so there was no need to x-ray or otherwise examine most of the items since their origins were verified by the actual receipts.

Caitlyn surmised that the chest of drawers was now where it had always been, never restored, never a cause for suspicion. Its age, not its design, were what made it of interest. Since everything else in the Hibbert House was also old, the chest didn't stand out. The secret drawer hadn't been detected and the pamphlet had remained undiscovered. Caitlyn said nothing about it to the attendant. Given its unsavory character, and the possible implications for a member of the Hibbert family, she wanted to pick the proper moment to discuss it with Conroy and the NEVS.

CHAPTER FIFTY

MARK

April 2017

Finding Junior without a single identifying characteristic remained a quandary. I weighed tactics while drinking coffee and watching the morning news shows. I talked to Dave's urn: *Any suggestions? Did you have any contact with the kid at all?* The urn didn't answer. Never did.

Perhaps a discussion with the doctor in charge of Dave's case would help. A business card with the name of the physician, Dr. Niles Monroe, was included with the stack of papers that Taylor had given me. Monroe was affiliated with a cancer clinic down the street from the Fenway Grand. I called the phone number on the card, and after I made my way through a gauntlet of automated and human obstacles, I ended up in the voicemail box of a physician's assistant named Elizabeth. I left my number and a rambling explanation of why I was contacting her, hung up, and then waited for a callback.

My mind wandered. Should I go to the place where Dave's body was found? Would that reveal anything? To the urn: *Do you have advice on this?*

Elizabeth rang back within a half-hour. I elaborated on my message and the purpose of my call. She responded with a protesting voice. "Dr. Monroe, his schedule is impossible unless it's an emergency. Besides, a patient's records are confidential."

The bureaucratic wall. So damn frustrating. "I have power of attorney for Dave's estate. Does that make a difference?"

Elizabeth was quiet for a moment before saying, "Yes. A power of attorney can help. As for your brother's case, I could try to get you an appointment with Dr. Monroe, but honestly, his calendar is crazy. He's an expert in his field, he travels, his patients. It could be months. David spoke here a few times with a hospital social worker. Charlotte McBride. Let me give you her number and email, and why don't you see where that goes? If she doesn't work out, get back to me, then we'll try the doctor."

Sounded good to me. I thanked Elizabeth for her help and then made another run through the fires of hospital phone hell before getting to Charlotte McBride's voice mailbox to leave yet one more message. Nobody answers their phones anymore. To double my chances of a speedy reply, I also sent an email.

About an hour later, almost noon, Charlotte McBride responded to my email. Very professional tone, expressing sorrow for my loss. An appointment for later in the afternoon had been canceled, she wrote, and we could talk then by phone if I was available. I got back to her at once and said, presuming that her offices were part of the clinic's complex and close by, that I would prefer to meet face-to-face. I suggested that we could go to a food court that served the hospital community. I hadn't left the apartment yet today, and I craved a connection with a human being. She answered, agreed to my request, and proposed an exact time and place. She asked me to bring a copy of the power of attorney for her files.

Progress! Now all I had to do was figure out how to ask about Junior without asking about Junior.

CHAPTER FIFTY-ONE

CAITLYN

February 2017

Caitlyn tried old-fashioned methods to find information about the Hibbert House's architect: library visits, files at the Boston Architectural Society, a search of contemporary newspapers and periodicals, that is, when she could find them. She compiled yet another list, this time of the men who worked at Burns Brothers, the firm responsible for the construction. So far, nothing had linked a particular architect to Hibbert House, although one of them, a man named Arthur Gannigan, caught her attention because he'd died young, in his early thirties, in a fall at a construction site. Details about the accident, however, were vexingly few.

As for the blueprints of Pearson Jeffries's Marlborough Street house, lent to Caitlyn by Lisa Allsbrook, they were faded and almost indecipherable. Even scanning didn't help. She was about 75% certain that the documents showed a room that mirrored almost exactly the Boston Box at the Hibbert House: a concealed stairway entrance leading to a chamber in the basement level. But she couldn't be sure due to the discoloration of the blueprint and the imprecision of the draftsman who created it. Was that indeed a solid wall in the basement? Or was there a door? She might be able to declare it a "Boston Box" definitively if she overlaid the anecdotal material about Jeffries's crimes in his basement.

Despite the stop-and-go-and-stop of her scholarship, she reminded herself that she'd accomplished plenty in a relatively short period—just three months. That all of the pieces didn't yet fit wasn't surprising. At least there were pieces to put together.

Her biggest ongoing frustration was the failure of Rumberg to answer her query. She didn't want to go over to his residence and bang again on the door without knowing whether he was home. However, random visits might be necessary to catch him.

Caitlyn decided to go to Professor Venda's office for a consultation about Rumberg and other tactics when she spotted her mentor in Harvard Yard having a conversation with none other than Dr. Bacht. The two of them walked side by side, and their discussion appeared to be heated, although Caitlyn was too far away to hear any of their words. She ducked into a classroom building to let them pass, feeling silly but happy to avoid Bacht. As she waited for them to move out of sight, Caitlyn realized she was disturbed to see Venda chatting with her nemesis, even angrily, but she couldn't pinpoint why.

The Boston Box wasn't Caitlyn's only preoccupation. The students had returned from winter break, and her assistantship duties had resumed. She continued to work on her thesis.

And then there were men.

Her night with Andrew, the booty call, had been almost two weeks ago. The physical chemistry had been incredible. She wondered if he was always that good, no matter whom he was with, if he was a skilled lover who brought all of his partners to such a peak. She preferred to think that their connection was special, that she made him play his best game. But a question about their attraction wasn't one she could ask. *Is it special with me?* Yuck. She'd never hear from him again.

She wanted more, of course: more meetings, more Andrew. But after that night, he'd more or less disappeared.

On the other hand, Henry was persistent. Henry would take "no" for an answer, but only as a response to an individual invitation, and not as a prohibition against another attempt. They'd dated a few more times, and it was increasingly evident that he was really into her, much more than she was into him. She liked Henry. She just liked Andrew more at the moment, and so she asked herself whether hanging out with Henry was settling for second best, a deliberation that was the kiss of death for Henry.

She and Henry were at a point where her conscience was delivering sermons about leading him on. Caitlyn had steered clear of having "the talk," the one with declarations that "I'm not in love with you," the one where she'd emphasize that she dated other men.

Valentine's Day loomed, and Henry had hinted at a date. Going out with Henry on VD would send the completely wrong message. But if she refused him, what else would she do on that most awful day of the year to be single? Stare at the phone, hoping that Andrew would text? She'd spent other VDs in that manner, and they were miserable. Knowing that she had turned down time with Henry and chosen to be alone wouldn't help.

And nagging at her was the fear that she'd regret Henry someday. "How much" was unclear. Part of her wanted to ask Henry to give her time, let her head clear. Maybe she was needing sex, lots of it, just temporarily, more than she needed love. Sensation. Why did she feel that way right now? Was it good or bad for her psyche? The impact of David Chieswicz?

Speaking of which, when her mother called, they talked mostly of day-to-day matters, their ordinary checking in. Since the holidays, they had only discussed David Chieswicz once, when Sylvia had said she'd told him that Caitlyn did not want to meet. If her mother had any other details, she hadn't offered them. Caitlyn was grateful for her mother's discretion. Any further mention of David Chieswicz was unwelcome. She wished she could imagine him out of existence.

CHAPTER FIFTY-TWO

MARK

April 2017

With reluctance, and relief, I left the gun at the apartment when I headed to the appointment with Charlotte McBride. Since I would be entering the hospital complex, I wasn't certain whether or not there would be bag inspections or metal detectors. During the short walk to the clinic, my mental radar was tuned to the shape of Clarence's black Mercedes, but no blips ever flashed.

Boston's Longwood medical area has a cluster of what seems like dozens of hospitals, clinics, medical schools, and other related businesses. Years ago, these institutions were distinct, but now, thanks to mergers and cross-collaboration and connected indoor pathways, they all run together like a big city that has swallowed its suburbs.

The food court where I was to meet Charlotte McBride was at the junction of two of the largest buildings, and it catered to staff and hospital visitors. Except for the fact that half of its customers wore scrubs, it wasn't too different from what you'd find in any mall. There were fast food hamburgers, pizza, and a place with vats of Chinese food, with free tastes of bourbon chicken on top of a counter. Every person living in the USA has sampled that dish. The air was scented with sugar and grilled meat.

I stood in front of a Starbucks and waited for Charlotte McBride before ordering a drink; if she wanted something, I'd treat. She arrived a few minutes late, not enough for me to be annoyed. To the contrary, some people are instantly likable, and Charlotte McBride was one of them. Very slender, dark brown hair styled with a short frizz, probably dyed, trendy black framed glasses, thin-lipped. Around forty years old. Wedding band with a matching engagement ring. Nice-sized rock. She smiled warmly, looked intelligent and sensible, and she radiated trustworthiness. She insisted I call her "Charley." My offer to buy her a coffee was refused with a rueful declaration that she couldn't handle caffeine after noon. I had no such concerns and got a cup, and then we found a table removed from the noisier fray.

"Let's take care of business," she said. "Can I see the power of attorney?" I retrieved the copy I'd made and gave it to her. After a quick scan, she said, "Great. I can keep this?" I nodded yes. She continued, "So how can I help you?"

Because I felt comfortable with her, I thought I could be honest. Well, almost honest. "My brother and I hadn't spoken for years. I know nothing about him anymore. I was hoping, maybe, you could tell me about him, like maybe people I should notify. I just feel like I walked into the life of a stranger and now I have to tie up the loose ends without a clue. The police said he listed me. Total surprise."

"This must be so hard," she said. "Emotional."

"No. Not really. At least I don't think so. I'm not heartless. The truth is it was over twenty-five years since I last saw Dave. We were virtually strangers."

She nodded. "He mentioned that. I think he felt really bad about it."

"He was sick and getting sentimental, I bet. Not that he did anything about it. With me."

"Lots of things come out when people die," Charley said.

"Yeah? What came out for him?"

"For David? He was scared, I think. Wouldn't you be? He was hard to read. Lots of bluster. 'If I go, I'm going in style.' But I was thinking more about the people they leave behind sometimes. Someone like you. If you weren't at peace with your brother, that chance to heal, to come to an understanding, maybe a reconciliation, that's over. You're left with the emotional mess. He's gone, though, and it becomes a time to act out."

"I reconciled with Dave a long time ago. In my head."

"How did you do that, exactly?"

"I wrote him off. Just like he did with me. Turnaround. Fair play."

"That's sad," she said. "I'm sorry. But death is another matter entirely. You should watch yourself. Anger, grief…they do strange things. Feelings you thought were over and done with all come back. Especially with surviving family members."

When I had set up this appointment, I hadn't anticipated being analyzed myself. I drank my coffee. It was scalding hot and singed my tongue and the roof of my mouth. "Shit," I muttered. And then, "Sorry. He mentioned me? The police said he did."

"Part of an intake. Nearest living relative."

"He told you but didn't tell me."

"I think he was about to get to it. Actually, he didn't mention you at first. It was only recently. Prodding. It was just a matter of time until he reached out to you."

I was silent.

"So, Mark," she said, "do you know what I do? With patients?" I shook my head no. "I'm not a therapist. That comes into play, the counseling, handholding, I have credentials, but my chief function is more about bureaucracy. Helping patients through the system. Social work. With your brother, because he was on his own, we were working out his care plan for his treatment. He was about to start chemo. It would be debilitating."

"He hadn't begun?"

"No. His health insurance wasn't in order, moving from state to state. Another thing we were doing. We were waiting for authorizations. He wasn't good with things like that. Using a computer. Treatments like your brother's would be tens of thousands of dollars, especially if he were to be hospitalized at any point. As it was, given his lack of resources..." I must have looked surprised. "I mean, emotional resources, friends, family, like that, in the area. Providing home nursing visits would be costly. Treatment was supposed to start around now, actually. If he were alive." She shuddered and was visibly distressed. "His murder was such a shock. I was shaking when I first heard about it. Hard to believe. It must be horrible for you."

"It's unreal." Once again, as with Russ and others, I was struck by the oddity of being with someone who had interacted with Dave more recently than I had, who had seen how he, as a man in his fifties, had breathed, spoken, walked, moved. "For most of my adult life, it was as if he was dead already."

"It's tragic," Charley said.

"Just the way it was. But his treatments. He was taking pills, I thought. For his cancer. That must have cost him."

"He had some money, for the meantime, but he wanted to limit his liability. That made sense. I mean, if he lived, he'd need money, right? In his case, a few weeks to wait wasn't going to be significant, health-wise. I think the pills were for discomfort. It's the long haul, long delays, that could hurt you. Him."

"Why did he come to Boston? Do you know that?" I presumed that he was hiding from Russ but maybe he had another purpose.

"Treatment is what he said. He'd read somewhere, or heard it, that the clinic was the best place for his kind of cancer, so that was what he wanted. He was right about that, too. His cancer wasn't common, but there's research going on here. Some experimental protocols. Even so, it seemed peculiar to me, and I questioned him, since he would be a stranger here, but..."

"What?" I said.

"He was isolated. Maybe it was for you."

My body stiffened. I hated that I still couldn't muster any pity for my brother. "Or someone else?"

"He never mentioned anyone else. Obviously, he provided your name and number. David said you weren't close, but he didn't say you were completely estranged. Evidently, he didn't speak the truth. I could have sworn he said he saw you. But no?"

"What number did he give you?"

"I have to check." She took an iPad from a handbag and typed some info. In a minute, she read aloud a number.

"That's where I work," I said.

"Perhaps he was embarrassed to contact you."

"Or maybe he just didn't want to. Looking for any option other than his gay brother. Or maybe he was lying to you."

"You're gay?"

I nodded.

"He must have really done a number on you," Charley said.

"That's a way of putting it. Well, he's dead. Nothing more to be done. The police spoke to you."

"Yes. But he never called you? Interesting. We pushed him on it. He was facing some very hard times."

"He never talked about anyone except me?"

She shook her head no.

"How about his background? His work history?" My tone may have been mocking in saying that last phrase.

"You mean, did he tell us about his arrests? No. The police hinted at them. Ordinarily, it's not something we'd ask about."

"No?"

"It's not relevant," she answered. "We don't put ourselves in the place of refusing patient care because of that." She shrugged. "Insurance is another matter." A pause. "You look disappointed? Why?"

"Do I?" I asked. "Maybe. In some ways, I'm relieved. I'm trying to find out if there was anyone in Dave's world who I should tell about this. About him. I don't know if I can explain exactly why that's important to me. I'm trying to convince myself that I'm doing the right thing by Dave, it could be, even though he didn't deserve it. My own peace of mind."

"Death does strange things. I keep saying. Do you feel guilty?"

"About Dave? Absolutely not. He was the one who abandoned me. I'd nothing to do with his death. Just left with the mess. If anything, I'm pissed off. Brings back too many bad memories."

"I see," she said. "His end was so harsh. David and I met a few days before he died. That's such an odd experience. You wonder what you would have said had you known."

I sighed.

"You look disappointed, again," she said. "What's going on with you?"

"My brother," I answered. "I can't express it. I didn't know him anymore. It wasn't my fault. The separation. His choice. But my family is all gone now. There's no one."

She knitted her brow, hesitated. "Mark, get some help with it."

"Therapy? Done enough of that about Dave and the rest. Through with it."

"Not for Dave, then. For yourself. You're dealing with loss. Don't underestimate what you've undergone here. Trauma. Losing family."

For a moment I flashed on Paul. I'd seen a psychotherapist following my breakup, but my insurance coverage for therapy had maxed out. Maybe if I got the inheritance.

Charley continued. "If you're going to grieve, you should channel it in a way that's healthy, not destructive. He hurt you once, and he's done it again by coming back into your life, in a way, and then dying. I don't want to make judgments about David. I didn't know him well enough. Or what he did to you, with you. Just find someone to talk to." She frowned. "Can I say something?"

"Of course."

"You are a lot like him in some ways. I think much smarter than him. But you look like him. And you both have...I don't know. What? An air about you. He seemed a little lost."

"Doesn't everybody?"

She smiled. "Some more than others. Some people are just happy. Anyway, think about what I said. I have referrals."

"I'll keep it in mind."

With that, we stood, and I thanked her. We walked into a bracing April breeze, said our goodbyes, and separated. I immediately missed her warmth.

On my trek to the Fenway Grand, I should have been exhilarated. If I ran into dead ends in my search for Junior, the entire estate would be mine. Instead, I felt sad. And something else. But what? The fact that Dave almost reached out didn't change my feelings about him. He was only going to approach me if circumstances put a gun to his head.

A gun metaphor came into my brain because I spotted Clarence's car circling the block. How the hell was he able to find me? Did he plant a radio transmitter up my ass somehow? Sleep in a tent outside of the Fenway Grand?

He neared me in the Mercedes, slowed down, and gave me the finger. Because I was out in public, and close to home, he would be unable to harm me physically. He was only trying to intimidate me. And making good work of it.

Since I was unarmed, I quickened my step for about two hundred feet. But as my heart rate increased, so did my anger. Already been churned up by my conversation with Charley, my feelings pressed on me, ached for a release.

So I stopped hurrying, adopted a more leisurely pace, even slow, and waited for Clarence to pass by again. When he did, I pointed my right index finger at him and pulled an imaginary trigger. He didn't react, just looked like his usual dumb-fuck self. A college-aged female pedestrian walked by me. Her expression revealed that she thought I was scary nuts. She hitched up her backpack and scurried along. Clarence drove off.

Charley had suggested that I was like my brother. Dave was a criminal. I began to wonder about my own tendencies as I returned my imaginary gun to its imaginary holster.

CHAPTER FIFTY-THREE

CAITLYN

February 2017

An invitation to get out of town to Vermont for a brief ski trip with a friend from Penn State made it possible for Caitlyn to avoid her Valentine's Day problem. She mentioned her intention to go away a few times when Henry was around at the office, and he got the message. She read his reactions as amused, patient, exasperated, but he asked her for lunch anyway, didn't show signs of giving up. A difficult conversation lay ahead.

Meanwhile, Andrew was MIA. He had sent a text at 11:30 PM one Wednesday night, a "Hello," that she ignored, another booty call. For several days after that, she wasn't sure if she wanted to hear from him again. She hoped to be more than a friend with benefits with Andrew, even if their playing together felt somewhat mutual. An impulse to pull back from him to a more scholastically oriented distance was probably too late.

As for the Boston Box, over the past week or two, what drove Caitlyn was the idea that the architects she'd centered on—Adamston/Hawkins, Simpson—had had an alliance or professional relationships, that they had collaborated and exchanged information on things like a Boston Box. If present-day Boston was any indication, the circles of specialists in a field were small. Caitlyn crossed paths with the same women over and over again at events aimed at local architects. Declare an interest in Boston, especially in a very defined subject, and over time you would meet many of the others in town who shared your passion. That must have been true as well when the population of the city was smaller. Unfortunately, the records from the earlier era, such as those for architectural organizations, were either spotty or so broad in scope, like digitized copies of old newspapers, that searching through them had been, thus far, an unrewarding, time-consuming slog. And that was without including that other architect, Gannigan, who had died young in an accident and who still nagged at her.

Professor Venda, good fairy godmother that she was, floated by Caitlyn's office late one morning, and after an appeal, she listened to a summary of the problem.

"You are looking too narrow," Venda responded. "You look only at architecture."

"Yes, obviously." Caitlyn wanted to add, *Duh.*

"Open your eyes. Look elsewhere! What of other connections? Family? Marriages? Children? Or schools. Harvard? Even then. Or religion."

Caitlyn felt chastened and dumb. Her subjects could have crossed paths in so many ways. Genealogical tables had already helped with Josiah, and the tie to Andrew, and they could be beneficial here, too. And Harvard class records were mountainous and easily accessed. If any of her subjects had studied together here, the relationship would be easy to trace. "Common sense," Caitlyn said. "I should have thought of it."

"My heavens. Not to berate yourself! You move in a good direction! *Trés vite!*" She paused. "It is all very sinister. You must be careful."

"I'm not sure I understand," Caitlyn responded.

"Secret rooms, Boston Boxes, all very amusing. Yet the discoveries you are making! Women being tortured. Hidden sex practices. Yes, I know that some such sex practices are harmless. Yet one begins to believe that there is some unfortunate... what? Energy? Karma? Something sinister behind all of this."

"Even so," Caitlyn said, "we are talking of very long ago."

"Not so very long. You are young. It perhaps appears to be ancient history, like the Greeks, the Romans, but truly, it is just a moment ago. Yes, I know I am being superstitious and eccentric. And perhaps European. I have such blood in me. But one wonders. The sinister element, wasn't it what attracted to you initially to this study?"

"I wouldn't say that. It was just a rich topic. And fresh, unexplored."

"Do not misunderstand me, please. I have encouraged you before and encourage you yet. But I believe that one must recognize, must judge, if you will, the impulses that may have inspired this design. Inspired is the wrong word. Stimulated? Aroused? That there may be a kind of evil that led men to make these boxes."

"I don't disagree, but I don't know yet. Yet a room, in the end, is neutral. Not good, not evil."

"An interesting question. This thing you found, you talked about, this menu...is that neutral? It was a way to subjugate those women. There could be, if one looks at it in a certain way, an evil purpose attached."

"All of the rooms might not be for that," Caitlyn protested. "There was the Underground Railroad."

"I am simply asking that you are careful. There may be, even to this day, those who do not want any secrets to be revealed. I do not say this is true, I can see your doubt again, but this is just for your thought. That one must—that you must—take care. You must be open to the possibility that some of your explorations in the present will not be welcomed."

The conversation confused Caitlyn. Did Professor Venda believe the rooms were haunted? Evil? Was she referring to Bacht? Or was she giving into a poetic impulse, granting a personality to an object, an entity? Probably she was just revolted by some of the stories that Caitlyn had told. And she admitted to herself that at least one of them was horrible.

After they parted, Caitlyn used her laptop and looked at Simpson's information. He graduated from Harvard in 1852. She was able to pull up a class list but there was no reference to Adamston in that class—no surprise there, he was older—or anywhere else. But Gannigan was in the Class of 1854. She wondered whether, in those days, older students like Simpson mingled with younger ones like Gannigan. Venda's admonitions rung in her ear. It was silly to limit the possibilities. Harvard connections didn't stop at the Yard or at graduation. Whether or not the two architects had met while at the university was almost immaterial. Because of their common matriculation at Harvard and their living in Boston, an acquaintanceship was almost guaranteed.

That still left Adamston to be tied into the collaborative circle. Josiah Hawkins had no Harvard affiliation. But at least she'd just made a tentative link between two of them, and before she turned that victory into a failure, she decided to take a break and celebrate it, and she knew exactly how.

An exhibition ran at the Museum of Fine Arts, a show of watercolors by John Singer Sargent. Several friends had seen it and declared it breathtaking. She loved the MFA and could never visit it enough. The exhibition's end was nearing. Today would be the day to see it.

She'd have more fun with company. She thought of Sophie, or Svenda, and checked an online scheduler where she discovered they were in classes for the rest of the afternoon. As fate would have it, according to the scheduler, Henry was free.

She sent him a message: *"sup?"*

Hey. Sup?

"want to go to the MFA?"

Sure. When?

"now"

I can't do now.

"☹"

I could do in about two hours.

"☺"

Meet you at the kiosk? 3:30?

Knowing that they were to meet outdoors, with a definite plan, made her feel more at ease. There would be little or no opportunity to get physical. But having made the date, she wondered too late—even with some limits—whether it was a good idea.

CHAPTER FIFTY-FOUR

MARK

April 2017

I arranged to meet Clark for lunch at a coffee shop in Jamaica Plain, JP, a hipster Boston neighborhood, more or less halfway between our two homes. Afterward, if the weather cooperated, we'd go for a walk. I cleaned myself up and chose one of Dave's laundered shirts to wear along with my favorite of his sweaters. The bruises on my face were almost all gone. Measured on the Brad Pitt scale, I wasn't beautiful, but for me I looked good.

Because of yesterday's pissing contest with Clarence, my resolve to take no risks was firm, and I packed the gun. When I got into the BMW, I set the sack gently down next to me, nervous that the pistol and ammo would spontaneously combust. I parked the car near the coffee shop. Not having seen any sign of being followed, I considered whether to leave the bag behind, but the threat of an episode with Clarence outweighed my doubts. Of course, I'd only go for the gun if Clarence appeared, and only if threatened with violence. I judged the chances of another confrontation to be extremely slim.

The coffee shop was more like an upscale, self-service corner store that also offered salads, pastries, sandwiches, soups. About ten butcher-block tables were bunched in the shop's front corner near to a wall of windows. The customers were about as mixed as a crowd in Boston can get: a young couple with a child, some older Latinas, a jumble of Millennials and Gen Yers of various hues. Clark and I represented the gay community. JP is nothing if not diverse.

We ordered sandwiches and then huddled at a two-seater. At first, Clark did the talking, and his main subject was his son Oliver, who was almost eleven years old. Clark was a man for whom fatherhood was an avocation. He told about the grueling adoption procedure, how long it had taken, how he wished he had a second child. Oliver does this, Oliver does that. For me, who often wonders whether I could ever manage owning a cat again someday, Clark's assuming responsibility for a kid was admirable and inspiring, even when he spoke about parenting as fervidly as an evangelist. His insistent passion for being a dad was curbed by a sweetness about him, and by admissions that he was lonely sometimes, that he didn't have much of a social life outside of relatives.

I let him talk, enjoying the excuse to just listen and stare at him. Clark wouldn't turn heads on first glance, but on second glance, there was much to savor. Behind his hornrims were dark brown eyes, and rich, long eyelashes. An easy smile. By the end of our sandwiches, I was increasingly charmed and felt the onset of a crush. I hadn't been infatuated for a while, and I didn't want it to end. We finished our sandwiches. "Up for a walk in the Arboretum?" I asked.

"Let's do it."

We bussed our trays and bundled up, and I carefully slung the strap of my knapsack over my left shoulder. Metal clinked, probably some clasps, but I worried whether the sound was caused by the gun. I easily could have dropped the bag off at the car but reminded myself of the dangers and dismissed the idea. The noise, whatever it was, didn't last.

Outdoors, the sky was crisp, blue, clean, and without clouds, and the temperature in the fifties was practically tropical for Boston at this time of year. We strolled through the residential streets of JP toward the park. "So how old are you, anyway?" I asked him.

"Thirty-eight."

"I'm forty-seven."

"I know. From your application."

"That's a gap."

He shrugged. "I guess we'll find out. You seem younger."

"You seem older." Clark made a look of mock offense. "Not in appearance," I corrected. "Obviously. I mean, being a father. Doesn't it ever wear you down?"

"Sometimes. Sure. But it's what I always wanted. Oliver is the center of my galaxy. He feeds me."

It was too soon to ask if there was room in that galaxy for another star but not too soon to wonder. "You seem so together," I said. "That's good."

"Have to be. Once you're a dad."

We reached our destination, the Arnold Arboretum, a link in Boston's Emerald Necklace of parks. A 200-acre sprawl, the Arboretum is over a century old. The park holds thousands of species of trees, shrubs, and such, and serves as a learning lab for botanists, but for most people it simply offers a splendid opportunity to amble over a large expanse of well-tended hillocks. Not a hidden treasure, exactly—it's popular in Boston—but because it's a few miles from downtown, mostly locals—and not tourists—visit it. Everyone there today seemed to have a dog. Or a kid. Or both. But mostly dogs. All kinds of dogs.

As we ambled, Clark turned his attention to me, asked about my work, my relationship with my ex, and more about Dave. I tried to answer him truthfully, but at times I was uneasy, especially when we broached the subject of my brother and everything connected to him. I didn't want to scare Clark off by suggesting I was being stalked by a group of gangsters. Because the inheritance problems had to be resolved soon, one way or the other, I hoped that my omissions would reflect my ultimate reality of peace and prosperity.

Then Clark talked again, this time about his family on Massachusetts's south shore, a passel of parents and siblings who had become the village that helped him raise his son. I envied him his family.

We walked up a paved incline toward the park's highest point. The path rose in a gentle spiral that eased the climb. About midway to the summit, above us, standing like a sentinel in a clearing on a higher rise, was a solitary man, clad in jeans and winter jacket, his hands on his hips. I could have sworn that he was watching us, yet from the vantage where he stood, the view was marvelous, and it was possible that he was simply taking in a sweeping vista of the Arboretum.

This much I was sure of: it wasn't Clarence. But until that very minute, I hadn't considered the idea that Clarence might have a lieutenant or two. I couldn't tell my fears to Clark, or even signal them, but inside, I groaned. Playing cat-and-mouse was difficult enough with one cat on the prowl. How would I outwit a clutter of kittens?

"Are you okay?" Clark asked.

"What? Oh, sure. Just enjoying the fresh air."

"You seem distracted."

"Not at all. I'm enjoying this. Hearing your voice."

He smiled.

We continued to walk up the spiral, talking, when I noticed that the sentinel had reversed his course and was heading downward in our direction. My stomach tightened. I drew my knapsack more closely to me and calculated next steps. We were out in a very public area, people all around us. There was no way he would attack me. But that didn't mean he couldn't make a scene. Should I get out the gun? In front of Clark? Ridiculous. He would never forgive me.

The sentinel approached, his hands in his pockets. He knew I was watching him. Closer.

Clark spoke. "Hi."

The sentinel smiled. "Hi." He passed us and continued along the path.

False alarm.

"Did you know him?" I asked Clark.

"Him? Oh, no. Just being friendly. Probably second nature from the bank. You have to greet everybody."

I was troubled by my overreaction. Or maybe it wasn't a false alarm. Maybe, because there were two of us, the sentinel delayed an altercation with me and would lie in wait at another location. In any case, he was now out of sight.

At the top of the path was a flat patch, about a thousand square feet, with a circle of cement benches and a crude wooden railing held up by a series of uneven stone posts. You could turn around and see, off in different directions, the spine of Boston's skyline, the mountains of the Blue Hills, the Arboretum's full extent, and the nearby parkway that edged its borders.

"This is beautiful," I said. "I should come here more often."

"I'm here all the time with Oliver. Or it seems that way. Oh, hi!" I turned to see who Clark was addressing, fearing that the sentinel had returned. But no. A male couple, younger, sat upon one of the stone benches, petting a blissful Golden Lab, his leash on the ground. "Some friends," Clark said.

He strode toward them, and I followed. Clark's friends had the shiny smiles, symmetrical countenances, thin physiques, expensive haircuts, and labeled clothing of gay A-listers. One of them stood to hug Clark and then shake my hand, and the only way to avoid being awkward was for me to put my knapsack on the ground, where I lodged it between my feet. "Jay," the standing friend said. "And this is Robert." Robert remained seated, petting the dog. I leaned over and shook his hand. The Lab moved toward me, started to nudge my leg, sniffing my knapsack. "That's Max," Jay said. "He likes your bag. Get back, Max."

Max lifted his head, looked happy, and then lowered his snout again and poked the knapsack's front pocket. With my luck, he was probably a former DEA animal, trained to sniff out weaponry. The bag fell over backward. "I think there's a protein bar in there somewhere," I said. "He probably smells it."

Max barked, looked eager, the happiest pain-in-the-ass in the world.

I picked up the bag, worrying that my gun would somehow tumble out, and Max tensed, seeming to anticipate that I was about to play with him. "No sticks, boy. Sorry. No treats."

Max barked again.

Jay said, "He's protecting us, I think. Come back, Max."

Max backed off and took his place next to Robert at the bench.

"I'm harmless, Max," I said. "I promise."

But I wasn't. I was carrying a gun. As the other three guys talked about what a great day it was, the break in the weather, and other inconsequential matters, I pretended to listen. But my spirits tumbled and landed with a crash. Clark was good-looking, a nice guy, and by my mere presence I was bringing him into my sphere, a dangerous one, exposing him unknowingly to harm. He had a child, for God's sake! What the hell was I thinking? Why did I ever think it was a good idea to spend time with him? Bringing a gun! When did I become so warped? And I couldn't blame Dave for this selfish stupidity. It was all mine.

I suddenly wanted nothing more than for the afternoon to end, to get Clark away from me and safe. Once his conversation with his acquaintances drew to a close, I stopped dawdling, gave up on enjoying the view, and headed to a shortcut that led to the Arboretum's gate. What had been a leisurely stroll I turned into a sprint. I made some kind of excuse and assured Clark that everything was fine. He was probably confused, and while drowning in my own distress, I believed his puzzlement was for the best. I wanted him to dislike me, to stay away. He was a decent guy and unless I got my life in order, I wasn't a fit companion for him.

Not far from the park gate, the sentinel sat on a bench, hands still in pockets, watching the world go by. He was probably just another guy, outdoors and enjoying the day, but I had converted him into an evil being who stalked me. I felt scorched by my flawed suspicions, burned by my fear. *Clarence, if anything ever happens to Clark, I swear to God, I'll kill you, you son of a bitch.*

"Are you all right?" Clark asked.

"Yeah, sure," I said. *Hate me*, I thought. *I like you. But hate me. Get away.*

"You didn't care for Jay and Robert," he said. "I really don't know them that well. I was at dinner parties with them a few times. Mutual friends."

"No, not at all," I said. "They seem nice enough. Cute dog."

"What's wrong? Something's upset you."

"I'm not upset," I lied. I was getting good at that. "Honest." And then I fell silent.

We retraced our steps to the area near our cars. Knowing that my behavior disturbed Clark, I wanted to assure him somehow before we parted that he was not the cause. I wanted to tell him how much I liked him, how much I wished we could go back to my place or his place and hang out. I wanted to hold him in my arms for the rest of the afternoon. But I would rather that he thought I was overemotional and moody. The knapsack on my shoulder weighed a hundred pounds.

Clark hugged me, and I stood stiffly. I offered some token words about wanting to see him again soon. More lies. Maybe I could explain myself at another time. I didn't know when that would be. Some demons had to be purged before I was worthy. By then, I might have missed my chance, or be damaged goods. After today, he probably wouldn't want to talk to me anyway. We exchanged goodbyes, and I jumped into my shiny silver-gray BMW, the car I always wanted, and drove away.

It was better this way.

CHAPTER FIFTY-FIVE

CAITLYN

February 2017

The kiosk—the start of Caitlyn's rendezvous with Henry—was the home of a magazine vendor in the heart of Harvard Square. Arriving a few minutes early, she peered at the outdoor displays of periodicals. The air had weight. It was the worst time of year in New England, when—sick of cold—everyone yearned for spring. She tried to offset the gloom by listening through wired earbuds to a shuffle of energetic Mozart piano concertos.

As she stared at a copy of *Architectural Digest*, oblivious to her surroundings, Henry tapped her shoulder. His touch startled her. His grin was warm and toothsome, and he wore his Red Sox cap, of course. After she recovered from her surprise, he greeted her with a kiss and a tight hug held longer than usual.

Caitlyn removed her earbuds, stuffed them into her pocket. After the Mozart, street sounds were harsh. She resisted an urge to hold onto Henry's arm as they walked half a block to the place where the #1 Bus would stop. There, they waited amid a small passel of riders: some teenagers, a derelict, two women speaking Spanish, a middle-aged man in a black scarf who delayed everybody getting onto the bus because he didn't have the right fare.

Aboard the bus, she and Henry exchanged departmental gossip, as well as all the information they knew about John Singer Sargent, which was next to nothing. Henry used his phone to look on Wikipedia for more. Sargent, a renowned portraitist, had painted murals for the MFA, Harvard, and the Boston Public Library, and some of his greatest works were displayed locally. His father was born in nearby Gloucester. It wasn't clear whether Sargent's life justified calling him the most Bostonian of great artists, but the city claimed him ardently.

Along with several other passengers, the two of them got off the bus near Symphony Hall and wended their way along Huntington Avenue—a jumble of storefront restaurants, shops, apartment houses, and Northeastern University buildings—until they arrived in fifteen minutes at the MFA. The museum itself was a monumental neo-Greek edifice that didn't hold much interest for Caitlyn architecturally, but the collection inside was golden.

The Sargent exhibition was heart-stopping in its breadth and splendor, and they moved slowly through the galleries, at times together, murmuring words of awe to one another, at other times separated, entranced by one work or another. Exquisite washes of Italianate gardens made Caitlyn long to visit these places of sun and ruin and green, of languor, of style, of great beauty. Although the show was crowded, the paintings were luscious enough for her to block out many of the other visitors. At times, however, people were so close that she herself felt under observation.

When she and Henry finished viewing the exhibition, it was almost dinner time, and they went to the MFA's cafeteria, which had a less enjoyable ambiance than a restaurant in the massive, airy courtyard of the museum's new Art of the Americas wing, but the food was cheaper. Henry grabbed a burger while she gleaned a meal from the selections of the salad bar. Somehow, she piled enough stuff into the bowl to run up a ten-dollar tab, over a pound of salad.

They took two seats at a table with room for four, and Henry eyed her mountain of greens, veggies, and other selections.

"Don't judge me," Caitlyn said.

"Go for it. Makes my cheeseburger and fries look healthy." He bit into his burger.

"I literally can only do so much looking at pictures before my head explodes."

"Then it's good we stopped. Hate to see your head explode." He paused. "Do you like the Red Sox?"

She eyed his cap. "Is this a trap?"

He pretended to be indignant. "What do you mean?"

"Your passion is clear. If I say, 'no,' you're not going to argue with me, are you?"

"So you don't like the Red Sox?"

"It's not a question of the Red Sox. I'm just not into baseball. Maybe I could go on opening day, you know, something like that, or when they play the Yankees. I'd like to see that. The rivalry. More for the archetypal experience. Otherwise?" She shrugged.

"I have some tickets to an Orioles game in April."

She answered too quickly. "You should take someone else. Someone who'd really like it." Her answer did not please him. "Henry, I'm sorry. I'm just not into baseball."

"Unless it's with the Yankees. Got it." He sounded irritated. He looked over her shoulder.

"What?"

"Tell you later."

"What?" She turned around and saw nothing peculiar, just some other patrons, alone or in groups, eating their food.

He snapped. "I'll tell you later."

"What's wrong?" she asked. He seemed to be pouting. She looked at him with skepticism. "What? You don't want to talk to me because I don't like the Red Sox?"

"Drop it."

"What happened?"

He glared at her and pushed his plate of food aside. "You know, I think I'm tired. I'm heading home after this. You should stay and see some other galleries."

"I've had enough, too."

"No," he answered. "You should stay."

"Henry."

"I insist. Enjoy the museum."

"Henry, what?

He spoke sharply. "It'd be great if just once you acted like you were really happy to be with me. Just once. Not like I'm always second choice, some default. Red Sox, Yankees? Couldn't care less if you liked them. It would just be a chance for us to hang out. Doesn't appeal to you? Fine. Like you said, I'll find someone else who'd really appreciate it."

"That's not fair." She started to say that she'd invited him to the museum until she remembered that she'd first looked at Svenda and Sophie's availability. He wouldn't know that, but she did, and the reassuring words stuck in her throat.

They ate the rest of the meal in silence. All of the food on her plate had blended together into a big unappetizing mess, and she struggled to finish it, her lack of hunger as much a result of tension as from distaste. After five minutes, she was defeated by the salad's leadenness, and they left the cafeteria.

"The guy behind you was listening to us," Henry said. "Did you see him?"

She had no memory of anyone and shook her head. "Maybe we were making a scene."

"Right. That's it. I made it all up."

"Henry. I just didn't notice him."

They rode an escalator to the West Wing lobby. "I'm going to head back," he said.

"I've had enough, too," she repeated.

"No. Stay."

"Henry."

"I insist. I want to be alone right now."

"Okay," she said, voice low. "If that's how you feel."

"That's how I feel."

They said goodbye tersely and Henry turned and walked stiffly toward an exit, at one moment tugging at his cap. Caitlyn felt tears well in her eyes. He was right. She deserved his anger.

Absentmindedly, she ascended a staircase and wandered through some rooms, paying no attention to the art that hung on the walls, in an emotional state, until she found herself in a small gallery of medieval artifacts. A glass case held a statue of the Virgin and Child, although the Christ figure was more man than boy. Both figures, in an intimate embrace, wore sad expressions. Caitlyn felt as if this work revealed something to her, a sophistication about medieval art that she'd not appreciated before. She spun around the room, which held about a dozen items, a mix of paintings and statuary and objects. All of the characteristics that she had attributed to a lack of technique now appeared to be deliberate choices to her, more calculated, more meaningful. Suddenly she loved what she saw. She had a different view.

She wondered if she'd underappreciated Henry.

She sent him a text: *"sorry"*

No reply came back. Discouraged, she left the MFA. Night had fallen, but she felt safe because the streets were lit, and Northeastern students ambled and gabbed all along the sidewalks. Instead of a bus, she aimed toward the subway. Near the station, she reached inside her right coat pocket and searched for her earbuds, but they weren't there. More determinedly, she stopped and rifled through the rest of her coat without finding them. She had a spare set at home, but the lost pair were her best. *Great! Perfect! Fuck my life.*

Henry still hadn't answered her text by the time she got home. It was inevitable that their paths would cross again, probably soon, even tomorrow, and she hoped by then he would be less angry, past his unhappiness. Maybe this was just a spat, a crack in their friendship, but no matter. She couldn't lead him on any longer. If their affair was over, she sincerely hoped he wouldn't hate her. She also wondered whether she had just messed up her life. What was wrong with her? He was a good man.

A half-bottle of white wine was chilled in her refrigerator, and she finished it while playing on her laptop, looking at funny videos that didn't make her laugh, exchanging some messages with her mom and others but concealing her distress, catching up on Facebook and Instagram without liking any posts. She spent a few minutes reading *The New York Times* and *The Crimson*. Finally in bed, her sleep was fitful, and she woke at 4:30 AM, tossing and turning until the alarm clock rang two hours later.

Following a shower and breakfast, on her way out of the apartment, she came across a manila envelope with her name scribbled across it. Someone had slipped it through a mail slot in the front hallway door. Unusual. She unlatched the metal clasp. Inside were her tangled white earbuds.

Caitlyn smiled and sent a text to Henry: *"thx for returning my earbuds"*

A few seconds later came his response: *I don't know what you're talking about.*

CHAPTER FIFTY-SIX

MARK

April 2017

As I drove away from my date with Clark, my anger grew, my patience snapped. I wanted the matter of Dave's estate to be simple. Instead, Clarence and Russ had complicated everything. I wished they would go away, disappear, die. I negotiated the curves and swerves of the Jamaicaway with more recklessness than was smart, as if aching for an accident, some kind of violent catharsis.

In the whirlwind of my fury was an image of Dave. I cursed him, and at the same time I berated myself. *The man was killed, Mark! Do you care about that? Are you concerned about anything but the money?* And then the counterarguments. *What do you expect of me? He was the one who rejected me. I'm trying to find his kid.* And then: *Think of the money he's giving you.* Then again: *Illegal money. If some mobsters don't beat the shit out of me. Thanks a lot, you thief.* After that, revulsion. *I am a worthless son of a bitch.*

I parked the BMW in the Fenway Grand garage and took a stairwell that bypassed the lobby and entered directly onto the street. Lugging my knapsack, I walked to a nearby liquor store where I bought a six-pack of Sam Adams and a pint of whiskey. I wanted Clark, couldn't have Clark, so I was going to get good and smashed with boilermakers. Before returning to the apartment, I went about a block away to a fried chicken franchise, another craving. I didn't know why I wanted to be reminded of my beating in the KFC parking lot. It didn't make sense.

In the apartment, I took a shot and then swilled my first beer practically in a single chug. It was only five o'clock, and there was a long, lonely, boring night ahead of me. I didn't care. I went to the bathroom cabinet and took a Valium. No big deal. I turned on my laptop and searched for some stupid porn, turned on the television and searched for some stupid movie. I retrieved the gun from the knapsack pocket, removed the bullets, and toyed with the chambers. I wasn't yet high. Despite my mood I knew I wouldn't do anything to harm myself, but the feel of the gun in my hand satisfied me.

Where was Clarence now? I looked out the window onto the street below. The sun was lowering, almost gone, the stunning view at odds with my foul state of mind. Clarence must not be on duty. And if he had been, what would I do? Go out and shoot him? No. But it was pleasurable to fantasize about making him suffer.

On the television screen, Tom Cruise was running as an airplane exploded in the background. Courtesy of Dave's expensive speakers, the roar of the blast caused the apartment to shake, and the piercing horns of the soundtrack almost stripped the paint from the walls. The flames and smoke of the burning plane—costly special effects—made oblivion look beautiful.

CHAPTER FIFTY-SEVEN

CAITLYN

March 2017

The mystery of the earbuds remained unsolved. None of Caitlyn's acquaintances knew anything. She considered whether she might have dropped them near the apartment, whether a neighbor could have somehow deduced they were hers, until she recalled listening to Mozart several blocks away in Harvard Square before Henry had arrived. After a few days passed, with nothing else suspicious happening, routine concerns took over and she fretted less about the incident although, once in a while, she was perplexed by the oddness of it all.

During these same days, Henry ignored her. He was being childish, she thought, but she made no further effort to reconcile because she'd already apologized and didn't want to give the wrong impression, that she was eager to resume dating. She missed him, it was true, and felt some regret, yet doubt about the wisdom of her decision wasn't enough to overcome her determination not to play with his affections.

With Andrew MIA, two guys down. Downpour followed by drought. Depressing.

Academic work had prevented her from following up on Professor Venda's suggestions about other affiliations among the architects, in particular, that they might be connected through Harvard. Finally, with a free afternoon, she pursued this idea. In her office, Caitlyn first researched the matter online. The university's penchant for keeping track of its alums was almost scary. For example, one member of the class of 1853 had taken it upon himself to track down each of his classmates and then to compile a book with a brief biography of every one of them. Caitlyn flipped through the electronically duplicated pages of the book, written forty years after graduation. She was amazed that the lives of so many men had been saved from complete obscurity. But Simpson was Class of 1852, and no similar volume was online for him, nor for Gannigan in 1854.

She went to the website of the Harvard archives and tried to find items for those years. There appeared to be a compendium for the Class of 1852 like that for 1853, but it hadn't been digitized and would require a visit to the library archive itself. The situation with 1854 was less clear. She decided to follow this trail to its end.

The Harvard archive was in a corner of the campus she rarely visited, a block or two on a side street off the yard. She arrived there in ten minutes. The archive was housed in a building that resembled a concrete bunker a few stories in height. Once inside, she learned from a directory that archived material was in storage below ground. The elevator ride down was slow, taking so much time that she wouldn't have been surprised if, like some horror movie, the door opened and led to a subterranean laboratory where a mad scientist tried to bring corpses back to life.

Off the elevator, she was confronted by a set of locked glass doors, through which was visible a service counter, presently untended. A wall, painted the color of dark sherry and framed with stained oak, was behind the counter and hid everything else from view. She waved her Harvard ID in front of a scanner to see if the doors would open. They didn't. She rang a doorbell, which made a surprisingly old-fashioned sound, *ding-dong*, like that of a house rather than an office.

In less than a minute, a willowy man, maybe thirty years old, apparently a librarian, came to the counter and pushed a button. The door opened. The librarian's eyes, behind wire-rimmed eyeglasses, appraised her benignly. He wore a brown cardigan sweater, a white shirt, and a Harvard tie, and his complexion was colorless. His style straddled a line between geek and hipster. "Can I help you?" he said in a voice so soft that Caitlyn almost couldn't hear him.

"I'm trying to find some materials," she said, before the counter, briefly displaying her ID.

He nodded, knitted his eyebrows, like this was an unusual request that required contemplation, and then he whispered his response. "You are certain it's not at Widener?"

She wasn't sure why he was so quiet, and she spoke at normal volume. "I checked online. The book is in this archive."

His eyes opened wide, seemingly disturbed at the strength of the sound that came from her. After a pause, he retrieved a form from a wooden box on the counter. "Fill this out," he murmured, leaning his head toward her as he spoke. His expression suggested that her request would enlist her in a conspiracy. Although no "please" had been added to any of his instructions, politeness was embedded in his manner and intonation. While she completed the slip, the librarian stood at the counter and waited for her to finish. Caitlyn gave him the form. He read it and smiled. "Class of 1852," he whispered. "Good choice. Wait here."

"I'm also looking for 1854, if there is one."

He shook his head sadly, a no. "The legendary lost volume of '54,'" he said before he walked off.

Well, he's a little odd, Caitlyn thought. She checked her cell phone, read a text from her mother that she answered, and then scanned Facebook a few moments until the librarian returned with an old leather-bound volume, about the size of a college yearbook.

"This doesn't circulate, of course," he said.

"Of course. Where can I read it?"

A serious expression. "Go over here." He signaled a door to the right of the counter, headed toward it, and opened it from the inside. Caitlyn entered a room with a small row of individual study carrels, all unoccupied. The librarian led her to one of them, placed the book upon a desktop, and said softly, "There's Wi-Fi. Do you have paper and pen?" She nodded yes. "We are open till five o'clock." About two and a half hours from now. The young man left her alone with the volume. No one else was in the study area.

Caitlyn ran her fingers over the aged cover of the book, compiled forty years after graduation, like that of the class of 1853. The first few pages revealed the biographies that followed were for the most part obituaries, read during annual reunions held at Boston's Union Club. The bios ranged in length from a few paragraphs to several pages. To begin, she read some stories in alphabetical order: Addison, Ammens, Anderson...fascinating. One of the men had lived in Paris at the time of the 1870 commune. Another had a long career as a businessman until his body was found floating in a river. There they were: the descendant of a president; the valedictorian whose life was ended too soon in a shipwreck; the officers in the Civil War (there were several of these); the rich heir who became a philanthropist; the rich heir who frittered away his time in Europe; extraordinary lives mixed with ordinary lives.

She finally turned to the entry for Thaddeus Simpson.

THADDEUS BROOK SIMPSON

Son of Thomas Brook Simpson and Harriett (Jones) Simpson, born in Boston, Massachusetts, on October 27, 1829. Received his early education at Boston Latin School, and entered Harvard in fall of 1848. At the university, he was known as a witty companion, popular, and always desiring to explore the delights of Cambridge. Many of Simpson's class benefited from his familiarity with the cultural and recreational opportunities of Cambridge and Boston, and he could offer uproarious tales of the denizens of those localities. Upon graduation, he wrote that his "years at the school have been the most pleasurable of my life."

Having tried the merchandising business of his father and not finding it congenial, Simpson undertook an apprenticeship in the study of architecture and the building crafts at the offices of Hamilton & Smith. His education in this discipline was supplemented by a sojourn in Europe for a period of one year. He arrived in Paris in 1857, where he made a study of the French language and building trades with some success. He befriended performers celebrated in the Parisian theater. Spring travel in Italy included a delightful fortnight in Rome, where he saw services under the direction of Pius IX, and in the absence of railway, he traveled further by postilion, coach, and horse to the city of Florence, where he met up with Classmate Shaw, who reports that they much enjoyed that city. On the completion of his studies in Paris, Simpson also journeyed to Berlin, Dresden, Munich, and Vienna.

In partnership with Smith on his return to Boston, he began his practice of architecture. He was married to Elizabeth Greenwood, and they had two children before her unfortunate drowning during the summer of 1861 at

Nantasket. Desirous of enlistment following the commencement of the war, he was to his severe regret deemed unfit for service due to parental obligations and a childhood injury that rendered him partially deaf in his left ear.

His architectural practice maintained a high reputation. It is said that Simpson's cultivation of his many acquaintances was very important in obtaining commissions. The services of Smith & Simpson were sought by people of prominence during the early improvement of the Back Bay, and their designs could be seen along Commonwealth Avenue and Marlborough Street. The skills of the architects were such that their reputation grew much beyond the confines of Boston, and warehouses and factories in the towns of Lowell, Portsmouth, and Salem are their product.

It is at this time when the class secretary has the unfortunate duty to recall a matter of notoriety. Simpson's undoubted generous nature had led him to assist a young woman, who, as it became later known, was a person of sad impropriety. Her untimely demise, in time determined accidental and as a result of her own malfeasance, was a cause of speculation and allegations directed at Simpson, his relationship with her, and his share of responsibility for her death. Scurrilous newspapers reported that Simpson's past activities demonstrated a habit of undignified associations and inferred his guilt.

The school rose in his defense. The firm of Lewis and Thane represented Simpson. Several others including Lilly, Carter, Harrison, Gannigan, Shaw, and D. Williams attested to his character. This testimony went far in assuring the jury of Simpson's innocence, and the charges against him did not hold.

Simpson's legal innocence was established, but the imprecations of the press had unhappy results. He chose to no longer practice his trade in Boston and relocated for a time to Ohio, after which time little is known of his activities. He died following an apoplectic attack on January 19, 1887. His children, Mary Margaretta, b. May 14, 1859, d. Aug. 1, 1899; Brooks Thaddeus, b. May 25, 1860.

Gannigan! Bingo! He and Simpson were acquainted! But the reminder of Sally Morris's death tempered her excitement.

Caitlyn left the carrel and went toward the service counter that was, as before, unoccupied. "Excuse me?" she said. The librarian did not appear. "EXCUSE ME?" she repeated.

Finally, she heard a shuffle and the librarian re-emerged. Caitlyn could almost swear his sweater was no longer the same color as before, undoubtedly a trick of the eye from the adjustments to artificial light. Quietly, he asked, "Are you finished?"

"Not exactly," she answered. "I wondered, is there other archival material about classmates? I mean, there are a couple of men I'm researching, and the book was helpful, but is there anything else you might know of?"

He almost seemed frightened by her query, but then he took a deep breath. "May I see your Harvard ID again?" Caitlyn complied with his request. He examined both sides of the card, at one point lifting his eyeglasses and squinting at some markings on the back of the ID. As if accepting this final verification of her trustworthiness, he asked, "What are their names?"

Caitlyn wrote Simpson's and Gannigan's names on a piece of paper. The librarian scrutinized the note. "I will be right back." He started to go into the archives but stopped, turned to her, and said, "Wait here."

Where else would I go? she wondered.

In about five minutes the librarian returned holding two manila folders. "Here is one for Gannigan," he said, "and another for Simpson." He passed them across the counter.

"Thank you."

"We depend on your discretion," he said, without offering an explanation of who "we" referred to, or why she needed to be discreet.

Caitlyn returned to her carrel and opened the first folder, labeled "GANNIGAN." Inside was a single news clipping from the Boston Daily Advertiser, an obituary, headlined "Boston Builder Gannigan, 36, Dead in Accident." The story, several paragraphs long, said that Gannigan had fallen from the upper floor of a building on Newbury Street designed by his firm. Police investigators said at least one witness saw Gannigan enter the building alone, and no evidence of any wrongdoing had been found, but there was no structural cause of the fall. That is, he may have tripped. Gannigan's wife had survived him, as had several members of his extended family, but he had no children. His work with Burns Brothers was referenced but no specific buildings were attributed to him.

At this moment Caitlyn wished that the "legendary" lost volume of the Class of '54 was available because the other biographies that she'd read often had more intimate details, in addition to having forty years' perspective. This obituary left questions about the circumstances of Gannigan's tragic death.

Caitlyn next concentrated on the other folder for Simpson, much thicker than Gannigan's. Old newspapers clippings, brittle with age, brown, almost crumbled in Caitlyn's fingers. She wondered if they had been copied and preserved elsewhere. But that was a query for later. She turned the items over one-by-one and tried to get an impression of their content. Just about all of them related to Simpson's trial for the death of Sally Morris. Whoever had gathered the clippings for the file had arranged them, more or less, in chronological order.

The tone of the articles startled her. She had known vaguely that the press of the time could be almost slanderous but hadn't realized what that might mean in practice. Although a few of the newspapers took Simpson's side, many of them declared him guilty long before the jury delivered any verdict. The vitriol was startling. Behind the anger was the presumption that a wealthy cad had taken advantage of a very young and innocent woman.

A number of the articles offered strong evidence for that conclusion. Witnesses placed Simpson in the company of the unfortunate Morris for several months prior to her death. Simpson himself had denied any significant relationship with her, so he looked like a liar. But other papers that favored him raised questions about the character of those unfriendly witnesses and implied they were people known to be dishonest and open to bribes. Who, exactly, would pay those bribes wasn't clear: the yellow journalists, ratcheting up the level of scandal for sensationalism? The prosecution lawyers, to seal the case and their reputations? Some other enemy of the accused? Caitlyn surmised them unlikely to be friends or families of the victim since Morris wasn't wealthy.

Medical witnesses, with their detailed descriptions of Susan Morris's bloody body, added sensationalism to the accounts. Of course, the forensics of the time were much more limited than now, and physical evidence tying Simpson to Morris was at best inconclusive. But traces of blood were present in a carriage owned by Simpson, and a coachman testified that he had seen the vehicle near the spot where Morris's dead body was found.

The defense presented a parade of character witnesses. They were described as elites, and the list in Simpson's biography in the class volume was supplemented by a dozen others. Testimony was not reported verbatim, but Gannigan was named. For the populist papers, the upper social class of the witnesses was the pretext for more scorn. Given the "Not Guilty" decision, however, their avowals must have convinced the jury of Simpson's innocence.

The stack of articles about Simpson didn't end with the trial. A follow-up story, dated about four years after his acquittal, indicated that he had moved to Cleveland. The portrait was not one of a man who retreated to a quiet life after a trauma. Quite the contrary. Simpson was described as someone who attended every social gathering in the city.

A sudden rap on the carrel door startled Caitlyn. The librarian, responsible for the knock, said, "We'll be closing in ten minutes."

Caitlyn took pictures of some of the articles and then gathered her belongings. Her reading, particularly after that final piece, left her with the impression that although evidence had connected Simpson to Norris's death, powerful friends had lined up to rescue him.

Before leaving, Caitlyn asked the librarian about the opening hours for the archive and suggested she might be back soon. The librarian noted that she would be welcome and bid her a good evening.

As the elevator made its slow ascent, she felt somewhere in all this material was a way to link the murder to a Boston Box. But then she had second thoughts. Once more, she wondered if a conspiratorial web of architects existed, or if she was just weaving it in her mind, an occupational hazard for historians, seeing what she wanted to see.

CHAPTER FIFTY-EIGHT

MARK

April 2017

I was awakened by my phone. Gerry. My supervisor. "Where the hell are you?"

"Shit," I said. "My alarm didn't go off. I'll be right there."

"Doofus."

Beer was spilled on the night table, and a gnawed-on chicken leg bone sat on top of the bedspread. I didn't remember how it got there. It was gross. I slept with trash. The greasy bone made me want to vomit, not that it would take much this morning for me to puke. I suppressed the heaving, rolled over, muttered "Christ," and got out of bed. My head hurt; my brain cells must be committing suicide by the thousands. This was what I wanted last night?

I showered long enough to wake myself up. Seeing myself in the mirror was unavoidable. My eyes were bloodshot. Was it too early in the year to wear sunglasses? I dressed fast, threw the pistol—unloaded, security device on—into my knapsack without wrapping it up, and left. Total time elapsed since the call was about fifteen minutes. Driving to work was a waste of money because the distance wasn't far and the parking fee would be ridiculous, but five or ten minutes might be cut from my travel time. I hoped I wasn't drunk any longer. Luckily, because Sunday mornings are quiet, I was able to find a spot on the street, with not even a quarter in the meter required, even though I feared that Clarence might use the opportunity to perform some of his magic again.

I hurriedly entered a convenience store to buy a giant cup of black coffee and a big bottle of tonic because I needed both the kick and the hydration. Following that detour—elapsed time: three minutes—I reported to Gerry in the small onsite office where he was stationed. I prayed that I didn't smell like alcohol. He looked up at me. "What the hell, Mark."

"I know. I'm sorry. I've never been late before. It won't happen again."

"Last week, black eye. This now?"

I felt like a scolded puppy, yelled at for wetting the floor, and I wanted to escape getting whacked on the nose. "Can we talk for a minute? Here's the thing." I gave him a digest of the main event of the last weeks without too many particulars. I explained that Dave and I weren't close—and how many damn times had I said that in the past two weeks?—but that I was off-kilter. Using Dave's death as a justification for my irresponsibility wasn't the noblest thing I'd ever done in my life. But my excuse was partly the truth.

Gerry frowned. "Okay, man," he said. His tone was marginally sympathetic. "Look. Sorry about your brother. That really sucks. And if you need time off, whatever, we can manage that. But we can't manage you not showing up for work. Don't let it happen again. Or you're gone."

"Got it. It won't. I swear."

"Get out of here," he said, shaking his head.

"Thanks. Sorry."

I judged myself, ultimately, to be sober, and I went outdoors to find my Duck. There were wispy white clouds in the sky, and the air had an icy bite. Another driver had jumped onto my earlier run, switching times, so the riders on my tour weren't aware of my screw up or waiting impatiently for me to show.

Driving a couple of tons of heavy equipment around the streets of Boston was horrible treatment for a hangover. Especially in spring, when the streets, having buckled from cold and wet weather, are pocked with potholes. Each lurch and bump of the Duck was an invitation for the contents of my stomach to find a new home at a curbside. The choppy waters of the Charles during that part of the ride were unforgiving, causing a sensation akin to seasickness. The cold wind on the river saved me, like a damp washcloth on my face. I won my war against puking with frequent swigs of ginger ale from the double liter bottle I'd grabbed at the store.

By now my tour routines are well-rehearsed, including quips, so I could put my brain on automatic pilot and maintain a semblance of professionalism during the first run. With my back to the group, no one could see that my face was green. But just like the Duck, my brain and guts traveled in circles. The second trip was worse than the first, not so much in my performance but in my nausea. Before my next and final tour, I ran to a men's room and vomited. That helped, and my last run went okay, but my hangover crept back in increments, and by the end of my shift, I was miserable again.

The BMW wasn't damaged when I returned to it. My recognition that I expected an assault felt like a great insight, a sudden acceptance that yes, I was stressed, on edge, had been so for days, despite occasional victories, despite glimmers of better times ahead. My resentment grew. Yet knowing that I was off-balance didn't translate into being watchful about my own impulses. It's hard not to act crazy when you're crazy, even if you know you're crazy.

I drove back toward the Fenway Grand. Traffic was tied up on Boylston Street, the main drag, so I veered to a side street where travel was looser. I was almost home when I came across a sight that infuriated me: Clarence's black Mercedes, unoccupied, parked not far from my apartment building. My stalker was on the prowl.

After putting the Beemer in the garage, I promptly walked over to the Mercedes. Still there, still vacant. I swore. I had had enough of Clarence. If he wanted to play games, I was in a mood to comply. Dusk had fallen, and the Mercedes was on a street less traveled, away from traffic or any pedestrians. Maybe Clarence had gone to CVS, or to get a burger, or for a drink at one of the local watering holes, bored because I hadn't been around for him to torment.

I moved next to the car. There was no mistake. I was certain that it was Clarence's. After another scan of the neighborhood and seeing no one, I used one of my keys to make a nice long scratch along the driver's side. An almost noiseless act of malice. The groove was thin, but you couldn't miss it. I swiveled my head, checking yet again for witnesses. The sidewalks were still empty, and no one was in any of the windows of the nearby apartment buildings. So I reversed course, scraped the car a second time, adding more pressure for a deeper cut, and then I turned and scored it again, the final mark going up and down, a wavy line like an oscilloscope. I stood back and admired my work, but just for a second, before somebody appeared. I felt gratified, in a punishing-the-schoolyard-bully way. Had I been eleven years old, I might have been really proud of myself.

Instead, I just went back to the Fenway Grand, cleaned up my mess from the previous night for about ten minutes, and then crawled into bed. I needed to get rid of my hangover.

CHAPTER FIFTY-NINE

CAITLYN

March 2017

"It's such hypocrisy," Caitlyn exclaimed.

"Caitlyn," Professor Venda responded. "This occurred over a hundred years ago." They sat at a Starbuck's, the day after Caitlyn's visit to the archives, not far from Sandler.

"I know. But it's so typical. Men circle the wagons, hide the truth, and it doesn't matter. That girl was probably murdered."

"Of this, you can't be certain. Your outrage is admirable, but please remember it may be a distraction from your original purpose. With luck, because the details are sensational, this will bring attention to the research. And funding. You can channel your moral righteousness after you get a sizable grant." She delivered that phrase with a hint of irony. "Where are you so far?"

Caitlyn looked distractedly into the space of the coffee shop, seeing but not seeing as she gathered her thoughts. Every table was occupied. She found herself gazing at a man who sipped a latte, maybe in his fifties, dressed in an expensive looking topcoat. He was familiar. Or familiar-ish. He might be from the university, or a regular here. A folded newspaper was on his table, but he wasn't reading it. In fact, he was staring right back at her. He nodded. Shaken out of her reverie, embarrassed by her absent-minded rudeness, Caitlyn half-smiled in return and snapped back to attention, addressing the professor.

"At this point, I can verify some connections among the architects," Caitlyn said. "Gannigan spoke at Simpson's trial. I wonder if there are transcripts. But I haven't yet found anything that confirms an architectural collaboration on a building, much less a Boston Box. I'm not saying that there wasn't any exchange. I think there was. It's a question of documentation.

"I think I can say definitively that Boston Boxes," Caitlyn continued, "or whatever it is we want to call them, that Boxes were being built regularly, and that after the beginning of the Civil War, they were being used for clandestine behavior. That is, mostly sex. There's the paraphernalia from the Hibbert House, and the abducted women on Marlborough Street, and Josiah Hawkins's letters about the South End. Three examples, and three times connected to fooling around, and three different men. Like Victorian S&M dungeons or love-nests. Of course, the murdered women were a sexual perversion of the most extreme kind." Caitlyn wanted to add that men in the nineteenth century were just as sex-obsessed as their twenty-first-century counterparts, a rueful joke between women, but her own recent behavior made the denigration of men's appetites seem unjust. Maybe everybody was sex-obsessed, however, some people were slimier than others. "I bet that one night over claret at the Union Club they started to compare strategies for hiding their lechery."

"Sounds would carry, wouldn't they?" Venda said. "In these Boxes."

"Depends. Several floors between activities, maybe, or they just kept quiet. Or maybe wives were part of it? I suppose that's possible. I'll have to experiment with it at the Hibbert House.

See if voices can be heard. It's possible street noise would disguise it. Or maybe there could be padding."

"That house in…where is it? Chadwick Square? The one you wanted to see."

"Nine Chadwick Square." Caitlyn sighed. "Yes, that. The owner still hasn't answered my correspondence. I'd literally kill to get into it."

Venda raised an eyebrow. "Literally?"

"Figuratively."

"Tell me again why you think it's important."

"Adamston designed it. Or Hawkins. The only cited sample of a Boston Box—the legendary archetype, if you will—was an Adamston place, one that burned down. Chadwick is the only home I've found of his so far that's untouched. I think. You should see it. All the other homes on the square are beautifully remodeled. This one looks like it hasn't been updated." She sipped the coffee, which was cooling off and tepid. "It's almost odd, the way it stands out. The situation is so frustrating. If I had clear evidence of another room, more proof, to show these constructions were regular…I think people, like the owners, would find it fascinating, that what some may think is a quirky feature of an individual home was actually part of a much more deliberate, more widespread, architectural pattern in Boston. Might even increase the value."

"You don't know for certain?"

"No. But Chadwick is the best possibility. It would back up my assertion that Hibbert House isn't an anomaly."

The man at the neighboring table scribbled something on a piece of the newspaper. He tore the shred with his note from the newsprint, and then folded the scrap and placed it into a sweater pocket.

"And it's about sex?" Venda asked.

"I think so, yes. Some. And violence. Disappointed?"

"Eh, sex is not disappointing. Or surprising. Sex is just life. Perhaps some of the—how to say this—kinkiness is intriguing. Why would I find that disappointing?"

"Oh, I don't know. Sex is so commonplace. If they were all Masons and the rooms were outposts of a secret society... wouldn't that be more unusual? A great sexual political *Eyes Wide Shut* underground?" Caitlyn laughed. "Actually, now that I think about it, there's some of that. But sex. I guess there's the whole culture of sexual behavior in nineteenth-century Boston that I may need to research if I want to understand this."

"You have found nothing else?"

"Other uses? Actually, no. Maybe the Underground Railroad, but mostly it's all this furtive stuff. Of course, what would you expect from hidden rooms? By their nature they're furtive."

"Can I say something?" Venda asked. Caitlyn nodded her assent. "This is very good work," the professor continued.

The compliment was unexpected, and Caitlyn was pleased. "Do you think Dr. Bacht will like it?"

Venda laughed. "Is Allen ever pleased about anything? Other than an occasional woman?" She laughed, almost knowingly. "You can cite him as an inspiration. What is it you say? Full circle." She drank the last sip of coffee in her cup. "And so? Next?"

"I'm not sure," Caitlyn said. "I may try to construct a narrative out of what I've learned. Just to see what story I have to tell. See where the weak spots are, what needs to be filled in. And I'm probably going to break into Chadwick Square." She chuckled. The man at the next table looked surprised, as if he heard her comment and thought she was serious.

Caitlyn flashed on a memory. Maybe it was several. A man in a North End cafe. A bus, and the man Henry noticed at the museum. The returned earbuds. All of these odd events coalesced. She watched the man at the table. A mole on his neck looked just like hers.

And at that moment she knew who the man was. He nodded at her again, smiled. He'd obviously wanted to attract her attention, sitting where he had. He'd been following her, she realized, and today he had decided to come forward.

"I must run," Venda said, and she put on her coat. "Is everything fine?"

Caitlyn scanned the café. Dozens of other people were nearby, so it was safe. "Yes. I believe so."

"You look strange."

"Thank you, *merci*," Caitlyn said. "I want to stay for a few more minutes." The professor eyed her uncertainly. "I'm fine," Caitlyn said. "Some matters to take care of before I leave."

"I could have another cup of coffee," Venda said.

Caitlyn appreciated her mentor's kindness but wanted her to go. Caitlyn watched the man. "No need. I'll catch up with you later."

Venda left the café, wrapped in her colorful scarf. Without her presence, the distress that had Caitlyn stifled flooded in. She glanced at the man at the table.

"It's you, isn't it?" she said to him.

He looked almost bashful when he shook his head in response.

"My mother gave you the message. That I didn't want to meet?"

Without asking permission, David Chieswicz slipped into the chair that Professor Venda had vacated.

CHAPTER SIXTY

MARK

April 2017

In the stark light of Monday morning, my actions of the previous forty-eight hours seemed unreal, idiotic. The last dregs of alcohol remained in my body, bringing depression, and more than a smidgeon of regret, especially about the drinking and the pills, but also about the adolescent behavior, the impetuous vandalism. My remorse on that matter was shaded with trepidation, but not repentance. Clarence hadn't seen me, yet if he made a connection to me somehow, my next few days were going to be rough.

At times, I just didn't care.

I brewed coffee with the last scoops of stale Folgers. I wanted to remove my brain and heart and soul and air them out. The uncontrolled behavior couldn't continue, or I'd mess up irreversibly, with or without the inheritance. What were the stages of grief? Denial. Anger. What else? Can you mourn someone you detested?

My phone rang. Taylor. I must have been on his "To Do" list, leftover from the weekend: call the victim's family to update them about the investigation. I didn't know why I was so cynical. He was trying. But he didn't have any progress to report.

"Of course, we're continuing," he said. "We have no results yet. That's all I can tell you."

"Which suggests you've found something."

"I wouldn't want to get your hopes up. It's baffling."

"Have you found anything on the Boston Box?"

"Running a few things, but nothing solid."

"I was also wondering about where you found my brother's body."

"Dorchester."

"Specifically."

"In a parking lot. Not too far from an exit off the expressway."

"It would seem, then, there should be a lot of evidence. Tire tracks, or DNA, or something."

"Not on the macadam. No impressions. Presumably his body was driven there, but there were no blankets on him, or coverings. It's rained. If we can ever find the vehicle that transported him, yes, we might make a match, but DNA is trickier than you'd think, more time-consuming. Even supposing a sample of the killer's blood on your brother's body, there's no database where we could crossmatch, you know. You need a suspect to take that step. We still have your brother's clothes, if it comes to that."

"Has the site been cleared?" I asked. "Where he was found?"

"Yes. It's back to normal. It's a place of business. The owners were eager to clean up. Obvious reasons."

I asked for the address. "And his phone. Didn't he have a phone in Florida?"

"If he did in recent years, he must have used untraceable cells. Or under an assumed name. We've gone back as far as a year, I think, and come up cold. Trying to go back farther? We'll see. It's a manpower thing. Time and money. I know that's not something a victim's family might want to hear. We're working it as best as we can."

The untraceable cell scenario was a sophisticated tactic for Dave. It wouldn't surprise me if Russ had taught him that dodge. Since their arrangement about the money was illegal, and Russ was clever, he'd look to hide any contact. "I understand," I said.

Taylor continued. "We know he bought his car in Florida, and he made some stops during his travel on the way to Boston, but they appear to just be solitary, overnight visits for the most part, rest along the way. Some fun in NYC. No evidence of any kind of meetings. He arrived here in late December."

He had nothing more to add. I thanked him for the call.

I sat at the breakfast bar in the apartment, went online, and entered the address where Dave's body had been discovered into a mapping website. It turned out to be about a mile and a half from the place his car had been parked. Presumably, his death occurred somewhere between those two points. Chadwick Square was located along this axis, but so were dozens of other blocks and landmarks, including a housing project, a police station, a flower market, and some antique shops. Thousands of people, hundreds of homes. With the map function, street views of the area were available, although the pictures were static and dated from the previous autumn. The parking lot was sufficiently isolated so the murderer could operate under the cover of night and not be seen. He—or she, I suppose—must have scouted the vicinity for a place without cameras. Maybe he held onto Dave's body for a few hours until the coast was clear. In any case, Taylor had already said that they'd checked security videos without success.

Because of the memorial I'd seen in Blackstone Park for Emily, the girl who'd disappeared, I pondered briefly whether I should put flowers or a wreath or something in the parking lot where Dave was found. These days, it seemed to be the thing to do. Under the circumstances, that option was ridiculous. A week had already passed. Even if the lot owners allowed it, which was doubtful, nobody would see it, nobody would care. Besides, these kinds of memorials can be morbid and upsetting, blindsiding people with reminders of violent death in otherwise innocuous places.

My phone rang again. I recognized the number, the Florida area code, and almost didn't answer. No news is good news. But curiosity got the better of me.

"You know," Russ said, without a salutation, "you're not as smart as I thought you were. In fact, you're even dumber than your brother. I didn't think that was possible."

"Nice of you to call and say so. Anything else?"

"I wasn't happy before, and now our friend isn't happy."

"I don't understand what you're talking about."

"Oh, Mark," he said, exasperation in his voice. "You may be an idiot. I am not. And our friend you underestimate. This is going to cost you. To be exact, it's going to cost you $10,000. You have forty-eight hours. At most. Maybe less. I'd advise you to get moving."

"Cost me for what? What am I being blamed for today?"

"Play your game if it makes you feel good. I assure you the smile will be wiped off your face unless you have 10K in cash by Wednesday morning."

"I still don't know what you're talking about. And where would I get ten thou, even if I wanted to?" Sure, I'd be given money to service the estate, but I had to keep records. I was certain that a line item for extortion wasn't what the judge had in mind.

"I guess that's your problem," Russ said. "I don't care. And neither does our mutual friend. Forty-eight hours. Be grateful it wasn't twenty-four. Or immediate. You apparently don't know who you're dealing with. And it's not for me, baby. You're just buying patience from someone who is ready to smash your head on a sidewalk."

"Again," I said.

"It'll be much worse this time. Much worse."

"You know, if anything happens to me, you'll never see a cent." Not that I had any plans to give him a penny under any circumstances. At the same time, talking about my own death so matter-of-factly was an out-of-body experience.

"You stupid shit, wise up. Forty-eight hours. He'll find you."

"It's to your advantage to calm him down." But Russ had hung up again. That was getting to be a habit. I felt bad. He never said goodbye.

My bravado collapsed. Do I call Dietz? Run away? Draw on the account? Shoot the bastard? Ignore the warning? Do nothing? Any action I took had plusses and minuses. I tried to calm myself. However close the deadline loomed, I had two days to make what might be the most critical decision of my life.

I paced, then grabbed a chair, sat, and stared dumbly out the window. My post-breakup isolation was more acute than ever. In a better world, I'd have a shoulder to cry on, someone to talk with and weigh the pros and cons. I thought bitterly if Paul and I were still together, this entire situation would be different, that Russ and Clarence would have faced a more complicated reality. Holding onto the $633,215.28 became more desperate because I was alone.

Tough nuts, Mark. I was single, and that's how it was. And suppose that I did have someone to talk to? I was hiding money from thugs. I'd escalated the situation by vandalizing a car. I was carrying an unregistered gun. This illegal behavior would sicken and scare my old acquaintances. They were normal people who didn't cavort with criminals.

Outside the window, Boston spread before me, such a remarkable city that I ached looking at it. I wanted to have it, to own it. I closed my eyes and listened to my beating heart. As much as I desired a happy ending, only a sad one came to me. I needed to get out of town.

CHAPTER SIXTY-ONE

CAITLYN

March 2017

According to Caitlyn's mother, David Chieswicz was ill, but he still had the posture and appearance of someone in full health. His hair, metallic gray, was thick, gelled, and carefully combed, and his clothes, while simple, looked costly, a starched white shirt under a navy-blue cashmere cardigan. "I had to come to Boston," he started. "My health. You see? So I was here and I knew you were, too, your mother said. Sylvia. Harvard and all. And I thought I'd try. Maybe if you saw me, you'd see I wasn't such a terrible guy. I felt bad about things." His tone was ingratiating but not apologetic. His chin was tucked in and he seemed to peek at her as he spoke, almost a coy appeal to her good will.

"I don't really care what you want," Caitlyn said. She tried not to raise her voice. "I don't want to talk to you. I didn't want to meet you. I asked my mother to make that clear."

"Don't blame your mom. She told me. It isn't like I want to interfere. It could be worth my effort to know you, I just was thinking, and for you to know me." A pause. "You're a very pretty girl."

"Do not go there."

"Come on. I'm not a bad guy. Really. And I could help."

"Help with what?"

"That house," he said. "The one you talked to that lady about. The one you want to see. I could do something about that."

"How could you help? You were eavesdropping?"

"I was right there so I could hear. I thought today...that after that lady left, that today should be the day when I tell you. I sat right there. It's not like I was hiding."

"This time. The earbuds? You returned them. You followed me?"

David nodded yes.

"Let me make something completely clear," Caitlyn said. "You are not to come near me, or my research, or my apartment, or I will notify the campus authorities, or the police. I want you to stay away from me. You are never to follow me again."

"Okay, okay. I get why you're mad. It wasn't malicious or nothing." David shrugged. "I just wanted to see you. You're my daughter. Don't get mad. Kind of my kid. I thought maybe get to know her, you, a little. Least what she was like."

Caitlyn exhaled sharply, leaned her elbows on the table, and combed her hair with her fingers. A countdown started in her mind: *Ten...nine...eight...* "I am not your daughter," she said, her voice edged with fury, but quiet. "I don't know you. I don't feel anything about you. You have your life and I have mine. There might have been a time when we could talk. But that's over. I simply don't want anything to do with you."

"I have money. For school..."

"I don't need your money. Do you understand? I don't want your money." Her voice was rising, and a student, dressed very casually and working on a MacBook Air, looked up. He tried to appear as if he hadn't heard anything, but a split-second glance gave away that he'd been listening. Caught, he turned away.

"I'm in town to see some doctors," David said. "It wasn't like I was stalking you or nothing, you got it? Not why I came to Boston, I mean. Jeez. It's cold here. I'm getting treatment for the cancer."

It was such a manipulative appeal for pity that Caitlyn almost rolled her eyes. "I'm very sorry, but that's not my problem. Look. You don't have any chips to cash in with me. If you have money, you're sick, use it to find help. I'm sorry you're not well. But if you come anywhere near me again, I will make a scene. And then I will notify the police. Do you understand me? You are not to follow me."

"I can help," he said. "I know about getting into houses."

"I do not want your help," she hissed. The MacBook Air guy perked up again. She returned his interest with a toss of the head and a grimace, doing her best to communicate wordlessly that he should piss off. He received the message and lowered his eyes to the laptop screen.

"I thought if you saw me, face to face…" David said.

"Okay, I've seen you."

"You just need to cool down a little. Maybe you could think about it. You might change your mind."

"I want you to leave," Caitlyn answered. "And I'm not going to cool down. Are you kidding? After you ambush me? I'm going to get another cup of coffee and when I turn around, I expect you to be gone. I never want to see you again."

"You ambushed me. When you called."

"Please. That was not the same thing."

David scratched his head. He didn't appear upset or angry about her rejection. His expression seemed to say, *Well, I tried.*

"Listen," he said. "I'm not trying to work you up, like you are. Your mom, she didn't give me your phone number or nothing, and I just knew you're at Harvard, so I had to find you this way. I'm not good at computers and that shit. I mean, stuff. Excuse me. So, look, it's just that you're my kid, you see, and I thought I should try to meet in case I get sick or anything. You see? Before that happened. Win me some points with the angels. You never know. If I was in your shoes, I'd probably hate me, too."

"I don't hate you. I don't know you enough to hate you. I don't hate anybody."

"Yeah, well, whatever you say. So like, this room, what was it, Boston Boxes, that's interesting."

"You listened."

"I was just there," he answered, gesturing to the table.

She was tempted for a split second to talk about her work. She hesitated, almost yielded. He didn't appear to be threatening.

Two other patrons of the café, a pair of young women, walked near the table where David Chieswicz had sat before joining Caitlyn. His newspaper, coffee, and coat were still there. They looked around. "Is anyone using this table?" one of them asked.

Their interruption snapped Caitlyn back to reality. She answered them. "Sorry. My…my friend here. He was just leaving."

David Chieswicz stood and picked up his belongings, moving the coffee and paper to Caitlyn's table and draping the coat over his arm.

"Oh, no," she said. "Don't get comfortable." David remained still. "I think it's better that you go now. And I don't want you to get in touch with me again. I made that clear with my mother, and she told you." He nodded. "I'm sorry you're not well. But this is too much for me. This will only hurt me. I don't want this. I'd like it if you'd leave. No more. I have a father."

"It's just that…"

"I'm sorry. It's too late. I just don't care. Honestly."

He stared at her for a moment. She hoped that her eyes were hard. She wanted to show only anger, anger that would discourage him, anger that would hide any softer side. "I'm going to get a cup of coffee," she said. "I'd appreciate it if you were gone when I get back to the table."

David Chieswicz inhaled sharply, appeared to be calculating. "Okay," he said.

Caitlyn stood and extended her hand to shake his. "Goodbye," she said. His hand was calloused and warm.

"Right," he said. "Bye."

She walked to the counter. A large piece of coffee cake was displayed in a glass case, and she wanted it. She knew she should watch her coat and other possessions, but she looked forward, hoping not to see that man, David, her father…oh, what the hell? Her eyes watered. "That piece," she said to the barista, pointing at the cake. "That biggest one, please. I need it today. And a tall dark."

The barista, a young woman, looked sympathetic. "Oh, I know those days," she said. She placed the cake on a plate and then pulled a paper cup of the coffee. She leaned toward Caitlyn. "Don't say anything. The coffee's on the house."

Caitlyn realized her distress might be too nakedly visible, but that didn't stop more tears, this time of gratitude, from welling up. "Thank you," she said. She paid for the cake, and when she turned to the table, David Chieswicz was gone.

CHAPTER SIXTY-TWO

MARK

April 2017

My next maneuvers in the war between me and my stalkers were devised quickly. Since I'd prepped Gerry for a mental health break, chances were good that he'd give me some time off. A few days, or even a week or two, should be easy to negotiate. I also made a mental list of what I might need for my escape, and I decided to make a trip to my old apartment and grab some clothes and get my mail. I hadn't been there in a week, and I should check on it, especially if I planned to leave town.

My thoughts about Gerry must have energized some molecules in the atmosphere, connecting us, because as I prepared to leave, he called. Another driver was sick, and Gerry figured I owed him a favor for the previous day, so he asked if I could take the shift. With two days left before the expiration of Clarence's extortion deadline, I agreed without much hesitation. The tours would distract me, add some cash to my pocket, and give me more time to figure out where to go. And I could address the matter of my schedule with Gerry face-to-face.

I carried my knapsack, keeping the gun in it. In the interest of speed, Gerry had agreed to cover parking fees if I drove to work, this time to one of the company's alternate sites near the Boston Aquarium. The tours that started here were shorter than those by the Pru, and as a result, the balance shifted to the attractions along the harbor: Old Ironsides, Bunker Hill, the Boston Garden, the Museum of Science. This was one of the most enjoyable parts of the city. Being near the water made me think that I could run away to Cape Cod. In off-season, it would be easy to find a place to stay. I might have to search for stimulation, but the gay community of Provincetown could liven up my nights. During the days, I could go for long, soulful walks on empty beaches and plan the rest of my life.

Formulating my getaway while driving a Duck, I concluded I'd have to use the BMW. The alternatives weren't practical. Public transportation to the Cape was spotty before high season, so unless I changed my destination, I needed the car. If, by chance, Clarence checked up on me, he might see my escape and follow. To elude his observation, I decided to sneak off in the middle of the night. The risk was worth it. Presuming my success, I'd have more time with the only love in my life, the BMW, and more freedom when I arrived.

I finished up my tour runs about 4:00 PM and then talked over my request for a leave with Gerry. A decent guy, he agreed to a ten-day break, not a formal vacation but just a juggling of the schedule, which I appreciated.

I hit rush hour traffic on my way to Brighton. I parked along Commonwealth Avenue, a short distance from my place, but legal. The spots nearer to my apartment required a neighborhood sticker. Let no one say I wasn't mostly law-abiding when it came to small stuff. Nevertheless, as I cut through an alley, knapsack strapped on my back, I second-guessed my decision. The safety of proximity might have offset the cost of a ticket, even if the fine had been sizable.

I retrieved a stack of mail from the mailbox, most of it bills. I'd convert my payments to online for the future. Entering the apartment, I was struck by how shabby it appeared, how much it reflected my post-breakup depression, my post-breakup poverty. My tenancy here was over at the end of June. After that, for the rest of the year, I'd run out Dave's lease, for a few months anyhow, presuming I could return to town. I couldn't afford the Fenway Grand permanently, but the inheritance would allow me to live in some place better than this student dump. I was mindful that everything about Dave's accounts was tentative, yet it was time for me to grow up—past time, really, to take better care of myself. When I gave up this apartment, very few items would be worth saving. Almost none of the furniture.

I loaded a black carry-on suitcase with clothing that might blend with Dave's high-end wardrobe. I let the best of it stay on hangers for transfer to the Fenway Grand, and threw some memories into the knapsack: a framed photo of a deceased cat and a favorite coffee mug. For now, I'd leave behind a picture of Paul and me. I wondered why I'd displayed it in the first place, except out of masochism.

The hangered items gave me too much to carry in one trip, so I grabbed the carry-on, which was on wheels and easy to tote, and headed to the car. I was half-way there, in the middle of my alleyway shortcut, when I spotted someone walking toward me, less than a hundred feet away.

Clarence! *Shitcrapshit.* And he wasn't alone. Alongside him was another man, short and stocky, muscular. They sprinted toward me. The second man's features became more distinct; his skin was tawny, and his long coarse hair was pulled back.

I immediately realized my first mistake: not bringing my knapsack. I didn't have my gun. My second mistake was hesitating to run because of the suitcase, which I didn't want to drop and leave behind.

I panicked and hoped I'd have at least a chance to reason with Clarence. As the two of them approached me, I said, "Hey, what's up?" So insipid. My left hand hung onto the carry-on's pull handle. Clarence's companion smiled contemptuously. He had crooked front teeth.

Nearing me, Clarence responded to my greeting with a leather-gloved fist, a solid punch to the right side of my face. A boxer's swing, like being hit with an iron crowbar. My stunned disbelief about the attack was followed by an immediate throb of excruciating pain. I wheeled backward, falling over the suitcase, the second man's mocking laugh adding to my humiliation. I curled in agony, defenseless and frightened, in too much shock to cry out. Clarence tried to kick me in the stomach, but my fetal-like position deflected the worst of his attempt. Instead, the sole of his running shoe scraped my forearm.

"Get up," Clarence grumbled. I tried to stand, moving to all-fours, but I couldn't recover fast. "He needs some help, Edo," Clarence growled. Clarence's friend grabbed a handful of my hair and yanked me upward. My scalp was almost ripped from my head. Before I could yell, Edo put me in a chokehold that made me gasp and thwarted any attempt to shout for help. Edo was shorter than me, so I was unable to stand straight, instead leaning backward and wobbling in the direction of my assailant.

So far, the scuffle was strangely quiet and unlikely to attract any notice from the apartment buildings whose rear windows faced the rarely used alley. I was scared shitless but too woozy from the punch to fight or scream. They could kill me if they wanted to. There was nothing I could do.

"Going somewhere?" Clarence said.

I tried to speak, to lie and say I was just moving some clothes from one apartment to the other, but the chokehold made it impossible for me to be audible, understandable. The sounds from my mouth were little more than gulps for air. Edo loosened his arm without fully releasing me. "Just moving some things," I said with a rasp.

"Where's my money?" Clarence said.

"Wednesday," I whispered.

"What did you say?" Clarence hissed.

"Wednesday. Russ said I had until Wednesday."

"Russ was wrong."

I was doomed. "I don't just have it. I need to move some accounts to get the cash. I don't carry that much."

"I should fucking kill you for fucking with my car."

"It wasn't me," I said.

He frowned, caught Edo's eye, and moved his head upward, a signal. Edo tightened his chokehold again. I couldn't breathe. "Please," I tried to say. I'd almost blacked out when the hold loosened. I collapsed again onto the bumpy, broken surface of the alley and swallowed deep gulps of air. "Please," I begged.

Clarence said, "You was seen, asswipe. Don't give me this shit about 'it wasn't me.' You was seen. I am going to fucking kill you."

"Please!" I wanted to plead for my life like a sniveling wimp, yet I was too weak from the assault. *You won't get any money if you kill me. Russ won't get any money.* All of my resolutions about not paying them crumbled before the simple fact that I wanted to live. But even if I was willing to admit defeat, I couldn't talk.

"Edo has a trick to show you," Clarence said.

"What?" I wasn't sure if I actually said the word or just thought it.

"You should've thought twice before fucking with me," Clarence rasped.

Edo wedged my neck in the crook of his muscled arm once more, almost crushing my windpipe. *"You're choking me!"*

"Too bad, faggot," Clarence said.

Edo put his left hand on his right wrist and pulled, choking me harder. My breathing was tortured, inadequate. That was the last thing I remember. A strange thing about death, its blackness, the grace with which it can come, when you realize a struggle is useless, the surrender, the peace that you feel.

PART THREE

Caitlyn: March 2017 – May 2017

CHAPTER SIXTY-THREE

CAITLYN

March 2017

Returning to her chair at the café, Caitlyn sat down, used a plastic fork to break the coffee cake into crumbs, and then played with them absent-mindedly. She put a first morsel into her mouth—cinnamon and sweet vanilla—and ate the rest rapidly. Ten minutes later, she packed up her things and left. On the way to her office, the street was noisy and full of construction vehicles. Traffic seemed more treacherous than usual. She was on the alert for David Chieswicz's reappearance, but there was no sign of him. At least he had the decency to stay away.

She hid in her office, a safe place but not one where she could fall apart. She tried not to cry and started to text her mother. *"David Chieswicz just...."* What? Introduced himself? Trapped her? Followed her? She restarted the text. *"just met David Chieswicz. he's in Boston."*

She waited for a return message. Instead, her cell phone rang.

"What happened?" her mother said. "Are you all right?"

"Yes," she responded. "I mean, I'm not hurt. I'm upset."

"Did he call you? How did he find you?"

Caitlyn poured out the details of the encounter, ending with, "I told him to stay away from me."

"I don't think he meant to hurt you."

"You're not taking his side," Caitlyn responded sharply.

"No, of course not. I mean, I don't think he's the kind of man who will try to contact you if you told him not to. Again, I mean. I'm so sorry. I hope not."

Caitlyn heard her mother sniffle. "It's not your fault, Mom."

"I know. It's just, Squirrel, I don't want you to be hurt. I don't think he's dangerous. Do you?"

"No, I don't. But not trustworthy. Do you know much about him? What he does?"

"Now? I think he's retired. He's sick. I told you. I'm not sure what kind of work he did. Why?"

"Nothing to do with architecture?"

"I don't think so. Unless he worked like on a construction company. We didn't speak about that. I don't remember what he told me about his living in recent years. If he said anything at all about it. Why?"

David's comment about "helping her" with Chadwick Square nagged at Caitlyn. But when answering her mom, she said, "It's nothing. He said he had money. That's all."

"Can I do anything for you? Do you want me to call him?"

"No. I just needed to tell someone. For him to show up like that. I'm in shock."

"I'm so sorry. Now you've met him. I don't know what to say. Do you think you should tell someone? The university."

"If he tries again, I will."

The call went on for several more minutes. Her mother's voice soothed, calmed, and grounded Caitlyn, apart from some notes of anxiety. They closed with Caitlyn's promise to be in touch if she needed to, followed by Sylvia's promise to phone soon no matter what.

Caitlyn sent a few texts to postpone some student appointments. Then, exhausted, she left Sandler and headed to her apartment. The brief walk was refreshing, as if putting physical distance between herself and the café—and the unpleasant surprise that it had held—gave her an emotional distance from David Chieswicz as well. *So that was him. The sperm donor. My biological father. My father.* She wanted to put qualifiers on that term, even as she thought it. Not *My father* but *"My father."*

At home, she stretched out on the bed. With her head on a pillow, she reflected on David Chieswicz's actions and character. She didn't like him. He didn't seem especially bright. In itself, that didn't bother her. Caitlyn had friends and family back home who weren't sophisticated, but they had warmth or street smarts, a different kind of brains, emotional intelligence. David Chieswicz had come across as crude.

Yet she was partly a product of his DNA! They must have some traits in common beyond the moles on their necks. She turned on her iPad and used the cam to display her face. She stared at herself on the screen, and her imagination imposed his features imposed on her own. The resemblance was there. Oh, her nose was smaller, and her hair much different, of course, but if she pictured an outline of David Chieswicz's face, she could see how her own would fill it in. Suddenly, she turned away from the image, the notion, and dismissed the resemblance as a product of her distress. She was her mother's daughter, not her father's child. Her "father's."

Until this morning, David Chieswicz had been unknown, which had enabled her imagination to make him imposing, even frightening. Now, as the shock of meeting him began to wear off, he was scaled realistically, with dimensions and a size that were all too mundane. He was human, vulnerable flesh and blood, just like her, just like anyone on the planet. Almost sympathetic, pathetic.

She still wished fervently that he'd never approached her. But she decided it would be wrong—and unhealthy—to stay angry. She'd done that once. True, she needed time before she forgave him for his intrusion. Weeks, perhaps months. She wanted to be sure he stopped following her. Yet she found peace in the idea that forgiveness was possible someday, as long as it was far, far off in the future.

CHAPTER SIXTY-FOUR

CAITLYN

March 2017

Over the next day, Caitlyn immersed herself in her academic work, scrutinizing architectural studies, examining buildings and their concrete beauty, using whatever ways she could devise to dodge the emotional turbulence stirred up by David Chieswicz.

Late in the afternoon, at the coffee shop around the corner from her apartment, Caitlyn retrieved the pictures on her laptop of the clippings from the files that she had photographed down in the archives. Unfortunately, the images weren't clear. She'd have to make a trip back across campus if she wanted to read more. By now, that library's closing time had been passed, so that task was for another day.

She hadn't completed an investigation into Arthur Gannigan's accidental death. Then she remembered the librarian's comment about the "legendary lost volume of 1854." A book of the Class of '54's biographies would likely answer some questions. Another internet search for it uncovered nothing. Was there something peculiar about the class of 1854 that would account for the volume's disappearance? Probably not. Too bad for her that it was gone, but nothing suggested that it vanished because of a plot.

Even if the 1854 volume was lost, other records about the students from that class must still exist. She did an online search and found a list of names. Gannigan was there in the middle of it. She scanned the rest more closely. Mostly WASPs: Adams, Anderson, Andrews, Bacht...

Bacht?

Viktor Bacht?

She gulped her coffee and then typed madly into her laptop. Another search of some genealogy tables revealed that one of Dr. Bacht's ancestors was indeed a member of the Class of 1854. She wasn't really surprised, in retrospect, that Bacht had Harvard alums in his family going back several generations. He was the whitest guy on the planet.

She dug around on the internet and found little about Viktor Bacht. He was an architect, working near Philadelphia most of his life. If only the 1854 edition was available! Its "legendary" status, mentioned by the librarian, had to be facetious. Dozens of copies must have been printed, and some must survive. But she would have to track down all the ancestors of the class and determine whether any of them had held onto it as a keepsake. That could take months. The book wasn't a Gutenberg Bible in rarity or value, yet it might as well have been, as far as she was concerned.

Allen Bacht was such a snob, parading his sophistication and pedigrees, that he probably took the library's volume himself so he could display his bloodlines and impress people. Or maybe he had a copy, the logical owner of a family heirloom.

She leaned back, stared at Mass Ave through the window. A mellow song played over the coffee shop's speakers. She remembered that Bacht did have a stack of leather-bound books about Harvard in his office. Was it possible that he owned a copy of the "legendary" volume? It wouldn't necessarily be the one that disappeared from the archives. Since his ancestor was an alum, a copy simply could have been passed down from generation to generation.

With chagrin, Caitlyn realized that whether or not Bacht owned a copy was moot. He wasn't around. Plus he'd never share it with her, especially if he'd learned of her mission to prove him wrong. And she wasn't going to rummage through his office. It didn't matter that he was on sabbatical and wouldn't be there. Breaking and entering was a bad step on the path to a degree. Besides, querying him meant re-entering his orbit, and she hated that idea.

On the other hand...

It was late, and Sandler would be almost empty, and his suite was just above her own. Suppose she accidentally got off on the wrong floor, totally innocent, and before she realized it, oops, there she was in his office? And, look, there'd be that book she was searching for! She only needed it for a half-hour. Surely, he wouldn't mind if...

She flashed on the articles she'd seen years ago about David Chieswicz's arrest for housebreaking. Maybe it was a family predisposition.

Oh, forget it. The door to Bacht's office was probably locked anyway. She should just wait. Maybe he had a generous side and would share the book someday if he owned it. Of course, when she published her results, he might not look kindly upon her if she had tricked him. It really would be better if she could dig up a copy without his knowledge.

Yet the idea that Gannigan and the two others had colluded to build Boston Boxes was like a Holy Grail. Proof would be wonderful to have.

Caitlyn was at an impasse. She'd spent too much time at the coffee shop, had drunk too much caffeine. Her nerves jangled. She needed to get outdoors, or she'd start to dwell on David Chieswicz again and drive herself crazy. Later, she could track down somebody for a drink. Somebody not Henry.

Out on the street, she obsessed about Bacht's books. She walked across a Harvard campus green and headed to her office at Sandler. A guard, who recognized her, offered a greeting and waved her in. She was at a decision point: she could take the elevator, and push "3" and go to her own space, or she could push "4," and pretend that she'd gotten off on the wrong floor if anyone questioned her.

She pushed "4." She rehearsed an excuse in between thoughts like *I must be crazy. If I get caught, there could be disciplinary action. Or expulsion.*

She stepped into the fourth-floor corridor and walked toward Bacht's office. The hallway lights, controlled by motion sensors, came on, indicating no one had been there for a while. Taking a deep breath, she grabbed the handle to Bacht's door and pushed it down. Great luck! The door wasn't locked and swung open easily.

Shades were drawn, and the bulb of a desk lamp gave off a dim radiance. By the time Caitlyn realized what she was seeing, it was too late to withdraw. Bacht himself was sitting at his desk, his head buried between the legs of a woman straddled atop it, her legs propped on him, skirt hitched up. His head jerked back, mouth open, his eyes startled, then filled with anger. The woman, who had been leaning backward and supporting the upper half of her body by leaning on the heels of her hands, also twisted and faced Caitlyn.

It was Professor Venda.

CHAPTER SIXTY-FIVE

CAITLYN

March 2017

"Who is that?" Bacht lisped. He recognized Caitlyn and became livid. "What the hell are you doing here?"

Venda looked amused and repositioned quickly herself on the desk.

"Oh my God," Caitlyn responded. "I made a mistake...I thought..."

"You little cunt!" Bacht hissed.

Venda slapped him, a whack. The crack in the air was so sharp that Caitlyn almost felt its sting. Stunned by the blow, Bacht sputtered another curse. His face turned bright red, an imprint of Venda's forefingers outlined on his cheek. Turning to her, he said, "I'm warning you, Helene," he said. He rubbed his face.

"Oh, Allen," Venda said, the tone of her voice weary and irritated and like a shower of ice. "Stop behaving badly. Don't be so damn serious. This is Harvard."

"I am so very sorry," Caitlyn added, breathless. She froze, uncertain what more to say or do.

"Caitlyn, leave!" Venda commanded. The order shook Caitlyn out of her daze, and she retreated into the hallway and shut the door behind her, too fast, which made it sound like she'd slammed it on them, not her intention. She had meant to say "excuse me" before going. Under the circumstances, however, an accusation of impoliteness was the least of her problems. The evening would almost be farcical if not for the fact that she was doomed.

Caitlyn hurried toward a staircase, lurched down to the third floor and her own office, and shut and locked her door. Why hadn't Bacht secured his office if he was going to have sex? Why hadn't she knocked? *So stupid!* She stumbled to a chair. Bacht's wrath would fall upon her worse than ever. Even if he kept the details of the episode to himself—a possible outcome, since he wouldn't want to bring attention to the fact that he was going down on a colleague in his office—he would make Caitlyn's life miserable. She didn't know how he'd punish her, but he'd watch for any misstep and make her pay. And Professor Venda! Her mentor! Consorting with her enemy! Literally consorting!

The sense of betrayal Caitlyn felt about Professor Venda overwhelmed her. She was certain that Venda had told him everything about her research. How could she not? They were fucking, they were colleagues, they had Caitlyn as an advisee in common. She imagined the two of them collaborating on her downfall and groaned.

Her phone buzzed. A text. Professor Venda. *Harvest bar. 20 minutes.* She never texted, so this step indicated the gravity of the situation.

For the second day in a row, the universe had dictated that Caitlyn deserved to be miserable. Goddamn it! She was only trying to do some research. But her mental protests of innocence about Bacht's office were delusional and self-serving, she knew. The fate that she faced was one that she had invited. The sin of snooping around might have been venial, but it was still against codes of conduct and warranting punishment. She'd brought it on herself. A Harvard disciplinary board was unlikely to be sympathetic to someone breaking into a faculty office. She hadn't been thinking straight but she might have just ruined her life.

She grabbed her knapsack and used the staircase instead of the elevator, an effort to be secretive and avoid any encounters. Outdoors, evening, she kept her head down and walked toward the Harvest Restaurant. The sidewalks had a layer of winter dirt.

The restaurant was hidden in a passageway off Brattle Street near Harvard Square. Its name was announced on huge plate glass windows with a splash of neon. The dining area was about three-quarters full; its décor was contemporary; the same was true of its separate bar. Caitlyn told the host that she was meeting someone and then searched for Professor Venda. Caitlyn's mentor and executioner sat on a stool near the far end of the bar, drinking a green concoction from a martini glass. Caitlyn inhaled and slipped onto an empty stool next to her.

"What are you drinking?" Venda asked.

"Something strong," Caitlyn replied, meekly. "What are you having?"

"One of their house cocktails. Lots of alcohol and it swallows like candy."

"I think I'd rather have something painful." Caitlyn ordered a Manhattan. She usually avoided spirits. The drink would make her want to die the next morning, redundant, since she already wanted to die. The two women were silent while the bartender stirred the liquor and then poured the contents into a chilled coupe, close to a double. Under the circumstances, Caitlyn took hope when Venda raised her glass to clink. "Bottoms up," Caitlyn said. Venda shook her head. "Oh," Caitlyn said. "I didn't mean that." She took a big sip of the drink, which burned her throat and almost made her choke. She hated bourbon. "Should I pack my bags?" If she hadn't been tired of crying, she might have started again.

"What is it that you're saying?"

"Me. 'The little cunt.' Bacht wants to get me. And you?"

Venda grimaced. "Americans."

Caitlyn swallowed again, choked again. She asked the bartender for water. "I don't understand."

"*Ma chère,* may I talk to you tonight, woman-to-woman?"

Caitlyn nodded. She hadn't eaten for hours and the drink was going straight to her brain.

"Allen and I had an affair several years ago," Venda said. "It is true he is sometimes *un salaud,* a bastard. But he is not the personification of evil that you have made him. At times he is attractive, intelligent, and he is talented in certain ways. Tonight, we were talking about some other thing. The sex happened. It does occasionally. Old lovers. It's just sex. I was hungry, he was hungry, so we ate. Why were you in his office?"

"I made a mistake. A big one. I'd had a bad couple of days. I wasn't thinking properly." Another swallow. "I tend to avoid him."

"But not tonight."

"How is he now?"

"Oh," Venda said. "Bothered. He is all worked up. He did not like my slap. When I left him, however, I told him to forget it."

"Will he?"

"No. He cannot forget anything. But he won't report it. I told you. He is not a demon. Avoid him. But he's nothing you should fear. He is not precisely an innocent. I will handle him."

"Does he know?"

"What?" Venda asked.

"About my project. About the Boston Box."

"It's probable. Frankly, we don't speak of it. This drink is too sweet. But I may want another." She signaled the bartender. "So why were you there?"

"It was a mistake," Caitlyn repeated. "I was nosy. I guess it depends on how you define mistake. I was preoccupied. I was looking for a book. I'd had a bad day and wanted something to take my mind off my problems. I wasn't thinking straight."

Venda paused, appearing to weigh which hook she wished to bite on. Finally, she said, "What book?"

"A book about Harvard," Caitlyn answered. "History."

"I see." Venda tasted her refreshed cocktail. "Too sweet. *Eh, bien.* It is easy. Allen has lots of books about Harvard. I think there are several in his office. I believe he should have an 'H' tattooed on his ass. A big maroon H." Surprised by the candor of the comment, Caitlyn didn't know how to react to it. The professor continued. "He doesn't." She kept a straight face for a moment, and then both women laughed. They regained their composure. Venda said, "Perhaps you should ask him. About his books."

"Yes," Caitlyn said. "After tonight, I'm sure he'd love to help me." She giggled again. The drink was taking over. Then a crash. "Oh, what am I to do? I'm so sorry. It was embarrassing."

Venda said, "It was only sex. People do sex every day. You should finish the drink."

"But the situation." Caitlyn moaned and then complied with Venda's instruction and knocked back a long swig of the Manhattan, but much of it remained in the glass, and the drink was too strong for her to finish with one chug. Venda waved at the bartender and asked for the check while Caitlyn drank until the Manhattan was completely gone.

Venda stood. "Come with me."

"Where are we going?" Caitlyn said. She rose to her feet and felt a little unsteady.

"To my office."

Caitlyn didn't argue.

Night, with a chill, had fallen, and Brattle Street was eerily empty, although the hour was not yet ten. The stars blurred more than usual. "You know," Venda said. "Boston is a lot like a city in France, sometimes. The weather is not good, or the history so long, but in the United States, it is perhaps as close as one gets. There is New Orleans. Certainly not New York."

They reached Sandler, nodded at the guard, and gained after hours entrance to the building with the slide of Venda's ID card. Getting into an elevator, Caitlyn pressed a button for the fifth floor, the location of Venda's office, but the professor muttered a "tsk" and pressed the button marked "4."

Caitlyn said, "Huh?" but Venda didn't respond.

The two of them exited into the hallway where Caitlyn's earlier disaster had occurred. The lights clicked on automatically. "Wait here," Venda said. Caitlyn hung back, watching Venda as she approached Bacht's office. When the older woman stood in front of its door, she turned to Caitlyn and waved at her, an indication to hide, a precaution. Caitlyn walked around a bend in the hallway, which put her out of view.

Venda knocked. "Allen?"

Nothing happened.

She rapped again, more loudly, and once more. "Allen?"

Once again, no response. Venda called out. "Caitlyn? You can come out."

Caitlyn stepped into the hallway, clumsily tripping on the wall corner but righting herself before she landed on the floor. Venda played with a ring of keys and eventually slid one of them into the lock. The door opened.

"I have a key while Allen is on sabbatical," she said.

The two of them peeked into the office. The blinds were drawn. The hallway lights illuminated the room unevenly. "Perhaps it is best that we do not turn on a lamp," Venda said. She went in first, and with a gesture, beckoned Caitlyn to follow.

Venda walked to the bookcase behind Bacht's desk. A few dozen volumes lined its four shelves.

"What is the book that you are looking for?"

Caitlyn scanned the embossed titles on the books' spines. The volumes were organized in no order that she fathomed. Several copies of Bacht's own writings were on the top row, while in the second range were older volumes, almost all of them about Harvard. Caitlyn squinted at times because the room was dark, and she was dizzy from the bourbon. And then, there it was, on its side. CLASS HISTORY 1854. A Harvard insignia. She eased it from the shelf. "This is it," she said.

"That's it?" Venda asked. "That's all? Be certain. You will not have another chance."

Caitlyn turned back to the Harvard shelf. Most of the volumes were recent and widely available, and since the university's connection to the Boston Box was loose, at best, she didn't think taking any of them was worth the additional risk. However, at the end of the shelf was one book that looked like a ledger. She pulled it from the shelf; its cover was black and rough to the touch. She opened the book and examined it quickly. It appeared to be a diary of some sort, but the penmanship was dated in style, and she was reasonably certain, even in her inebriated state, that the handwriting was not Dr. Bacht's. Had it been, her scruples would have forbidden her to take it. But since that wasn't the case, on an impulse she grabbed this second book, too.

"Allen is out of town tomorrow," Venda said. "He returns on Thursday. I do not believe he plans on coming here, his sabbatical, but we should meet tomorrow evening and put them back."

Caitlyn nodded. "Of course. This is awesome. I don't know how to thank you."

Venda fixed her gaze on Caitlyn. "Nobody should ever call a woman a cunt when I can hear it," she said.

CHAPTER SIXTY-SIX

CAITLYN

March 2017

Had she been sober, Caitlyn would have rushed home, books in hand, and poured over the texts to find information on Arthur Gannigan and Viktor Bacht. But the Manhattan, chosen for its power, took its toll, and she was unfocused and feeling sick by the time she reached her apartment. She had enough foresight to take a pain reliever and drink a pint of water. Then, thinking with affection of her mentor and giggling, Caitlyn flopped onto her bed, fully clothed, and fell asleep. After about four hours, following a dream in which she was pursued first by a gangster and then by a ghost, she woke in a cloud of delirium, drank more water, and willed herself back to a choppy sleep.

She arose only a half-hour later than normal, and the drinking didn't exact as much of a penalty as she had expected to pay. As she recalled the night's events, she groaned, remembering the scene with Bacht and then the borrowed volumes. "Borrowed" was a gentle way of phrasing it. Had Professor Venda made the situation better or worse? In any event, it was done. Resignedly, Caitlyn brewed a pot of strong dark roast; ate some buttered toast; checked her calendar to be sure she hadn't forgotten any commitments; and then opened the "legendary" volume while curled on a beat-up upholstered chair that was her most comfortable piece of furniture.

Like the other class history she had read, this one had the now romantic look of a book set by hand, with irregular type. Gold edged the pages. She flipped back to the flyleaf where no Harvard Libraries insignia was imprinted. This wasn't the university's copy of the legendary volume after all. Dr. Bacht hadn't stolen it. This thought reminded her that she couldn't claim any moral high ground about borrowing material.

She went first to the entry for Arthur Gannigan. Much of what she read was familiar. But one detail in his biography was new: an implication that Gannigan had committed suicide instead of dying in an accident. He was *"a sensitive man who had been despondent over recent events."* Caitlyn did some mental calculations about the year of Gannigan's death. What would "recent events" have been? The Simpson trial had been a year earlier, and the case about tortured women on Marlborough Street would have come to light. But other factors—health, family problems, business—were possible, she supposed.

An interesting notation was that Gannigan, a man of some resources, had left a good amount of money to charities, particularly those that served women in distress. According to the yearbook, *"Our classmate, who changed his will shortly before his death, hoped that his money would assist those in need, keep them safe, and right past wrongs."* Caitlyn found that final phrase peculiar. What past wrongs? The women's? Society's? Or Gannigan's own? Since she'd not found much about him on the web, she assumed the charities that he had funded must be closed, and their histories and purposes lost.

Gannigan's despondency, the restitution for past wrongs, the timing: could he have been connected in some way to the

Marlborough Street house, which Simpson had designed, and where Jeffries had committed his acts of rape and torture? Could that have been enough to drive a "sensitive man" to suicide, for his contribution, maybe innocent and unwitting, to a murderer's plans? And maybe more than one murderer, if one included aiding Simpson in his trial? These theses felt like good possibilities to test as she went on with her research.

Next was Viktor Bacht. Apparently, some of the accounts in the volume were simply reprints of autobiographies submitted by the subjects themselves, and Viktor Bacht's was one of those. The man went on for a dozen pages. He wrote that he was born *"on a wintry coast where sea salt encrusted the windows of my domicile while storms raged."* His mother was a teacher whose *"repute brought students from miles away and she was valued across the countryside."* He was an architect, and whenever he received an appointment, it was always *"by unanimous consent."* If he mentioned any man, a notation of that personage's importance was included, a nineteenth-century version of namedropping. In his ego, he was definitely Dr. Bacht's forebear. At one point, he was clear to point out that his bloodline was not traceable to the Framingham Bachts, but to the Boston Bachts.

Boston Bachts?

Boston Bachts equals Boston Box?

The punning was delicious although—as far as Caitlyn could make out—irrelevant. Still, the coincidence reminded her that she'd not been able to establish where or when or how the Boston Box got its name. Maybe it just happened.

Viktor Bacht hadn't shown up in any of the studies of Boston architecture that she'd examined before this day. As she read his biography more deeply, it became clear that although he was very proud of his Massachusetts heritage, most of the work he had done was not in the metropolitan Boston area, but rather in Philadelphia, as she'd seen before, and sometimes in New York. Not a single building near Boston bore his imprint.

Still, he had been a classmate of Arthur Gannigan. She went back to Gannigan's biography, which indicated he'd done some training in France in 1854-5. Back to Bacht's entry. He had also done training in France in 1854-5. They had to be acquainted while in France. *Had to be.*

She checked her notes on Simpson. If he was there at the same time, it would be too good to be true. Disappointingly, he had studied in France two years later. Still how marvelous it would be if she could not only refute Dr. Bacht's contention that the Boston Box was a fantasy but, as a bonus, prove that one of his own relatives had contributed to it. Icing on the cake.

A text from her mother interrupted her. *How are you today?*

Because of Caitlyn's escapades with the "borrowed" books and her enthusiasm to read them, Caitlyn had put the encounter with David Chieswicz out of mind. To her mother: *"i'm fine. buried in work. good distraction."*

I'm glad, Squirrel. What are you doing now?

"more of same. how r u?"

I'm good. Worried about you, of course. Dad says hi.

"hi back."

Do you want to talk about anything?

"no i'm good."

Check in later?

"yes. ttyl"

Reminded again about David Chieswicz, Caitlyn's revisited her determination against a reconcilement. A countdown ticked, she knew. His illness was serious, and she didn't have unlimited time to come to an understanding if she desired it. But her resistance hadn't softened enough yet for that.

Before she returned to reading about Viktor Bacht, Caitlyn wondered if a French source for the Boston Box was possible because the four men under her investigation were Paris-trained. She put the volume aside and searched online for examples of secret rooms in Paris in the off chance that the Boston Box had a Parisian counterpart. The effort didn't succeed. The search results, tens of thousands of them, were for hotel bargains or other "hidden treasures" of the city. A comparable search using broken French, *chambres cachées à Paris*, also bombed. The hypothesis of a French source for the Boston Box would take time to investigate if she pursued it.

She did yet another search, this time about Viktor Bacht's work in Philadelphia. Despite the man's self-importance, none of his buildings was deemed notable. Many of his designs had been torn down. Looking at their images, she found the buildings ordinary, no beautiful details or hint of creativity, just big brick boxes with dull ornamentation. At least his descendent had some flair.

Resuming Viktor Bacht's autobiographical entry, she saw again that his mediocrity didn't prevent him from boasting. His children, named Alfred, Abraham, and Edith, were remarkable.

They lived in enormous mansions, traveled everywhere, cured illnesses, stopped world wars, and were kind to dogs and children. Insufferable man. A note by the class secretary at the end of the autobiography mentioned that Viktor Bacht had died in 1907after a stomach illness, possibly cancer.

Viktor Bacht's story disappointed her. Given that she had risked her future, not to mention her ethics, on obtaining the volume, the payoff was so small as to be useless.

But there was still the other book to examine, the ledger. She poured another big cup of black coffee and once more settled in her chair. A gust of wind rattled the apartment windows. The knocking sound was comforting because it highlighted that she was in her own nest, snug and protected.

Caitlyn opened the ledger. It had no title page, just an inked signature on the inside cover, "A. Bacht." For a moment, she felt sick. Had she, despite her intentions, stolen a volume of Dr. Bacht's diary? To her relief, she determined the author was not Allen, her professor, but Alfred Bacht, Viktor's son. She flipped through the handwritten pages and skimmed the content. The narratives contained in the entries were mostly mundane: family gatherings, some travel and entertainments, work travails. The tone was matter of fact, without Viktor's self-aggrandizement, but without much style either, or intimate details. Sometimes several weeks or months passed before any item was recorded.

But, toward the end of the diary, the pace accelerated. The matter that precipitated the increased number of entries was Viktor's final illness. In between the lines in which Alfred told of his father's sickness and of his weakening and growing frailty, Caitlyn sensed distress. The tone changed. Alfred wrote more emotionally.

And then she turned to the final entry in the book.

CHAPTER SIXTY-SEVEN

CAITLYN/ALFRED BACHT'S DIARY

March 2017/1907

This is the story my father, Viktor Bacht, told me on his deathbed.

During his years at Harvard, where he applied himself to his studies diligently, particularly in those classes required in his first year, my father became a member of the college boat club. At the time, the club itself, while popular, was without many resources. He described it, with much fondness and irony, as a group of beggars, despite the wealth of some of its members. It was here that he first became acquainted with another crewman, two years ahead of him, Thaddeus Simpson, whom, during the recitation of his story, my father called "Thaddy."

Thaddy Simpson had a peculiar reputation at the college. Personable, intelligent, proficient in his courses, he was also known as a rogue and sometimes a troublemaker, although the exact nature of his sins was not known to my father when they met. Indeed, Thaddy had a lack of guile that endeared him to many, including my father, who was charmed by Thaddy's wit.

On an October evening, after a racing meet with the boat club, my father first encountered the darker side of Thaddy's character. I must say this description, "darker side," is attributable to me. In his accounts, my father insisted on saying that Thaddy was adventurous and only naughty, but, to my mind, "naughty" is simply a word for "immoral" disguised with a playful wink. My father was persuaded to join Thaddy and a few others in the pursuit of a red wine of a label that Thaddy insisted was the finest product of France. Before this moment, it was unlike my father to take part in such pastimes, but he and the other lads were in very good spirits, having had a successful race earlier in the day. The young men went to several establishments in Boston, high and low, in search of this wine. It was not the first instance in my father's life in which he imbibed alcohol, but it was the first when he drank too much of it. The warmth with which he recalled this night indicates that he regretted it not a whit. These were his times of youthful high spirits. He was also pleased to be in the circle of Thaddy and his friends, who were among the liveliest and most sought companions at Harvard.

One episode of revelry led to others. My father was not as rich as many in this group and was often dependent on Thaddy's generosity, which was apparently offered without comment or expectation of repayment and with an open hand. As for why, I can only offer that my father was handsome and much devoted to his wardrobe, and his allowance, neither stingy nor extravagant, allowed him to fashion himself in a way that attracted many compliments from his fellows. That is what he has told me. "Clothes make the man," I have often been advised by him, in a misquote of Shakespeare.

On one such evening of over-indulgence—again, my word—my father embraced vice more deeply. After much whispering among the cohorts, my father was invited to join Thaddy and a few others at a house in the North End of Boston. This journey was to be undertaken by foot and was a matter of hilarity to the young men, except for one named Gannigan, of a nervous disposition. My father agreed to the walk, although he claims that at the time to be naïve about the visit's purpose.

That was the night, my father said, that he "became a man." He viewed it as a rite of passage. Others might say it was the night that he became *less than a man. I love him and I try not to judge, all too aware of my own failings, which, however, do not match precisely with those of my sire. Had I admitted to a similar rite in my youth to him, I believe he would have been in a rage.*

For much of the time that followed during the next year, my father became a libertine of the kind that Harvard often breeds. Nevertheless, he managed to complete the college curriculum, which often was based on the memorization of facts and texts, at which he was adept. After this schooling, he pursued studies in the mechanics of building and architecture in Paris, a trip that was then (and is yet) an indication of more profound intellectualism and training. Gannigan, the nervous man of the night of my father's "maturation," had overcome his lack of experience and scruples and was now a sophisticated companion in Paris, although my father deemed him of a guilt-ridden temperament. I cannot speculate with certainty on the source of Gannigan's misgivings unless they were only the manifestations of remorse that must trouble any man of good character when he has sinned. I do not believe he was a Papist.

The money was not available to provide the orgies (my word) that Thaddy had sponsored at Harvard, but my father said that Parisian women, including some of great beauty and skill, did not demand the same investment, especially if a lover was young and handsome and presentable, as was he. Thaddy was to spend time in Paris as well, although his stint did not occur at the same time as my father's. I was given to understand that my father arranged for many romantic introductions for Thaddy.

There follows a break in their quotidian relationship, due to distance and circumstance. My father wed my mother and moved to Philadelphia, and I was born. Thaddy also married. Their acquaintance was renewed annually at gatherings held at the Union Club, once at a time when Thaddy mourned the premature death of his spouse, who was a beautiful but unfortunate woman.

And now I must tell of the murder.

I am ashamed to say that my father resumed his more profligate habits when away from Philadelphia, away from his family. Is there some beast that is released even in men of good character when they travel? Even to Boston? As if the distance gives permission for behaviors that would never be considered during their day-to-day life? In truth, my father's confession to me, undertaken in his final hours, like a Roman Catholic in search of absolution, was often bemused, except for the parts that I now relate, for which I believe him to have been both regretful and frightened of divine judgment.

On an evening before he was to depart from Boston and return home, my father arrived after dinner with companions at the Union Club, and he was about to retire to his quarters when he was called upon by Thaddy, who was distraught. Thaddy's conversation was incomprehensible. My father ordered a brandy from a club attendant and insisted that Thaddy swallow the drink. Other than the club man, a longtime employee known to both of them, no one else witnessed Thaddy's distress.

Thaddy drew my father outdoors and prevailed upon him to walk across the Boston Common to his home, built less than a year earlier on the new Commonwealth Avenue. Their destination was achieved in good speed and without explanation on Thaddy's part. The home was entered quietly. Thaddy warned my father that an elderly servant slept above on the fourth floor of the mansion and efforts need be made not to disturb her. His children also slumbered.

Thaddy led my father to a room in the basement, achieved through a staircase concealed from general view behind a bookcase cleverly constructed in a drawing room on the first floor. Inside the room, across a crude bed, was a young woman, little more than a girl, wrapped in bloody sheets. The girl's skin had the grayness of death. She was indeed lifeless.

Thaddy was on the fringe of a hysteria, although his sobs went unheard elsewhere due to my father's efforts to make the other man contain them. How they themselves avoided a soak in blood my father could explain only by the abundance of sheets and bedclothes used to contain the repulsive mess.

Thaddy said the girl was a factory worker who had entertained him for a price and that she was without family. He alluded to times that he and my father had enjoyed during their days at Harvard, saying with this girl was no different, a comparison that my father did not at the time dispute. The girl was to have a child. Her crude attempt at ending the condition— a notion that horrifies me in so many ways that I can hardly write the words—had ended with the girl bleeding to death, under Thaddy's witness. Thaddy, to his shame, had not sought help. He pled with my father for help and prevailed upon the memories of when he had sponsored my father's share of their college times. He claimed the girl had initiated the foul act by her own will, that he had found her in this state after leaving her briefly to attend to a matter in the upper house.

I am unsure of the logic that led my father to agree to assist. It is certain that his affection and loyalty to Thaddy account in some measure for his participation. Yet I am in great pain to disclose that I believed my father was convinced that the girl was worthless. She was a harlot, of no great background, willing to perform acts that good women would not consider. He believed her to be weak of character, of worthless stock, a threat to society due to the looseness of her morals. She was too ignorant and lazy to work honestly. (How he reconciled this estimation with his own behavior, equally lustful, confounds me.)

They acted quickly. The girl was swaddled in more linens and removed to a rig that Thaddy kept behind the house. It was very late, and due to the sparse population along Commonwealth Avenue at this time of its creation, they were little noticed. The girl had a room on the back slope of Beacon Hill that Thaddy had once visited, but there were too many others of her sort in residence and it would be impossible for them to return her to that place. They took her body to the Charles River, where they disposed of it by dropping it by the riverbank. The linens were kept and later destroyed. They contrived as best they could that the girl had bled to death after her unspeakable act. There was some truth in that, albeit not a whole truth.

The events that followed are more well-known. Thaddy was accused in her death, but he invented a story in which he was a generous protector, not the source of her misery. His innocence and good character were attested by several of his peers and former classmates. My father, having returned to Philadelphia, was not among them. Due to apprehension, he never contacted Thaddy again. Thaddy was deemed not guilty by a jury and escaped the punishment of men. Almighty God has, by now, made His own decision about Thaddy's actions.

My father intimated that his old friend Gannigan, haunted by his alliances with Thaddy in many personal and professional matters, eventually suffered from madness, as haunted as Hamlet. Moreover, in regard to my father's need to admit to his sins, he believed that there was a chance to make amends by confession and public exposure but unfairly has placed that burden on me. It is one that I cannot fulfill without harm to my own innocent children. I heard his words, and I prayed with him for God's grace before death claimed him. As for the young girl, that friendless young girl, I wish that her soul will rest well, knowing that someday these words will be read, and the truth of her fate will be told.

CHAPTER SIXTY-EIGHT

CAITLYN

March 2017

Caitlyn let the ledger slip from her hands. She was angered by the men; horrified by their crime; outraged by their sense of superiority; saddened by the girl and her awful life and death; and furious for all women. With so many crimes being revealed over the course of her research, it felt as if the Boston Box had been transformed into a Pandora's Box, with one story of evil escaping after another.

Because of the solution uncovered about a classic Boston mystery, she should have felt a surge of elation. For here was a discovery that was sensational yet of historic value. A surefire attention grabber. But, of course, due to the way she had found the material, she couldn't use any of it. Directly, in any case. Perhaps it could guide her in other ways.

One thing seemed certain. The ledger helped to explain Bacht's opposition to her research. This account of evil by his ancestor must have led him to protect his heritage, his family's reputation. Caitlyn pitied Bacht. The criminal behavior must have been difficult for such a proud man to stomach.

It was almost the hour when she was to meet with Professor Venda to return Bacht's books. Clouds hid the sun as she left the apartment and walked across Harvard Yard to Sandler Hall. There, Venda asked about her efforts, and Caitlyn mentioned that she'd uncovered interesting material that she needed to absorb before discussing. A bustle of activity at Sandler—some kind of undergraduate mixer was underway—would require them to wait before returning the volumes to Bacht's shelf. Venda offered to undertake the task by herself, shielding Caitlyn from possible discovery or punishment, and allowing her to return home.

CHAPTER SIXTY-NINE

CAITLYN

April 2017

After more research, Caitlyn believed she had sufficient material for a draft of her findings. Undoubtedly, holes needed to be patched, but crafting a paper would help determine what other areas needed investigation. One deficiency was glaringly apparent: her failure to see the interior of Nine Chadwick Square. It was time to go there again, ring the doorbell, explain her mission, and beg to enter. Because of Rumberg's unresponsiveness, the task made her nervous. Caitlyn considered whether to ask one of her colleagues in the department to come along but decided that two people on the doorstep might be more intimidating than just one, and she wanted the situation to be as free of tension as possible. She didn't want to scare George Rumberg away.

Her departure was delayed when a student conference ran overtime. A broken-down T train held her up even more. Finally, in the South End, the sun had almost set, and she rushed to Chadwick Square, foregoing a more leisurely stroll through the local streets and squares because she'd hoped not to be knocking at the door in the dark. Besides, all of the stories about the evil that had taken place in Boston Boxes made her anxious, and she felt that she had to stay focused or an irrational fear would grow. Despite her resolve, when she was finally at the head of the steps of Nine Chadwick, she was tenser than the situation deserved.

She saw no lights inside, heard no noise, noticed no movement. She poked the doorbell and waited.

No one answered.

Other homes on the square had lower entrances that led to garden level units. Caitlyn looked beneath her. A grimy door was hidden beneath the steps at Nine Chadwick, on the left, and it didn't look as if it was used, but she went down to it, another place to try. On the base of a column next to the door was an intricate design, covered in dirt. There was no doorbell, so she knocked, the chipped paint on the wood almost abrading her knuckles.

Again, no answer.

Discouraged, Caitlyn wondered if another entrance was at the rear of the building. She walked around the block. The alley behind the row of brownstones wasn't paved, and mud from an earlier rainstorm clung to her shoes. She identified Nine Chadwick easily. Light came from one of the windows. A basement door looked similar to the one she'd seen when she'd visited the condo for sale, many months ago, but remembering that the condo didn't have a welcoming back hallway, this entrance wasn't a logical place to use.

Nevertheless, the light in the windows gave her hope. Maybe Rumberg, or whoever lived there, had come home while she had circled the block. She walked around to the front again and rang the doorbell once more. Funny. When she pressed the button, she heard no sound. She'd never noticed that before. So she knocked, this time on the main entrance door.

Nobody answered.

She could hardly hang out on the doorstep at this time of day. Having made several attempts, she gave up. Maybe Rumberg worked at night, and lamps were on a timer, and her next try should happen earlier in the day. She went back to the subway, disappointed yet again, but still firm in her resolve to see the inside of Nine Chadwick Square, no matter how many visits she had to make.

Arriving in Cambridge at Harvard Square, she was hungry, so she bought a couple of slices of pizza and carried them to her apartment. On reaching her doorstep, Caitlyn retrieved her mail, and among the pile was a plain envelope, unmarked with anything except her address. Indoors, climbing the steps to her place, balancing the pizza and other stuff, she opened the letter. It contained a single sheet that held in its folds, without any explanation or note, a ticket for a Red Sox game with the Yankees.

CHAPTER SEVENTY

CAITLYN

April 2017

The ticket cost almost $200 and was for a match-up to take place in early May. Caitlyn stopped on the staircase and looked more closely. Occasionally, information about a buyer was printed on a ticket. Not this time.

Inside her apartment, perplexed but calm, she shed her coat, sat down on her couch, and munched on the pizza. Who had sent the ticket? She reasoned only three possibilities existed, or maybe four. First was Henry. On the day they had argued, she had confessed her desire to see the Red Sox play the Yanks. Since then, Henry had been frosty except for those times when academic work or situations threw them together, and they affected cordiality. The ticket might be his attempt to rekindle their affair, or at least make peace. Arguing against Henry was the price: $200 times two was expensive for a student. Plus his continued aloofness. Overall odds it was Henry: 10-to-1.

The second possibility was David Chieswicz. The method of delivery mimicked what he'd done with her earbuds. She thought it was unusual for him to have selected a Red Sox-Yankees game until she remembered that a man had eavesdropped on her and Henry at the MFA. Sneaky, but that fit his character.

If David Chieswicz were the sender, to her own mild surprise she couldn't bring herself to totally reject the idea of going to the game. As time had passed, and as the shock of his appearance had lessened, her opposition to him had eased. She hadn't yet decided to speak with him or to seek him out actively, but his illness added pressure, gave her almost a literal deadline. This could be a good way to chat with him.

Or perhaps he wouldn't be there. Maybe it was a single ticket, an attempt to do something nice. A peculiar approach, but more bearable than being caught off-guard. Or, if he was at the game, with the offer of the ticket he was almost saying, *Should you change your mind, here I'll be.* He'd given her time to think it over. And by sending the ticket anonymously, he assured that she wouldn't rip up the envelope, or return it, without examining the contents. Or contact any authorities for stalking her.

Would she go if David Chieswicz was her companion? Possibly. Odds on him being the sender: 2-to 1.

The third choice, Andrew, was one that she discounted almost immediately. This ploy was not like him. He'd be more direct in order to impress her and then move in for the grand seduction. 100-to-1.

Final possibility. An unknown admirer. Stranger things have happened on the road to romance. It could be another student, or one of her advisees, or a teacher. This idea tickled her but was dubious. 100-to-1.

So, were she placing a bet, she'd go with David Chieswicz. She wished he initially hadn't upset her so much, that she could use the ticket without emotional complications. Selfishly, she was interested in seeing the Sox play the Yanks at Fenway.

She hadn't looked up David Chieswicz on the internet since her undergrad years. She tried again. Not surprisingly, no new items about him showed up. At least he hadn't been arrested in the last three years. More hits featured a Mark Chieswicz, who was in Boston. She'd forgotten him. He could be a cousin or distant relation. Mark had a Facebook account that she tried to examine but his page was blocked except for the cover image, which showed the picture of a Duck Tour vehicle of the sort she'd seen lumbering around Boston. She couldn't imagine contacting Mark Chieswicz since a connection was improbable. And difficult to explain: *I want to talk to you but not to my father.* Sometime in the future, she might approach Mark Chieswicz out of curiosity to see if any relationship existed. Not now.

She tacked the ticket for the game on a bulletin board with a push pin. She had time to decide whether or not to use it.

CHAPTER SEVENTY-ONE

CAITLYN

April 2017

Over the next two weeks, as the semester neared its end, Caitlyn finished the first draft of her essay about the Boston Box. She tried to construct a coherent story out of her research: the various architects: Adamston, Hawkins, Simpson, Gannigan; the documentation supporting her thesis: blueprints, letters, clippings, visits; the crimes and assignations she'd uncovered, from love nests to torture chambers to S&M rooms. For now, she included the material about Viktor Bacht, although she doubted that she could use it in whatever she submitted for publication.

The Nine Chadwick Square visit had yet to be accomplished, a big gap.

She thought the draft was fascinating, yet something was missing, something she couldn't put her finger on, besides Chadwick Square. She sent an email to Professor Venda and asked if she'd be willing to review the manuscript. Her mentor agreed to meet in a few days to discuss the material.

At the time of the appointment, Caitlyn went to Venda's office. Since at this stage everything was preliminary, Caitlyn was at ease as she awaited Venda's judgment.

"What's here is very good," Venda said.

"What else?" said Caitlyn.

"It is not enough."

Caitlyn paused a moment, prepared herself, and then bowed her head, an encouragement for Venda to say more.

"You have gone almost as far as you can go," Venda said, "You have limited yourself to those things you can discover on your own. You need to come out of your closet."

Caitlyn looked shocked.

"No, I do not mean that," Venda said. "I do not think you are lesbian. Whether yes or no on that, *ça ne fait rien*. What I mean is that you need to ask the world to participate in your work. You must ask if others know about these Boston Boxes, these secret rooms. All kinds of homes were being made at the time of your study. I am correct? I understand you cannot physically see all of these places. The amount of research is impossible. Unless…"

Caitlyn waited. "Yes. Unless?"

"Unless you get help. Do what other researchers do. Ask in journals. Put up queries. In the *Journal of American Architecture*. In things like, what it is…Craig's List? People might be very happy to volunteer information. A chance to talk about their homes."

"That's enormous."

"Truly? You think this? Maybe not. You are to be very specific in your query. You say, 'I am looking for such and such a room, built in such and such a time, in such and such an area.' Think, Caitlyn, of that book you like so much, *Back Bay Houses*. You do realize, don't you, that at some point, the author…the name slips from my mind. I'm getting old."

"Bailey Munce. No, you're not old."

"Yes, Munce. He must knocked on every door in the Back Bay. It must have seemed enormous, like you think. But finite.

And look at the result. It could be a way to distinguish yourself, make your career, in academia, here at Harvard possibly."

"And what about Bacht?"

"Oh, Bacht, Bacht, you have to stop worrying about Allen! He is just a man. You have worried enough about him. It is time for you to move on. He is not Satan. Time enough for your anger. Use it now in a better way. Be a better woman. Be a better researcher. I will handle Allen. I keep telling you this. I will handle Allen. Listen to me."

Caitlyn found herself, just for a moment, to be frightened. Venda was offering her a much larger vision of work, of possibilities, than she had given herself. Could she do it?

"As long as you bring him up," Caitlyn said, "what did you think about the Viktor Bacht material?"

"It is disgusting. But it is the truth."

"And for Dr. Bacht?"

"In reality, it has nothing to do with him. For now, of course, you cannot use it. But move forward. Maybe, when he learns of what you have done, we can convince him to participate."

Caitlyn sat back into her chair. "Wow."

"Why is that? What is this 'wow'?"

"You have given me a lot to think about," Caitlyn said.

"You are capable, Caitlyn. You are here at a very young age. You have drive and intelligence and enormous curiosity. You can do this. You have the time. Think about what I have told you. Make some plans. Aim for the moon. Let's talk more."

Briefly, Caitlyn wished that the universe had warned her that this moment was approaching. That there were always going to be times when life offered unexpected invitations. Lately, it seemed as if they came to her regularly. "Thank you," Caitlyn said. "Thank you for saying this."

Venda said, "You are welcome."

After the two of them chatted a while longer, Caitlyn once more thanked her mentor and left, with Venda's admonition to be ambitious lingering in her mind. And as she walked down the stairs to her office, oddly, her thoughts turned to another question. Caitlyn suddenly knew that, no matter what happened at Fenway Park, a couple weeks away, she would be ready and able to handle it.

CHAPTER SEVENTY-TWO

CAITLYN

May 2017

Fenway Park! Soon after Caitlyn had arrived in Boston, she was aware of the important place that the stadium had in the hearts of New Englanders. Did other cities dote upon a baseball park the way locals did with Fenway? She didn't think so. True believers, like Henry in his Red Sox baseball cap, were legion. Living in the epicenter of Sox worship, she almost found it difficult to believe that Fenway, the oldest major league baseball stadium in the country, wasn't revered by everybody, including people who never set foot in Boston or watched a game.

She had done homework before the big day. Fenway had been built in 1912, and over the years, it had expanded; had been damaged in a fire; had been patched up and expanded again, and yet again. Proposed plans to replace it more than a decade ago with a new structure had been abandoned in favor of renovations. Fenway Park would remain the capital of Red Sox Nation for the foreseeable future.

Even though she'd told Henry that she was only mildly interested in seeing the Sox play, as she neared the stadium for the afternoon game, her excitement soared much more than she had anticipated. Nearby Lansdowne Street had been roped off and turned into a street fair, with vendors pushing hot dogs, bottles of water, souvenirs. The crowd was buoyant.

She just wished someone were by her side to share the experience. Of course, that circumstance could change very soon. Admittedly, the excitement of the game was complicated by her uncertainty about the ticket. She could be spending the next three hours sitting next to David Chieswicz. If that happened, she was determined to make the best of it, to focus on the game, to remember that the man could be dying. She would use this chance to make peace with him and their situation.

And, of course, the possibility existed that it wasn't David Chieswicz at all. In her heart, she hoped Henry would be by her side.

She passed through the entrance gate and offered her maroon backpack for inspection to a good-looking guy with a metal detector. After ambling in the interior arcade, she eventually bought a Fenway Frank from one of several look-alike stands and then dressed the hot dog with relish and mustard. Nothing about the wiener was pretentious, which made it great.

The crowd grew, and the time came to head to the stands. Figuring out the stadium's layout wasn't difficult. A short ramp led her outdoors again into sunny, brisk air. Her nervousness mounted. As she found her way to her section, she looked over the crowd and searched for any familiar face. About half of the red seats were still unfilled. She maneuvered through some narrow aisles until she reached her row. Her seat was the first one in, on the aisle. The next was empty, and in the two beyond it were a man, maybe in his late thirties, and a boy of grade school age, presumably the man's son.

Her seat had a clear view over third base to the pitcher's mound. Marvelous. Players were warming up, and there was a lot to take in: electronic scoreboards that flashed ads and stats and shots of the crowd; yellow-clad vendors selling pizza, popcorn, beer, lemonade; snippets of high-energy recorded music; other ticket holders continually shuffling past her to get to their places. The fans were a sea of red. If she ever came here again, she'd be sure to adorn herself with some red garment. She took pictures of everything with her phone, and checked in on Instagram, noting that she couldn't believe she was at a baseball game.

Pre-game activity began: a sentimental promotion of a charity brought tears to her eyes; a powerful rendition of the National Anthem caused tears again; the Red Sox starting line-up was announced, and even that made her cry, it seemed so epochal, so full of tradition. The dad in the nearby seat took pity on her and chatted in between moments of attending to his son.

Red Sox Nation booed a few of the New York Yankees when they were announced. And as the first of their batters took his place at home plate, the seat next to Caitlyn remained empty.

By the fourth inning, Caitlyn resigned herself to being alone and tried not to be distracted by the puzzle of the ticket. The score seesawed back and forth until the Sox pulled ahead in the seventh with five runs. She found herself robustly singing "Sweet Caroline," the Sox's unofficial anthem, at the bottom of the eighth. Although the lead didn't change, she stayed in place until the end, savoring the event, despite her confusion, despite the mystery.

After the game, she walked to Back Bay Station, about half-mile away, to avoid the worst of the post-game crush at the Kenmore Square T stop. As she absent-mindedly looked up at the buildings of Back Bay, she tried to make sense of what had just happened. Or, more accurately, what hadn't happened. Perhaps someday she'd hear from whomever sent the ticket and get an explanation. Perhaps the sender had simply forgotten, or gotten lost, or gotten cold feet, or had a conflict, or maybe it was all a mistake. She wanted to know the truth, of course, but she had no idea how to find it.

CHAPTER SEVENTY-THREE

CAITLYN

May 2017

The day after the game, in mid-afternoon, following a session of coursework at her office, Caitlyn boarded the subway and aimed for the South End, for another try at Nine Chadwick Square. Dark clouds gathered, and she checked a weather app on her phone. Rain was predicted. Yet she felt an unusual optimism about this attempt and the prospect of a storm didn't deter her. She intuited that today her knock would finally be answered.

When she exited at Back Bay Station—the same station she'd used after the game—the rain had begun, not yet a downpour, but steady and uncomfortable. Many people on Dartmouth Street walked swiftly, heads down, caught off guard, without protection against the weather. She opened a collapsible umbrella and aimed to Chadwick Square. She second-guessed her transportation choice. The #1 Bus might have gotten closer to her destination, kept her dryer. An Uber to Chadwick Square was an unnecessary expense, however, since the walk would only take ten minutes. She hoped her slacks wouldn't be soaked by the time she reached the door.

She walked down Washington Street, crossed Blackstone Square, and passed a makeshift memorial to a young girl that she'd never noticed before. The pile of teddy bears and flowers was a sodden mess. A picture of the girl, a blonde named Emily, was protected by a plastic page holder but it, too, had suffered from damage by the elements, the ink at its edges starting to run. At a different time, Caitlyn might have stopped and looked more closely, but the rain caused her to rush.

Another block took her to the edge of Chadwick Square. She approached the steps of Nine Chadwick. The force of the rain increased. In the storm, no one else was visible, except another pedestrian more than a block away. A flash of lightning surprised her. The skies became very dark. She folded her umbrella and knocked. She hoped Rumberg would answer, if for no other reason than to get her out of the storm. Well, that wasn't exactly true. Shelter would be an added benefit to finally seeing the building. But she waited, as she had many times before, and as with all those other times, no one responded.

Positive thinking was the key, she told herself, and she tried to imagine Rumberg, or whomever, opening the door. A visioning exercise. She knocked again, this time more strongly. She could hear something rustling on the inside but after a minute the place was still shut tight.

She went downstairs to the basement entrance. Below street level, a small puddle had gathered at the foot of the steps, and she had to stand off to the side to avoid putting her feet in the water. She was unsteady. She rapped sharply on the splintering door. *Dear God! Why won't he answer?*

The dirt-covered design on a column caught her eye. The rain had washed away some of the soot, and the pattern was like an interlocking series of "C's." She'd seen this pattern before: on the grave of the Carter family, where Josiah had been buried on Cobb's Hill. And on the church plans. A realization came to her. The Carters had been builders. This might have been a signature. And she flashed on the biographical material she'd seen on Simpson. Someone named Carter had testified on his behalf. Theodore Carter's son would have been of college age in the 1850's.

This was it, the connection she sought! Josiah Hawkins could have introduced the Carter's son to the Boston Box! And he could have carried it to others: Simpson, Gannigan, architects for whom he did the construction. So obvious! Why had she not made this link before? Then again, as a builder, not an architect, he would have flowed through her initial filtering. And Carter was such a common name.

She wanted a picture of the design. While trying to juggle her umbrella, she withdrew her phone and took some pictures of the chain-styled ornamentation.

A window near the steps was covered by a white opaque curtain, and the panel closest to her had been moved aside, leaving about an inch between it and the window frame. It was rude to peek inside, but frustration got the better of her, and she peered into the sliver of space. There, she saw, not three feet away, a stocky man, standing still, looking at her with the phone in hand.

He startled her. He moved toward the entrance. She'd waited for this introduction for months now and swallowed her excitement. She hoped he hadn't seen her take the picture. That might not be the proper way to open a conversation, with her being defensive.

The door opened. "Mr. Rumberg?" she asked. Whoever it was, he was a heavy, unsavory looking man. He smelled.

She thought she could hear some noise out in the street and turned to face it, and the man in the doorway, presumably

Rumberg, heard it, too. Before she knew what had happened, she felt him yank her hair and pull her into the house. *"OUCH!"* she shouted. But the shock was such that she was disoriented. He swung his arm downward, pulling her off-balance, and in a second, she was tossed upon the floor of the basement, a dimly lit room with a threadbare rug. She hit her head. She heard the door slam.

Caitlyn was stunned by the pain, and the surprise, and for a few seconds, she couldn't speak. While on the floor, Rumberg punched her in the face.

"What do you know?" he hissed. "Why are you taking pictures?"

She wanted to scream but he was on top of her now. His sweat was fetid. She struggled. He hit her again.

"What are you doing here? What do you know?" he demanded.

"Please don't hurt me," she begged, crying. "I'm just a student...please!" She struggled to sit upright, but then Rumberg struck another blow, fierce, and her head hit the floor with a thud. Whether it was fright and shock, or the force of the punch, or the impact on the floor, she was suddenly in the dark, falling into space, no longer sensible, no longer conscious.

Caitlyn couldn't tell how long she had been knocked out. Perhaps seconds; perhaps hours. She opened her eyes but that made no difference. Total blackness surrounded her. And then remembering what had happened, she moved her head with a start, raising her body, alert for another attack. If Rumberg were there, she would not be able to see him. But she didn't smell him now or hear his breathing, so not sensing his presence, she unclenched her body and crumpled back onto the cold floor.

In moments, more awake, she stretched her right leg and felt a shoot of pain. It must have banged against something, but she didn't recall any blow. Her face was wet. She touched her head, which was throbbing. Stickiness. Blood? Her fingertips ran along a gash in her scalp, an inch or more. In the dark, she couldn't tell if the blood still oozed, or how fast.

She uncurled more, moving onto her knees, and felt around the floor with her hands. Tile? Her leg hurt again. She groaned. The layout of the room was impossible to see. Her palms slid across a wooden riser, a step. She seemed to be at the bottom of a stairway.

Heavy footsteps pounded elsewhere in the house. They moved fast.

She heard breathing. Had she become disembodied? She herself was indeed moaning, but was it the ringing in her head that made her think the sound came from somebody else?

Was he there? Suddenly she screamed. "OH, GOD! HELP ME! SOMEBODY HELP ME!"

She twisted and yelled again, crawling, moving around on the floor, desperate, afraid to stand, one hand extended in front of her, the other propping her up. She touched a wall. It was padded. Back on the floor, she felt debris and she knocked something over, a bowl, and putrid liquid covered the floor.

Urine. Feces.

She recoiled, cried out once more, her throat torn by her yell. She swept her arms around wildly in the absolute darkness. She stumbled and fell. Her right hand knocked against an object that was soft, warm, pliant.

A body.

She screamed again.

PART FOUR

Mark: May 2017

CHAPTER SEVENTY-FOUR

MARK

May 2017

What I remember. Some sort of hard pillow hitting me in the face. Doors slamming. Or was it just one door? An engine whining unhappily.

I smell whiskey. I smell hot.

Sirens. Murmuring voices. Some man tried to speak to me. I remember that, too. I couldn't answer. I know I was put on a stretcher. Hoisted by my shoulders, hands gripping my lower legs. Or maybe I remember that because it had to happen. I am tired and want to rest.

It was all so quiet and then it was all so noisy. Sirens? The only thing that really hurts is the side of my face. Like before.

But mostly I don't remember much. Please let me sleep.

When I awoke, I was in a single patient hospital room, on my back on a bed. Everything was as white as heaven, and my eyes hurt. My ex, Paul, sat nearby, which confused me. Were we together? Was our breakup something I had hallucinated, the last year just a nightmare? Were all of the events surrounding Dave just a dream?

"Hi," Paul said. His voice was tender. "How are you?"

"What happened? Where am I?"

"You were in a car accident, Mark," he said. "You're not hurt. Not too bad, anyway. Lucky. The car is totaled. Front-end. You're at Saint E's." Saint Elizabeth's Hospital was in Brighton, not too far from my old apartment.

"The BMW?"

"Yes."

"I'm alive?"

"Yes."

I tried to recall any of it. There was the alley with Clarence and his accomplice. But after that…

"Why are you here?" I said.

"I'm listed as your emergency contact."

I'd meant to take care of that detail but never got around to it. Lack of urgency, I supposed. Or denial. Mostly, I didn't know who I should put in his place. "Sorry," I said. I was hoarse. "I'll change it." I felt extremely tired, like from a hangover, complete with headache. An IV was in my left arm; the veins in my right arm showed bruises from being pricked for blood samples.

Paul touched my shoulder. "It's okay. I'll get the nurse."

In the next moments, a swarm of medical personnel buzzed around me. I passively obeyed their commands: move, lift, say my name, remember my birthday, wiggle my fingers, wiggle my toes, count backward from ten. Everyone wanted to know the last four digits of my Social Security number. Enough monitors for a rocket launch were wired to me and repeatedly checked. Plastic things were put in my mouth, under my tongue. I was prodded, patted, and pinched. After this examination gauntlet had been traveled, a young doctor—short woman, short hair—sidled up to my bedside and told me that under the circumstances, I was fortunate: no broken bones, mostly cuts and contusions, a small concussion. I'd been knocked out; drugs afterward may have kept me under. Some x-rays had been taken while I was unconscious, and they showed no sign of serious brain injury. I'd stay another night or two for observation, but if complications didn't arise, I'd be released soon. I was told that someone had to pick me up. With a glance, she implied that Paul would take on that duty.

"I'll work on in it," I said.

The doctor glanced back and forth between the two of us. "Think about it."

The doctor, nurses, technicians cleared out of the room, except for an all-white woman—clothes, skin, hair, shoes—who futzed around at a small table in a corner. White was the color of the day, or the lack of color. So bright.

Paul neared me. "How you feeling?"

"Confused," I said. I had to concentrate, almost as if performing a 28-point mechanical self-inspection before I could answer accurately. "Hungry," I added. Another pause. "Sore."

"Do you remember anything?"

"No, not much."

"Were you drinking?"

"No. That's not it."

"They said they smelled alcohol. You could be in trouble. A DUI."

My last clear memory was getting abused by Clarence and his friend, and I hadn't drunk anything before that.

"I'll call my lawyer," I said. I addressed the nurse. "Is my phone around? But I wasn't drinking."

"Perhaps you should rest," Paul said.

I knew he meant well and that I should have appreciated his attention. To some degree, I did. But it was very difficult to have Paul by my side. His help was false to who we were to one another now. I didn't want to lean on a broken crutch that was going to crack any second and leave me sprawled on the ground. "I'm sorry you got involved. I'll change the papers. I really appreciate you're being here. But you can go. I'll be okay."

I couldn't tell if he understood, whether he thought that I was ungrateful or that I wanted to hurt him. When we were together, I often sensed what Paul felt, but that time had passed. I no longer knew him.

"Don't be that way," he said.

"I'm not any way in particular. I'm fine. The doctor said so. I'll call my lawyer. You've already gone to too much trouble. You were very good to come here. Thank you. I mean it."

"You're upset."

"Yeah. I think it's safe to say that. But not with you. I'll be in touch when I'm in better shape."

"Mark."

"Paul," I said dramatically.

He didn't laugh. "I'll give you some time alone, okay? Call me if you need something. Seriously. Straightaway. I'll come back."

"I will call. Thank you." He kissed me on the forehead. I was grateful, after how he had reacted to my getting the BMW, that he didn't say *I told you so*.

The white nurse had tried to fade into the background during my conversation with Paul. After he had gone, she said, "He seems like a nice man."

"Yes," I confirmed. "He was. Is. Is a very nice man."

CHAPTER SEVENTY-FIVE

MARK

May 2017

With the ashes of my dead relationship brushed away one more time, I turned to the still raging fires of my very fucked-up situation. My cell phone had been recovered with me and it had enough of a charge for me to call Dietz. I told him I could be in trouble. He said he'd come at once.

In the moments before his arrival, anxiety overtook me, with my worries ranging from my lost suitcase to whether Clarence would continue to beat me up until he got his money. Would he want more and more after that? Was I going to be arrested? Get fired? Were any of my injuries permanent? And the car was gone. My BMW! That list made some of my problems of a few weeks ago, loneliness and bankruptcy, seem like cupcakes.

I got out of bed, assisted by a nurse and dragging the IV pole, in order to pee, and I saw myself in a mirror for the first time since the accident. After my injuries two weeks earlier at the KFC, the banged-up face in my reflection was almost familiar. You know that life isn't good when black eyes become a way you recognize yourself. At least I wasn't dead. Yet death had come too close. I shivered. If being murdered could happen to my brother, it could happen to me.

I returned to my bed, yelping as I crawled under a sheet, one of the bruises in my side aching like a bastard. Soon Dietz arrived, his reassuring unflappability on full display. While he approached me, he peered over the frames of his glasses. "Fell on a sidewalk again?"

"Same sidewalk," I answered.

"So what happened?" He slid a metal chair near to me and sat down. "I'm sorry for your injuries."

I told Dietz what I knew, starting with my vandalism of Clarence's car—a story that elicited a deadpan look shaded with disbelief in my idiocy—and then went onto the extortion threat, my visit to the Brighton apartment, and Clarence's assault. I mentioned Russ by name. I confessed honestly that I didn't remember anything about the accident, and that I believed that I was set up to take a fall for a DUI.

"Why didn't you tell me about the threats?"

"I'm not used to having a lawyer on call. I'm not rich. Not to mention, I was a moron."

"Are you holding anything else back?"

I had known that question would come. Although I'd told Dietz of Russ's claim that Dave owed him money, I hadn't yet revealed the possible illegality of my inheritance. Nor had I told him about my gun, which was still back at the Brighton apartment. Even though he had sort of recommended it. Or about Junior. "I'm not holding anything back," I lied.

"Do you have any criminal record? Felonies? Arrests?"

"None."

"Driving violations? Accidents?"

"The vandalism to my BMW I told you about," I said. "Not my fault. The only claim I've ever made. Other than that, not even a ticket. Well, some parking. All paid."

"This guy. Russ Celano. Contact information?"

"Yes." I retrieved Russ's cell number from my phone. "My charge is running down."

"Okay," Dietz said. "Here's what I'm going to do. First, I'm going to send a message to Mr. Celano to have his lawyer give me a call. Unless he's very arrogant or stupid, we should be able to get you a break from any intimidation and extortion. It may not last forever. But if they contact you again, you let me know. Got it?"

I nodded.

"Your biggest problem is Hudson," Dietz said.

"No shit," I answered.

"Again, I think we can get Celano to put a lid on him for a while, but Hudson is not a rational man."

I shuddered. "Can you get some kind of restraining order against him?"

"You haven't filed any charges prior to this. I can rattle that cage but dubious. You'd have to provide a lot of details."

"It was a thought."

"Everything helps. Next, I'll be in touch with the police about the accident and see what's pending. If they come by, do not speak with them. Tell them to get in touch with me."

"I don't even know where the accident was."

As if our conversation had caused them to materialize, a pair of uniformed cops—both of them middle-aged white guys—appeared at the door of the hospital room. Dietz stood, grimaced, and managed the introductions. The fact that he was a lawyer didn't surprise the police. He suggested that the two policemen speak with him in the hospital hallway, which brought forth half-hearted belligerent retorts, almost mechanical, like the cops didn't have enough energy for a battle with an attorney but they had to put on a show. Their chat in the hallway lasted about fifteen minutes. When it was over, Dietz re-entered alone and sat near my bed again.

"So?" I said.

"I told them you didn't remember anything, which, as far as the accident is concerned, has the important advantage of being true. You'll have to give a statement, probably in the next day or two, but I explained that you were in no condition yet to talk to them. Which is also true enough."

"Thanks. Did they say anything about the accident?"

"You were found behind the wheel of your car on a bypass road near Soldiers Field. No witnesses to the accident. There was an open bottle of whiskey on the passenger's seat, and a strong smell of alcohol on you. My guess is that Hudson and his pal splashed some around. Circumstantial. But unless they force fed you, chances are your blood alcohol level isn't going to back up an accusation. We might say the bottle broke in the accident. Don't know yet."

"What about the truth?" I said. "That I was set-up?"

Dietz shifted in the chair. "Don't know yet about that either. Could be a bargaining chip when I talk to Celano or his attorney. Your silence for their cooperation. Cross that bridge when we come to it. It's not exactly a story that's immediately credible, even if it's true."

"Do you have any idea what happened?"

"You were set-up, like you said. They wrecked the car and put you in the driver's seat. Little complicated with airbags, but there are all kinds of specialists these days. Maybe they put you there first, before the crash. That guy, Edo, never heard of him, but if I did some digging, I wouldn't be shocked if he was a go-to man for this sort of thing. No report of excessive speed, at least yet, but fast enough to damage the car and a brick retaining wall. Don't take much these days to total a car. Let's just say they're sending you a message."

"Like pay up?"

"Or maybe you just don't get artistic with a hit man's car again. I'll talk with Celano. Or his attorney, like I said. We should find a short-term solution. For the long term, we'll have to see."

"Should I leave town?" I asked.

"Don't know. Maybe. Not until you talk to the police. I'd lay low. Stay in the apartment. Get a disguise."

I always wondered how I'd look as a blond.

"If I lose my license, I don't have a job," I said. Thank God, several days in my leave were still ahead.

"We'll try to keep that from happening. They, Hudson and his pals, probably know that. A little cherry on the top of their coercion sundae. I can't make promises. Just don't say anything to anybody, to the police, to Celano, to anybody. Got it?"

I nodded.

"Anything else?" he asked.

"One more thing," I said, tentatively.

"What is it?"

I was embarrassed.

"What?" he asked again.

"Can you pick me up tomorrow?"

Dietz made no promises. He was my lawyer, not my friend, and at $325/hour, he would be an expensive limo driver. I didn't think the hospital would release me on my own. Dietz said he'd check with his administrative assistant, who was a do-gooder and might be willing to help, if I could put up with getting a religious pamphlet at the end of the ride.

I was able to borrow a charging cord for my phone from one of the nurses and kept it working. I became agitated when I got two hang-ups over the course of the evening. The numbers were blocked so I couldn't tell if the calls came from either Clarence or Russ, but they spooked me. Any hope I felt from Dietz's visit and his efforts to protect me ebbed away. I reminded myself that he hadn't had much time yet to work on my problems. Yet even if he was eventually able to ward off Clarence for a while, my longtime viability as a living and breathing human being was in doubt.

On the ever-shrinking positive side of the ledger, I still had claim to the money. And I still had a gun.

I probably would have tossed and turned all night were it not for a sedative or something that the doctor had prescribed, which, combined with emotional exhaustion, put me into a deep sleep. I dreamed about owning a dog. I wasn't sure where that came from since I hadn't had a dog since childhood, back when the four Chieswiczs still were a family.

CHAPTER SEVENTY-SIX

MARK

May 2017

After an inconclusive x-ray of my head, the doctors decided to hold me at the hospital for another night. In the intervening period, Dietz called and reported that his receptionist had agreed to help me. He also said that he'd had a conversation with Russ Celano's lawyer, and while no agreements had been formally brokered, my situation had been reviewed in unpleasant detail. Reading between the lines, Dietz thought a virtual safety barrier would shield me from harm for a short period. He could make no promises about forever. I told him about the hang-ups. I also asked him if there was any sign of my suitcase in the car wreckage. He didn't know.

I sent a short text to Paul to tell him that I didn't need a ride.

The following morning, after several brief physical examinations with more reassuring results, I was permitted to leave. Although bruised, I wasn't in bad shape. Dietz's receptionist turned out to be a talkative, not unintelligent woman, who, in between the moments of our chatting, had long discussions with the National Public Radio commentators who came over her car radio. Her viewpoints didn't jibe with NPR. I prevailed upon her to drive first to my Brighton apartment so I could pick up a few things, and she waited in the car while I got my backpack and the gun. I smiled innocently on my return. At my request, she also swung by a grocery store to allow me to grab some sustenance for the stay at my luxurious bunker on the Fenway. I threw a box of hair coloring into my grocery basket. Quizzical looks, invited by my black eye, prompted me to buy some makeup.

Dietz's warning to the contrary, the receptionist offered no religious pamphlet at our parting. He might have been kidding. Neither Clarence, nor Edo, nor any black Mercedes showed up during the journey.

Because the Fenway Grand was a doorman building, I was safe as long as I stayed in the apartment. I tried to figure out something worthwhile to do with my time. I couldn't think of how to trace Junior online, so that diversion was ruled out. But I had the gun, and a bigger incentive to become accustomed to it. I'd never be as fast as a cowboy, but I needed to be better than I was. No more fumbling. I put on the shoulder holster, which kept the gun close to my upper body. I rehearsed drawing the gun, first without wearing a jacket, and then with one, because that would be the only way to hide the holster when I left the apartment. Unzip, grip, stance, fire. Over and over again.

I wondered whether a way existed for me to become the hunter, not the prey. If I had a picture of Clarence's car license, I could use it to uncover his address and track him. To strike first. That scenario was a flight of fancy. All of my wounds and suffering had not turned me into an offensive player. I was still on defense. I was never going to hunt down Clarence and shoot him.

The sports metaphors—offense, defense—reminded me of the Red Sox ticket on the refrigerator. The game was two

days away. I'd see if there was some safe way to use it. Worse
case, I would give it to one of the staff at the Fenway Grand. It
shouldn't go to waste.

Unzip, grip, stance, fire. My body was sore from the accident, and after a time, I was exhausted. Being smashed to a pulp
took it out of you. I rested. Then more unzip, grip, stance, fire.
If Clarence tried to beat me up again—no, *when* Clarence and I
had another encounter, I'd be ready.

The next day, the cops came to the apartment to take my state-
ment. This time, the duo included my friend Detective Taylor.
He was difficult to read. He knew about the tire slashing, and
this latest incident must have signaled that all was not right in
Chieswiczville. But so far, he hadn't deduced the whole story.
Not surprising, since I wasn't fully forthcoming.

Dietz was present, and we had rehearsed ahead of time. I
stuck to my earlier account: I remembered nothing as a result of
the accident, my last memory was my trip to my old apartment
to gather up some odds and ends. I didn't say anything about
Clarence. Dietz helped me with this tactic, part of the agreement
he'd worked out for now with Russ Celano's attorney in return
for my safety. I did deny any drinking. My blood levels backed
up that claim. A DUI would be disastrous for my Duck job. I
wasn't cleared yet, however, since that other circumstantial evidence, the bottle in the car, supported a possible charge.

In the end, I was betting $633,215.28 that Taylor would be-
lieve me, even if that figure was being nibbled at by legal costs.
When Taylor and his partner left the apartment, it wasn't clear
if I'd placed my money on a winning proposition.

Before Dietz went, he advised me once more to lay low.
He repeated that Clarence's participation in the brokered agree-

ment was by no means assured. Dietz didn't forbid me from leaving the Fenway Grand—that wasn't within his power—but he did say that if I ventured out, I should be vigilant and take whatever precautionary measures I could.

After that, I was alone again. I still had to work things out with the insurance company about the BMW, but I decided to put off any action for a couple of days. As much as I loved the car, it had been a curse since the beginning. I was considering a more sensible vehicle to replace it. A Subaru. A Mini-Cooper. Or I might accept my destiny to be a T rider for the rest of my life. Rent Zipcars. Use Uber.

I was glad that Dietz's warning wasn't absolute because after a short time in isolation, I was stir crazy, and the ticket to the Red Sox looked more and more inviting. Going to the game would be a calculated risk. The crowd offered a type of protection, and the stadium was barely a five-minute walk away. The biggest complication was that because of Fenway's security measures, I couldn't bring along the gun.

A disguise could help in evading Clarence. I retrieved the box of hair coloring, stared at it, and wondered about the wisdom of going blond. Nothing guaranteed that I'd fool anyone. And I'd never tried to dye my hair before. According to the internet, I'd unintentionally made the right decision in my choice of product: a semi-permanent dye, so if I fucked up, the color would wash out after several shampoos. On the other hand, I'd picked a tone that was well beyond the recommended "three shades lighter" than my natural color. In the end, because of the dye's short life, I asked myself how bad it could be.

The answer: pretty bad.

The results proved two things. First, despite stereotypes, not all gay men are born to be hairdressers. Second, the internet isn't always a reliable way to learn how to do something. My now almost platinum hair could best be described as refugee-meets-David Bowie, circa 1973. Once I applied makeup to hide my black and blue marks, I had a pallor not unlike my brother's when he rested on the stretcher in the morgue. For added style, I hadn't worn latex gloves during the dye job, so my fingers were yellow from the chemicals, as if I'd doused them in iodine.

What was done was done. I decided to live with my new look for a few days. Nobody important would see me anyway.

I poked around the apartment and found two more items for my masquerade: Dave's pair of the horn-rimmed reading glasses, weak enough for me to use, and, praise God, a baseball cap. No one would ever recognize me, but it wasn't a great disguise because I was so ugly that I'd possibly attract negative attention. No anonymity. However, should I decide to go to the game, I needn't worry about anyone attacking me. No one in their right mind would want to get near me.

I convinced myself that the game was a good idea. I hadn't been to Fenway in a long, long time. The Yankees were the classic Sox opponents. I didn't see what could go wrong.

You would think that dyeing my hair would teach me a lesson about how things can turn out much worse than you expect.

CHAPTER SEVENTY-SEVEN

MARK

May 2017

The second I saw her, I knew she was Junior.

To be cautious, I'd gone the stadium at the last minute, the crowds at their peak, safety in numbers. I was on the way up the steps to my seat. When she came into view, I was moving slowly because of the swarm, and I spotted her without being observed myself. She tapped away on her phone, sending a text, and her eyes were lowered. The mole on her neck was what reminded me immediately of Dave. But more dramatically, had I compared her to a photograph of my mother at the same age, like the wedding picture that Dave had in the apartment, the two of them could have been twins.

I hadn't considered that Dave had made arrangements to meet someone at the game, least of all his kid. Caught off-guard, I was shaken and uncertain about how to handle the situation, or if I was capable of it. Fortunately, because of the stadium's bustle, she didn't make out who I was. Not that I had any reason to think she could know that I was a relative. I didn't know crap about what she might put together. She might not even realize I existed. Or if she did, buried in my dreadful disguise, whether she'd recognize me, or guess who I was.

Instead of taking my seat, I continued up the steps, located myself near the rear of the section, and watched her from behind. She seemed to search for someone. Dave, perhaps. That suggested she had no idea that he was dead.

The situation was confounding, to say the least. I was threatened, upset, worried, and even intrigued by the idea that I'd found Junior. A niece. Or maybe I had had too many bangs on the head, or too many pills, or hair dye had seeped into my brain, and I'd jumped to a wrong conclusion. In the moment, it was too much for me to sort through. I needed to chill. I needed to think.

I didn't want to walk up to her and introduce myself. My space-aged hair and thick make-up made me looked awful. A troll. Moreover, if she didn't know about Dave's death, and apparently she didn't, this wasn't going to be the place to tell her. And my guess, that she was Dave's daughter, still had to be confirmed. My presumption was based on instinct, and without more information or proof, it could simply be a fabrication of my injured brain and circumstances.

And self-interest had a strong grip on me: The $633,218.28 was slipping away. I was conflicted. If the money was hers, so be it, but I wasn't going to hand it over without certainty.

I waited in the background for a while, riveted by her. An attendant approached me and asked if I needed help finding my place. I showed her my ticket to prove I wasn't homesteading and then said no, that I had to stretch my legs. She didn't question my claim, but to put off another query I checked out the rest of the section and homed in on three empty seats from which I could keep an eye on Junior. Obviously, she was no longer "Junior," but that name would have to work until I learned her real one.

I slipped down the row over the knees of about a dozen other fans, sat in one of the empty seats, and shot a few pictures of her with my phone. Easy enough to do without attracting attention since everyone was snapping photos. Under the circumstances, it should be no surprise that the situation distracted me from the play on the field. The good news was that the Sox pulled ahead and were on their way to a win over the hated Yankees. I had some further good luck because Dave's daughter appeared to enjoy the game and stayed in her seat, which gave me time to plan what to do next.

This could be my only chance to learn who she was. I had to follow her and hope that she would lead me someplace where I could discover her identity. I'd be taking a big risk because, of course, I hadn't brought my gun, thereby exposing myself to an undefended attack. I imagined a little parade of spies: Clarence following me following Junior. Offsetting the danger was that I'd seen no evidence of Clarence. And the crowd would obscure me. I worried that Junior had traveled by car because I wouldn't be able to chase her in that case. I might get a license plate number.

The baseball game ended. Along with everyone else, Junior moved from her seat and out of the stadium, down Lansdowne Street. She was dressed casually, in jeans and a dark blue jacket, which at another time might have been difficult to keep track of, but in this throng, with its dominating red for the hometown boys, she stood out. She also carried a small maroon backpack with a trace of bright silver reflecting tape that I could follow without getting too close.

As she walked along, I watched for hints about her personality. Her hair was styled professionally and fashionably. A pair of white earbuds was plugged into her ears, and she occasionally typed something into her phone. Interestingly, and most unusually, she often had her head up to look at the buildings of Boylston Street, a habit that was especially noticeable in a crowd where everyone else either chatted sideways to a companion or watched the pavement.

She turned onto Dartmouth Street, walked a block, and entered Back Bay Station, an Orange Line subway stop. I panicked because, far behind as I was, she could get on a train before I caught up. I quickened my pace. The Charlie Card I used to pay my fare caused the turnstile to bleat. It wasn't loaded with enough value to cover the charge. I hastened to a ticketing kiosk where I could add ten bucks to the card, rudely pushing ahead of some foreign tourists. I acted like a creep, but I'd been behind others like them too many times before and it could take forever for them to figure out how to buy passes. I didn't have the time to help. This was urgent.

A digital sign above the turnstiles indicated a train was arriving for Oak Grove, one of two possible destinations. Four endless minutes had passed since I'd lost sight of Junior, and I rushed down the stone steps of the station to the lower level just in time to see her enter a car at the far end of the train. I wouldn't be able to reach her compartment, but I could jump on one closer to me. At the next stop, I stepped off to see if she had exited. She hadn't. I had enough time to move a few cars down the line, nearer to her. We went two more stops before she got off at a station, Downtown Crossing, which connected to the Red Line.

Once more, I dashed after her. The bruises from my accident pinged me with pain, and some internal voice berated me for pushing my body's abilities while I was supposed to be in recovery. I was sweating, and my make-up was probably runny, a new problem for me. When I reached the platform where the Red Line train would arrive, she was near the entrance and toying again with her phone. An alternative entry was available, around a wall, and I took it. She didn't notice me. I spotted a Harvard emblem on her backpack, and we were heading in the direction of Harvard Square, so I considered with wonder the possibility that my dumb brother Dave had fathered a Harvard student.

The train, making a racket, pulled into the station, and I went into the same car as she did, but at its farther end. The crush of passengers, mostly ballgame fans, helped me to remain undetected. She got out at Harvard Square and aimed toward a spot underground where she could grab a bus. This was dicey for me because the crowd would be sparse and there'd only be a single bus. I could be seen, but I didn't have much choice. I tried to hold back until the bus pulled up. Then I mingled with about fifteen other passengers who were gathered at the stop. I pulled down my baseball cap and hunched my shoulders. She had taken a seat at the front and I did my best to avoid eye contact although it would have been impossible for her not to see me.

I sat several rows behind her and stared out a window, leaning on my hand to hide my face. The bus left the station and made its way down Mass Ave. The sun had set. She stood up to leave very early on the route, and she and I would be the only riders getting off. She'd have to see me, but I had no choice other than to continue trailing behind her.

I kept my head down and avoided looking directly at her. When we were on the street, I went in the direction opposite to hers, a ruse, until she was far enough away for my behavior not to be too noticeable. I reversed course and shadowed her again. She turned down a street near a coffee house. I went into a trot;

I desperately prayed that she wouldn't go into any building before I saw which one it was. As soon as I negotiated the corner, I spotted her climbing the front steps of a triple-decker.

Bingo.

I waited. A light on the uppermost floor came on. I snuck onto the porch of the house where a mail slot had three names on it: L Freedman, C Gautry, and B Harris. I used my phone to record the names and heaved a sigh.

One of them was Junior.

CHAPTER SEVENTY-EIGHT

MARK

May 2017

I'd taken enough risks for the day, so I bypassed the subway for my trip home, instead ordering an Uber. Immediately on my return to the apartment, I went to my laptop and searched the three names from the mail slot. It didn't take long to winnow the list down to one: Caitlyn Gautry. She was easy to identify from her Facebook page. Although much of her content was blocked, several pictures of her face were available, there and elsewhere on the web. The more I stared at the photos, the more I saw my mother, my brother, myself. I set my mother's picture next to Caitlyn's image. Dead ringers.

I started to cry. I can't fully explain why. Maybe the loss of my claim on the money. Maybe the fact that Caitlyn existed. I had a niece. Someone in whom I saw so much of what I'd lost. Even if she came at what could be a very high price, she was my family. I buried my head on my folded arms. Minutes passed before I regained control of my emotions.

I became absorbed in learning whatever I could about her. She grew up outside of Philadelphia and was very accomplished: *summa cum laude* from Penn State, a doctoral program in architectural history at Harvard. One summer she apparently worked in Italy on an archeological dig. She played on a championship high school soccer team. A dynamo. A good woman. I was fascinated by her, yet after an hour, I felt overwhelmed and exhausted, and I moved away from the computer.

I faced my dilemma. Caitlyn had a moral, and probably legal, claim on Dave's inheritance. Of course, I'd no idea what her position would be on the matter, or what, if anything, she knew about Dave. But I couldn't deny her birthright. That had been done to me, in a fashion. Unless I wanted to forget her and be haunted by my deceit for the rest of my life, I had to be better to her than my family had been to me.

While in this state of mind the matter of the Boston Box resurfaced. Was there a connection between Caitlyn and the note in Dave's pocket? Maybe the Boston Box was misleading, with no link to Dave's death at all. Nevertheless, I needed to let Detective Taylor know about what I'd found out. But not before I talked it over with Dietz. And more importantly, and first, not before I talked it over with Caitlyn.

In bed, I wrestled with my pillows and my sheets as if they represented all of the issues in my life. I had ideas about what to do next, none of them perfect. At five o'clock, after a little sleep, I'd come to no conclusions except to learn more about Caitlyn and find a way to introduce myself.

In my web searches the night before I'd been unable to track down a phone number for her, and her email address at Harvard was protected behind a wall. I was sure I could find some way to reach her when the moment was right, but first I wanted to learn more. I had to be sure that I'd not created her and her relationship to Dave out of nothing but an overactive and possibly damaged imagination.

I rose and showered, and washed my hair several times, trying to get rid of as much of the dye as I could, in the event that I'd meet my niece. I dressed quickly and put on my holster and gun. My escape from the Fenway Grand, I believed, was undetected, except for Hesh, who was on duty, and whom I asked to call a cab. The Fenway Grand had connections for that kind of thing, discounted. I instructed the taxi driver to take me to the café that I'd seen at the corner of Caitlyn's street. It had had big windows bordered by counters where I could sit and watch her building.

At the café, I bought an extra-large cup of French Roast and some coffee cake and took up my observation post. Of course, I couldn't be sure that she hadn't already left even though the time was barely past seven when I'd taken my place. I reasoned that the worst-case scenario was that I'd missed my chance and would have to come back another time.

I tried not to use my phone too much because I didn't want to run down the battery. Someone had abandoned a copy of *The Boston Globe* at a nearby table and I retrieved it. An hour and a half later, I'd finished the coffee, had a second cup, had eaten the cake, plus a donut, and I'd read through the paper twice. My hope was evaporating, and my bladder was exploding. I had to break my vigil to pee.

A restroom was available at the rear of the café. I was only away for a few minutes but as I returned to my seat a surprise greeted me: Caitlyn stood in line, ready to place an order. A bulletin board hung on the wall near me. I swiveled toward it. A slew of makeshift flyers offered everything from yoga classes to cat sitters to learning eight languages at once, and I pretended to be absorbed by them. Surreptitiously, I glimpsed at Caitlyn. Once again, the family resemblance was unmistakable. But

I didn't stare for long. My appearance had changed from last night so I doubted that Caitlyn would recognize me from the subway or be aware that I stalked her. But I had to be cautious. As the day progressed, we might be in situations where I'd be more visible. If she noticed my presence now it might trigger suspicion later.

With coffee in hand, Caitlyn left the café. I said a silent prayer of thanks that she didn't sit at one of the tables at the café to do work, as had several other students, because hiding from her would have been impossible. I counted to ten and went out to the street. Caitlyn had crossed Mass Ave, and I dodged a stream of morning rush hour traffic to catch up with her. She eventually went onto Harvard property, near its law school. I trailed far behind as she walked on some sidewalks that intersected a college green and led onto a side street. She passed by beautiful, Gothic Memorial Hall and then soon entered what looked to be a classroom building.

I was stalled. It could be hours before she came out, and she could use any of several doorways. I wasn't certain whether an ID was needed to get into the building, and that seemed like an unwise move for me in any event. I'd already lost track of her—she was on one of several floors by now—and I was carrying a gun. I was pretty sure getting caught with an unregistered concealed pistol on a college campus wasn't a great idea.

The classroom building faced a small open space for pedestrians with a few park benches. I decided to sit there and wait. I hoped she'd reappear quickly. I really wasn't ready for a prolonged stakeout, but I didn't have anything better to do with my day. Or much of a choice.

After an hour, I wondered whether I should stay. My internal bargaining began: *Don't give up so easily,* countered by *Just what's the point of all this?* Answering my own question, I told myself that many pieces of the puzzle were still missing: Who killed Dave? What, if anything, did the Boston Box have to do with it? Did Caitlyn play a role? Was she who I thought she was? And then I considered that I could walk away, keep the money, and she'd never be the wiser. I told myself I didn't have the patience to just sit outdoors for hours on what was a fool's errand.

I checked a weather app on my phone and the forecast called for rain in the afternoon. The skies looked ominous. I'd been smart enough to bring my gun but not an umbrella. I should go.

In the end, I couldn't convince myself to leave. While sitting, I decided that somehow, somewhere, I would introduce myself to Caitlyn. If academia was anything like the real world, Caitlyn might leave at twelve o'clock to get lunch and sit, and that would be my chance. Soon, my brilliant thesis was confirmed. Caitlyn appeared and went to a nearby grocery store. I spied on her. She threw together something at the salad bar. Huge meal. Looked like a square foot of forage. But then she returned to the classroom building before I got the balls to introduce myself.

No big revelations from my spying, except that her eating schedule was the same as everyone else's and that she had no control at salad bars. It was going to take her at least a half-hour to finish that mound of food, so I ran back to the same market, used a customer restroom, grabbed a prepackaged sandwich and another cup of coffee and a *New York Times*, and returned to my bench. I tried to ration my distractions, so lunchtime was spent nibbling the sandwich in small bites.

The time crawled. I took out the paper, which was chock full of detailed articles, and read. Darker clouds had gathered and drops occasionally hit me on the head or splattered on the paper. At about two o'clock, I was bored out of my mind and on the edge of battiness, but miraculously, she reappeared. Fantastic!

Her pace was fast. She seemed determined. I followed her to Harvard Square, where she went into an entrance for the subway. I ran to the station gate and headed down to the platforms. She waited for an inbound train to Boston. In my hurry, I was reckless, and she noticed me. My mistake. I didn't think she made any connection to any of my earlier appearances, nor did she recognize me, but from now on I'd have to be careful and lag behind, or she could become suspicious. I didn't want to scare her. I hoped that she'd end up in a situation, like a bar, where I could approach her and not freak her out.

In my obsession with tracking Caitlyn, however, I'd made one big miscalculation.

I hadn't realized that I, too, was being watched.

CHAPTER SEVENTY-NINE

MARK

May 2017

Caitlyn switched trains at Downtown Crossing, once more to the Orange Line, just like after the Red Sox game, and got off at Back Bay, again as before. By the time she walked out of the station, rain was steady, and I was miserable because of my lack of protection. On the upside, her black umbrella was easy to see, even from a distance, so I was able to hold back and remain out of her sight.

With increasing confusion, I realized that she was going toward the neighborhood where I'd retraced Dave's steps, that is, the South End, in the vicinity of where I had speculated that Dave had been killed. Caitlyn obviously didn't live there. What could be drawing her? From her evident academic success to her blasé demeanor at the ballpark, being a murderer didn't fit with what I'd seen. My belief that it was a coincidence was contradicted by my memory of Dave's book markings.

I was more than a block behind her when she had stopped at the house of George, the pudgy man I'd encountered, and was knocking on the door. I stopped. This was very bizarre. I had a clear line of vision as she moved down to the lower level and rapped again. The rain was by now a full-fledged storm, clearing the streets of any pedestrians except me, and bringing the skies to a black almost like night. I was soaked.

Because of the rain, at first I didn't believe what I saw, the violent movement George used to pull her into the house. I uttered a cry. It happened so fast that I could have been mistaken. But my vision is good, and her disappearance had been sudden, a backward fall, and not in any way normal. It was as if I'd seen a plane crash or a pedestrian hit by a car. Unreal yet real.

Whether or not I'd misinterpreted the incident, I knew at once that I had no choice but to make sure that Caitlyn wasn't in any danger. After Dave's murder, after all of the circumstantial evidence that had led me here before, I didn't care if I made a fool of myself. If she were hurt, and I could have prevented it, I would never forgive myself. I was scared, yes, and the situation was awkward. But that didn't matter; this wasn't a time to be neurotic. I searched my pocket for my phone, in the event I had to call the police, and I started to run in the rain toward George's house. I tapped the gun under my jacket.

Unfortunately, I didn't get far. Clarence's Mercedes cut in front of me as I crossed a street and blocked my way. Jesus Christ! I wasn't able to get around him. I didn't know how he'd traced me. He pulled up to a curb, and shouted, "Get in, asshole." The Mercedes was still scratched.

Making a mad dash to George's place without a confrontation wasn't an option. Clarence could reach me without trouble and probably batter me to a pulp. I hesitated, not from any question that I'd get into his car—I wouldn't—but from weighing whether to draw the gun, the moment that I'd done all that my preparation for. I didn't have much time to decide. Deep down, despite my bluster, pulling the trigger on another human being would put me in a club that I never wanted to belong to.

But Caitlyn could be in danger!

"Not now," I said. I wish I could say that Clarence didn't scare the shit of me, but he did. I toyed with my jacket and edged around the car and away from him.

My words and movements were bright red flags in front of a chemically enhanced bull. *"Ten grand!"* was all he said. He looked ready to leap from the car.

Scared, resigned, in a rush to get to Caitlyn, I unzipped my jacket, grabbed the gun, and pointed it at Clarence. Bad for me, my phone fell from my hand as I did so. I was afraid to pick it up because he might use the diversion to strike. I wasn't speedy in drawing on him, but it didn't matter. He was still behind the wheel. "Drive off, fuckwad!" I said. I prayed that Caitlyn wasn't being hurt while Clarence and I compared dick size.

Clarence's expression was one of utter hatred. A countdown seemed to be ticking off in his brain as he decided how he was going to pulverize me. He reached for the door lever. I only had a second left to determine what to do. I took a stance, not as if I was going to fire my gun, but as if I was going to sprint, yet not away from him, but toward him.

As soon as he put his left foot on the ground, midway in the act of getting out of the car, I bolted toward him and threw myself against the half-open door, body-blocking a Mercedes. His head was smashed between the door and the car's frame, and his right hand, which he had placed on the edge of the door, was pinched in a wedge of metal. There was blood. He was stunned. I had inflicted some serious damage, but at least I hadn't shot him, hadn't killed him. My own bruises screamed at me in outrage.

I didn't have any time to second guess my reluctance to pull the trigger. Besides that fast check on his injuries, I hadn't a moment to lose, and I immediately bolted toward George's house. A string of curses and yowls echoed behind me. My shoulder hurt like hell from my attack. It'd be more black and blue soon, but at this point, what was one more bruise?

I worried that Caitlyn might be seriously hurt by now. I glanced backward. Clarence, a few hundred feet away, had tumbled back into the car.

My wet shoes squished like sponges on my feet. I reached George's door, the one on the lower level, and knocked on it loudly with my fist. "Let me in!" I shouted. I tried the handle. It was locked.

I checked the street. Clarence was standing in the rain, holding his injured right hand in the left. I went back to George's entrance and banged again. A window was adjacent to the door, and through a drawn curtain I looked into the room. A cell phone lay there. I thought I recognized it. Blood stained the floor. I couldn't call the police. My own phone was somewhere on the street behind me.

"SHIT! FUCK! SHIT!" I yelled.

I walked back up a few of the steps, gripped the gun, took my stance, and fired at the door handle. The pistol almost jumped from my hand. It was the first time I'd actually shot something. Some splinters struck my skin. An acrid smell of gunpowder stung my nostrils. The door flew open. I probably just made a fool of myself and assured a stay in a jail. I was lucky that the bullet hadn't ricocheted and hit me.

Adding to the sick feeling in my gut, Clarence was moving again.

I went down and pushed my way into the house. I didn't have much of a chance to assess the situation because George appeared from nowhere. He had a good sixty pounds on me.

Animated by anger, fear, madness, and God knew what other evil energy, his size became formidable. His gaze was wild, a desperate creature caught in a spring trap. Hell. I'd just blown my way into his house. The only *good* thing about seeing him was that it confirmed I was right to fear for Caitlyn. The really, really *bad* thing was a hefty chef's knife, ten-inch blade, very sharp point, that he held in his right hand. It gleamed even in the dim room. Oh, Christ! I hoped he hadn't used it on Caitlyn! At least, no blood dripped from it, but the stain on the floor was fresh, as I'd feared.

"Stay calm," I said. The timbre of my voice made it clear that I wasn't following my own suggestion. "Where is she? What did you do to her?"

George breathed heavily, his bald head glistening with sweat. "Who the hell are you?"

"Where is she?" I said, my voice raised. To emphasize the point, I waved the pistol in his direction. "FUCKING GET HER!"

"Who told you?" he said. "Who told you about her!"

"Told me what?" I shouted.

He didn't answer. From somewhere in the house came a muffled scream. I'd never heard Caitlyn's voice, but it had to be her.

"Look," I said, urgently. "Whatever's going on, it's over. The police will be here. The neighbors must know there's trouble by now. Tell me where she is." Maybe if I kept him talking, I'd be out of danger, in time for the cops to handle the situation. The rain splashed behind me in the open door. Thunder cracked.

George let out a cry of anguish. And then he took a swipe at me with the knife, but missed me, not even close, but that was small comfort. I remembered now that Dave had died of stab wounds. Is this how it happened? Was I about to follow in my brother's footsteps?

I backed away, avoiding a second attempt at a stab. George wasn't a man protecting himself against an intruder. This was a crazy person. What the fuck drove him? He lunged at me again. The knife almost landed but missed. He was aggravated by his failure. I was frantic, tried to back away. Our positions had reversed. He was now beside the doorway. I was about to pull the trigger. I had to! Goddamn it!

Then Clarence appeared in the entry. His forehead dripped blood. His right hand was twisted. In the left was a shiny steel handgun about twice the size of mine. And he was aiming at me.

I was facing two men who wanted to destroy me. With a sick jolt of fear in my stomach, I resigned myself to dying.

But entering the room that way, in a fit of anger, blinded by a need for revenge, Clarence couldn't immediately comprehend the situation he'd happened upon. He had no fucking clue about George. His few seconds of delay while taking measure was all that was necessary to determine my destiny.

George, lathered to insanity, defending himself, confused, seeing Clarence's gun, striking out at every threat, lunged at Clarence, the knife in front of him like a lance. It went into Clarence's chest all the way to the hilt. Clarence, looking bewildered, fell against George. Blood pumped from his wound and then gushed like vomit from his mouth. He had to have died almost immediately. Almost. It turned out he had enough life to do one last thing.

He pulled the trigger on his gun.

Bundled together as the two men were, George holding onto the knife and near his victim, Clarence's aim wasn't completely true. But true enough. I would learn later that the bullet entered

George's belly and exited through his nuts. It didn't kill him at once. He would spend a few days in the hospital before going to a well-deserved demise. But the injury sent him into immediate shock and rendered him harmless.

Clarence had saved me.

The two of them collapsed upon one another, Clarence's blood gurgling like a fountain, George's guts slipping onto the floor. Two devils in a puddle of viscera. It was sickening, a bloodbath. I almost puked. George, in agony, moaned loudly and then fainted.

All of this insanity had occurred in a matter of two or three minutes. I learned that violence is like that: over almost before one could comprehend what had happened. I was practically crazy myself and I tried not to lose my nerve. I was frantic to find Caitlyn. I was sure that some neighbor must have alerted the police about the gunshots by now and that they'd arrive soon. But I had to know whether Caitlyn was all right. Her screams were coming from somewhere else in the house. I dashed around, headed up a staircase, but as I did so, the screams became fainter. I ran back downstairs.

"Caitlyn! You're okay! It's okay. You're safe! Where are you? If you can hear me, bang on a wall!"

She pounded. It sounded as if she were beneath the staircase but there was no door anywhere. I looked around confused. I remembered what I'd read about the Boston Box and hidden rooms and headed back up the staircase again. There was an opened small door underneath the upstairs staircase, some kind of closet, and I ran to it. A light shone. Another, even smaller door, was in the back of the chamber, like the entry to a cubby hole for storage. It was latched with several bolts and Caitlyn was pounding against it and yelling. A safety lock had not been snapped shut; my guess is that George hadn't had time to secure it when I had shown up. Thank God. I didn't want to blast another lock open with my gun.

I pushed back the bolts and swung open the door. Caitlyn, on the other side, just about fell into my arms, but she was near hysteria. "Don't worry," I said. "It's okay. You're safe."

Caitlyn looked terrified, bewildered, tears flowing. Her head was bloody. She struggled.

"Honest," I said, urgently. "It's okay. I'm a friend. Your uncle." She was startled. It was probably the wrong time for that announcement, but I'd hoped to reassure her. "I'm Mark. I'm related to Dave Chieswicz. I'll explain."

Sirens were getting closer.

She started to stumble out beyond the door. "Stay here," I said. "Please." She looked frantic. "You don't want to see what's out there. The police are on their way."

She shook her head up and down and inhaled sharply, gasping between sobs. "Take care…" she said.

"Yes," I said. "I'll take care. I'll take care of you."

"No." She pointed at the staircase. "NO! Take care of her."

I didn't understand. "I don't want to leave you."

"Please!" Caitlyn said. She looked distraught.

I stepped carefully to the cubby door. I flicked on a light switch, and moving cautiously, I went down into the basement. The steps creaked. The place smelled awful, of shit and piss. The small room I entered had what looked like mattresses nailed to its perimeter.

It took me a moment to comprehend that the bundle of rags I saw in a corner was an adolescent girl, chained to a wall.

CHAPTER EIGHTY

MARK

May 2017

When you're up to your ass in trouble, it's good to have a smart lawyer. And one who's forgiving when you tell him a few things you've been holding back.

And on some matters, it's even better that a couple of people think you're a hero.

Emily's rescue, and the fact that she was alive, were reasons for joy and celebration in her family, and I got some of the credit. For, indeed, it was Emily, the girl from the memorial, in the corner of the room where Caitlyn had been imprisoned. George Rumberg had kidnapped her. The circumstances that led to finding her were remarkable, mostly due to Caitlyn's research on architecture, a completely coincidental crisscross. Because Rumberg lived in such a populated neighborhood, the discovery of his crime was bound to happen. If it hadn't been Caitlyn knocking on his door, with me in pursuit, sooner or later it would have been someone else. Just maybe not in time.

I wish I could say that Emily's story had a completely happy ending, one of recovery and a return to her parents. But the trauma from her captivity and abuse has enclosed her in a shell. And medical examinations have determined that her suffering was severe. As days have passed, it's uncertain whether she will break through and join the world again. Her father, a remarkable man whom I've spoken with several times since the day of her rescue, has a mantra, that where there is life, there is hope. He said there are glimmers of the old Emily now and then in her eyes. If love can be a cure, Emily will be cured. I pray so.

Two other families, whose daughters' bones were found in Rumberg's house, have no such hope. At least they have some closure in learning of their children's fates. They have thanked me for helping to solve painful riddles that they have lived with, in one case for many years. I don't think for a second I deserve any of their gratitude. My role was chance. And their grief is intense. I've never much believed in God, but they do, and they are not bitter toward Him. He comforts them.

As for Rumberg, he never regained consciousness, so the exact details of his depravity, which appear to have been so horrible as to be unfathomable…if there could ever be an explanation for his evil, it died with him.

Finding Emily in the middle of a populated neighborhood prompted soul-searching in Boston about the horror that can happen under one's nose. Letters and editorials in *The Boston Globe* asked whether the neighbors should have noticed that something rotten was occurring, or should have heard the cries, or brought Rumberg's insanity to the attention of authorities. All of those judgments ring hollow to me. The neighbors in Chadwick Square are actually pretty tight. Good people. Rumberg did not behave especially crazy; the room that he used to hide his victims was insulated and sound-proofed; his victims were evidently terrorized, always under the threat of death and often drugged and gagged. He is the only one culpable for these tragedies.

Ah, that room. The Boston Box. The police—and me and Dietz, for that matter—have pieced together, eventually with Caitlyn's help, that Dave knew of her research, and that in a misguided attempt to ingratiate himself, he may have broken into Rumberg's property to see if a Boston Box existed there, as Caitlyn had supposed. Breaking and entering was part of Dave's criminal record. With his illness, maybe he wasn't thinking too sensibly. Maybe he was bored. Or who knows? Maybe, like Caitlyn, he just knocked on the door, asked questions, and triggered Rumberg's protective insanity. In any case, Dave probably didn't expect that he'd tripped into a hellhole. We've guessed that he hoped to have information about what he'd found, which he'd present at the Red Sox game, an offering of goodwill. That said, the precise scenario of his murder will never be known unless Emily witnessed it and someday can speak of it.

However, blood samples found in Rumberg's car matched Dave's. The police consider his case, if not exactly solved without a confession, then concluded. Every once in a while, I shiver with the thought that the two Chieswicz brothers almost met exactly the same fate. What happened to Dave, I'd nearly experienced myself. In my guts, I know how he died.

As for the surviving Chieswicz boy, me, I had some explaining to do. On the night of the bloodbath at Nine Chadwick Square I was taken into custody, and I surrendered without protest, as long as I got to make my one phone call. Dietz, of course. I had to endure a stern lecture from him, and he told me if I lied one more time, he'd be gone. I deserved his anger, but it was worth the discomfort, for it kept him on my side after I swore I now knew everything. With his advocacy, along with Caitlyn's testimony on my behalf, and the rescue of Emily, I was given some slack and no immediate charges were filed.

I told the police—specifically Taylor—that Clarence had claimed Dave owed him money, and I didn't go to the cops because he'd threatened me. The car crash, with Dietz's maneuvering, became evidence of my claim. I said I was afraid.

As for my tracking of Caitlyn, I told Taylor that Clarence had dropped a comment about Dave having a child, which I'd dismissed until I went to the ballgame. I said although I had suspicions about Caitlyn as a result of the game, they were by no means confirmed. The date of the game, a little more than 24 hours before the Chadwick Square horror, gave believability to my contention. I claimed I would have contacted the police eventually, but it was too soon because I wasn't sure if I'd guessed right about Caitlyn. I sneezed once while I talked and nearly put poor Taylor into shock.

Of course, Clarence wasn't who had told me about Caitlyn. That had been Russ. Dietz made a call to his attorney and said that I would keep Russ's name out of my conversations with the cops, but there would be a price. To be exact, $633,215.28, adjusted for expenses. The deal was accepted. I do not expect to hear from Russ again. He has plenty of money, I think, so maybe he'll chalk this one up to experience, and get past his ego. By my keeping silent, he gets his money's worth. He'd have a hard time with his claim anyway, now that Caitlyn is part of the calculations.

My biggest legal obstacle turned out to be the gun, which came with a mandatory one-year sentence since I'd purchased it without a license and concealed it. Charged and convicted, it'd be '*Goodbye Mark, enjoy your stay in prison.*' And I can't argue that the sentence would be unjust. I knew what I was doing.

This is where my role with solving three murders and a kidnapping came in handy. Many people spoke to the police on my behalf. And another, more oblique argument arose for leniency in my case. I got the sense that the cops didn't cry too long and hard after learning that Clarence was out of the way. I overheard a comment that I'd done them a favor. Don't get me wrong. I didn't kill Clarence. I was connected to his death by chance, by his determination to harass me. But the situation possibly worked in my favor with a certain subset of the BPD.

To make short a very long story, the gun charge was swept under the rug. I had to promise that I'd be very well-behaved if I didn't want to see the threat of an indictment resurrected. Those guarantees were easy for me. I had learned I was chicken-shit when it came to firing a pistol. Frankly, I don't ever want to hold a gun again.

Before I talk about Caitlyn, one more matter has to be explained. A number on Clarence's phone belonged to none other than Hesh, the doorman at the Fenway Grand. Seems like he was taking money on the side from my stalker to report on my comings and goings. The morning of Chadwick Square, he'd told about my departure and destination to Clarence, who had a lackey follow me until he was free to confront me himself. I hope that Hesh's payoffs from Clarence were healthy since he won't be working at the Fenway Grand any longer.

After I had discovered Emily on that stormy day, Caitlyn and I didn't speak much. Our encounter was a matter of a few minutes. She was distraught, hysterical, and injured from being thrown down the flight of stairs. She was taken away by ambulance. In the chaos, she couldn't fully understand what had happened, who we were to one another.

Soon after my questioning and release, I made my way to the hospital where Caitlyn recovered. Her mother, named Sylvia, and her father, Ed, had rushed to her side. I negotiated with them out in the hospital corridor. At the time, with so much other noise around George Rumberg and Emily's rescue, and with Caitlyn's sedation, piecing together the story of Dave and her wasn't straightforward. Several more meetings would be necessary to figure it all out. But on that day, we had enough to start.

While I waited outside with Ed, Sylvia went into the hospital room to prepare Caitlyn for my visit. Ed, who was a good-looking man with a gentle air, spoke.

"Before we go in," he said, "I just want to say thank you." He choked up. "If she had…if she had…"

I looked at this man, who had so much love for his daughter, and I was certain that the ways things had worked out for Caitlyn, without Dave, had been for the best. Ed touched my arm. We hugged.

Sylvia opened the door and invited me into the room. Now, under less fraught circumstances, I was about to meet Caitlyn. My niece.

My family.

CAITLYN/MARK

August 2017

After a few weeks of rest in West Chester, under the care of her mother and father, the nightmare of Chadwick Square receded for Caitlyn, not forgotten, or completely healed, but better. A black mood had prevailed at first. But binge-watching television shows—for a while, a welcomed, mindless diversion—became unsatisfying and boring. Eventually, she accepted that a full recovery could not happen in her parents' home. She had to return to Boston, to Harvard, to work. And so she had come back. Her mother stayed for a week at her apartment to ease the transition. Once Sylvia left, many friends and classmates were on call for those first few nights alone. She saw a therapist regularly. And then she was more or less okay.

But not always. Waiting now on a dock at Boston Harbor, by herself for a moment under the grandiose coffered arch of Rowe's Wharf, Caitlyn had to fight to be alert, to stay buoyant. The attack on her had been too awful an event for her to always coat it with sugar, and anxiety, all of a sudden, threatened to engulf her. At moments like this, she tried to keep her ears—and her heart—open, in order to receive messages from the universe. She touched a small bracelet on her left wrist that her dad had given her as a reminder of his love. And a message came through loudly, one that she'd latched onto in the past, one that she and her dad had talked about: that good can come from bad.

A seagull flew near her and alighted upon an ornamented cement balustrade. The bird twisted its head and examined Caitlyn, looking for food. Its feathers were wet, and they glistened in the bright sunlight. They had an intricate pattern of black, white, and gray, almost like diamonds. The gull looked at her, curious. *What have you got, Caitlyn? What have you got for me?*

She hunted in her backpack, found an uneaten portion of a granola bar, and threw it on the dock. The gull hopped to peck at it. A few others swooped down, but too late. Nothing was left. Caitlyn motioned with her hands, showing that they were empty. "Sorry, guys." Most of the gulls flew away except for the one with the diamond feathers.

Good from bad. In the last couple of months, many good things had happened. For instance, when a reporter had mentioned Caitlyn's research project on the Boston Box in a story, and the role it had played in the crimes and recovery, she suddenly heard from people in Boston who had hidden rooms in their homes. The advice that Professor Venda had given, about expanding her research, had come forth almost as if summoned from the ether. This avalanche of information was not without a negative side. Her experience at Chadwick Square wasn't one she wanted to recall by going into dark spaces alone. But she could do it with company. After all, she still loved architecture, and still loved Boston and Harvard, and still loved research. They were salvation. Most of the time before Chadwick Square, her explorations had been fun, an activity beyond work, stimulating, and that enjoyment hadn't been spoiled. And she told herself that when you had a bad plane ride, fell off a horse, tumbled on a bike, discovered some evil in a hidden room—when you've had the worst experience of your life—you just had to get back in there, or you might as well shrivel up and die. She was too young for that. She loved life. She loved her life.

On one matter, the nature of the Boston Box, Caitlyn decided Professor Venda was wrong. Nothing was inherently wicked about a room. A room was just a room.

Caitlyn fought to move past her pain.

Summer sessions at Harvard had begun, with their casualness, their lack of crowds. A comfortable time to readjust. Venda, and everybody back at the university, had treated her gently, with kindness. Even Dr. Bacht, during those office appearances when he broke his sabbatical, was more solicitous and less of a martinet. He didn't mention her intrusion into his office. He didn't discuss the Boston Box. Maybe he felt she'd been punished enough. Maybe he wasn't as bad as she believed. Of course, Caitlyn hadn't said anything about what she'd discovered regarding his ancestor. Could she ask for Bacht's help? In any event, she'd done plenty of work already, and she certainly had the material for a unique story without that anecdote. A publisher was interested.

Good from bad. What else?

The breach with Henry had healed. And Andrew had been in touch, expressing his concern. For now, both men had put aside their desires for love or sex, giving her space but expressing their willingness to be around if she wanted companionship. So many of her acquaintances were stalwart.

Good from bad. She held onto the phrase.

Of course, there was the inheritance that her Uncle Mark had told her about. She thought he was crazy to insist on her claim on the money. If it belonged to anyone, it belonged to him, reparations for the awful way his immediate family had treated him. She had absolutely refused it. But Uncle Mark was persistent. She struck a deal with him. Halfsies. She'd get $316,607.64, before taxes and other expenses, and so would he. There might be some other assets thrown into the mix, but she was more than satisfied with the base sum. It would take care of her educational costs and set her up with a nest egg, or give her a chance to travel, see the great buildings of the world. And the half that remained with Uncle Mark made him happier. He deserved it. Some reward money for finding Emily and the other girls had also come his way.

Where was he anyway?

Uncle Mark. She felt like she got a fair deal from the universe with him, too. She was still getting to know this man with similar genetics to her biological father, but a better person than David Chieswicz, and someone who was blameless with regards to her, who hadn't abandoned her. In fact, she could almost say Uncle Mark had given her life again by rescuing her. Furthermore, he had become a benign way to learn about her biological father, with none of the emotional weight that David Chieswicz would have carried.

The gull rested on its haunches and settled in.

When she thought about the way Uncle Mark's parents had behaved, the way David Chieswicz had rejected Mark, she seethed with fury. She didn't care that times were different back then. They were wrong in doing what they had done. For her, the situation was uncomplicated. Uncle Mark was a good man. Being gay just wasn't a factor. And while she could never make up for the distress that her biological grandparents had caused him, she would make sure Uncle Mark would know that he was family, that he was loved, that he'd always have somewhere to go at Christmas, if he needed it. Her mom and dad, grateful to Uncle Mark for rescuing her, were okay with that. He was the best thing that came from the worst thing that ever happened to her.

She'd survived. Money. She had this new, special relative. Good had come from bad.

Now, where the hell was Uncle Mark?

She got a text: *Be there in ten.*

The used Mini-Cooper I'd bought to replace the BMW was probably more my type of car anyway. More me. The BMW was bad luck from the beginning. And the Cooper was fun, plenty of room, easy to park. That's important in Boston.

Make that "usually easy to park." My morning shift giving tours was supposed to be over by noon but took longer than usual. A good run had been extended by a gabby, inquisitive group of bankers. Then, because of what I needed to carry, I had to drive to the harbor instead of taking the subway, and I'd thought I'd be able to get into one of the city lots near the wharf that didn't cost an arm and a leg. My mistake. After swallowing my fate, a $35 fee, I had left the car and was about a block away from Rowe's Wharf when I realized that I had carted along the refreshments for our sail but had left behind the most important piece of cargo. I had to run back to the Mini.

I grabbed a plastic bag and its contents from the rear seat. "Okay, Dave," I said. "Time to go swimming."

At Rowe's Wharf, I spotted Caitlyn before she saw me. She was staring out at the water. I can't get over how beautiful my niece is. My mother had been beautiful, too, but time and her curdled disposition had given her mouth a downturn, made her ugly. In looks, Caitlyn was my mom transformed, by intelligence, by spirit, by generosity. Even after the incident, Caitlyn's best qualities survived. Okay, I couldn't exactly be sure of that, since I hadn't known her before, didn't know what she was like before the horror. Throwing comparisons aside, however, she was special. And strong. Remarkably resilient. And, as I said, so very beautiful.

"About time," she said, a smile on her face. She gave me a big hug. "Are you ready?"

"More than ready," I answered, and looked at her. "Are you getting muscles?"

"Self-defense class," she said.

A seagull trailed us as we walked to a nearby office on the wharf. Neither Caitlyn nor I knew much about sailing, so we'd made arrangements with the Boston Harbor Club to rent a boat and hire a crew. We checked in and then met the two young men who would manage the excursion for us. Both of them were tanned and shaggy and friendly and, in the familiar way they casually handled some gear, already evident as competent.

A small motorboat, driven by another Harbor Club staff member, carried the four of us a short way on the water to our sailboat, a 33-footer named *French Contentment*. We made the shaky jump from the motorboat onto our sailboat. The crew spent about ten minutes setting up: unlocking the quarters, uncovering the sails, taking care of the navigational equipment, explaining how to use the head. They assumed that our mission was solemn and our abilities minimal, and they didn't ask for much help.

After disengaging the sailboat's mooring rope from a buoy, we cast off. The water was calm, and the harbor surprisingly empty of many other crafts.

"How's it going with Clark?" Caitlyn asked.

"He's good," I answered. After Chadwick Square, I had called Clark to explain myself and asked to try again. Clark said yes. We're only dating, but I've met his son, a good sign that I've been forgiven. Oliver's a lively boy. I'm not quite comfortable around him, not having had many kids in my life. On an outing together, the three of us had gone to an amusement park. Roller coasters ended up being a great unifier. They scared the crap out of me, but I rode.

"I brought some sandwiches," I said. "And some drinks. A good bottle of champagne. And cookies."

"And I brought the music," Caitlyn said. She retrieved a small portable speaker from her bag and Bluetoothed it to her phone. Great sound. Some soft R&B.

"Modern technology is awesome," I said.

"Not exactly funeral music," she answered.

"This isn't exactly a funeral."

"There's some classical, too, in the playlist."

Caitlyn and I had talked a good deal about where to spread Dave's ashes. We both agreed that we had no desire to fly to Florida or to the town in Pennsylvania where Dave and I had been raised. Dave might have felt differently but he wasn't there to vote. The conversation came around to our own favorite spots in Boston. The MFA? The Gardner? Harvard Yard? The Public Garden? Somewhere along the river? Along the Emerald Necklace? Of course, several of those places were absolutely impractical. It wasn't possible to put Dave anywhere in the MFA, even on the sly. That the harbor became our point of agreement seemed almost inevitable.

The sailboat traveled under engine power for about a half-hour until we were farther away from the city. Spectacle Island, with its hills that looked like eyeglasses, was to our right. The shoreline to our left…was it south? North? I can never tell. The crew member at the helm cut the engine. As best we could, Caitlyn and I helped to raise the sails so we could move with the wind. Soothing waves lapped at the boat.

"Shall we just get this over with so we can relax and enjoy ourselves?" I said.

"Sure," Caitlyn said.

The helmsman eased the boat into a gentle circle and we now faced the city. Caitlyn and I climbed out onto the bow, which dipped up and down jarringly in the wake of a passing motorboat that had created large ripples on the surface of the water. After some heavy keeling and unsteady steps, we righted ourselves and took our place on the pulpit, side by side, at the prow. I removed the urn with Dave's ashes from the plastic bag. The sad violin of a classical piece came from Caitlyn's speaker at the stern.

"What's the music?" I said.

"Mendelssohn," Caitlyn answered.

A seagull flew above the boat and swooped close to the sails. I removed the top of the urn and upturned it, but not so that Dave would disappear all at once, but in a way that let his ashes flow softly onto the water. When I finished, Caitlyn draped an arm around me and leaned her head upon my shoulder. "Bye, Dave," I said. I choked up despite myself. Off in the distance, Boston's skyscrapers reflected the sun.

ACKNOWLEDGEMENTS

The Girl in the Boston Box is a work of fiction, but obviously, it blends actual locations and some Boston history with details that I've imagined. As a rule of thumb, anything connected with the architectural phenomenon "the Boston Box"—including murders—is invented. There was no Gregory Adamston, Josiah Hawkins, Arthur Gannigan, Theodore Carter, Pearson Jeffries, Sally Morris, or Thaddeus Simpson. Some details of Chadwick Square, the Old Pilgrim, and the Hibbert House are derived from actual locations but changed to such an extent that they should not be construed as anything other than fictional. Harvard may have an Art and Architectural History Department, as well as library archives, but any similarity between them and my depictions is purely coincidental. Sandler Hall is an invention. Class books from Harvard for the 19th century do exist, and I used them to formulate some language and entries in this novel, but the people and incidents described are completely fictional.

Some resources that informed the book are *Boston A to Z* by Thomas H. O'Connor, *Houses of Boston's Back Bay* by Bainbridge Bunting, and *AIA Guide to Boston: Contemporary Landmarks, Urban*

Design, Parks, Historic Buildings and Neighborhoods by Michael Southwick & Susan Southwick. That said, any errors in the descriptions of neighborhoods or other details are all mine.

I often imagined scenes and processes that may not reflect how they play out in real life but provide the dramatic elements I needed. So for their indulgences I respectfully thank the police officers, lawyers, tour guides, Harvard associates, real estate agents, funeral directors, librarians, architects, medical personnel, and other professionals who may question my portrayals here. I hope that my flights of fancy did not interfere too much with your enjoyment.

Along the way, several people read drafts of this book and contributed insights, corrections, and suggestions. Among them are Jeff & Karen Kita, CJ Arasin, Mary Bagg, Nancy Crochiere, Paul Fallon, Billy Fleming, Hugh Gabrielson, Paul Lewis, Franco Mormando, Travis Müller, Lisa Nazarian, Ed Orzechowski, Carl Seglem, Anne Starr, Cheryl Suchors, Dana Torrey, and Lee Varon. I am grateful for their interest and help.

Many thanks to Alex Peltz, my generous, talented cover designer.

Support comes in lots of ways. To that end, I would like to thank David Aronstein & Steven Tamasy, Giliane Bader, Tom & Judy Bakerman, Paul Beaulieu, Judy Borak, Dom ("Nicky") Bovalino, Mary Jane Casey, David Colton & Hsien Khoo, John Cormier, Peter Epstein, Carolyn & Jim Giaccio, Thom Harrigan & Mike Lew, Beth Kantz & David Silva, Stephen Kuehler, Rick McCarthy & Franc Castro, Jeanne and Maggie Mishkofski, Ken & Fran Roller, Ruth & Howard Smith, Adam & Ping Wiener, and Rich Yurko.

There are many others who I am honored to call "friend." If I missed you here, I'll catch you next time!

ABOUT THE AUTHOR

Chuck Latovich worked as a diversity and communications executive during his corporate life. He has degrees in Journalism and Education from Boston University. He lives in Cambridge, Massachusetts. *THE GIRL IN THE BOSTON BOX* is his first (published) novel.

Follow the Boston Box on Facebook (@TheBostonBox) and Twitter (@Boston_Box) for more information about the book (and Boston).